CW00409606

# No Shelter for the Wicked
# Peter Chegwidden

Copyright © Peter Chegwidden 2019

The moral right of the author has been asserted.

No part of this publication may be reproduced, stored in a retrieval system or transmitted in any form or by any means without the prior permission in writing of the publisher, nor be otherwise circulated in any form of binding or cover other than that in which it is published and without a similar condition being imposed upon the subsequent purchaser.

This book is a work of fiction. Names, characters, businesses, organisations, places and events are either the product of the author's imagination or are used fictitiously. Any resemblance to actual persons, living or dead, events or locales is entirely coincidental.

ISBN: 9781795325059

Three unexplained, seemingly motiveless murders in different parts of the country. No clues, no murder weapons, no meaningful DNA, no useful forensic evidence. Nothing to connect them.

Then the police discover a bizarre and tenuous, wafer-thin link. But how to progress it with nothing to go on? Or is it all coincidence? The police don't think so.

A private eye, an ex-cop, doesn't believe in such coincidences either. He's a suspect in one of the murders, and by chance he becomes more deeply involved in the investigations. In a remarkable set of circumstances he forms an unlikely alliance with a supposedly disreputable woman, an ex-con, who is desperately seeking her sister, and they set out on a quest that eventually leads to peril.

And a terrible shock for this woman he has befriended.

The trail heads from Kent to Hertfordshire, Suffolk, the Derbyshire Dales, north Devon and the Lake District, and eventually to a life or death situation and heartbreak.

A tale of murder, mystery, of love and passion in many guises, of deceit, betrayal and vengeance, played out across the country as the tension mounts inexorably towards its horrifying climax.

# Author's note

The action takes place in various parts of the country so inevitably real police forces are mentioned.

I would like to make it clear that the forces , the officers, their ranks, their behaviours and the procedures as detailed in this book are products of my imagination. They are simply part of a fictional tale and exist solely for the purpose of the story.

If I have inadvertently used the names of real serving officers I am truly sorry but it is by pure chance and therefore quite accidental.

Please also see my 'Afterthoughts' at the end of the book.

***

Although this is primarily a murder mystery it is also a tale about relationships; how different people interact with each other on matters of love, friendship, family, workplace camaraderie, the mutual enjoyment of shared interests, and so on.

And it explores how people can react to changes in those relationships, how circumstances can force people apart, make them wary and untrusting, and conversely how it can bring them closer together, often to form stronger bonds.

Occasionally change brings irrevocable harm, dreadful irreparable damage, the consequences sometimes unimaginable and horrible. There can be vengeance and violence. Betrayal can be the hardest to accept and overcome, and it can eat away at the mind of the betrayed.

This is a story about the way people can set about destroying the harmony of both sound associations and the ones that are precariously balanced between success and failure. It is a story of how strong relationships can be fashioned when so much seems to be against their development, when there are so many barriers to be surmounted.

We can find friendship where we thought there could be none, we can find love in a seemingly barren wilderness, just as we can find our faith misplaced and sometimes destroyed.

It is indeed a narrative about life. And, of course, death.

# NO SHELTER FOR THE WICKED

Just one brief hour.

It was all the time she could risk, being out while her husband was home. When he was away she would go to her lover's house but such visits were infrequent, which made today's meeting all the more poignant.

One precious hour, here at their special place, here where they would share heavenly kisses and feel indescribably glorious passion, here where today they would suffer the frustration and desperation of unconsummated love, here where there was little chance of detection.

Her scream should've woken the dead. But this dead was not for waking. She had stumbled over the lifeless body of her lover, the raw, livid marks on his neck all too clear and horrible.

# Contents

# Prelude

I am standing alone.

Just me. Nobody else. Laura's not here.

I am staring across the wide, wide Solway Firth, and the south west of Scotland beyond, to this fabulous and most incredible golden sunset and wondering if I shall see the sunrise.

It's quiet on this late November afternoon, this bitterly icy cold afternoon, yet nothing can take away the sheer beauty of a wonderful sunset.

It is not the sun's fault.

I used to be a policeman, some time ago now. It doesn't matter which force. I had to forfeit my job, the work I loved, because I spoke out.

I'd made it to Detective Inspector; might have gone further. Now I'm just plain David Canbown, private investigator.

Had this dream about apprehending criminals, protecting the public, all that kind of thing, which is why I joined up in the first place. It gets in the blood and the reasons for being a policeman have never left me, even now, long after I left the force.

That's why I'm here on a deserted part of the Cumberland (sorry, I'm old-fashioned, and I should say Cumbrian) coast, knowing that tonight it may be me or the murderer who must perish before the dawn.

Hopefully, if anyone has to die it'll be the killer so that other lives might be saved. Too many have been lost already. With any luck I'll be able to present the police with all the damning evidence as well as handing over the villain still alive. That's the plan.

Only the wrong-doer will be armed in any way. I have nothing on me, so the dice is a wee bit loaded.

For me it all started in Kent earlier in the summer, but the rotten tentacles have spread far and wide, from North Devon to Suffolk, to Derbyshire and the Lake District. A trail of blood, I suppose you could say.

And tonight it ends here one way or the other. It's been a long journey, with the last few days both exciting and frightening with only the adrenalin thrusting me forward.

I can't even recall when I started to suspect who the killer was. It wasn't a light-bulb moment, no blinding flash, just a gradual realisation of the possible truth, the sad and horrendous truth.

Think I might like to retire to Silloth if I get the chance. Like it here. Like the glamorous sunsets!

I liked where I used to live, all those years ago, until I made a decision that cost me my job. Then, as now, I just wanted someone behind bars so he couldn't offend again.

He had brutally raped two women and the Prosecution thought it was cut and dried, so much so that it turned out their case was woefully under-prepared. Perhaps they didn't realise they'd be up against a really smart defence barrister good enough to work his socks off for his client.

Not guilty!

He walked out of court, fist pumping, with a Cheshire cat of a grin and gave me two fingers just for good measure. I lost it, but I didn't take it out on him.

I ranted at the barrister. I really let fly. Asked him how he could sleep at night knowing a dangerous criminal was back on the streets. That kind of thing. No bad language; not my scene. Just a raging emotional explosion of anger.

But it was very public, made the local paper, and he complained to a higher authority.

So that was my lot, I had to resign.

Within two months the monster had raped again, this time almost killing the girl, but he was caught in the act and finally he's inside. I wonder if that barrister ever considers this animal's third victim, a victim he could've saved if he'd allowed his client to be convicted.

Still, innocent until proven guilty, anyone and everyone entitled to legal representation, da-di-da-di-da.

I was soon to meet Laura, an ex-druggie jailbird who then supplemented her income by being on the game. Maybe we both needed someone, who knows? But they say opposites can attract and we got on together. Somehow. Eventually. But good grief, were we opposites!

Funny thing love. Sometimes you just can't stop it, it simply happens. Can't always choose the person you find you love.

Cannot imagine the relationship would've done my career prospects any good anyway, but if I hadn't left the force I wouldn't have met her, wouldn't have been where I was that morning.

Such is life.

Reluctantly joining forces with Laura as my sort-of partner made the whole business that much more successful. She calls us Cagney and Lacey; don't know which one I'm supposed to be.....

Between us we have a wide diversity of knowledge and experience as you could well imagine! Ex-cop, ex-con, tracking down the missing and the straying and making a bob or two. Yes, a pretty corny idea really, and totally lacking in originality, but it's what happened and that was just the start.

After a mediocre but fun existence, just getting by, we've finished up in a deadly business hunting down a malicious merciless serial killer who has evaded the police. We won't even earn any money!

Sod's law, really.

I mean, it might have been what I wanted to do when I dreamed of being a policeman, but not once I'd had to give it all up. Let me tail an errant husband by all means.

And it was precisely that sort of business that got me into trouble, and why I'm here now, shaking like a leaf. Yes, I'm scared and not ashamed to admit it. An amateur cop up against a professional killer with a hell of a track record.

It was a simple enough job. My contact was a solicitor working for a self-made man of great wealth who wanted his shapely and very attractive wife followed. Apparently she came from a very ordinary background and had clearly married the guy for his money.

He gave her all she asked for, but he was extremely busy (self-made men often are) and she had nothing but leisure time on her hands. And he became suspicious and wanted to know what she actually did with that time, if you understand me. Little did I know where it all might lead.

Yes, to begin with a simple enough job.

# Chapter One

# A Fresh Start

With an ex-wife and an ex-job tucked neatly behind me I decided on a completely fresh start.

There wasn't enough money from the divorce for me to a buy a property so with rental in mind I thought I might as well move somewhere completely new.

And so David Graham Monckton Canbown moved to Kent and Minster on the isle of Sheppey.

John Donne may have written that *No man is an island entire of itself* but living on Sheppey felt as if I'd put distance and a barrier between me and the past, this was my kingdom, my retreat despite the fact I was sharing the place with over thirty-thousand others.

From here I could go forth on my new chosen path, except that I didn't have one.

Tried my hand at a few jobs that never really grabbed my imagination or tested my ability, let alone my intelligence.

The only thing I really knew was police work, so until I could get myself sorted out and maybe look for something more permanent I elected to be a private eye, unaware of the danger I was later going to place myself in.

Now, politicians have debated the regulation (licensing) of these people, but it hasn't quite happened yet. There are plenty of rogues and scoundrels out there. I realised I would have to work for at least two years before I could apply to join the highly regarded Association of British Investigators (and there is much more to it than that), but hoped my past as a police officer would help my integrity with a watchful public in the meantime. At least I had a good understanding of law but knew I would have to keep up to date.

I pondered what I would call my business. *Canbown Independent Detectives* had the initials CID so perhaps not a good idea. Then I concluded that it might look more professional to simply use my name and mention that I was a former Detective Inspector, and that seemed to do the trick.

As I quickly discovered potential customers assumed I had retired early. The public perception is that officers can retire at fifty-five.

I didn't feel fifty-five, maybe because I was fifty-one, but in all probability the job and a failed marriage had aged me.

Getting my first case was, nonetheless, a tough experience.

Any newcomer trying to set up a business will know the form. It's a struggle but if you believe in what you're doing you'll get there eventually if you persevere and never give up. Failure after failure dogged my every effort until one day I had the call I'd longed for.

When it finally happened I bought a bottle of *Cava* and drank it all by myself one evening by way of celebration.

An elderly couple in Herne Bay engaged me to locate their estranged and only daughter who had been lost to them since a family fallout years and years ago.

In due course I tracked the woman down. Her parents thought she was married but didn't know her surname or if they had any children, and desperately wanted to hear from her before their demise.

I found her in Mablethorpe on the Lincolnshire coast.

The only trouble was she didn't want to be found and her husband (her second, by the way) emphasised the matter by threatening me with considerable violence if I surrendered the information to my clients.

I did manage to learn that Mrs McAllister as she now was had five children, two from her first marriage, three from the second, and two had married and produced offspring. So the couple in Herne Bay not only had grandchildren, they had *great*-grandchildren.

It took all the diplomatic skills I've never had to overcome the problem.

So I told a lie. Well, sort of.

I explained to Mr and Mrs McAllister that I *believed* there was a matter of inheritance involved and that her aged parents wanted to change their wills. That did the business. Usually the hope of money does. In truth such an occurrence was on the cards as it had been hinted at during my meeting with her parents in Kent.

After all they had their own property and apparently nobody to leave it to.

I suggested to Mrs McAllister that she write and detail her feelings and provide her parents with an address to reply to. Maybe she could tell them about the children and so on. And that is what she did.

I've no idea of the outcome. The couple were overwhelmed with the letter and both wept openly when, having accepted their invitation to call for a glass of sherry one afternoon, I popped in 'for a few minutes only'. Of course they wanted me to fill in the gaps but I only went so far. Fair's fair.

They hadn't yet decided on what to say in their reply but I did take it upon myself to suggest some tact and to tread with care, and they were in wholehearted agreement.

My cheque arrived a few days later. Maybe this type of work was just the ticket but then I'd reckoned without events of the coming weeks and the impact they would have on me.

It was about the time that I casually noticed a newspaper report of a murder in Barnstaple. Little did I realise the death would have important consequences for me sooner rather than later.

***

Across the other side of the country from Devon Evida Prada hung up the cat-o-nine-tails, went to her dressing room, changed out of her red basque and black stockings and showered as was her habit. Wrapping herself in a thick, warm and soft white fluffy towel, she walked back to her place of entertainment, poured a glass of *Sancerre* and sat quietly contemplating the evening's proceedings. Madonna's *Confessions on a Dance Floor,* her client's choice, still played throbbingly in the foreground.

At least the evening had been very profitable. Successful architect. Excellent tipper. Down here on business, back home to Derbyshire tomorrow. It was difficult to describe how much she'd enjoyed humiliating him, yet easier to remember how much she'd adored inflicting so much pain. And there was Madonna to submerge his pitiful squeals.

Wonderful! Him strapped down helplessly as she'd beaten him to his own specifications. She sipped at her wine musing sadly that she wished she'd been allowed to draw blood. Lots of it.

That was the only drawback to the job; she had to be controlled, thoroughly professional.

Oh well, perhaps one day. Tomorrow her client would be a wealthy middle-aged lady who wanted to be spanked and caned but playfully so. Boring for Evida, so one for the mortgage as they say. And now it was time for her to dress, lock up and drive home through Suffolk's quiet country lanes.

***

I'm a good cook.

Well, no, let's clarify that. Not so much *Cordon Bleu* as *Gordon Bennett*, with an appearance on *Bake Off* unlikely in the appreciable future. Yes, alright then, uninspiring, unoriginal, basic.

But what I do, I do well.

I could make your mouth water with one of my delicious Sunday roasts! I can create simple dishes like Shepherd's pie (precisely cottage pies, as they are beef) that would blow your mind. My home made vegetable soups, often containing eight or nine different veg, are not only nutritious but filling and a delight to the taste-buds. And inexpensive.

Bangers and mash, check. Ham, egg and chips, check. Salmon en croute with salad, check.

And for a fruit intake how about an apple and raisin crumble made with oats? Which reminds me, I do love a large bowl of porridge in the morning particularly in winter. Followed by a slice of toast and home made marmalade.

Yes, that's right, I make my own marmalade too! Just can't buy marmalade the way I make it.

I try to balance my diet so that I have plenty of fresh fruit and veg, with an occasional naughty treat. Sad to relate I do like baking my own cakes. So my balance does get a bit out of kilter every now and then!

None of this stems from a failing marriage I hasten to add.

Being a police officer fast food was the order of the day, hastily snatched mouthfuls, sandwiches and things like bacon rolls the mainstay, and only then if practical and time allowed. Tasting home cooking was a rare luxury.

It wasn't exactly the conversion of Saul, but one day I woke up to the problems I could be making myself in later life having read a newspaper article that might have been illustrated with red flashing lights.

To her credit my ex-wife kindly guided me as divorce approached. She taught me my cooking skills and I had plenty of time to practise once I was out of the force. It was a learning curve that in the early days of my culinary education pointed downwards, and my efforts were all too often accompanied by failure on a grand scale.

Still, it gave Penny something to laugh about.

Odd though, she always said she'd fallen in love and married me because I made her laugh; it was just that there weren't enough laughs in those last few years. And there were no children which I considered to be just as well, but which represented a sore point (well, a very painful one) for Mrs Canbown.

She's remarried now, a divorcee with two of his own kids, and I wish 'em well.

***

Elsewhere, someone with a guilty secret was setting off for home and reminiscing about the pleasure the last few hours had brought them. If the first killing had been enjoyable the second had been magnificent. Did it get better and better each time you eliminated someone?

If so there were happy times ahead. Right now there was to be a brief meeting with a trusted associate and the chance to make sure he knew how things stood. That was vital. Communications had to be few and far between and then they had to be pithy. Also the fewer people involved the better, less chance of mistakes, less chance of leaving evidence.

The killer had the army to thank for the strategic precision with which the operation had been planned and, to use a pun, executed. And afterwards no feeling of regret, no imposition of pangs of conscience, no sorrow that someone's life had been ended so swiftly, so brutally.

Perfect! On that basis this show could be set to run and run.

***

You won't be surprised to learn that I do my own washing and ironing, although overall the latter art has come at the cost of a couple of shirts, a pair of pants and a sock, and five handkerchiefs.

At times like that I really missed Penny! Now that's not only a typical male viewpoint surfacing, my reliance on my wife to do what I felt were the womanly duties helped bring down the marriage. If I am honest then, for the record, I didn't like the idea of women getting on in the force. What a pig, what a bigot! I see things very differently now.

I look back and think about how convention (and nature) dictated the role of women. Over the centuries how many great doctors and surgeons, architects and engineers, business entrepreneurs, politicians, military geniuses ... the list is endless .... have been lost to the world because society decreed that convention be followed.

At least some of our greatest female writers broke through.

The Brontes have been inspirational to me, and I'm not ashamed to admit I've enjoyed Jane Austen. *Sense and Sensibility* is my favourite. And I've discovered that I have a strong romantic side that's been buried and lying dormant since I courted Penny.

So, in due course, I started dreaming of some female company, especially as I now held the opposite sex in high esteem, viewing ladies in a very different light.

How I wish I'd kept in touch with DS Mitchell. We always got on well and she was a damn good detective, but I was afraid of her because I knew she was better than me. I felt threatened and I think she was aware of my animosity. My own fault, I know that.

Somehow I didn't want to be a typical male any more.

I tried my hand at online dating but packed it in quite swiftly.

The first lady I met had lied about her age on an astronomical scale. Not that I would've worried, but she was so wary of me and eventually told me the last person she'd trust would be a policeman. So much for the public image of the force.

A couple of ladies were happy to exchange messages but shied away from a meeting. I guessed these were products of the website's imagination, designed to keep you hooked and keep paying the subscription.

My second date, despite all that she said on her profile and in her messages, was less interested in a Long Term Relationship than a Long Night's Wham-Bam. And I thought it was us men who were supposed to be like that! A wiser man than me might've realised when she asked in one of her early messages if I still had my hand-cuffs, truncheon and taser ....

I must be getting old!

It was only much later that I came to accept that love isn't necessarily about finding a near-perfect match. Love happens, sometimes whether you want it to or not. You can't always choose who you fall in love with.

And the catalyst for this revised thinking was about to make an appearance.

# Chapter Two

# Laura

I'm not, and have never been, a keep-fit fanatic.

I do possess a rowing machine but its use is occasional and it is rarely employed for as much as ten minutes.

But I am an active person and do love a good walk.

Since leaving wife and job and now renting a small property with an equally small garden I have, for the first time in my life, taken an interest in gardening. The housekeeping's going well, or at least I think it is.

Of course, there is now nobody to criticise my efforts!

So I do get plenty of exercise, at least by my own undemanding standards.

On this particular morning, and taking the Met Office's local forecast at face value (you'd think I'd know better) I parked opposite the Ship On Shore pub and walked along the sea wall prom into Sheerness to get some items of shopping I required.

I remember the tide was in and the sea wasn't looking particularly rough; just very grey, reflecting the dull overcast grey sky, and with the faintest ripple and swell to disturb it. There were one or two other walkers, mostly with dogs.

Approaching Neptune Terrace I passed an object that I have always considered strangely out of place on this concrete promenade, this sturdy sea wall, this first and last line of defence. The front of the prom circles out a little way and there is a bench and above it a blue painted shelter, a simple device comprising some upright stanchions and a roof.

From the outset I've felt it was a curiously romantic spot in a sort of *Sound of Music/Mary Poppins* way, if you follow me. At odds with its setting, especially being in Sheerness which does not have much of a romantic feel to it at the best of times.

Any sensation of the shelter being romantic is sadly often dispelled by the detritus left around and about overnight.

But it was here that I met Laura a little later on, a meeting that was far from romantic by any means of definition.

On my way back from town the heavens opened and the rain cascaded down vertically, there being no wind of note, and I quickened my step to reach my shelter and the comfort of the seat.

There I deposited my shopping, myself, and stared out to sea in a state of hopelessness, only too pleased to know I wasn't in a rush. And there I sat and sat, and there it rained and rained.

Typical September. No Indian summer on our horizon. And so I waited and waited and waited...

***

"I'm Impressed."

The impressed man sat in a quiet corner of the bar at a table away from the few other drinkers.

The room was dark with precious few sources of light to improve the situation. The man was small and tubby with untidy and greasy looking short black hair, and although he wore a brown suit and a shirt and tie he managed to appear less than clean.

And he looked older than his forty-odd years. Much older.

There were beads of sweat on his forehead and his cheeks were red.

He picked up his pint glass, half empty now, and gulped down the other half as his companion spoke.

"I want you to be impressed. I'm efficient and effective and I want you to remember that at all times. Serve me and serve me well. Fail and you'll be my next victim. This is one of the few and very rare times we will ever meet. Just as long as we both understand each other.

"We don't leave clues for Mr Plod. Understand me?"

The speaker sitting opposite was a complete contrast being tall-ish and athletic in appearance, smartly dressed, well groomed and handsome, and well-spoken. The chubby man noticed particularly the highly polished shoes. My how they shone!

The chubby man sweated some more to visually express his growing anxiety, and in the hope his companion would accept his explanation. "Yes, yes, yes, I know the score. I'm anxious to help because what you're doing is right, right and proper. Count on me, count on me. I know the score."

"Yes. Just making sure you do," the companion replied before slowly sinking an Islay single malt with the care and attention such a drink demands. "I'll be away now. Never been to North Devon before but I've no wish to stay. I've seen enough and now I want to see the eastbound A361."

"Quite, quite, quite" gobbled the chubby man, quickly realising he was talking to a retreating back.

***

"Mind if I sit here, love?"

My reverie was interrupted as I was completely taken by surprise.

Looking over the estuary towards Southend all I had heard was the rain falling on the ground, on the pebbles on the shore, and on the roof of the shelter.

It was as if she had crept up on me.

"No, no, of course not. Make y'self at home," I replied quickly as I regained my senses and pulled myself together, shuffled along the bench and moved my purchases to the ground out of the way and out of the rain.

She sat down quite close to me (well, it wasn't a large seat) and we shared a brief glance and an equally brief polite smile. She was dressed in a thick black coat, black gloves and black boots and her black hair hung about her head and her round face in disarray.

Clearly she'd been caught in the rain and her hair had suffered.

"Jeez," she exclaimed, "I wasn't expecting this."

"No," I replied, "neither was the Met Office!"

"Just thought I'd pop out for a walk on the front, get some fresh air, and *this* 'appens," she added.

Hearing her explanation I added my own story to the dialogue.

"I know. I parked at the Ship On Shore and walked into town but didn't quite make it back."

There was a pause.

"Where'd you live then?" she asked.

"Oh, Minster. Just off the Broadway, the other end, near the shops. Take it you live in Sheerness?"

"Yeah. Crummy flat in a crummy town, but hey, I'm livin' the dream!"

I risked another look. She was staring straight ahead and yet I knew she was seeing nothing, not conscious of the view, such as it was, just staring ahead. Her mind was elsewhere. There was sadness and resignation etched in her face and resounding in her voice.

She moved her right hand and brushed some sodden hair from her face as I spoke.

"What dream's that?"

"Always wanted to live at the seaside, ever since I was a child, and I've finally made it after all these years.

"Used to go out for day trips, as a family like. Went to Allhallows. Came here once or twice. And Leysdown. Loved our summer holidays to Dymchurch. Sandy beach, and a ride on the little train. Knew then I wanted to live at the seaside."

"Yes, I can imagine Sheerness would be a bit of a compromise in that dream." But she was elsewhere, she had her own thoughts, probably her own troubles. For some reason I wanted to keep this conversation alive although I sensed she wasn't bothered either way.

"Where did you live originally?"

"Strood, born and bred."

"How have you ended up here, if you don't mind me asking?"

"Long story, love. Lived mainly in the Medway towns and one or two other places. Came here to get away from me past. Sometimes," she sighed, "the past comes with you, don't it? Like there's no escape. You from round here then?"

I decided to outline my recent history, including the demise of my marriage, if only to turn the conversation away from the mundane, so told her, very briefly, about being a copper who did something wrong and where I was in life now, divorced into the bargain.

"What you do wrong, then?"

It was almost an inevitable question but I'd hoped she wouldn't be that interested. I explained about the rapist, the barrister, my burst of anger, and everything that happened afterwards. It was my turn to stare straight ahead.

When I looked round she was looking directly at me.

I was at once struck by a kind of raw loveliness I hadn't noticed before. This drowned rat was letting some inner beauty rise to the surface. Difficult to describe, really. She wasn't beautiful, I wouldn't want to give that impression, but there was something attractive about her features, and her expression had changed from passive to concerned.

"Yeah, see, I know what it's like to be held down and ... well, y'know ... against yer will, and it ain't pretty. And you got the push, like, for standing up for the victim like you did? Fu ... I mean flippin' awful. You're a good cop in my book, love." And she turned her head away and her eyes returned to the sea.

Neither of us spoke for a while.

"I'm sad to hear of your experience," I eventually added lamely.

"Don't be sad, love, don't want yer pity and yer sorrow. My life. The way I chose to lead it. Known some real bastards in my time. My first bloke, absolute brute he was, put me in hospital three times. Had to say I'd had an accident at home. Don't think they believed me.

"Thought I'd landed, me. Smart dresser, got all the moves, expensive car, splashed the cash and then some. Good looker, great body. Big businessman, so he told me. Yeah, thought I'd landed.

"Took me on holiday to the Gambia and then the Seychelles. Wow, this was it, this was living. He was the man for me. But he was a crook and a drug dealer, that's where the dosh came from.

"Got me into drugs and when I was hooked he got me into all the attendant crime. You know what I mean, being a cop and all. Had to work as a prozzie. He got the customers. And I learned early to be a good girl and do as I was told, like." She was still staring aimlessly across the water.

Her voice was a mixture of bitterness, regret, and defeat, a voice of loss and emptiness.

"Anyways, you don't wanna hear all this...."

"If you'd like to talk I'm a good listener and I'm interested, and we aren't going anywhere in this weather." I could've bitten my tongue for I knew it wasn't the right thing to say but some unknown force drove it from my mouth.

"No love, I've said too much. I'm just a boring old tart. You got any kids, love?" The question surprised me but I guessed she was changing the subject.

"No. No close family. Had a younger sister but she died tragically years ago. My poor old dad died less than a year into retirement, so some pension firm must've been clapping their hands. Mum went much later. What about your parents? You got any children, man in your life?"

She looked at me, pondered me and my question, and after a while replied.

"No kids. Glad I never brought any into my world. Parents dead long ago. Me elder sister deserted me, wanted nothing to do with me. I tried to keep in touch. She kept her distance and I've no idea where she is now. What happened to your sis, then?

"Died for love, I suppose you could say. Story for another day." It was my turn to look ahead and in reflective mode as the memories flooded back and lapped at my mind like the incessant lapping of the waves on the pebbles in front of me. Ceaseless. Unstoppable.

"Sorry, love. Sorry and all that. No, there's no bloke in my life these days, other than me clients, that is. Still do a bit of part-time as a prozzie. Brings in some extra dosh, know what I mean.

"You know the old song, *Nobody loves a fairy when she's forty*? Well, there ain't many blokes want a prozzie when she's fifty. It's like I just get the old dregs these days. Still, as the song goes you just look at the ceiling." And she laughed, a hollow laugh, obviously devoid of humour.

"Are you trying to tell me you're fifty?" Ye gods, I could've kicked myself. I felt so stupid and embarrassed. As silly questions go that was right up there in the top ten, and my enquiry received the contempt and condemnation it deserved, delivered in a real put-down.

"I'm fifty-five, love, and you can turn off the charm, that won't get you in me knickers. Cash will. If you fancy a bit we could, y'know like, slip back to my flat when it dries up. Be nice to have a sexy bloke like you after me favours. 'Course if you just wanna chat some more, well, as you must know, you're only paying for me time. Anything else that happens between consenting adults blah, blah, blah."

I declined as politely as I could. She continued.

"Anyways, give over, love. You don't want to be seen with an old jailbird like me." She saw the surprise in my eyes. "Yeah, been inside twice. Last time I decided to straighten my life out. They can help you do that. Got off the drugs, started to learn things, started some half decent education.

"They can help alright. Fixed me up with accommodation and a job when I came out. Who could ask for anything more." I sensed the sarcasm. "Nothing job. Got sacked when the staff found out who they were working with. But I didn't give up. Came here. Didn't want me old mates, if you know what I mean, coming after me. I've had some jobs. Offices, factories.

"One place I worked one of the girls learned about me but kept it quiet. She started stealing things, well, so I reckon, because then it was me got the blame when she told everyone about me past. The manager would've kept me on, but I knew it was no good.

23

"Got a part-time job in the dockyard. Supplement me income as a prozzie, for what it's worth. At least I don't pay tax on them earnings! You ever been in love? Did you love yer wife?" I nodded, surprised if nothing else. She continued.

"Never known love and never will now. Sad innit?" I nodded again. It was all I could do.

***

In time the rain eased up and we went our separate ways.

We'd exchanged names and mobile numbers for one reason.

Having told her about my work as a private eye, and my success with the Herne Bay couple, she wondered whether I could find her sister.

For the first time I heard her giggle as if she was truly amused, and that was when she suggested giving up her job and the game and going into partnership with me. I nearly laughed out loud too.

Her brainwave was supported by the concept that me, as an ex-cop, and her as an ex-con, with all our differing knowledge, background and widely varied expertise and experience, could just about crack any case. We certainly ought to find the estranged sister who had abandoned her.

At long last her whole face was alive and, I must confess, it excited me in a way I can't easily recall. She positively beamed when she smiled. Her dimpled cheeks made her so very attractive.

Not long ago, I knew, when I was a different me, I'd have shied away from this, thought her to be a disgusting, worn out old hag. But this was the new me and I wanted to help, and furthermore I wanted her to help me. Don't ask me why.

Of course, there was no way I was going to go in search of her sister let alone adopt her as a business partner.

Or so I thought.

We had laughed together when she said my reward for finding sis would be a 'freebie'. I didn't cotton-on at first, but as her face cracked into a grin it dawned on what she meant.

Then we laughed together. A really good hearty chuckle.

Her parting words as we set off in different directions were:

"Don't forget you could always come and pay for some companionship sometime!"

I didn't imagine for one moment I would hear from Laura McCaffield again, forgetting she now had my mobile number.

We'd really opened up to each other. Amazing for two strangers. And I began to wonder where my discretion had vanished to and why I had revealed so much about myself. I usually keep my own counsel and would never normally talk about private matters as I had done with Laura.

So where had my common sense gone? Why had I been so daft?

When I got into bed that night, turned the light off and curled up warm and cosy and closed my eyes, all I could see in my imagination was Laura smiling and giggling.

And I found I rather liked the image.

# Chapter Three
# Barnstaple and beyond

"Sorry to disturb you on your day off, Geoff."

"No problems, sir, we were only going to the mum-in-law's so Maisie can go on her own with the kids. I might actually be grateful." The two detectives shared a wry grin.

Sergeant Geoff Alcock's voice had that beautifully rounded, gentle, fluffy west country burr that marked him out as a true Devonian.

"So, what have we got?" queried his Inspector as both officers looked down at the corpse.

"Name's Edward Nobbs, sir, and we know that as his wallet, including his driving licence, was on him. Probably rules out robbery as a motive. Notes in his wallet, coins in his pocket as is his mobile phone." The Inspector nodded. Alcock continued.

"Discovered by a lady who, according to Constable Nicholls, overdid the hysterics and has since been showing all the signs of heartbreak. I've seen her myself. Genuinely heartbroken, I'd say. And she knew him.

"Now that's interesting, sir, as his fiancée had told us he went out for a walk, as he often did, and the fact he was gone over two hours wasn't unusual. Might suggest the lady who found him was his lover and they had an arranged meeting."

"Right. That's a start. Not likely she killed him, but who knows."

"Strangled, according to the doc, but the rope marks are all too easy to see, sir, or at least that's the doc's preliminary observation. Rope, that is. About two centimetres thick and no sign of it. In my opinion, Mrs Kethnet, that's the lady who found him, wouldn't have had the strength to do it. Y'know, hold him down and throttle him, and there's no signs of a struggle."

"Kethnet you say, Geoff?"

"Yes, that's it, sir."

"Anything to do with Nathan Kethnet?"

"His wife."

The inspector sighed and then blew air out of inflated cheeks.

"The millionaire. Funny how we think about people with money having everything they want and being extraordinarily happy." It was of course a sarcastic joke and Alcock dutifully laughed in an ironic way to illustrate that he understood the Inspector's humour and found his superior's comment amusing. The Inspector continued.

"See, Geoff, Mrs Kethnet, married a man with money, probably loves the cash more than she loves him, and still risks it all by having an affair. Cathy Stailes, if I remember rightly. Daughter of a couple who run a B & B up the road in Ilfracombe.

"I suppose I'm not allowed to say it these days but she was widely acknowledged as sex-on-legs and it was no surprise when she foisted herself on Nathan. Trophy wife, was Cathy, someone to be shown off. Mind you, Geoff, here I am, a police officer, speculating when we don't know for sure she was seeing Mr Nobbs on the quiet.

"Her presence here could be quite innocent."

Both officers nodded again. Both were smiling.

\*\*\*

I wasn't expecting a text from Laura.

In fact I hoped I wouldn't hear again.

The memory was fading fast and didn't need revival. We had been two complete strangers, meeting by chance circumstance, and talking quite freely about the sort of things most folk would keep hidden at first acquaintance.

You just don't talk to a stranger about a marriage break up, or about being inside. Things like that. Well, maybe I'm out of touch. Perhaps people do reveal their life histories and problems to those they are unfamiliar with these days. Maybe it's to do with that chemistry thing, y'know, two people hitting it off like they've known each other years.

Could be where the idea of love at first sight comes from.

There was no love at first sight between me and Laura.

Her text was full of the abbreviations typical of the medium, but basically it was to tell me she'd turned out all the info she had on her sister, born Lorraine McCaffield, two years before Laura, and had tried to arrange the data together with appropriate notes to help me.

To help me?

She really thought I was going to try and find Lorraine.

Even abbreviated it was a lengthy text, and it ended with the words *wen we goin 2 meet?*

I sent a reply.

'2nite @ 7 ur place. Tx address pls'

I hoped it wouldn't be convenient, but best to get it over with. Have a chat and as nicely as possible tell her the facts of life. No freebies from either party!

Beep! In came the response. It was convenient. Blast! Oh well, never mind.

An hour later I had a phone call from a solicitor. A man wanted his wife tailed. I made an appointment to meet the solicitor at her Ashford office the next day.

\*\*\*

In the meantime another successful case had come to a satisfactory conclusion. I scanned the resultant cheque for my files, finalised my records and then filled in a paying-in slip ready to go to the bank.

It had been a complex search but a rewarding one, finding someone, anyone, who might have an interest in the affairs of Donald Arthur Payfold, deceased. The poor chap passed away alone and unloved, neglected for years by those who might have cared.

He named a woman in his will and all the usual attempts to find her had failed.

So as a last ditch measure the executor commissioned me to have a brief scout round, and I'd run her to ground, if that's the best expression, in Seahouses, Northumberland.

Twice married, twice widowed, she was now all but bedridden and suffering dementia.

The sale of Mr Payfold's house and the rest of his estate would enable the woman's children to place her in an expensive but highly-rated nursing home, to live out her days in some degree of comfort and not end up like her benefactor.

None of the children had heard of Mr Payfold.

How the sad old lady came to be a beneficiary required a deep dig, and I won't bore you with the details. Maybe it wasn't a happy ending but at least I knew she would be properly cared for now, with the added bonus that when she passed away the three children would inherit any residue.

No wealthy families were involved here.

Just ordinary people getting by modestly.

I think my success added to my reputation. As I looked again at the cheque it occurred to me that I might just be able to find Lorraine McCaffield. If I had to.

Laura had described her flat as crummy but it turned out to be surprisingly clean and tidy, and she had made the place look like home. She was as welcoming as the flat, the latter being warm and cosy this cold September evening.

Yes, the actual building was nothing to write home about, and perhaps the immediate environment fell within the descriptive realms of the word crummy.

But Laura had made the most of it, even doing some tasteful decorating.

"Landlord don't mind. Well, increases the value I suppose," she'd said.

She was a good host and quickly made me feel at ease, comfortable and relaxed. Then I remembered her part-time work and realised she might be well versed in making men feel like that!

The more I looked the more I knew she had the flat exactly as she wanted it. She'd made it appear larger and more spacious than it was, and it was light and airy. I told her she could make money as an interior designer and she laughed as she placed the coffee mug on the table next to where I was sitting.

"Do you know anything about *feng shui*?" I asked, quite innocently. It struck me I was looking at a work of art, and better than that, I was feeling *part* of it. And my mind was at rest.

"Who's he?" she replied with equal innocence.

"The origins are Chinese. It's about harmonising people with their surroundings. So there's ways you can decorate your rooms and arrange your furniture to help achieve that aim, induce a sensation of being at peace, that kind of thing."

"Oh" she commented, "how very interesting." She could not have sounded less interested.

"Just wondered," I persisted, "as your flat seems to exude the principles of feng shui. Is it all your own work?"

"Yeah. And if it's fenged itself then it's happened by accident. Are you going to be boring all evening?"

All evening? Where did 'all evening' come from? I queried it.

"Thought we'd have a good time, get to know each other. You driving? If not I'll open some wine later if you like." The matter seemed straightforward and settled with or without my agreement, and I elected not to argue. When the time was right for me to depart I'd be off regardless.

"No, I've walked." She picked up her coffee and sat next to me and as close as she could.

"Cosy eh? Drink up, I'll show you me work on Lorraine, and then we can talk about us before I uncork. Well, tell the truth, unscrew. It's only cheap wine but it's Soave. And it's chilling right now as I speak."

And for once it was me who was speechless.

Wanting to move things on and make good my escape I polished off the coffee and was led to the table where Laura had her documents on display. There was an eagerness, a liveliness about her. She was alive, and therefore completely different from the miserable, careworn woman I had met on the front.

I was simply playing her along, merely patronising her and I wasn't prepared for the shock yet to come.

Everything was laid out in good order and I was surprised at her diligence. There were photos of the girls in their youth, various documents and handwritten items, and evidence of cross-referencing.

"She takes after me mum," Laura explained, "so these photos of mum, matched up with Lorraine as a teenager, might give us a clue as to how she looks today." Their parents had both died while young (Laura had been in her early twenties) and most of the estate had gone to 'sensible' Lorraine. "They weren't leaving much to me knowing I'd only waste it. Don't hold it against them. They was right, weren't they?" I didn't comment.

There was a list. The columns were headed 'known facts' – 'reasonable assumptions' – 'guesswork' and 'my thoughts'. I was beginning to be impressed; a lot of work had gone into this and nothing seemed to be missing.

Laura's enthusiasm was washing over me and breaching my defences.

I asked questions and received immediate responses. But nothing could've prevented me being stunned by the surprise just on its way.

We'd discussed a number of features and had thus been able to make one or two minor amendments to the items on the list. And I'd started a list of my own, mainly to satisfy her and to give her the impression I was interested.

Then she sat back and produced an envelope.

"Look, Dave, fact is, been busy. Had to do some seasonal offers, like, to get some business in, if y'follow me. But I've been putting some money by anyway. Don't like these new plastic notes the punters give me, but every little helps as they say up Tesco.

"Anyways, I've got seventy five quid here. Don't know what you charge. Hoping it might be enough especially if we work together. Whaddya think, pardner?"

I knew my eyes were out on stalks. I could feel tears welling up and I had to control those. I looked at those excited, pleading, hopeful eyes and realised I was lost. This meant so much to her, so very much. I was slightly dazed. I could've cried for her naivety and her sad hopes.

I told her to hang on to the seventy five pounds and pay me when we found Lorraine, but she seemed reluctant no doubt assuming I would renege on the arrangement if I didn't accept the cash.

This was Laura's new world, her new being, her optimistic way of putting a sad past behind her, and finding Lorraine was core to that. She desperately wanted to tell her sister she'd changed, made something of her life, had shaken off the darkness and despair. This I knew. She looked down at my business card.

"What's the G and M stand for then?"

"Graham and Monckton"

"Monckton? That part of your surname?"

"Nope, it's a forename. My great grandfather's first name. He was a world war one hero. Saved a dozen soldiers lives in one heroic action. Got a medal for it. Posthumously. He was killed in the action. I was named after him."

"Monckton, eh? I shall call you Monkey Monckton. My little Monckton, you are. What an up-market handle! I like it, I like it," she exclaimed as I blushed to the roots.

"Don't be embarrassed, love. I'll only call you Monckton in private, don't worry yerself. You can be a little monkey with me any time you like," and she sniggered in such a childish yet magical way that I automatically joined in.

And I surrendered.

"Okay, we'll do it. Do you have any other names, Laura, names I can take the mickey out of?"

"Oooo ... sensitive are we? You silly monkey. Nope, plain Laura McCaffield me. Been called all kinds of names in me time. What friends I got often call me Law. You can call me what you like if it makes you feel better." She giggled again, a very girlish giggle.

In a moment of weakness I said, "I shall call you lovely lady Laura," and regretted it upon the instant. She laughed and laughed. Then I laughed.

In that moment I believed I might have surrendered not only in the case of her missing sister.

"Right, my little monkey, we shall open the wine and celebrate." This was Laura as I thought she should've been all her life. Had the badness repressed such a joyous, fresh and colourful personality, or was she purely masking her unpleasant real self for my benefit?

Perhaps, perhaps, perhaps she really had turned her life around when last inside but the real world kept giving her a good kicking to remind her of her lowly station and her wickedness.

Far from wanting to add to the real world's efforts to keep her underfoot and undermine her every attempt to better herself, I actually wanted to praise her, encourage her and believe in her. I wanted to support her yet comprehended this was something she had to do herself, and that, in a way, was why she wanted to be part of the search.

Contrary to my intentions I stayed most of the evening, helped demolish two bottles of wine, the second not satisfactorily chilled as its use had not been predicted, and politely declined her invitation to stay overnight.

"I know, Monckton, you don't know where I been, do yer?"

That comment naturally shrivelled me up and I helplessly spluttered the best kind of reply I could manage, and saw from her expression that I had not saved the day with my feeble words. I decided it would be prudent to say nothing more as that might only serve to pour petrol on the fire.

But she did corner me at the door, throwing her arms around my neck, and thrusting her mouth against mine. I hadn't shared a kiss with anyone for a long time and I allowed her passion to overwhelm me. Consequently I floated home, gliding like a hovercraft, and narrowly missed being run down crossing the road.

It was only when I walked into my darkened property that I felt very alone, sad that I had not stayed, and remembered I had an appointment in Ashford tomorrow. Ye gods, hope I won't be over the limit for driving. I didn't think so; Laura had drunk most of the wine.

Climbing into bed I felt lonelier still, became conscious that I was missing her, yes, really missing her, and allowed warm, tender and enchanting memories of that glorious kiss to flood my mind and send me into the arms of Morpheus.

The next morning I was starting to wonder if I was being used.

Was Laura's keenness and friendliness just an act to get what she wanted?

# Chapter Four

# The man with a straying wife

Jacqueline was pleased the school holidays were over and the kids were off her hands during the day.

Neville doted on them but it was left to his wife to entertain them throughout August, with the exception of the week when they took a holiday together.

This year it had been a Greek island; just eight days in all. Jackie couldn't remember the name of the place but, of course, it didn't matter. Fly there, fly back, stay at a hotel with everything you could possibly want, and between them look after their teenage offspring.

Who cares what the place was called.

Generally the offspring looked after themselves as teenagers are apt to do. There were moments of boredom and then Jackie and Nev stepped in and happiness was restored.

Neville Gradling, being a successful businessman, was often away from home leaving his wife to look after two adolescent and occasionally troublesome teens. So she welcomed any opportunity to enjoy freedom, and the period between the kids going to school and coming home therefrom was about the only chance she had.

And she made the most of it.

Jacqueline Gradling was not a bright or well educated woman. Her mother had worked as a cleaner and her father had rarely worked at anything at all, being adept at working the country's benefits system.

Although Neville came from a not too dissimilar background he'd made it in the world, and with his entrepreneurial skills came success and wealth. He decorated himself with the trappings of prosperity for everyone to see, from a country pad adorned with those hideous massive iron gates, to expensive motors of expansive size.

So it was only natural that his wife, when he chose one, should be a specimen that he could show off.

He'd eschewed the idea of a woman of celebrity status. Not our Nev. He wanted one that would be totally subservient, totally dependent, and overcome with her elevation to Mrs Gradling. And he would keep her happy and docile with money, the answer to everything.

Neville had known Jacqueline from childhood.

They'd often played together and, as they grew older, played adult games together. She was sufficiently thick to be ideal for his purposes. But boy, did she have a body on her! Perfect.

And so they married and Jackie was relegated to the role of baby producer and nanny, and arm candy.

Yes, she had all the things she wanted that money could buy. There were school holidays when she was able to take the children away without him, work being a greater calling for Neville.

They'd done Disneyland, gone skiing in Westendorf, relaxed on a beach in Bermuda, been to Iceland to see the northern lights (fancy naming a country after a shop, she'd remarked), and a host of other destinations, too numerous to recall.

As the kids became teenagers Jackie started to love these holidays even more, for as long as Jayde and Jason could amuse themselves with a hint of safety she could wander in search of pleasures of the flesh.

And she never had to search far.

Back home she had a vague idea that she lived somewhere twixt Ashford and Canterbury, up a country lane somewhere, not far from, what was it, the A28. She knew the way to the schools, of course, and she knew her way to Chilham. That was important because that was where Alistair lived and Alistair was her lover.

Utterly devoted, Alistair was an athlete in bed, quite capable of exhausting Jackie in a way she liked being exhausted.

How she loved the days when she spent a few hours with Alistair Bourne-Lacey!

Unfortunately, for her, Neville had a suspicious nature.

*** 

The thought that Laura was just using me haunted me that next day.

Then I decided to be merely cautious, keep my wits about me, and keep her at armslength.

She'd wanted to be named on my business card! I had to explain as gently as possible that she was one of the last people likely to get become an approved private investigator.

Perhaps the real reason lay in her desire to track down Lorraine, and wanted to feel that I couldn't get out of my commitment, not that I viewed it as such.

The meeting at Ashford was good.

I wasn't tendering for the work; my reputation preceded me and the job was mine. The remuneration package was exceptional. The solicitor provided me with a file with everything I required, and I was on my way back to Minster before I knew it.

Back home I studied the file.

This guy wanted the bloke nailed. Every i dotted and every t crossed. A report that would have legal standing. There was, I understood from the solicitor, no question of divorce, and I was almost afeared for the wife for the most dreadful retribution would be hers. At least that was my reading of the situation.

Neville Gradling, millionaire and then some, was not a guy you messed with. And I didn't fancy the lover's chances either!

I spent some time at my computer, opening a series of new files, adding relevant data from the info I'd been given, and thinking through my strategy.

But Laura was hiding in every nook and cranny in my mind. She would not be expunged.

And then she phoned me.

"Hi Moncks, when do I see you again? We's partners, remember, that's what we are. So hows about it then?"

"Laura, I have other work to do as a private investigator, and I'll get round to Lorraine, I promise." There was silence on the line. I waited. There was a sigh and a short whistling noise and then she spoke in that very resigned manner she has.

"Okay, come round and discuss your other work. We're partners, and I might have some bright ideas. Listen, I can go places you can't, like ladies toilets. Not even with all this LGBT stuff would you be comfy following some bird into the Ladies. I can help you there."

There was some truth in that, not that I was going to tell her, but why she should ever imagine I might need to follow a woman into the Ladies I had no idea.

"Look, I'll come round tonight if you're free..."

"I'm free," she interrupted.

".... and we can talk. But no wine and I'm not staying."

"Suit yerself. Got Frascati chilling. Listen Moncks, I'm good for you, but you just don't know it yet. Come round when yer ready." And she hung up, leaving me exasperated although anything but annoyed. Hey, I was beginning to like this woman, and that wouldn't do.

All the same, for reasons that deserted me, I took the Gradling file with me. Stupid or what?

***

DS Geoff Alcock sat in the Inspector's office.

"Drawn a blank so far, sir. No weapon left behind. Post mortem and DNA confirms rope. This guy was strong, big build, no way did his lover do for him."

"Okay, Geoff, so let's see if Kethnet knew what his wife was up to. Might be a connection there. At least we know Edward Nobbs and Cathy Kethnet were lovers, just don't see how we can keep it from Nathan."

"Not our worry, is it sir? She was misbehaving, that's tough on her, full stop. We're pretty sure robbery wasn't a motive. There was over a hundred quid in the wallet. God, what is this all about?"

"Well, Geoff, we have to find out. Let's start with the fiancée. But tread carefully with Nathan Kethnet – powerful man, man of influence."

Neither officer was looking forward to this task.

It was unlikely in the extreme they were going to be able to keep the truth from Nathan Kethnet and there was the chance he might react badly where Cathy was concerned. He had a reputation for violence, although the police had never received any complaints or been called to any trouble where he was involved. It was purely a reputation.

Still, as Geoff Alcock believed, if Mrs Kethnet was having an affair she must face the music, and that might include a divorce symphony. So be it. Play away at your peril.

***

Laura was wearing jeans so tight it looked as if she'd donned them at age six and had grown into them. That they were for my benefit there was no doubt. I was astonished she could move in them.

"Okay, Moncks, what's we gonna do then? You got it all mapped out?"

"Look Laura, I've other things to deal with, and I've started a new case today, and Lorraine is currently on the back burner. Sorry and all that." She looked at me sideways with an expression that said '*I don't understand*' and '*I understand only too well*' all at the same time. I knew I was in trouble.

"Well, as your partner, and I don't seem to be involved in anything else, I've put some ideas together." She turned round and picked up a box file, bending over and making sure I was watching the rear view. "See," she said, showing me the label, "this is the Lorraine file, and there's a bit more in there than when we last discussed it."

Her resolve was clear in her voice. Once again I set my mouth in motion without briefing it.

"Right, we'll look at file Lorraine and then we can look at file Gradling which I've brought with me." She looked surprised and almost bewildered, and then suspicious.

"You want me to sort of, like, be involved in what you're doing, am I hearing that right? Only don't mess with me, Moncks, cos I won't be messed about with."

My mouth, having run away on its own course continued its journey unabated without any input from my mind, let alone my brain.

"Laura, two things. As my partner I'm responsible for you. So you can start by giving up the part-time employment. I don't want my business associate entertaining men for money."

"That one thing or two?" she queried sarcastically adding, before I could interrupt, "And you're not responsible for me. Don't want charity, don't want you running my life. Understand brother Moncks?"

"You misunderstand me, I'm not offering charity and I don't want to run your life. But I'm top dog and I run the show. That's primarily because I'm an ex-cop, I'm a private investigator, and also because I know what I'm doing. It also means that I pay you. That's reasonable, isn't it,"

"And you're a typical alpha male." That stung. This was the new improved me, and I was making poor fist of it. She continued. "If you wanna be top dog you go right ahead and be top dog, and I'll be top bitch and one day I'll be number one and you'll do as I say. Got it?

"Now, I'd like some wine while poor alpha male monkey smarts and licks his wounds." And she stuck her tongue out in my direction as she went to the kitchen, calling back, "You want some Frascati or do top dogs only lick up gin and tonics?" I had to laugh.

"Yes please. Top dog has his tail between his legs and is very sorry. Tell you what, a compromise, top bitch can be my equal for now. How does that sound?"

"Not good enough, Moncks, I wanna be top everything," a disembodied voice called from the kitchen. Then she appeared with a filled glass in each hand and came and sat next to me. "Play yer cards right, top dog, and you might find this bitch is in season tonight."

Once again my eyes were out on stalks, and looking everywhere except at Laura. She giggled raucously, the way I liked.

"Okay, my little Moncks, I'll let alpha male have a little victory. I'll give up the game. There, does that make smarty-pants feel any better, mmmmm?" She was using her 'little girl' voice and trying to sound seductive. And succeeding. "Now what's you going to surrender?" she asked as she snuggled much closer.

"Right, how about this?" I was playing for time and my brain wasn't interested. "I'll give Lorraine equal status with my new case. Promise."

"Those are the right words, and you win tonight's prize. Thank you, top dog. Here, just thought of something. Hear us talking about top dog and top bitch people might think we're barking!"

\*\*\*

The police had been spared a Vesuvian eruption at the Kethnet home.

Faced with the inevitable Mrs Kethnet had confessed her infidelity to Mr Kethnet who had certainly erupted, but with laughter knowing the lover was dead.

"Serve 'im right," he managed between guffaws.

"Mind you, if he's stiff he might still be of some use to you!" And his laughter at his poor and unpleasant joke went up to the next level and definitely approached potential heart attack country. Cathy Kethnet wasn't amused.

Eventually, with Nathan Kethnet bright red in the face, his laughter turned into a coughing fit in which he came close to choking. His heartbroken wife looked on devoid of sympathy and hoping that, before he changed his will, as he surely would, he would be carted off by one medium or another.

Unbeknown to her he had already changed the aforementioned document.

For he had employed a private investigator who had only recently reported back with details of Edward Nobbs's liaisons with Cathy. Dates, places, times, photos.

Currently he was explaining this to Sgt Alcock.

"I'd rather my wife didn't know, sergeant. My sole purpose in using a private tec was to be sure of my suspicions and to surreptitiously change my will. I would've had a few well chosen words with the missus, which I have done now anyway. She won't stray again."

Alcock hoped the message hadn't been supported by violence.

Kethnet supplied contact details for the private eye. The sergeant, who believed that right and wrong were not separated by grey areas, and who usually spoke his mind even if doing so proved tactless, managed to raise Nathan's hackles.

"Some might think, sir, you had good reason to want her dead, as indeed you might've wanted Nobbs dead."

Controlling himself, and it took some supreme effort, Kethnet retorted sharply, full of himself and going onto the attack as the best form of defence. Out tumbled all the usual nonsense police officers have to face when confronting people of supposed influence.

"What are you suggesting, sergeant? I am personally acquainted with your Chief Constable." Calming, he added, "I love my wife, she's been stupid, but she won't be again. She's too good a wife to want to do away with her, and I'm not going into details for your benefit. How dare you!"

Taking Nathan's words in order, Alcock was suggesting the possibility Nathan had Edward Nobbs killed, didn't give a damn about Kethnet's relationship with the CC, and was actually quite pleased intimate details of the marriage were not going to be made known to him. And yes Alcock dared because that was what made him a good policeman.

His next stop was the private investigator.

***

"I'm going to give up asking you to stay." Laura feigned annoyance with one of her looks.

Good, I thought. The message is getting through.

"Ain't got no more wine. You're drinkin' me outa house and home." In reply I offered her some 'wine money' which she accepted, noting she quite fancied the twenty pound note she happened to see in my wallet. The twenty changed hands.

"Don't spend it all on wine."

"Can't mate, me rent's due soon and I promised not the raise funds me usual way."

"I'll pay this rent instalment. Let's say for office use; that is, using your flat as an office."

She smiled. She liked that. More money changed hands.

"So how do we catch this Gradling woman?"

"We know where she lives. The husband says she must go out between the school runs, so we keep an eye on the place and follow her when she leaves. Simples."

"Won't she realise what you're doing?"

"Not if I do it properly. You come with me, you can make notes, look after the camera, provide an extra pair of eyes. And I'll teach you to do it correctly. How about that?"

"When you starting?"

"Tomorrow."

"Can't. Got me day job tomorrow."

"Day after?"

"Yep, fine with top bitch."

I was happy taking Laura. There were odd occasions when you needed to take a picture with the car on the move, and she could certainly act as my secretary! It was harmless enough providing she didn't try to blackmail me.

She could, for example, threaten to sell the story to the local press, if they were interested.

I had to be prepared for that.

As I lay in bed so many things raced through my mind. Why was I involving her at all? Why, why *why*? I could still look for Lorraine. The best answer I could come up with was that I liked being with her. Worse still, maybe I liked her, liked her a lot.

After all it was never going to become an intimate relationship. Was it?

# Chapter Five

# **Southwold**

Grayden Optics was thriving.

Almost anything Jayne-Marie Panahan had a hand in thrived.

The daughter of an engineer she was proved to have the Midas touch where commerce was concerned. Her father set her up in her first business which grew and grew to the point where she was bought out by a large company, and pocketed a tidy sum.

She repaid her father and set off on other projects. Grayden Optics was one of them. Just one.

Tireless and restless she strove to make money, never wasting a second if there was profit to be earned. Ruthless and heartless in business she didn't hesitate to close down any part of her empire that wasn't pulling its weight, and would make employees redundant without further thought. She had eyes that could cut a man in two.

Her relentless pursuit of success was renowned and failure was rarely her companion.

It was at Grayden Optics that she took on William Bailey as head of Marketing. She went after him and lured him away from employers who clearly valued him highly. He cost her an arm and a leg but he proved his weight in gold.

Brash, cunning, determined but above all else able, and with a solid track record.

Jayne-Marie was not unattractive although looks were unimportant to her, except when she wanted to use her considerable feminine charm and allure as a means to an end. She always looked incredibly smart, almost elegant, and knew she could employ her appearance and the raw sexuality she exuded to great effect. But always, always to get what she wanted.

But there was another side to Ms Panahan.

She was quite capable of making herself look like something the cat had brought in, and therefore anonymous and not worthy of a second glance. There was a reason for this.

Not only did she give large sums to charity she did voluntary work when she could. All of it anonymously, for she sought no glory, no fame, no praise. She had worked with the homeless and vulnerable people. Once she took in a young mother and baby, the woman terrified of her boyfriend who used his fists too freely.

Jayne-Marie changed nappies, cleaned up when both mother and child were sick on the lounge carpet, and eventually found her a flat and safety, putting her in touch with those who could help her further.

This was the sensitive, loving and caring humanitarian, and possibly the genuine Ms Panahan.

She could divorce the cut and thrust of business from the need to help those in trouble.

William Bailey was a cold but effective business associate. He now drove Grayden Optics forward with power and might leaving competitors in their wake, and Jayne-Marie adored his no-nonsense thrust and utter professionalism.

Although he wore a smart, expensive and perfectly pressed suit he never wore a tie. He was tall and slender and obviously paid enormous attention to his grooming. Ruggedly handsome, sporting a little designer stubble, which only served to accentuate his craggy features, always upright and with eyes that darted everywhere, missing nothing, he spoke crisply and precisely and rarely wasted words.

His short dark hair, neatly parted to one side, completed the picture, and other staff discussed the possibility of his being an ideal *James Bond*.

He dedicated himself to his work and it was rumoured that, like Ms Panahan, he never slept.

Her only interest in him was in his ability to earn his monstrous salary, and he seemed to be doing that. It was known that he had dated girls but nothing serious had ever arisen. They were just for fun, just for the here and now, and easily discarded.

But in an extraordinary and unexpected occurrence Jayne-Marie discovered she had a kindred spirit away from work.

It was the night she drove into town and went in search of the homeless who might be in desperate need. In the doorway of the shoe shop was Sally, one of her regulars, who had been lucky enough to be given an old single duvet by a local resident. Sally was in her fifties and life just hadn't gone right for her.

There was a man she stayed with sometimes but the price was to share his bed. And she was sick of men and the way they had wrecked her life. Occasionally she'd go to a hostel if she could get in.

The council wasn't much good, for Sally had family but they didn't want her, and she wasn't a priority for that reason. Jayne-Marie had wept private tears for

Sally once. Sleeping in a doorway was preferable to a warm bed shared with a demanding man.

Tonight, as she'd slept, a passer-by had urinated on her while his mates looked on and laughed. Jayne-Marie could smell it on Sally's treasured possession, her duvet.

"I'll get you another one Sal. Here, got you your favourite cheese and pickle sandwiches."
"Bless you love. Got any money? Could do with some weed." With reluctance Jayne-Marie handed over some cash knowing she was doing wrong.

Not far along the road was Alvin (although she didn't think that was his correct name) and he had nothing to put over him. He was huddled next to a railing by an alleyway.

Alvin had been in and out of trouble since birth. His father taught him all he needed to know about crime and introduced him to burglary as a teenager. Failure to conform always led to horrific beatings. There was no *Childline* when he was young, nor it would seem any form of help.

He boasted with humourless pleasure of the different hotels he'd stayed in, all bearing the initials HMP. When he was given accommodation he used his Benefit payments for anything but the rent and was habitually evicted. He was, as ever, delighted with the hot home-made soup Jayne-Marie decanted from her flask, and the crusty roll that went with it. Like Sally he would've liked some cash, and for the same reason, but this time all he got was the usual polite refusal.

Janine was propped up against a gravestone in the churchyard where Jayne-Marie expected to find her. She had good news for the young girl whose family had made her early life a misery. An address to go to for accommodation and help.

Jayne-Marie had set up a small hostel in another town and hoped to do so here, but there were planning problems and, of course, she wanted to do it anonymously, and that wasn't so easy. In the meantime she gave what practical help she could, often little more than words and of scant comfort, but sometimes she really could assist and she knew Janine would be off the streets and cared for.

She heard an owl hooting in the trees that surrounded her, and the chime of the town centre clock to remind her it was 2 a.m., as she left the churchyard and turned back along the main street. It was there that she noticed someone talking to another homeless man in a shop doorway.

He was handing over a roll which the man set about with a vengeance, obviously hungry in an indescribable way. As she drew near the other man stood up and turned. He was dressed like a tramp but in the darkness it was difficult to tell accurately.

They looked at each other and their jaws dropped open. She was looking at William Bailey.

Later they went back to her town apartment and talked endlessly about social injustice and the true tragedy of the homeless, and the problems that led them onto the streets. With a busy day ahead they grabbed some shut-eye and William left before sun-up, back to his home near Saxtead Green. But an alliance had been formed, an alliance of love and concern for the less fortunate, and it was an alliance that had a positive future.

***

Over the following months that alliance proved a worthy one with some astonishing results.

And nobody who worked for Ms Panahan or was merely acquainted with the lady knew about her alter ego. Or indeed about William's.

The alliance, for that was what united the real people that they were, was cemented during a quiet couple of nights away in Suffolk. They revelled in each others' company, dined and wined modestly, and snuggled up in bed together for the first time, lost to the world, but gripped by extremes of happiness.

Both had made excuses for their absence from work and nobody put two and two together, so carefully had they covered their tracks. Of course, most staff believed Jayne-Marie would be the last person to enjoy a passionate escape unless, naturally, some business benefit could be achieved.

And so the secret side of their lives flourished and in due course they married. In secret, of course.

They spent their honeymoon, if three days off work could be described as such, in the same hotel in Southwold, on the Suffolk coast, where love had begun its wondrous journey. But it was three days of paradise, spent in a blissful timeless heaven, where they floated on spectacular rainbows that coloured their love and brightened their passion.

Rejuvenated by their time together, their vital precious time together, they returned to work with renewed vigour and hurled themselves into successes anew.

And that night they went out amongst the homeless, as was their wont.

To the staff, and the rest of the world, there was nothing to suggest any sort of relationship between them other than a purely commercial one. And so it remained.

Grayden Optics continued to grow, and the Marketing Director, as he now was, was leading from the front while Jayne-Marie privately glowed with pride and left much to William, leaving her to concentrate on her other businesses and acquisitions.

Unfortunately, William Bailey got rather above himself, and started to fancy the idea of being the big businessman. He took an interest in a small company in Suffolk that, whilst not in competition with Grayden Optics, made precision components that would add another string to Grayden's bow.

So, with his wife's permission, he opened discussions with the Chairman and Managing Director, one Phyllis Downport with a view to a possible take-over. Now Ms Downport was well endowed with physical attributes that many men had lusted after but so very few had experienced.

Never one to flinch from having to take harsh business decisions, William concluded that a closer rapport might yield better results, principally a lower price for the purchase of course. And thus he set about seducing the fair Phyllis.

It had been his intention to snap up her company for as little as possible, to the agreement and pleasure of his wife, whilst ensuring Ms Downport came out of the transaction with a small personal fortune. Everybody happy. If he had to trifle with the intimate favours of Phyllis so be it. He could dump her afterwards, full stop.

Except that he didn't.

The deal went through, much to Jayne-Marie's delight, but William found he couldn't resist continuing the personal arrangements with the now reasonably wealthy and physically blessed Phyllis Downport.

It wasn't long after that Jayne-Marie first began to have doubts about her husband. Call it intuition, for she fairly had no evidence, nothing to challenge him with. What to do? For an extremely busy woman there was only one answer; employ a private investigator.

And her report, when she gave the evidence to William's wife, was dynamite.

She had hoped the exercise would clear her husband of any wrongdoing, but alas it rather condemned him.

To make matters worse, and her explosion nuclear, was the fact the pair had enjoyed trysts at the very hotel in Southwold where Jayne-Marie and William had consummated their love.

But Ms Panahan had not so much been born as hewn from solid rock. She was, as they say, one tough cookie. She didn't want William to know she'd had doubts but she wanted an end to the affair with Phyllis, not to her marriage.

To begin with she took a chance and confronted Mr Bailey, saying that her intuition told her he was up to something with another woman. He denied it but she left him in no doubt about his life expectancy should he ever dabble. She concluded by adding that he should say goodbye to Ms Downport pronto.

This took him completely by surprise, but he recovered from his shock, not before his body language had given him away, and once again denied his involvement.

"Just be warned," her parting words.

The subject seemed to be closed, and William considered himself well and truly warned.

He never strayed again.

But it didn't end there. Someone needed to suffer for all the terrible emotional pain Jayne-Marie had been through. She did not seek revenge on William but on the woman who had usurped her. Now, how to achieve that?

***

Nosey. That's what she was. Nosey.

Laura has been asking me all manner of questions about me, my marriage and my work in the police force. My mind was wandering and I had no interest in her own past, so I answered briefly each point and asked no questions of my own.

In fact, I was restless. Perhaps Mrs Gradling would not be going a-calling today. I was getting peeved at Laura's endless banter, the questions, the comments. This was why I liked working alone. Phew!

The Gradlings lived along a narrow country lane, which was narrower still beyond their abode, so I reasoned Jacqueline was most likely to drive out the easier way, and gambled on the assumption, reversing into the entrance to a field about a hundred yards away.

Oh yes, I'm sorry, but I've no idea what a hundred yards looks like in metres. We still measure road distances in miles so surely it's no big deal. Work it out for yourself, I don't care. Get over it.

Laura then asked the question I'd been dreading.

"Spose she goes the other way?"

"She won't. She's got a bloody great tank called a Range Rover Evoque that looks as if an elephant has sat on the back, and she won't, according to my information, want to drive that any further than she needs to on these lanes. Trust me."

"Don't trust men who say Trust me."

"Well get out and walk then...."

At which point the bloody great tank drove past. And we were off.

"Spose she sees us?"

"She only uses her rear view mirror to check her hair and make-up. Besides, I noticed she was on the phone. At the mo we're mere coincidence. We all get other cars behind us." I nearly added a Trust me and decided against the wisdom of doing so.

"How d'you know she uses her mirror like that?"

"Cos that's what women like her do. You read my briefing documents, you must know what kind of woman she is."

"Moncks, you's making assumptions. What assumptions you made about me?"

"None at all."

"Bet you have and I bet you're wrong."

"Laura ..... please be quiet."

Wisdom? I'd demonstrated a complete lack of it. And now I'd lit the blue touch paper. At least my companion was quiet for once.

We had no problem following Jacqueline Gradling.

"I still think she'll see us and get suspicious."

"Look, put yourself in her place. You're going to see your lover. You are going to spend some hours in his arms. He is going to take you on a trip around the stars, give you feelings you didn't know you could get, send you right off the planet. It's the most exciting thing that ever happens to you. Even now you might be on the phone to him letting him warm you up, teasing you, electrifying your sensations, arousing your passions so you're ready to go off like a pressure cooker when you arrive. Would you be bothered about a battered old Ford Fiesta behind you?"

Laura thought for a few moments and then answered.

"Yes."

I sighed one of my best and most audible sighs and she sniggered, even putting a hand across her mouth in a childish fashion.

We were soon on the outskirts of Chilham and she was turning off. I'd given Laura lessons with the camera without any confidence my instructions would be correctly carried out. She could take pictures on her phone but this was different.

Mrs Gradling pulled up outside a fairly ordinary property as I slowed. I'd told Laura to use the zoom and she'd starting snapping away. Well, one or two of her mass of photos might come out okay.

"We need pics of her leaving the car and going into the house, and if we can get a pic of the guy that would be wonderful. At least we've got an address. Of course, it might all be innocent. She might be visiting a female friend or a relative, or calling to discuss flower arranging in the local church....."

But it didn't look very innocent. I slowed right down as we approached her car and Laura was clicking as Mrs Gradling walked up the drive, the front door opened, and a youthful looking male, all beaming smiles, embraced her on the doorstep. Then a quick but full-on kiss was shared before she vanished inside and the door was closed.

"Don't give the church flowers much of a chance," Laura commented. I parked up ahead and took the camera, dreading the outcome. I worked my way back through the photos, most of which were, quite frankly, useless for one reason or another but, joy of joys, there were a few good ones, very good ones, and they were the ones we really needed. I congratulated my assistant.

"What we do now. Go home?"

"Nope, we need to know when she leaves. Now have you made a note of all the timings?"

"Ssshhhh ..... I mean, blow it, no, but I think I can remember so I'll start the diary, right?"

From day one Laura had always managed to avoid using obscene and filthy language in my presence. Why, I don't know, and the odd word had slipped out. Maybe she thought I'd be offended, especially as I didn't routinely use bad language myself.

"Yes, and I'll check with you as we go. I can remember as well, so we should get it right."

She started writing diligently, going over the various details with me and trying to behave as an efficient secretary might, as if failing to make notes as we went had never happened. She has this way of making failure look like part of the correct way of things. Very handy, I suppose, when you're often wrong!

***

That morning I had picked Laura up along the road, but on the way back she wanted to see my place and I wasn't over-keen.

"You've got all the files, and we're sposed to be partners and, well, I wanna help you get everything written up, photos done and tagged, and all that. What's wrong? Don't worry, I won't outstay my welcome. Know when I'm not wanted. I'll walk home; it's a nice day."

Once again I sighed. I'm doing that quite often when I'm with Laura.

"Okey-dokey, come in for a drink and we'll get everything sorted, then I'll run you home. That okay?" Another weary sigh, a sigh of defeat.

"Don't force yerself. But, yes, I'll come and have a drink. Besides, I'm dying for a pee."

Jacqueline Gradling had left Chilham about 1.30 p.m., and gone straight home. I'd taken some photos from my stationary car, these pictures being of better quality than the earlier ones but of rather more mundane substance.

She'd left the house, closed the door (no sign of him this time), climbed into the motor and set off. She looked on cloud nine. Very happy. Home first and then the school run. We'd tucked into some sandwiches I'd made followed by a treat of chocolate éclairs.

"You do well for yourself, my special Moncks, this is delishi-oh-so and then some. I like you all the more. Do you always have éclairs on a stake out?"

"A stake out? Not quite that, is it?"

"Yummy, yummy, way to girl's heart is through her tummy. And éclairs might get you to one or two other organs as well!"

I had a flask of coffee but Laura had brought a small container of vodka and orange so declined my hot drink.

"Never driven," she revealed, "never had a licence. Not going to start now, especially now I've got a chauffeur. Imagine little old me, Laura McCaffield, with a chauffeur! What shall I call you? Jeeves? Parker? Lewis?"

"Lewis?"

"Yes, you know, Lewis Hamilton."

"See Lewis Hamilton in a ten year old Ford Fiesta."

Once at my place the first thing she wanted to see (after the bathroom) was my bedroom.

"Wowee, double bed, eh? You expecting company, babes?"

"It's left over from my marriage. My ex didn't want it, so I've got it."

"Can I stay the night and sleep in this?"

"If you want to, but I'll sleep in the lounge."

"Spoilsport."

She located my drinks cabinet without effort and without my agreement opened a can of IPA. She held another and dangled it in my face but I said I wouldn't drink before driving her home, thus emphasising the fact she'd be leaving later.

We settled down to do what she called our homework, namely making up the files, and she watched intently as I used my computer. She commented on the computer.

"I use one up the library now and then. That's how you learn things. I've learned a lot of things on the library computer."

"Such as?"

"Dunno. Can't think of anything off-hand. Oh yes, I know. One of the main constituents, if I've got the right word, of plastic is oil, so that gives it a calorific value similar to coal. And they're actually polymers, poly means many, so they are monomers joined together, and there's loads of different types of plastic."

Not for the first time I was utterly speechless, eyes wide open. She's developing quite a habit of leaving me like that! Where this knowledge of plastic would ever take her was beyond me, but she was quite right, she was learning things and I admired and respected her for it.

Later we watched the early evening news and there was an item about a prominent business woman, a millionaire, having been stabbed to death somewhere in Suffolk. Laura's new found knowledge did not extend to intimacy with east Anglia so I had to explain, and did so with my road atlas in support.

"What was 'er name again?" she asked.

I said I thought it was Phyllis Downport, if I'd heard correctly.

# Chapter Six
# A lack of evidence

Unfortunately I had to explain at length why we hadn't got nearly enough on Mrs Gradling.

Laura couldn't understand.

"We caught 'er in the act. We got the pics. Sorted."

No, we hadn't anything anywhere near enough. She could've been visiting a friend or relative as I mentioned before. And we needed evidence of adultery.

"What you mean, hide in his bedroom and take pics?"

Not a very practical solution. I said that it was generally accepted in a divorce court that a man and a woman sharing a hotel bedroom was tantamount to catching them red-handed committing adultery, purely by presumption.

"So you and me together, my place or yours, and if nothing happens it's as good as read, we doing adultery?"

Yet another one of my sighs. I told her that as she's single and I'm divorced we can never commit adultery together.

"Shame. Good word, that. Adultery. Conjures up all kinds of pictures of throbbing passion. Wish you and me could do adultery. Sounds more exciting than sex."

Sigh. Sigh of exasperation. Long sigh.

Then I detailed how we could come by other information, such as the man's name. We tried to find Jacqueline on Facebook and there she was. As Laura belonged to this so-called 'social' medium I told her to find out what she could and what she could surmise from the entries.

"Do I ask to be her friend? Do I like her?"

Sigh.

Then a handsome thought occurred to me. I suggested she go to the library and find out all she could about Neville Gradling, and about Neville and Jacqueline as a couple. After all, we had all the info Neville had supplied on his wife but we didn't know a lot about *him*. And there might be clues.

For example, a wedding photo might include Mr Chilham Man. Laura beamed, and looked excited.

"Yeah, great idea, oh wise monkey. Love it, love it. I'm on Neville's case. Leave it to me, babycakes."

Sigh.

So I left it to her and later took her home. She insisted on kissing me as she alighted and I have to confess that I didn't discourage her. Well, alright then, I responded, fair enough? I've been deprived of female company for a while and although Laura might not make my top ten of ladies I ought to try and date she sure did taste nice. And her kiss made me tingle all over.

Later that night, as was becoming my custom, I snuggled down in bed enjoying memories of her kisses as I drifted to sleep.

***

The solicitor told me Neville Gradling was a happy man.

He had the lover's name and address and he had photos. That, I was assured, was all he needed. His intention was to pay the lover a non-violent visit, and then explain the facts of life to his wandering wife in the hope she would mend her ways. Pronto.

Once again I sighed.

Job done, BACS transfer completed, bank balance instantly healthy, close the file.

It was only very much later that the file was found to be very open indeed. And I was to find myself in the thick of things that would lead to jeopardy.

***

There was a lull in proceedings.

In fact, all I had in my lap right now was the case of a woman who was convinced her partner had become involved in something illegal. Well, it made a change from chasing straying spouses.

This woman had even been to the police but they felt she lacked any reasonable evidence to investigate. Or, as I suspected, they were unconvinced she wasn't completely round the bend.

There was an added complication: she wanted her partner to stop what she was doing, not have her arrested and charged. The police may well have had a bit of a problem with that concept.

Having a lull in my work unfortunately kept the Lorraine McCaffield affair to the fore, and Laura was a-nagging me, especially as she'd been laid off looking into Neville Gradling, a task she was finding absorbing to say the least. It didn't mean anything at the time but her digging was to prove valuable later on. But I'm getting ahead of myself again.

Clearly Laura adored going to the library and looking things up, and I have to admit she did have a good way of recording and filing her information.

I'd been in a bit of a dilemma, actually. I wanted to know what she'd been inside for but didn't want to ask. Of course, I had one or two friends on the force who would've found out for me, but then I knew I'd have to confess if she ever confronted me, and I didn't feel I could go behind her back. For some reason I didn't want to appear that way. Not to her, anyway.

Strange.

Was she getting to me? Did I mind? The more I tried to expel her from my mind with the view she was nothing to me, the more stubbornly she refused to budge.

No, I needed to make some progress with Lorraine. Perhaps that would keep Laura off my back.

You're right, of course. It was a vain hope. So one evening, thinking I was safe from Laura's intrusions into my life, my home and my work, I opened a can of chilled Holsten Pils and looked through all the information she'd supplied me with.

The phone rang.

"Hi Moncks, what you up to babes? Cos I'm at a loose end, like."

"I'm sorry, Laura, but there's things I need to get my head around tonight and I'm off limits." There was a long pause before she spoke again.

"Can I walk round and just sit quietly in a corner somewhere, and not speak to you or nothing?"

"No you can't. Sorry."

"Hmph. So that's all you care about me, is it? Well, know when I'm not wanted. Bye." And she put the phone down.

She was infecting my well-being. It was an annoying habit. And now I found I couldn't concentrate. I emptied my can and stared into space unable to collect my thoughts. If I'd told her I was studying the 'sister' file she'd have come round regardless.

The day before I'd paid her for her work in the Gradling case and she'd whistled at the eighty pounds in her hand.

"Blimey, I'd have to spend a few hours on me back to earn that as a rule." Her words sent a pang of pain through my feelings. I could've shed a tear at my sadness of that aspect of her life. I was shocked at her comment but also sorrowed and found myself hurting for her.

On the force I'd learned that what is euphemistically called an escort could command upwards of a hundred pounds an hour, and it was obvious Laura had never operated in that market sector. Far from it.

Right now I just wanted time to myself, time to re-examine all the clues, precious few though they were, and try and locate an avenue worthy of investigation. Lorraine, Lorraine where the hell are you?

✳✳✳

"Stabbed clean through the heart, Inspector."

"And no sign of the weapon. Looks like a full frontal attack, Steph. I guess she saw the killer, even if only at the last moment. Doc got any idea what sort of weapon?"

"Just a chance it might be a carving knife. Doc says one side of the weapon could have a serrated edge."

"Crime of passion possibly? Lovers' tiff got a bit out of hand?"

"Maybe in a kitchen I'd go along with that, sir, but in the back garden?"

"Chased from the kitchen, perhaps?"

The two detectives smiled at each other acknowledging the black humour that helped them keep their sanity and a clear mind in cases like this. DS Stephanie Broome spoke again.

"Always that, sir. Anyway, we're looking at a successful woman here. Phyllis Downport. Made her own fortune. Sold a couple of thriving businesses she'd built up and made a packet. Not married. No time for that I would hazard a guess."

"So, this could be business related. Unhappy employee or ex-employee or a commercial rival even. Where do we start then?"

A handful of gulls flew past, all pursuing one that had a lump of bread in its beak, all squawking furiously hoping the food would be dropped. Stephanie Broome looked up.

"They don't give a damn do they? Long as they get fed, that's all that matters. They just don't realise they shouldn't be eating bread. They're seabirds. Bread has no nutritional value for them and can make them ill, yet idiots still throw it out for them"

"Thanks for that, Steph."

"Oh ... sorry sir," she quickly responded, recognising the sarcasm and frustration in his voice, "but it's so simple for the gulls, life I mean, and so complex for us."

"Yep. Mind you, thrusting a knife through someone's heart is simple enough, and we often find the reasons for murder aren't at all complex."

"No, agreed, Inspector. But the situations that lead to killing can be truly complicated, can't they?"

"Yes, and right now we need to make a start on the enforced demise of Phyllis Downport regardless of any complexity. Any signs of an intruder?"

"No sir. So that means, to state the obvious, she let her killer in. Maybe knew him or her."

"Yes, unless he or she was lurking in the garden. Complex? I'll say! Let's look into her family, her work, known friends and business associates, neighbours .... the lot."

And in the meantime the handful of gulls continued their quest across the dull skies that made even this loveliest of east Suffolk countryside seem grey and uninteresting.

They certainly didn't give a damn for the woman lying dead in her back garden in this quiet Suffolk village, just five miles from the coast.

***

Hundreds of miles away another Detective Sergeant was going through details of an interview with a private investigator, and doing so for the umpteenth time.

He was pleased that, these days, and this side of the Atlantic, private eyes didn't tend to get in the way of the police and try and do their job for them. John Wapernod couldn't have looked less like one of the fictional American gumshoes, as he believed they were known as, or indeed behaved less like one.

Quiet, totally unassuming, smart in his three piece suit, well spoken and precise in all he said, he handed over his file on the wayward Cathy Kethnet and her lover, Edward Nobbs, and offered every possible co-operation to DS Alcock.

The Sergeant was surprised to learn he was only forty-three as he looked at least ten years older.

He was also surprised by the watch-chain worn on the man's waistcoat, or rather by the watch it bore, as both were silver, family heirlooms (Wapernod explained) and were worth about five thousand pounds, for which they were insured.

Alcock couldn't help asking about Wapernod's career, he was so fascinated by the man.

He'd worked for a local council as a jobsworth (his own description) and became weary of finding fault, antagonising ratepayers, and bowing and scraping to jumped up councillors too full of their own importance to be anything other than impotent.

"The thing is, Sergeant, I've always loved anything requiring painstaking research. It was how I came into local authority work. From there it was but a short step into the library service but that eventually palled. I was having a drink with a friend who's a solicitor and the conversation turned to matters of the carrying out of detailed research. Some of his work ate up too much of his time.

"Well, I said it was right up my street but knew I had no qualifications to work in a solicitor's office and on issues of a confidential nature. To cut a long story short I finished up working for him on a part-time basis, just every now and then you understand, and found the library's resources extremely useful.

"In time I proved my worth, I suppose, and it was then that he jokingly suggested I become a private investigator. But from small acorns, eh Sergeant? He helped me build my reputation, gave me confidence and I've never looked back. However, this is the first time I've been in any way involved in a murder and I'm deeply shocked. I'm not that sort of detective."

"Well I am, Mr Wapernod, and we have to find the killer. That's our job as you appreciate. So you handed your file over to Nathan Kethnet, or at least his solicitor, and received due payment?"

"That's right. I heard no more until I learned of the murder. Dreadful business. I sincerely hope my work didn't lead indirectly to that poor man's death.

"We don't know just yet, but we will be talking to Kethnet and everybody else we can lay our hands on. So if you think of anything that might be of interest to us......"

"Yes, of course, Sergeant, and in the meantime I'm at your service." Noticing Alcock's wedding ring Wapernod glanced at the Sergeant with an unnerving glow in his eyes and asked if he was married, receiving a nodded reply. As he rose he sighed and added a simple comment.

"What a pity, Sergeant, for you are a most attractive man. Good-day to you." Without another word Alcock escorted him from the premises, warily shook hands, and returned to his desk almost shaking.

Alcock exhaled noisily as he tossed the notes on his desk, recalling only too vividly Wapernod's thinly disguised pass. Time to move on. In his heart of hearts he wanted to believe Nathan Kethnet was responsible for Edward Nobbs's killing, having had his wife's infidelity confirmed thanks to Mr Wapernod.

But the evidence? Oh, how he wanted to get his hands on Kethnet's computer! Still, even then it might provide no clues, no answers.

He glanced out of the viewless window at the dirty and higgledy-piggledy rear of other buildings almost so close you felt you could reach out and touch them. The back of shops, flats over, a muddled terrace of unattractive architecture. Nothing inspiring.

DC Eva Pellaman brought him a coffee.

"What's up, Geoff?"

"The killing of Edward Nobbs. As yet not a single lead other than the fact he was having an affair with a rich man's wife. And a private eye had just handed over his condemning file. All circumstantial, and I know I shouldn't jump to conclusions, but it all points to Nathan Kethnet, Eva. But I think I need to know more about the victim so that we don't end up looking in the wrong places. Let's go see what the boss has to say."

***

One thing was obvious.

Laura had tried to keep in touch with her sister, had tried to find her, and had failed utterly. Alright, she was wasn't a professional detective, but I had to admit she'd done her homework with a commendable amount of skill, culminating, after years of searching half-heartedly, in the effort she'd put into making up the current file.

The front of the file was headed 'Lorraine – missing presumed alive'. A nice touch, I thought.

But the sad position was that Laura had done all that might be reasonably expected of her, limited as she was by available financial resources. And now it was up to me and I didn't have a clue where to start.

Yes I did, what was I talking about?

Those very connections in the force that I mentioned earlier! But could I ask? Would they help for old time's sake?

One or two might. They were true friends or so I considered them to be. Therefore I worked out a simple list of questions and of information sought and telephoned two old comrades.

Both had supported me in my trouble, sharing the view that justice was not done, sharing the view that I was badly treated for standing up for the victims. Both agreed to help but with the proviso that if there were matters they couldn't touch that would be the end of it.

I emailed my list as attachments. One mate called me straight back.

"Okay, Dave, got it. I'll do what I can and ring with anything that clicks. Don't want to commit anything to paper, you understand that?" I did. "Hope the lady's worth it and proves grateful."

"Cheers, Ali, but it isn't like that with Laura." I heard him snigger. "Anyway, appreciate your help, and I really mean that."

"Yeah, no probs, Dave. And I still hope she's grateful." The call ended with some typical masculine banter in which I did my best to defend my relationship with Laura. Wasted my time!

Meantime I decided to use other connections to check birth records in line with the info Laura had supplied, and I really got the feeling I was getting things moving. Deep inside I felt it wasn't going to lead anywhere, but at least I was trying and could tell her so.

Come the morning it would be back to the other case, the woman with the partner allegedly into crime. I also needed to think how to keep Laura out of it. Using her was a threat to my current career. I needed a diversion and there was nothing she could now do about Lorraine that she hadn't already done, that is, until more data came to light.

Ping! Another text. I looked at the clock and discovered it had gone eleven p.m. This text she printed out in full recognising my ignorance and misuse of text-speak.

"Goodnight top dog. Love and kisses top Bitch." I had to chuckle. She was irrepressible. I composed what I hoped would be viewed as a neutral response.

"Goodnight TB. Sweet dreams."

Back came the reply. "Rather have wet ones!"

# Chapter Seven
## Suspicion, paranoia and murder

If two people are so madly in love why should it be so hard for one to say to the other 'are you doing something criminal'? I mean, fancy paying a private eye to pursue the issue. Maybe it's a difficult question. After all, if your partner sort of accuses you in that manner wouldn't *you* be offended? Perhaps I'm answering my own query here.

Oh dear. Never mind. Press on.

Linnie Yatesman of Faversham wants me to look into the activities of Michelle ('Shel') Crackby and I'm meeting the former shortly. I nearly always take the back way to Faversham, round the industrial part of Sittingbourne, past Tonge Mill and Teynham station, over the level crossing and down Bysing Wood Road to the Western Link.

It's an interesting route once past Sittingbourne and Murston, mainly country lanes, often narrow with muddy verges, lanes that twist and turn but don't deter motorists in a rush. The word reckless could've been invented for such idiots.

The countryside is varied, an occasional view of orchards, hops and sheep to remind me I'm in Kent, and is pleasantly undulating I think the word is. Past Tin Shop Hill and the site of the gunpowder works and I've reached the Western Link, a comparative motorway after my country lanes!

I have to cross over, still on Bysing Wood Road, as the address I'm looking for is off this route into the town centre.

Miss Yatesman, as she informs me she is, welcomes me at her door and invites me into the lounge.

"It usually surprises people," she explains, "that a woman of my age should use Miss rather than the curious and almost unpronounceable Ms, but we are a bit old fashioned in our outlook, Mr Carnbrown, me and Shel, that is, Miss Crackby, my partner."

As she indicates an armchair I wonder just how young she is. She is tall, taller than me and I'm five feet nine in old money. She has no obvious beauty, none that would send an artist rushing for the paint brushes, yet she exudes loveliness and has a face that demands attention and, I dare say, worship. I realise (in my typical masculine way) that she's alluring, and I've only got as far down as her neck. I try to stop myself scanning the rest of her elegant form while she's looking at me.

She has brown eyes, full of vitality, and I know she is looking into mine perhaps seeking my soul.

"Tea or coffee, Mr Carnbrown?"

"Coffee, black, please, if that's alright. And it's Canbown, David Canbown. Please call me David."

"Oh I'm so sorry, David. I don't usually get names wrong, please forgive me. Please call me Linnie. Black coffee is fine, I won't be a mo."

I watch her turn and leave. She has a figure to die for. Linnie is wearing a smart pin-stripe suit with extremely tight trousers. Her jacket is fastened by two buttons and underneath she has a simple white blouse. Smart, elegant, desirable.

Be honest, I'm not making a very good job of trying not to be a typical man, am I?

I've already guessed she's probably in her forties despite her efforts to appear in her twenties. That's the detective in me coming out. I have a feeling that her eyes have discovered more about me than I could ever hope to learn about her! She should be the detective.

Sitting down I take a quick look at my phone which is set to silent running and, sure enough, there's a text from you know who. I'll read it later.

Linnie returns with a small tray, two coffees and a sugar bowl, and a plate of various biscuits. She brings a small table to my armchair and off-loads my coffee, offering me sugar which I decline.

She sits right opposite and stares into my eyes as she seductively crosses her legs, slightly wiggling her hips as she does so, almost daring me to divert my gaze downwards. I resist and the tiniest of grins appears on her lips and that tells me she acknowledges the painful struggle I have just been through to avoid taking my eyes from hers. Linnie wins either way.

Either way, I'm still a typical man. Should've looked anyway.

"Thank you for coming, David. Do you know Faversham well?"

"Not very. Not been in Kent long enough to get to know all its nooks and crannies."
"Interesting you should think of Faversham as a nook or cranny. We're rather proud of it and think it an historic town worthy of far greater note than other better known towns. I would rather live here, for example, than in Rochester."

Her smile told me she was playing with me, teasing me, trying to humiliate me. No, that's unkind, but I still think she's testing me and I'm out of her league. I'll just go along with this; she's my customer, after all.

I asked about her partner and what she might be mixed up in, thinking it best to change the subject and get down to business, but it was clear from her facial expression that she knew she'd won that little exchange and that I was in a tangle.

"Well, David, I think she may be into money-laundering, possibly on behalf of a gang, and it may also include drugs. I fear for her, I really do. I did try talking to the police but I had to be over cautious as I don't want Shel getting into trouble with the law. That's my dilemma and why I've brought you in.

"Michelle, she's always known as Shel, is twenty two and we've been living here together for three years, very much in love. I know you won't ask so I'll tell you; I am forty five. We are both care workers, though for different companies, and I'm on night duty at a home this week. The odd hours we both work means that our times together are precious and to be cherished, but that we spend long periods apart when it's all too easy for Shel to get into mischief."

There was a photo above the fireplace and Linnie saw me glance at it.

"Yes, that's us, taken this spring on holiday in Florence." Michelle Crackby (an unfortunate name for one possibly caught up in the illegal drugs business) was facially stunning, truly beautiful, but was far more rotund than her partner who was lean yet curvy. Linnie's black hair is very short and shapeless in the photo, a little more curly now, whereas Shel's is blonde, long and fluttering in the wind. Almost the archetypal picture of a young woman with long flowing hair that you might see in a shampoo advert.

"Why do you think she's involved in something?"

This woman, who had appeared so precise and clever, so intelligent and, to use a phrase, switched-on, now took me on a long ramble round the houses. The basis of all this, I began to believe, might have more to do with the fact she had a young and attractive partner she didn't want to lose. Of concrete evidence there was no sign.

Just the fears of a woman who might lose her lover.

They shared an email address.

"We have, or thought we had, no secrets from each other. Then I found an email forwarded from a hotmail address and there was just something about the address itself that led me to believe it was her own. I challenged her and she admitted it. Very flippantly, in an everyday matter-of-fact way, trying to deflect my concern by asking if I had one.

"I wanted to know why and she just said it was handy, lots of people have them, and it wasn't a way of deceiving me. But I can't understand that. Why, David, why? Why would she need what amounts to a private email?" There was now a look of despair, frustration and grief on her face, reflected in her voice.

"Well, people do, I know, and as far as I'm aware deceit doesn't usually come into it, but naturally it can be used for that purpose. I don't have one, but a friend does and he uses it when he signs up for something online, like Amazon and so on. Then all those sales emails go to his hotmail address keeping his home one completely clear." She didn't look convinced, and I didn't expect her to be.

It transpired that she'd overheard phone calls that were whispered affairs, calls allegedly to friends and family. But why keep them secret? Why use her mobile when there's a landline, Linnie argued? And Shel had recently taken to guarding her mobile.

"Worried I might get my hands on it and check some numbers," Linnie concluded. I felt that this could well be jealousy borne out of that fear Shel might be ready to move on. And Linnie's behaviour was more likely to drive them apart and achieve exactly what she didn't want, but I couldn't very well tell her that.

I made a show of making plenty of notes including a few meaningful ones. But there simply wasn't any evidence whatsoever of anything illegal, and definitely not involving drugs and money-laundering. So where did this idea come from? I tried chatting to Linnie about her own life and turned the conversation around to interests and what she liked on TV. I'd always been good at that, getting people, usually witnesses or suspects, to talk about themselves.

Perhaps unsurprisingly I discovered she liked crime novels (Alex Gray, Gillian Galbraith and Rebecca Tope her favourites) and TV crime (*Prime Suspect* et al) apart from a love of watching tennis on the box and the pursuit of bird watching, none of which, curiously, interested Shel.

Enquiries were made about Shel's general behaviour, as I wanted to know if she displayed any signs of drug usage, not that I explained my reasons to Linnie. But there didn't seem to be anything pointing that way. Linnie was quite put out and upset when I asked if any money or minor valuables had gone missing, but addicts will steal from their own family, no problem.

I took some details as I would need to follow Shel at some stage, and made arrangements with Linnie to call me if Shel went out suddenly and unexpectedly after one of these quiet phone calls. I knew that, being miles away on the isle of Sheppey, I wasn't going to be able to fly to Faversham to go tailing, but I thought planting the concept in Linnie's mind might help.

When we parted gone was the stable, practical and self-assured woman who had opened her door to me. The transformation was complete. It was almost a worried, fretful, careworn mother saying goodbye on the doorstep, fearful for a teenage daughter's safety. Yes, I was now convinced this was an unfounded issue that had arisen because one partner thought the other might be unfaithful or, maybe worse still, about to say farewell forever. And Linnie couldn't cope with either possibility.

Whispered phone calls, a hotmail address, and all Linnie had needed to do was add an assortment of ingredients from her beloved fictional crime stories, and Shel was suddenly up to her eyeballs in wrongdoing!

The only thing that worried me right now was that I might indeed uncover evidence that Shel had another lover (or more!) and intended to call time on her partnership with Linnie.

Sad, but real life in the raw.

And, with equal sadness, that was the job I knew I might be embarking on.

Getting into the car I remembered the text and checked the phone. Although I'm not up on abbreviations used in texts I gathered this message was a crude invitation to enjoy personal pleasures, if I was free. I won't bore or offend you with the details!

But I declined. I had work to do, and on two fronts.

*** 

I never did ask what Linnie's real name was. Linda, Lindsey, Lynne? Well, no matter, it was Michelle Crackby I was after.

Her work schedule was in front of me, together with a current photograph, and the best thing I could do was to find her and watch her for a couple of days. Linnie had showed me the Facebook page they shared and I'd noted anything that might be interesting, not that it appeared very obvious. I was convincing myself Linnie was getting paranoid.

Perhaps she suspected her partner of infidelity and dreaming up the crime nonsense was her mind's way of dealing with the unimaginable.

So, managing to keep Laura at a distance (not easy), I devised a plan of action which is why you find me sitting in a pub, reading the local paper, and keeping an eye on Shel. I'm struggling with a pint of lemonade and lime (yuk) and, as far as I can see, she's on fruit juice. She's reading a book and I notice she is in a position where she can easily observe anyone entering the premises.

Shel looks up every time someone comes in, which is often. She's waiting for company. Otherwise why not go home after your shift and read at leisure in your lounge with a glass of your own fruit juice to hand?

She takes out her phone and reads a text. I guess the mobile isn't ringing, maybe just vibrating. Isn't it incredible what you can do with technology today? She types a reply, and seconds later receives a response and puts the phone away.

A few minutes later a young woman walks in, buys a half of lager, and leaves it on the counter to head for the Ladies. Shel gets up and follows her. The young woman walks straight out of the toilet and the bar, leaving her refreshments untouched. A minute later Shel departs the Ladies, book in hand, and also strides out of the pub.

Something has taken place. Probably drugs, unless Shel really is into nasty business. She gets in her car and goes home to an empty house (Linnie is at work) and, as it's getting dark, pulls the curtains, so that's the last I shall see of what's afoot.

Driving home I'm reminded of something Laura said about me not being able to go into Ladies toilets.

Laura, I might have a job for you after all!

\*\*\*

Before anything else could happen a roof fell in somewhere.

Well, it fell in metaphorically on Alistair Bourne-Lacey.

I saw it online, on the local news, and at once realised the implications. Here was the man who had been providing extra-marital services for Mrs Gradling in Chilham, and I had given proof to Neville Gradling, the cuckolded husband. And Alistair Bourne-Lacey was dead.

Reeling with shock I telephoned the police to explain my position. They weren't giving anything away, such as likely cause of death, but I wouldn't have expected that, and within minutes I'd gathered up my file and set off for Sittingbourne police station. My co-operation would be much appreciated, I was told. The number of times I must've said that to a person who quickly turned into a suspect!

I didn't bother calling Gradling or his solicitor and switched my mobile off altogether.

Later, much later, I arrived home feeling I'd been grilled to a turn, whereas in fact the police were no more than very interested in what I had to tell them. Perhaps that was how I used to come across when interviewing innocent people, probably making them sweat unnecessarily, possibly making them feel horribly guilty!

They looked at me almost contemptuously when they heard the story of my departure from the force (not the Kent police) but I knew it wasn't meant. Well, I hope it wasn't. I willingly left my file on the Gradling case having answered a mountain of questions and I was thanked for my prompt attention. I know from my own experience that the police are not always keen on private investigators.

However, I was treated with respect on this occasion and told my information was very useful. But I learned nothing of Alistair's passing beyond the fact his lifeless body had been found near a level crossing just off the A28.

The officers would want to speak to me again and I didn't doubt that would be sooner rather than later. As yet I'd kept Laura's involvement from them. I'm not quite sure how they'd react to my 'business partner' and it would all but mean the end of my career if her part in proceedings came out. That was another headache, and half a dozen text messages and two voicemail's from her wasn't helping my state of mind.

A voicemail from Neville Gradling helped it even less. He'd first heard the news on the radio. When I called him back he came across as quite shaken, speaking gently and in a restrained manner, a man much upset by the murder. The police had phoned him as a result of my information and he was to be questioned. All in all he gave the impression that he was being quite reasonable about it and only too anxious to help, probably to emphasise and prove his innocence, of course.

He never did make it to meet Alistair, but he freely told me he'd had words with Jackie, warning her to end the affair.

"Mr Canbown, I did threaten her. Made sure she knew I wasn't kidding, if you follow me, and she understood. Now it doesn't matter, I suppose. She's had some tears, but y'know, difficult to cry your eyes out over the death of a loved one when you've been bad behind your husband's back. Still, the price to be paid, eh, Mr Canbown?" I made no comment on that.

"But apart from you and my solicitor, and now Jackie of course, nobody else knew you'd worked for me and what the outcome was. I didn't want the fella dead; just out of my wife's life. So I'm thinking this had nothing to do with the affair. He's probably been done in by some bloke he's annoyed, who knows?"

It was a good point. Was Neville hinting that I'd stirred things up for him? It was possible the killing had nothing to do with Alistair and Jackie, but I still had to do my duty, do the right thing, not that I mentioned it in those words to Neville. It was up to the police to assure themselves Neville Gradling had nowt to do with Alistair's demise, and they would have to make full enquiries in the light of my revelations. It was they who had to clear Gradling when they were certain of his innocence.

And my innocence too.

For all they knew Gradling might have hired me to find the truth and to deal with Mr Bourne-Lacey in a style my employer would approve of. Gawd, keeping Laura out of this could prove tricky.

After my call I braced myself to ring Miss McCaffield.

She was unaware of the murder but shocked into silence as I told her the story so far. At one point I thought the line had gone dead, but she was genuinely speechless, an unusual occurrence, but one I was not in a fit state to enjoy at the moment.

"On me way, Moncks, don't you worry none. Be there in forty-five. Top Bitch knows how to look after a poor little frightened puppy." This time the line really did go dead. What was the point of trying to stop her? Let her come, at least I could bring her up to speed with the Shel Crackby case and the role I wanted her to play.

## Chapter Eight
# Too many suspects

"Bullet straight through the forehead. Instantaneous death. Close range. Lady up the road reckons she might have heard a gunshot about six a.m. but wasn't sure. Cars backfire, noisy motorbikes, busy main road, sir."

"And the doc?"

"Six a.m. might fit the bill, timewise. We'll know more later. No cctv hereabouts; found out from the railway their cameras don't cover this bit."

"Handy for the killer. Perhaps deliberate, of course. Looks as if the deceased was facing his executioner, even if only at the last moment. When was he discovered, Jamie?"

"Seven-thirty-ish. Pretty much hidden in the grass. Guy been out all night fishing, stopped his car thinking he'd seen something, and he had."

The two detectives looked at the corpse and all around them.

"No sign of a car. Did he live here, was he brought here, did he live nearby? Got everyone out asking questions, right up in the village as well, Jamie?"

"Yes sir. Otherwise we've no idea who he is at present."

It wasn't long before Mr Bourne-Lacey's absence was drawn to the attention of officers in nearby Chilham and descriptions matched the body. And it wasn't long after that his aunt, who lived not far away in Selling, was located and asked to carry out the identification, there being, according to her, no closer relative.

The police had little to go on until a certain private eye from Sheppey turned up with his revealing information, and at once they had a motive even if it possessed only the most tenuous links to Neville Gradling and David Canbown. They had to keep an open mind and consider what else might've led to the man's death. He had no wallet or other personal items on him although the former was found during a search of his home.

So theft seemed unlikely, unless the thief was, to put it mildly, disappointed Alistair had no money or cards on him.

Gradually the life and times of Alistair Bourne-Lacey were laid bare and with them came an extended list of suspects that thus expanded the police investigation. A former business associate who admitted 'hating Ali's guts but not enough to kill him' emerged. Allegedly Bourne-Lacey had swindled him when they were partners in a failed money-making project a couple of years back, and it was not the sort of situation in which lawful retribution could be sought in the courts.

Jacqueline Gradling was not, it came to light, the only lady he entertained, and another disgruntled husband had actually sent Alistair a threatening letter, now in the hands of the police.

He currently worked at a fruit farm but in a kind of supervisory role, having wormed his way into such a post whilst possessing neither the knowledge nor experience necessary. It was said he could talk the talk, and by such a medium had been promoted over the head of a more capable and worthy candidate. This candidate therefore had a motive, particularly as he'd had to take orders from Alistair and had fallen out with him on a number of occasions.

One of these occasions had led to an unseemly fight between them in which the other candidate had been beaten to the ground. Two other staff members had overheard the threat he made to kill Alistair.

"Course I didn't mean it," he now explained to the police.

The list of suspects grew and with it the chances of Neville Gradling being the villain, either directly or indirectly, receded down the list.

The police awaited greater precision on time of death, type of bullet, maybe type of gun, and the distance the killer was from his victim. DNA from the crime scene was vital too, and that included checking out Alistair's clothes. A full post-mortem was due.

Another victim of murder was also being shown to have led a most interesting life, a life which also produced an accumulation of enemies and therefore suspects.

Edward Nobbs, resident of Barnstaple, had been divorced twice, and on the grounds of admitted adultery, and even though he was engaged to a woman in Bideford, still couldn't manage to achieve monogamy.

He had been dallying with Mrs Kethnet for the entire six months of his engagement to Fae Darnlett. It might be presumed that he had something very few other men possessed to be so widely sought after. Police interviewed both grieving women who spoke of Nobbs as being kind, considerate, very romantic and passionate, a man who could make them laugh and forget all their woes. The stereotypical ladies man.

By trade a self-employed carpenter he had met most of his ladies in the course of his work.

However, Fae Darnlett's elder brother had discovered his sister's fiancé was dabbling elsewhere and, in his own words, was 'out for blood'. Not that he meant it, of course, as he now told the police.

"I'm not one for violence, Inspector, I just wanted to make sure he knew he'd either got to give sis up or call time on this other .... this other ... this other ... *bitch*," he spat out having searched for an appropriate word.

Nobbs had also upset a competitor, and a more competent one, by deliberately undercutting on the price for a job knowing full well his own standard of work would fall well below the other man's craftsmanship. The competitor could be said to be spitting nails as he'd lost a piece of work that would've enhanced his reputation and made him a tidy packet.

Into the bargain he told Edward Nobbs, in front of two witnesses, that if he wasn't careful and kept well clear in future, he'd nail him to his own front door. Not a death threat, but the words of an angry enemy, one that was added to the list of suspects.

Nathan Kethnet topped the list, but obviously not because he'd carried out the deed himself. He had a watertight alibi for his own movements, but the police conceived it was possible he'd ordered the assassination. For that reason his private eye, John Wapernod, was also in the frame, especially as he owned a dubious alibi relating to a female client who was now busy trying to keep out of the way.

"Blimey," the Inspector exclaimed, "are they all at it round here?"

\*\*\*

Now you will have realised most of this was going on without my knowledge. I had no idea who was being 'looked into' in connection with the death of Bourne-Lacey, apart from me and Neville Gradling, and even less idea of the investigation under way in north Devon.

It was back to the day job and the only day job I had in hand was Shel Crackby.

Whoops! Nearly forgot. And the missing Lorraine McCaffield. Her sister, Laura, was wearing a smug grin when I invited her to aid my mission on the subject of Shel Crackby, mainly because I'd pointed out that, as she'd predicted, I couldn't very well go into the Ladies toilet, not even in these supposedly enlightened times. She didn't say anything. She didn't need to.

But at least I'd been honest with her.

"Now what's we gonna do 'bout Lorraine, Moncks?" she'd queried instead.

Lorraine had been placed on the proverbial back-burner in my mind but Laura was never far away to turn up the heat to try and get things to the boil.

"I really don't know, Law, but I'll think of something." She managed to look disappointed and then annoyed and then resigned. Her black hair hung all around her face just as it had that day we met and today it made her look sad again. I brushed it gently out of her face and she bristled.

"You don't do that ever again unless you're proposing marriage at the same time," she snarled, and I didn't know whether she was serious, joking, or a bit of both. But then she grinned. "Got yer going there, didn't I, lover boy? Sorry Moncks, just don't like me hair touched like that. It's like you're saying I'm untidy. This is me. Take me as I am, with my hair wherever it is, and not where you want it. Okay?"

It was the first time she'd showed any signs of mild aggression with me, and I reckoned my action could've been construed as patronising, although I had not intended it to convey criticism. The more I thought about it, the more I knew she was right. It was an unconscious act of saying 'your appearance is untidy' and so I apologised profusely.

"No, no, no, Moncks; no apologies. Just understand where I'm coming from. I'm me. You're you, and we're the people we are. Full stop." Duly admonished I came up with an idea that I hoped might get me a combination of brownie points and of level pegging. Some hope.

I said I was going to get various records checked in relation to births, deaths and marriages, and use my connections to do so. That pleased her but only up to a degree.

"What good's that?" came the spanner thrust into my works.

"Well, let's see. We've got nothing else to go on, and I can get to data you've got no hope of reaching. Now do you want me to do this or not?"

"Ouch! Alpha top dog doesn't like being bitten, does he? Okay, we'll run with it."

Having sorted that out pro tem we returned to the case of Shel Crackby, and our next move.

***

If there had been too many suspects in the unconnected cases of Edward Nobbs and Alistair Bourne-Lacey, there were hardly any in relation to the killing of Phyllis Downport.

In Suffolk the private eye engaged by Jayne-Marie Panahan did not come forward, unlike her counterparts in Devon and Kent. In fact nobody did anything. Jayne-Marie and William Bailey decided to wait and see. So initially the police had nothing.

However, the police are pretty good at digging out something where the untrained eye might indeed see nothing, and in due course the business dealings between Phyllis and Grayden Optics came into view and Ms Panahan was approached. Purely a matter of routine, it was explained.

Both Jayne-Marie and William were interviewed and gave statements, but neither mentioned the involvement of a private investigator nor, more importantly, the outcome. It was a private matter they wanted kept quiet, especially now Phyllis was dead, and it suited their purpose. That it was a deliberate move to stall the police and hinder them in their enquiries was dismissed as unimportant.

When the private eye phoned to ask if she should contact the police, Jayne-Marie suggested not. There was no need. It was nothing to do with Ms Downport's demise. There was no discussion and no argument. It was left like that.

Sadly for the three of them hotel staff at Southwold knew Phyllis Downport and were able to advise the police that she'd stayed with them in the company of a man, a description of said gentleman being supplied. And so the world of Jayne-Marie Panahan and William Bailey began to unravel.

\*\*\*

The days were noticeably shortening now. Autumn, having rested its weary soul for several months, decided to mark its advent with a cold snap that took many by surprise.

For sufferers of SAD (seasonal affective disorder) this is a time of worry and concern, if not blind panic. Non-sufferers tend to take one of two stances. On the one hand the view is that it's non-existent rubbish in which the stricken should get a grip, pull themselves together, and get over it. But on the other it's recognised as a very real and debilitating health problem.

Like all mental health issues you either believe the mind can be ill to varying degrees or dismiss it as nonsense. If you've got a cold there's no mistaking it. If you've broken your leg and it's in plaster you're bound to get some sympathy. But suffer from clinical depression and there probably aren't any obvious symptoms for people to see.

In fact, you can be the life and soul of a party, but the agonising suffering is still in your head.

Mental health problems can lead the victim into crime once the mind ceases to function properly.

I'd known cases of 'diminished responsibility', as they call it, produce lenient sentences in the courts, even when murder and violence was involved. There was the one involving a Peter Aulton that I recall. He stabbed and killed his wife in a terrible frenzy as she sought, bravely, to calm him. He was so mentally ill that the charge of murder was reduced to manslaughter and a lenient sentence passed.

He had a complete breakdown. He'd lost the great love of his life and by his own hand.

It was all down to drugs, y'know. After the weed came the crack and the heroin. He'd gone through detox and was off the drugs but the damage to his mind, the mental scars were there for life. The damage was done. And it cost his loving wife her life.

Aulton finished up in a secure mental unit but somehow conspired to take his own life a few months later.

So I was pleased that Laura had seen the light and had finally found the help and support she needed to get off the drugs and try and turn her life around. It must've been a struggle, a real struggle. It's not just getting off, it's staying off, especially when life just keeps on kicking you back.

It could be that Shel Crackby was just starting out on the dark descent caused by these illegal drugs, and if so she might yet be rescued, particularly if her lover, Linnie, was there for support. In a way I hoped that was the only difficulty I might uncover. I still wondered if Shel was as loyal to Linnie as Linnie wanted to believe. I dreaded discovering she really was into something worse.

In the meantime my enquiries into Lorraine McCaffield scored in a different and pleasing way.

A friend in need is a friend indeed, and my old mate Steven Appleyard came up with the goods.

I've known Steven since childhood but whereas I went into the police force he went into local government and then the Civil Service. Strange really, he always fancied being a copper and never had any time for red tape. He has a lovely wife, Sally, and two children he can be very proud of as they set off on their chosen careers after university.

Steven and Sally live in Ightham, west Kent, these days, Sally having returned a few years ago to her profession in advertising. They're rolling in it; both drive

BMWs with personalised plates. I don't envy them their success or wealth, I just have no interest in the way people have to boast about it. If I had a personalised plate on my car it would probably read ME 00 SAD.

Anyway, as a result of his efforts on my behalf, and on the basis the source was never ever revealed, on pain of death, I now knew Lorraine McCaffield, born Strood (Kent), married one Gary Wimbush in Hemel Hempstead (Hertfordshire) but a long time ago.

Hertfordshire beckoned. Laura was like a dog with two tails, as befitting Top Bitch, but wouldn't be able to get time off work to accompany me as I might be away for a few days. But before that we needed to do something about Shel Crackby.

And that was the next step.

***

"Withholding information from the police is a serious offence, sir. As you say your wife knew about your affair with the deceased so there can be no reason not to tell us. Unless, of course, you're actually implicated in Ms Downport's murder.

"Thanks to you our investigations have been stalled and you've ended up as a potential suspect. How does that sound to you, sir?"

"Look, Chief Inspector, I've apologised. I've been stupid, but I wanted to protect my wife's reputation and that of her businesses. I know I've gone about it the wrong way, but I'll do anything you ask of me now."

"Perhaps, Mr Bailey, you could offer to reimburse the taxpayers for the wasted time we've spent on this."

"There's no need for sarcasm. I'll co-operate fully, but I need to contact my solicitor."

Contacting ones solicitor, the words investigating officers just love to hear.

Nonetheless a complete search of his Saxtead Green house, DNA tests, and an interview at the station were just the starters on the Chief Inspector's menu. And he hadn't even got to Jayne-Marie Panahan yet, one other person with a motive, albeit a slender one.

But he couldn't justify searching her just yet. Nowhere near enough evidence.

At present Jayne-Marie was in Antwerp but preparing for a rapid departure, leaving business unconcluded, and all rather annoyingly.

William Bailey surrendered details of the private detective Jayne-Marie had hired, Yvonne Pratt, and DC Grant Hadlesome was despatched post-haste to her home in Needham Market.

Of the three murder victims it was only Edward Nobbs who appeared to have any close family. His parents were distraught and his two sisters had arrived with all due speed to comfort them. Alistair Bourne-Lacey, in Kent, had an aunt who had identified the body, and Phyllis Downport had a brother in New Zealand and little else. He made no rush to book a flight to Britain and gave every impression that he might make the funeral only if he could.

The question of wills arose, especially as they might add to the list of suspects.

Edward Nobbs hadn't made a will, not that he had much to leave, and Bourne-Lacey left his estate to his aunt with a request she should favour charities of her choice. The Last Will and Testament of Phyllis Downport was quite, quite different.

Her entire estate was bequeathed to William Bailey, and that, coupled with his earlier behaviour, moved him into a class of his own at the top of the list of suspects, and since he was the only person on that list at present he was in for a grilling and a half.

Needless to say Ms Downport's estate represented a fortune.

And needless to say William's good fortune was going to be a complete shock to Jayne-Marie Panahan.

***

We'd followed Shel Crackby to the pub where once again she sat sipping a fruit juice, apparently absorbed in her book.

"Fine detective you are. No loss to the police, Moncks. You're watching her; tell me what you've learned."

Laura was entering into the spirit of covert surveillance. As I was driving I was enduring a modest lemonade and lime and she was sinking her second pint of Abbot, which she commented on.

"Don't know if they still do it, St Edmunds Light. Anyway, mixed with Abbot, renowned witches brew."

"How do you know that?"

"Used to drink it in me day. Bloke I knew got me going on it. Mind blowing it was."

"Regarding our subject," I interjected, keen to get back to the job in hand, "I think she's very nervous, that's my observation."

"Half way there, kiddo," Laura beamed. "Two things. She ain't turned a page all the time she's been here. Notice that, wonder boy, did you? Second, that ain't nerves, that's clucking, needs her fix. Anything else you wanna know, Poirot?"

I stared at the bar and breathed in very slowly, pursing my lips. Top Bitch was outscoring Top Dog and my in-built nature didn't like it, but the new improved me wanted so desperately to love it and to admire her talent. Turmoil! And she was lapping it up. Out of the corner of my eye I could see the smirky grin. No, truthfully I couldn't, but I knew she was smirking.

Just then the woman I'd seen before entered and walked to the bar and ordered a half of something or other. Laura was off to the Ladies. So too was the woman pursued by Shel.

Woman exits, Shel exits, Laura exits, the woman and Shel (separately) leaving the pub directly, with Laura retaking her seat next to me.

"Do we follow her or can I have another pint? Cos if there's no pint there's no information, Morse."

I didn't need to follow as I was sure she'd be going home so I bought Laura another pint of Abbot. I was pleased there didn't seem to be any St Edmunds light, for the Abbot by itself didn't seem to be affecting her. Some girl!

A third of her drink went in one sitting and then, having wiped her mouth on the sleeve of her coat, she gave me the answer.

"Weed, maybe skunk, and a couple of round pills. Didn't recognise them, couldn't see how much she paid the woman. No words, well, they knew someone was in there, didn't they?"

"And how exactly did you come by all this information, Dr Watson?"

"Who? Never mind, tell me later. Used me make up mirror, didn't I? Held it over the cubicle, from the inside, obviously. Took loads of care, but they was too engrossed, weren't they."

I was impressed by the count of eleven out of ten. And I told her so.

"That's what you get for being a good boy. I'm good at this job, Moncks, and you need me, like I told you before, but as long as I'm always Top Bitch, like." She turned away and polished off her pint without further ado. "Wanna come back my place, Moncks, and do lots of fun things?"

Once again I declined, but I did call in for a coffee when I dropped her off. She had a glass of wine, a large glass.

"Gawd, Laura, your stomach."

"It's a one-off, ain't it? Bit of a celebration, don't ya know?" The last line was delivered in her best impression of an up-market voice, frankly a total failure, but the drink was at last taking its toll.

I left for home, tonight without the customary kiss goodbye, for which I was grateful.

On the drive back she'd been expounding all her theories about how to deal with Shel's situation but I'd concentrated on my driving and it had gone in one ear and out the other, and I'd thus been able to offer no recommendations much to Laura's chagrin. It was all too obvious to her that I hadn't been listening.

Fatal.

So I wasn't flavour of the month.

# Chapter Nine
# Not enough clues

"First of all, Ms Pratt, why didn't you come to us with this information?"

Yvonne Pratt, private eye, was late middle-age, pleasantly rotund with short, dark red hair that utterly suited her round and rather pretty face. She wore an expression that said butter-wouldn't-melt and don't-mess-with-me all at the same time.

Facially she was at once little-miss-innocent and a creature of fiery menace. DC Hadlesome felt slightly overawed and unsure of himself, not his usual state of mind. But there was something about this woman that he found unnerving, that was for sure.

"Oh, officer, I'm so sorry, but it would never have occurred to me to be relevant to the poor woman's murder. Why should it? Why should the two be connected? But I'm so very sorry, I really am."

The contrition was undoing Grant Hadlesome's best efforts to be professional, and undermining his best efforts to be scolding. She looked as if she might cry and feminine tears had always been his downfall. The trouble was that too many women had taken advantage of his aversion over the years. He had a natural urge to comfort and to give in when confronted by the waterworks, particularly if he believed he was responsible, which he was usually told he was in order to add weight to the ladies' imagined grief.

By this sorry medium he had often surrendered ground, money, possessions and any moral rights he might feel he had at that given moment. His love life had been one disaster after another. Nearly all his liaisons ended in tears as most of his lady friends discovered that was a good way to achieve whatever they wanted.

So he was most concerned Yvonne Pratt might break down similarly. The tears of a woman were his one weakness as a police officer, but he was struggling gamely to overcome his disadvantage.

On this occasion the woman in front of him saved the situation, first by not bursting into tears, and second by offering to hand over all her files and accompany him to the station if required.

In that moment he just happened to look at her eyes. Her whole face was alight. Her eyes twinkled with fun and mischief. Her lips looked ready to devour him with passion. In that moment she was indeed the most beautiful and desirable woman he'd ever seen. And in that moment he wanted her madly. And in that moment she knew exactly what he was thinking, and that she had him where she wanted him.

What is good for the goose is not always good for the gander. By the same token what will work with one man won't with another, and Inspector Gregson was not for being worked.

If Hadlesome had shown any leniency, Gregson was merciless and launched a ruthless and scathing attack at the private detective. She did actually shed some tears but every drop of water was wasted. The Inspector had the bit between his teeth and tore into her, quietly but effectively, keeping his own self control perfectly yet ensuring Yvonne Pratt might feel well and truly admonished.

William Bailey was feeling well and truly admonished.

Back home after being roasted over an open spit he had turned to the bottle. He cursed the police with a vengeance as he prowled around the expansive lounge with nobody to listen to his words. Where the hell was Jayne-Marie when he needed her? He cursed her as well. Then he cursed Yvonne Pratt, and finally he cursed Phyllis Downport.

That brought him back to near normality. She had, after all, left him a dirty great fortune (his terminology), and if he shared it all with Ms Panahan she ought to be well pleased. And forgiving. Perhaps she would properly forgive him his wandering. She'd never quite led him to believe he was completely forgiven. Maybe this would help, maybe it would.

***

Laura busied herself, when time permitted, she did have her part-time job in the dockyard to attend to, looking into Gary and Lorraine Wimbush, late of Hemel Hempstead. Possibly still of Hemel Hempstead. Facebook and the usual social media suspects drew a blank.

It was always possible her sister had been divorced from Gary and had remarried. There was a chance she might be dead and Laura was prepared for this, and not attempting to blot her worst fear from her mind.

She visited the library and used the computer. She used her mobile phone until the credit ran out, as it did often, and persevered like a creature possessed. Secretly she was hoping to get to the truth before David Canbown, always assuming he might do so.

I, David Canbown, had never been to Hemel Hempstead. I'd passed through on odd occasions, usually on a high speed train, and had not felt the desire to make a visit. Neighbouring Berkhampstead could be different. From the train, on a fine day, the canal made for a picturesque scene in which a reasonable town played the part of a reasonable backdrop. There was countryside, so I had regarded Berkhampstead, rightly or wrongly, as an acceptable meeting place for town and country.

And the Grand Union Canal added the finishing touch.

No plan of action existed in my mind and I had nowhere in particular to start any sort of search of Hemel Hempstead. Instead I'd been thinking about Linnie and Shel, and whether I should simply give the former my report and walk away, or try and offer a solution. But then I didn't have one, a solution, that is.

There had been plenty of time for thinking as I'd encountered a couple of long-term traffic jams on the M25. The Dartford Crossing had been horrendous as usual. It had taken ages to reach Hertfordshire, yet I was almost rewarded at once.

A small cycle shop bore the legend 'Wimbush Cycles' and I duly made enquiries.

No joy. The owner knew of no family member called Gary, never mind a wife named Lorraine.

So near and yet so far. But he did recommend talking to a man who worked in a local baker's shop.

"Ian Prensell's his name. Lived here a long time. Been a good friend so mention my name. I remember, many years ago, he had a run in with a guy called Gary, and now I come to think of it I'm sure the wife's name was Lorraine. Might've been Lorraine. I'm just not sure, but worth you asking Ian."

As a copper I can tell you it's amazing how many times you hear someone say they're certain of something and then qualify it in some way. In one paragraph the man in front of me said he was sure it was Lorraine, then might've been, and finally he wasn't sure. I had a feeling he was just trying to get rid of me.

My story had been perfectly true. I was trying to trace a long-lost relative for a client, and, as my ID confirmed, I was a professional private investigator. I knew it wouldn't matter, I knew I'd be viewed with suspicion, the same fate for my mission.

I didn't find Ian Prensell at once as he wasn't at work that day. Try again tomorrow.

So it was time to find some accommodation and have a wander round, because you never know what you might stumble upon. And I stumbled (metaphorically speaking) across the grave of Arnold Walton Wimbush, much loved husband of Sheila and father of Gary and Norma.

The death occurred three years before so there was a chance widow Wimbush was still alive and still in the area. This was a lead I couldn't let go.

That night I phoned Laura with the news and she updated me with her efforts. She'd been on the computer, as agreed, and found numbers for all the people named Wimbush in the area I was searching. There weren't many. Well, most folk are ex-directory these days. So I was left with the merest handful and a quick ring round revealed precisely nothing.

Once again I spoke to Laura and I could hear the disappointment in her voice.

"Wish I could've come with you," she wailed softly. "We could've shared a room and investigated each other." She was never down for long! I skated over both issues, coming with me and sharing a room, and said I'd be in touch tomorrow. Now for a pint or two and a meal.

Unbeknown to me 'tomorrow' was going to have unexpected contents and be positively hazardous.

*** 

On the flight to Stansted Jayne-Marie Panahan was totally preoccupied and anxious. ·

What had William told the police? What information had Yvonne Pratt passed on? Neither person, in her opinion, could be expected to 'use their loaf', meaning that she was worried both might tell the truth and not let tact and diplomacy come into their thinking.

She was a woman of note and influence and she was determined not to be treated poorly by police officers. She must have the upper hand at all times, and with that in mind had already put her solicitor, Sumitra Bhatia, on permanent standby under orders to be at the airport to meet her.

Jitters. That's what Jayne-Marie had. The jitters.

A delay to the landing arrangements only fuelled the fire. She needed to know what the other two had been saying and what the police were up to. Unsurprisingly, when she landed, reclaimed her suitcase and cleared formalities, and met up with Sumitra she was ready to explode and did so all over the poor girl and with a horrible degree if venom.

The solicitor simply accepted this. Ms Panahan paid well for her practice's services, and this latest escapade would bring handsome rewards and possibly, if she did really well, a leg-up for Sumitra.

The drive to Suffolk was not pleasant for various reasons, one being the traffic and another being Sumitra's decision to travel east on the A120 to pick up the A12 in the direction of Ipswich.

Pouring rain added to the discomfort. Jayne-Marie, living life in the fast lane, believed any journey of distance should be undertaken by motorway where possible as these offered the opportunity to exceed the speed limits by appreciable margins.

Her route home would've been north on the M11 and then east on the A14, an altogether longer run, a fact she refused to acknowledge. Her grumpiness increased when it became clear that her driver had no intention of exceeding the speed limit at all. Eventually she screamed.

"For God's sake get me a solicitor who will do a hundred on this wretched road."

But that, temporarily, did the trick and calmed things down, so much so that Jayne-Marie was full of apologies, even offering to make it up to the object of her aggression. A couple of traffic jams helped raise tension levels again, but each time she allowed herself to cool down. In standing traffic she did once look Sumitra right in the eye and felt a pang of regret. It was in that moment that she was overcome by the woman's simple beauty.

She spent the rest of the ride home in silence, thinking how lovely Sumitra was, and occasionally risking a sustained glance in the solicitor's direction. If anything it was these actions that more unnerved the girl than all Jayne-Marie's rantings.

Once indoors, her eyes blazing, she ignored William's attempted greeting and avoided his kiss, and the three of them sat down in her office, ready for business.

"Where's Yvonne?"

"I don't know. Did you want her here?"

"Of course I want her here, you idiot. How unbelievable! I organise my solicitor and you can't think to get Yvonne over. Men? Useless, the lot of you."

"Shall I phone her now?"

"It's too bloody late now, isn't it? My God, where did I get you from?"

William Bailey was beginning to wish that wherever she'd got him from he wouldn't mind being put back. But it wasn't long before the police arrived, far too quick for Jayne-Marie to conduct a proper de-briefing. And now she had the extra worry about what Yvonne Pratt might have said without any immediate means of finding out.

***

"He's having you on, mate. Probably don't trust you and neither do I."

I'd had to wait at the baker's for fifteen minutes before Ian Prensell could be spared, and now we were standing on the pavement a few yards from the shop. He was referring to the man in 'Wimbush Cycles'.

"He knew Gary, but I don't think the lad was family, not his anyway. Gary and his missus are long gone, pal, long gone. He got some job in Matlock or somewhere, as far as I know. Don't remember wife's name."
"What *did* he do for a living, when he was here?" I asked, hopeful of an answer that might be of assistance. I hoped in vain.

"Can't remember. In and out of work, that one. If I remember his missus did some domestic cleaning. Sometimes, like."

"Any children?"

"Nope."

"How did you come to know him, Mr Prensell?"

"Well, you're not the police and I'm not telling you, and now I gotta get back to work."

I stood deserted on the pavement. I was further on in my enquiries than I'd really expected to be. Naturally I still wanted to find widow Wimbush in case her son Gary was the Gary I was seeking, for she might know his whereabouts.

The problem right now was that as soon as I briefed Laura she became over-excited. I knew from experience that such optimism can be misplaced and can lead to disappointment magnified a hundred times. It was a good job she didn't have a car or I'm convinced she'd be up here, exactly where I didn't need her.

"Just one thing," I'd added in deflationary mode, "how come you didn't find the number for Wimbush Cycles? Top Bitch is slipping." The distance between Kent and Hertfordshire was sufficient for me to risk such a comment and the silence that followed did not bode well.

"All make mistakes, Moncks. Never looked at businesses. I mean, who'd call their shop Wimbush Cycles? Stupid man." I had a silent chuckle and threw her own words back at her.

"Ouch! Top Bitch doesn't like being bitten, does she?"

"Wait till I get you home and you'll see precisely where Top Bitch bites for maximum pain." It was time to call a truce. I smoothed things over by saying I'd take her to Derbyshire if we had to go and if she could get the time off.

82

"That's the right answer, Moncks. You get to stay alive. See, Top Bitch wins every time." And I had to confess she was right, for I had succumbed again, afeared for the consequences of my remarks.

Now for widow Wimbush, little realising widow Wimbush had remarried, a fact that was to darken my skies as I soon discovered.

*** 

The knowledge of the type of pistol and bullet used to murder Alistair Bourne-Lacey was currently of little value, although such intelligence was obviously vital in police work. There was nothing to suggest either was out of the ordinary and that meant a wider search. He'd been shot from about eight feet away and almost definitely left where he fell, face down in long grass by the roadside.

No sign of the gun. Enquiries centred, for the present, on where he'd been last seen and when, and the closest they'd got so far was his next door neighbour who'd seen him enter his house at about seven p.m. His car was parked outside where it had been since the previous day.

That not only left a gap of nearly twelve hours betwixt sighting and death, it also posed a mystery as to why Bourne-Lacey was killed where he was. How did he get there? Was he taken there for the purpose, did he walk there (not expecting to be executed), had he just arrived on site or had he been waiting some time prior to being shot? Forensics were baffled but they were good at turning up the unexpected and, well, you never knew.

DS Jamie Harggest was studying the transcript of the interview with Neville Gradling and slowly shaking his head. He had an orange marker pen in one hand but had so far managed to highlight exactly nothing, a possible reflection of the fact he'd not found what he was looking for. He guessed he was looking for some weakness, an issue that did not add up, a secret message the transcript wasn't yet prepared to give up.

"He didn't pull the trigger but my money says he paid someone to do it. Threatening Bourne-Lacey was never going to be enough for a man like Gradling. I just know it wasn't."

"Your famous intuition, Jamie?" queried the eager DS Holton Okafor, sprinkling the edges of his remark with a light dusting of sarcasm.

"Yeah. Alright, I know I've been wrong before, alright, alright, but this one is speaking a thousand words of guilt to me. I just don't know why."

The two detectives shared a wry grin across the cramped office.

"What do we know about the private tec, what's his name?" Okafor looked down at his notes for the answer. "Ah yes, David Canbown?"

"You've seen the report, we know why he got the push, and he's not been long as a private eye. Now his story I believe. I think I know when someone's telling me porkies and I've got him down as genuine. But, being the good coppers we are, Holton, we're not about to erase his name from our list, are we?"

Both good coppers exchanged another set of wry grins.

Both good coppers went back to what they were doing, which in Harggest's case was speculating on Gradling's interview and the prospect of actually having to use his marker pen.

***

In Devon another 'good copper' was musing on the sum of his knowledge.

DS Geoff Alcock had a nagging doubt. Nathan Kethnet was not the sort of person to lie down meekly while authority trampled all over him. After an initial outburst, the usual sort of rubbish about knowing the Chief Constable and all that rot, Kethnet had calmed and seemed completely at ease with the prospect of being a suspect. It was almost as if he'd made a brief fuss because he ought to – man of position and wealth and influence – but then he'd settled down to actually enjoying the role of being under suspicion.

He'd laughed at his wife just as he'd laughed at the loss of her lover, Edward Nobbs.

And he now didn't appear to mind being fully investigated. In truth he was so co-operative that Alcock's nagging doubt was probably well founded.

This was a strange situation. It was true that the remaining suspects were behaving just as the falsely accused should. Kethnet had an alibi so watertight it would've survived the sinking of the *Titanic* and come up bone dry. So, Alcock wondered, did he hire a hit man?

By coincidence a similar thought was being arrived at in Kent.

"Right, everyone, listen up. This has all the hallmarks of a professional job. Nice and clean and tidy, no forensic, no DNA, no weapon, no clues. Looking at the possible suspects I would venture to suggest none had the money for a pro. *Except* Neville Gradling.

"Powerful people tend to get right up my nose, and that's putting it politely. They invariably know the Chief Constable, probably the Prime Minister, maybe the Queen, possibly even God! This guy's got an alibi that an atom bomb couldn't disturb. May have bought that as well, of course.

"We've got to keep plugging away at the suspects, but keep an open mind guys as there could be others we haven't unearthed. And we need answers about Alistair Bourne-Lacey's last journey. I'm going to call him ABL, let's all do the same, can't be doing with that mouthful. But I am going to centre our efforts on Neville Gradling, and that means we also give his missus a good looking into, and that goes for the private eye too.

"If Gradling paid someone there's got to be links. We don't actually know how well Mrs Gradling was getting on with ABL. She's afraid of her husband, no question, so let's not ignore the possibility of her wanting ABL off her back, so to speak. Did she arrange his shooting?

"No matter how unlikely anything seems, don't dismiss it. I don't know about this private eye. Normally I hate them just less than I hate powerful people. But this guy told a smart-arse lawyer what to do with his conviction. Normally I hate smart-arse lawyers more than I hate powerful people, but it cost a good bloke his job and, in my book, he was proved right when another innocent woman was viciously attacked.

"So I'm giving this David Canbown the benefit of the doubt, but only up to a point. He came to us straight away, gave us every co-operation. Usually the work of the guilty! We all know that, but, well, I'm not writing him off, but y'know guys, keep an open mind.

"Right now I'd like permission to search Gradling's place, do his computers, the works. But I need some sort of evidence as you all know. Let's go get it, shall we?"

The senior officer's briefing continued in much the same vein with work details being handed out.

Questions were answered and the meeting closed. A case with precious few clues, too many alibis, and enough suspects to make an Agatha Christie mystery. They were currently up against it and they knew it.

DS Holton Okafor was given the task of searching out this type of modus operandi amongst the killer-for-hire fraternity, and that involved contacting other forces as well as delving into the police's own computer systems. Although it was a search destined to produce so little it did manage to light a small fire in the Detective Sergeant's mind, and it wouldn't take a lot to fan the flames and render up an answer of sorts.

\*\*\*

At long last I departed Hemel Hempstead, older and wiser.

It proved an easy task tracking down widow Wimbush, now Mrs Peterson. However, Mr Peterson was far from welcoming, refusing me access to the former Mrs Wimbush.

"Gary, right little toe-rag he was," he explained in his own delightful and complimentary terms. "Led his mum a right dance. Anyway, he's pi ... I mean he's gone off with that wife of his. Slut, if you ask me. Went years ago, Derbyshire or somewheres, I don't know. His mum don't want nothing to do with him or that .. that ... *tart.*

"She never hears from him, nor don't want to. And that's all we're telling you, sunshine, so get on yer bike if you know what's good for you." I did wonder just how long Mr Peterson had known Mrs Wimbush before she was a widow to know so much about her family affairs, but I took his suggestion and rode out of town.

I hope my brief visit helped improve the incoming tourism statistics for Hemel Hempstead as I guessed they might need a bit of leg-up. And I was on my way home with all the information I could reasonable hope to gain.

And to face a woman excited and anxious to receive my news. That was the worrying part!

## Chapter Ten

# Progress

The interview with Jayne-Marie Panahan was strained and fraught with good reason.

The interviewer was frustrated by constant interruptions by Sumitra Bhatia, the solicitor. Ms Panahan was being objectionable and awkward (in the officer's opinion) and was making it unequivocally apparent that she was from the do-you-know-who-I-am, I-know-your-Chief-Constable school of unreasonableness.

Opposite her sat a senior detective who had risen to her exalted station by virtue of being highly successful, a woman who had outclassed those officers around her, and who now enjoyed and took advantage of a wealth of experience. Her next question sizzled into Jayne-Marie's mind.

"No innocent person would behave as you are. No innocent person would need such a smoke screen around them." Suddenly leaning forward across the desk before an open-mouthed Sumitra and a wide-eyed Jayne-Marie could respond, she spoke in a menacing and a loud, whispered tone.

"Don't you realise the damage you're doing yourself? Your attitude alone makes me suspicious, and you don't want me to be suspicious, do you? You don't want to be a suspect, do you?"

And with that she leaned back and suspended the interview before anyone else could react.

"I know it's all on tape, Ms Bhatia, don't bother telling me. I'll leave you and Ms Panahan to have a chat and we'll have another try. Tea, coffee or hot chocolate?"

\*\*\*

Being nigh impossible to grab a parking slot anywhere near Laura's flat from early evening I drove to a town centre car park, these being free after six p.m., and took a walk of less than ten minutes to her home. I was welcomed like a long lost friend. She'd gone out of her way to tidy herself up and with her hair properly organised looked an attractive treat. Steady on boy, I said to myself, there may be an ulterior motive.

Wine was offered as usual, declined as usual (as usual when I was driving), and a tray of snacks placed in front of us. Home-made delights including jam sponge, cheese scones, sausage rolls and bacon twirls adorned the tray of many pleasures. Bacon twirls, I remembered telling her, are a favourite of mine.

There was a selection of cheeses and biscuits, celery and tomato, and a dish of crisps.

I changed my mind and said I'd have one glass of wine.

"Don't force y'self, Moncks," she intoned as she sped to the fridge. "Cheapo Soave okay?" I called out my agreement and she was back in seconds with a very full glass. "Right, hit me, pal. Tell Top Bitch all about it."

A full and frank account of my travels and travails followed in which I omitted very little, an account that featured a number of pauses for the intake of sustenance, mastication and swallowing, and swigs of cheapo Soave. She hardly removed her eyes from me, save when she collected up some food.

It had been agreed she'd supply tonight's supper so there was no need for me to eat on the way home. I just had to ring when I left my place so she could warm that which needed warming, like the bacon twirls. These were the first items to completely vanish, rapidly pursued by the hot home-made sausage rolls.

I felt so at home. The meal was delicious and I told her so.

"Thank me in bed tonight."

"I'm not stopping."

"Fine. I'll come back to your place."

"Sorry, that's a no-no."

"You ain't listening brother."

"Sorry, but we are not sharing a bed."

"Look, Moncks, I'm clean in every sense. Used to go up the GUM clinic regular, like. And I've scrubbed ev'ry last millimetre of m'body to be hyper-clean for you tonight, babycakes."

"Then I'm truly sorry to disappoint you. It's got nothing to do with you being unclean, and it's not that I don't fancy you......"

Ooooo. Bad mistake. Once again, in trying to painlessly extricate myself, I'd said the wrong thing. When will I learn? Top Bitch wins again. I am starting to think she might just be a tad more clever than I am. As my voice trailed off betraying my failure she manufactured the broadest grin I think I've ever seen on a human being.

"Wahay, my little monkey. That took a lot, didn't it? So you fancy Lovely Lady Laura do you? Then my day will come. Alpha Male going to keep me simmering until he decides when to bring me to the boil, eh? Okay, Top Bitch will play along, no probs." And she giggled in such a seductive way I could've ravished her there and then.

Then I laughed. Once again I'd been done up like a kipper, as my aunt Clara used to say.

"So when we off to Derbyshire?" she interjected swiftly.

"Hold your horses," as Clara also used to say, "we've got unfinished business down Faversham way. I'll ring Linnie tomorrow and I'll pop over as soon as it's convenient."

"Hold your *own* horse, my lovely. Laurakins is involved, remember? We's partners."

"Sorry, but I have to see her alone. That's the way it is. Sorry. She mustn't know about you. I appreciate all you've done, I really do, but, even though we're partners, you're not official. Please understand."

She looked crestfallen and curled her bottom lip, then spoke.

"Let you go alone if you stay tonight."

***

Fae Darnlett's brother had been eliminated from police enquiries, and Nobbs's commercial competitor also appeared to have a cast iron alibi.

Cathy Kethnet didn't but would she have wanted Edward Nobbs dead?

It was widely believed she did not possess the strength to wrap a rope around Nobbs's neck and pull it tight until he perished. He was a tough, strong lad, tall and well-built, and would've fought back at the very least, but there were no signs of a struggle.

And why slaughter your lover? That was difficult territory for DS Geoff Alcock. Cathy had discovered the body and reacted exactly as an innocent person would, and reacted exactly as he assumed a lover would. She was heartbroken. Alcock could not understand why anyone would want an extra-marital affair but he accepted that it was a zone of human nature he knew least about, having never suffered the desire to be unfaithful.

Unless they had fallen out, and it was always possible Cathy had found out about Fae Darnlett and was thus the woman scorned, and unless Cathy found some incredible strength from somewhere, she was more than likely in the clear.

If she was going to hire a hit man she surely wouldn't want to be in the vicinity when the deed was carried out.

Alcock's thinking returned once more to Nathan Kethnet, now Mr Nice Guy, and the prospect of an ordered assassination. Time to talk to Mr Wapernod, the private eye, again.

John Wapernod sat impassively and listened to the Detective Sergeant putting forward his thoughts.

"Sergeant, setting aside the fact you are only telling me what you want me to know, it is, and I say this with great respect, your job to hypothesise, not mine. Nor is it my job to comment on your theories. I am, you'll remember, something of a suspect myself." Alcock considered this all very carefully, realising Wapernod had the measure of him.

"Alright, Mr Wapernod, what I really need to know is whether Edward and Cathy had a falling out, and whether Cathy or her husband paid for a hit man. Are there any matters in your own investigations that might point the way? There, that's being open and honest with you."

"Well, Sergeant, you have my files. I cannot add to the material there. I have no evidence to suggest a hit man, and Cathy and Edward, as you'll have seen, behaved like star-crossed lovers all the time I was watching them. The last occasion was a full week before his death, so I've no idea what occurred after that."

Alcock left it at that. This was all going nowhere fast, and annoyingly so. No forensic evidence at the scene of the crime. Nobbs was dead no more than fifty minutes before his lover found him.

No witnesses had come forward relating to Nobbs's movements in the hour or more prior to his slaying. No witnesses had seen anyone else in the vicinity, and that included Cathy.

But of course she was going to a secret liaison so didn't want to be seen.

Damn! There was a killer out there and nobody noticed anyone?

***

Laura sat in the car while I went in to see Linnie Yatesman.

This was another compromise in which I had surrendered and she'd been victorious. It was the price to be paid for not staying the night, and even though it might appear she was the loser she'd still come up smelling of roses. We went together to Faversham.

Laura was all for having a chat with the errant Shel Crackby, and I have to admit she had a good point. She knew more about the sharp end of drug abuse than I did, and was likely to be able to speak the language of the addict, that is, speak the language they would understand. Better than someone 'in authority' or some righteous bastard like me, I suppose.

But I needed to talk to my client first.

It wasn't easy. I told her I'd found no evidence of involvement in crime other than being a drug user. She was so shocked, so very pale, and so very shaken that I was frightened she could fall victim to some sort if medical attack. I explained what I knew about drug addiction, for she was much in ignorance, and also enlightened her to the desperate and difficult road to remission.

"It isn't about deciding to come off the drugs. If, Linnie, you decided, for arguments sake, to give up eating biscuits then with a little willpower you could probably manage it easily. Not so the drug user." Then I hit on an idea. "Look, Linnie, this is up to you. I've brought an ex-addict with me. You don't have to see her but she could explain it all far better than me, and she'd be the ideal person to talk to Shel."

Miss Yatesman looked at me so forlorn, and with such a hangdog expression, that I really couldn't see this business getting very far.

"The thing is, David, how do I tell Shel that I know? I can't tell her I've had her followed."

"Take a chance, Linnie, and expect her to lie to you at first. We know she brought the stuff home so she must've smoked the weed here, perhaps outdoors. Perhaps indoors and then a trip round with the air freshener. Just challenge her on the smell you sometimes detect. Tell her that you know, and that it's no good lying.

"But you've got to be prepared for the worst. She may storm out, it could spell the end of the relationship, things might not be the same again." At this point Linnie dissolved into torrents of tears. Her shoulders heaved, she wailed a dreadful noise, and she curled into a ball on her settee as if she was enduring the most awful of agonies, which in a way she was.

I moved across to try and comfort her but she brushed me aside, and rolled herself up in a sobbing heap. I felt so helpless. After a few minutes she regained enough composure to ask me to leave, telling me to submit my bill, and then rolled up again to give the seat another soaking.

This what not what I had wanted to deal with when I elected to become a private eye, and I was ill-equipped to deal with it as a human being. I left feeling empty and ashamed, and cross with myself because I hadn't handled it well. Back in the car I told Laura everything.

"Well, y'did yer best. Sometimes I reckon our best just ain't good enough. Drop me home, you'll get parked this time of day, and let's have a drink together." And that's what we did. I felt as if I'd been kicked in the guts. "Look, Moncks, that's life, ain't it? Thanks for offering me, anyways, I'd have liked to come in but maybe it's for the best. Bad shock for her. But better than you telling her Shel's a hardened criminal, or a gangster's moll, is that the right word?"

We tried to share a mournful chuckle and failed.

I gradually recovered my spirits and set off for home, Laura having tried, as usual, every trick in the book to spend more time with me, a vain effort.

During the evening I had an unexpected call from Linnie Yatesman.

She'd talked to Shel, gently and kindly, and received lies and animosity in return. But Shel had finally confessed and, having done so, flung herself off to the bedroom and pleaded with her partner not to enter. Linnie was after advice. For one thing Shel was having a fix and Linnie was acquainting herself with the aroma of drugs, and didn't like them emanating from the bedroom she shared with her lover.

"I just wondered, David, if your friend or whoever she is, could come and have a chat with her. I'm so desperate and I'm so afraid she'll walk out on me and I couldn't bear it. David, she's my whole world, my whole life, the only true love I've ever known....." The words faded as the sound of agonised sobbing took their place down the line.

"Shall we come straight away?"

"Oh, please, please, *please*. I just don't know what to do and I'm sure to say the wrong thing. Please help me, David, please come now, please." The despair was engraved into every word, the pain felt tangible even through the medium of the telephone, the wretchedness was soaked into her pleas.

"Be there as soon as we can." I was taking it for granted Laura would be willing and I knew, as she'd informed me all too often on the way home, she had a free evening.

***

After brief introductions Laura went up to the bedroom and we held our breaths. Linnie was a picture of a heartbroken soul, wrecked and washed-up, her face a map of anguish, fear and hopelessness. She cried but no more tears would come. She sat on the armchair and screwed her hands up in her lap, her head bowed, her heart torn asunder.

I've never felt so sorry for anyone in my whole life, and I knew she didn't want my comfort, so I sat on the settee and silently watched Linnie reduce herself to a crumbling heap of desolation.

It was some time before both girls came downstairs, Laura ordering me to put the kettle on. Therefore I could not witness the immediate aftermath of affairs, but Laura later described how she'd handled the situation, and how Shel had thrown herself into Linnie's arms, apologising, swearing undying love, crying fit to bust.

As it happened my drink making skills weren't needed. Laura fetched me from the kitchen and took me straight to the car.

The upshot was that Shel was going to seek help with Laura's support. But most importantly Laura had not merely won her over, she'd re-ignited the love Shel had for Linnie by explaining exactly what her partner was going through. She'd emphasised the serious nature of things and how the continued addiction would ruin the relationship, and probably finish her career as a care worker just for good measure.

She had been prepared to listen to Laura, and was genuinely concerned about the grief she was causing Linnie. I couldn't have achieved that, and neither could Linnie. Laura was the right person. And I was very, very impressed.

However we both knew only too well the odds were against Shel making it. An addict doesn't just walk away from their comforter, and even the devoted love of a dedicated partner can make no difference, but Laura believed Shel had been caught in the early stages. We didn't find out what the pills were. Hoping they're not as dangerous as some of them.

In the back of my mind was the impending trip to Matlock and the removal of Laura McCaffield from the front line. She would be needed in Kent not Derbyshire. Still that was a problem for another day.

*** 

DS Holton Okafor was musing on the joys of present day policing, and revelling in the experience.

How did they manage in the old days, he thought, without computers, radios, mobile phones, tasers et al?

Here he was, possibly on the cusp of something interesting, and all down to technology and its advanced application.

He'd been busy studying all kinds of police activity on the system, searching records, looking for established tie-ins, anything and everything. And there it was. A woman recently stabbed to death in Suffolk. No clues, no evidence, but she'd been investigated by a private eye who was following a straying husband.

Soon he was talking to DS Stephanie Broome and the prospect of the cases being pure coincidence began to recede. The more they learned about their own murders the more the parallels emerged and took shape.

Wealthy spouse, worried about their partner playing away, hires private detective to find evidence. In neither situation was divorce on the menu. They simply wanted to know so that they could warn their unfaithful other halves, and perhaps warn the lovers too.

And it was the lovers who were killed. No DNA, nothing much for forensics to go on, no evidence.

The hirers had alibis, as did the private eyes. Paid killers could be an answer.

Stephanie Broome suggested they issue a joint report and log it around the country's forces to see if any similar murders had occurred. Holton had put forward the idea that, despite the different weapons, they could be dealing with the same hit man. Or woman, of course.

Both consulted their immediate superiors who were ready to agree any course of action that might move the investigations on. Steph said she'd check out any known hired killers who might be at large and who were known to use various weapons. It was almost a tongue in cheek venture but every avenue needed pursuing. There could be a convicted killer out after their imprisonment picking up where he or she left off. It had been known to happen.

A variety of other enquiries were instigated.

In the west country it was DS Geoff Alcock who picked up on it.

"You see, sir," he said to his Inspector, "this looks almost an identical situation to the one surrounding Edward Nobbs."

"Agreed, Geoff. Another weapon as well. Wonder if any other forces have responded? Anyway, talk to Broome and let's get the ball rolling. Offer all co-operation, and in the pious hope they'll share everything with us!"

It wasn't long before Geoff, Holton and Steph were on a conference call. No, there hadn't been a response from elsewhere, but they were able to discuss and assess all three cases and the alarming similarities.

The upshot was that they could, *could* be dealing with a serial killer, an assassin perhaps specialising in dealing with the lovers of wandering spouses. And there they began to realise that they were entering the realms of the surreal and looking at the stuff of crime novels and tv crime series.

Suddenly it didn't seem such a likely idea, and mere coincidence reared its head again.

But seeds had been sown and many more enquiries were to be made, but for the time being more pressure needed to be applied to the wronged, two male and one female, all of whom had hired private eyes.

And that pressure also needed to be applied to those private eyes, because you never know.

# Chapter Eleven
## Questions, questions, always questions.

It was Thursday.

Yes, I know there are nigh on fifty-two a year, and I can't remember exactly which one it was, but I do know it was a Thursday. It's just one of those things. We can all recall what we were doing on certain days in our lives. And this happened on a Thursday, and it caused a marked change in my life.

A mate from my old force called me up. Adam Pensfield, now a DCI.

After a bit of chat about how we were both getting on, all that sort of thing, he said something that startled me.

"Main reason I'm ringing is I notice you're involved in a murder in Kent. Private tec followed the victim who was having it off with the wife of some wealthy bloke. Can't tell you any more, you know the rules, but there's been a couple of other recent killings elsewhere and, surprise surprise, both victims were being followed by amateur super sleuths like you, and both had been caught having it away where they shouldn't."

"Felt I had to ring, Dave, you know how these things come up on the system, and just wondered if the locals have mentioned it to you."

"No Adam, and I can't see them sharing that with an amateur super sleuth like me, you sarky old sod," I heard his faint chuckle.

"Well, don't tell 'em I told you or you'll be the next victim."

"I can't tell them at all, can I, cos they'll know it's come from a mate on the strength."

"Hoped you'd say that."

"And I don't suppose you can tell me any more, and there *is* more, isn't there? Like these three murders could be linked, or at least performed by the same creature of death?"

There was a brief silence.

"My lips are sealed."

"That tells me all I need to know, Adam. And at the same time tells me precious nothing."

"Yup. But you know more than you did before I called, and I really did think you'd want to know."

"Can't tell me where these other two were?"

"Nope. Told you more than I should. Anyway, changing the subject, you know me and Angie went to Devon for a holiday last year, well, we're thinking about Suffolk this time."

I wasn't going to be able to tease more from him, but it was a valuable tip-off, and he'd kindly slipped me two very obvious clues. After more matey chit-chat and the exchange of friendly abuse he did agree to pop over sometime and buy me a pint. Now to find out about the other two killings.

I'd taken to Adam from day one. Keen, clever, with an eye for detail that meant he could spot things others (myself included) had overlooked. So he was always going to make an accomplished detective, and he'd certainly enjoyed a successful career.

On the downside he represented a dying breed of copper who probably mourned the fact he hadn't been around when interrogation methods had included accidental use of the truncheon. A complete bigot, he resented women getting on in the force and for that matter getting on in any walk of professional life, and so, unsurprisingly, resented fast-track graduates in the police.

"University of life, that's where you learn," he used to say, and all too frequently, "and that takes time and experience. Nowhere is experience more important than in the police."

As a young man, as I remember him, he'd been beefy and yet incredibly fit. He turned down opportunities to play rugby, for which he was unquestionably suited physically, saying he didn't like sport much. Square-jawed, his head seemed to narrow towards the top where it was covered, in those days, with a thick clump of short black hair.

He may well have detested women getting on but he didn't detest women per se. On the contrary, he never appeared to have any difficulty finding a lady, and there were plenty attracted to his manly physique and brusque, no-nonsense manner.

Angie is his third wife. As thick as a plank, all her principal attributes must be physical. I could never see any other reason why a man would be attracted to her. They usually go on holiday to places like Orlando, Minorca, Sardinia and, on one occasion, Thailand, and I don't suppose either of them knew where their destinations were. Not once had I known them to even have a short break in this country, so the chances of Angie wanting to try Devon and Suffolk would be nil unless she thought they were in the Mediterranean!

So thanks for the clues, mon ami.

I'll say this for Adam, he's kept in touch with me and we've met a number of times. He was prepared to stand up and be counted in my support which is more than could be said of some of them. Certain 'friends' in my force were almost embarrassed by the prospect of voicing support, maybe because they thought it would damage their own careers. Very genuine, Adam. What you see is what you get.

I didn't know his first wife, Veronica, but the marriage lasted barely a year, so I was told. Then, after a prolonged period rummaging in the market place, he married Natasha, a matronly lady, tall and as well built as Adam. I guessed (he certainly never told me) that he married her hoping she would be everything, in his opinion, a wife should be. A homemaker, chef, cleaner, washer-woman, nurse, rampant lover, confidante, counsellor, and mother if so required.

There were indeed two children, both little more than infants when divorce came, Natasha winning custody easily, almost a relief to Adam. The break up arrived when he started dating Angie behind Natasha's back. She was having none of that, and he was shown the proverbial door. Angie came complete with a teenage daughter who, by dead reckoning, must've been born when the woman was fifteen.

Yes, Adam was probably born about a hundred years too late! Things have changed, at home and at work. I never subscribed to his view of the role of women, but I have to admit, as you know, that I've moved on because I started thinking for myself and gradually eliminated all, or most, of the bad inbred, ingrained ideas about men and women. I'd like to think I'm a better person but I still have the odd lapse.

Now, who do I know who would love researching these other two cases? Yes, you're right.

*** 

DS Okafor was getting up my nose and under my skin which must sound like a rather nasty and unpleasant invasive experience.

The man showed his contempt with his facial expressions and with his tone of voice and sometimes his choice of words. He didn't like the concept of private detectives and he didn't like me.

Most of my own questions went unanswered. For instance:

"Is there anything to suggest the killing was related to Mr Bourne-Lacey's affair with Jackie Gradling?"

"We're investigating all possibilities, it's what we do well in the police. *Sir.*"

"I just wondered if there'd been another similar murder somewhere. This one seems devoid of any real clues."

"What makes you say that, *sir*? Why would we share our information with the public, with you, *sir*? You're not a policeman now, *sir*." He had to drag the word 'sir' out of his throat where it was in danger of remaining stuck, and when he did achieve it he completely shrouded it with a mixture of sarcasm and contempt.

"Sergeant, you almost certainly know why I left the force, and it has nothing to do with being unsuccessful. In fact I had a good track record ...."

"Let's stick to the matter in hand, shall we, *sir*?" he interrupted, loudly and abrasively. My blood was beginning to boil and I could sense from his look he was pleased with the results of his efforts, there being the tiniest hint of a smug grin on his lips. He'd wanted to annoy me.

Right. I took a few deep breaths and allowed myself to relax and my blood to return to its normal arrangements. He wasn't going to win. His bold blue eyes bored into mine and I knew he was trying to outmuscle me with a stare. I wondered if I intimidated suspects the same way when I was asking the questions. Perhaps I did.

We ran through a number of matters and then he threw the ace of trumps on the table.

"Looking at your photos, by the way thank you for letting us have them, I felt one or two might have been snapped from your car while you were driving. That's a bit dangerous, *sir*. Unless someone was with you using the camera. If that was the case we'd need to interview them as well."

"Nobody was with me, and I took no pictures while driving." The first item was a lie, the second was true, of course.

"I hope we don't find out otherwise because firstly that'd make us suspicious and secondly you'd be in trouble, and we'd expect better from an ex-policeman. And I'm already suspicious that you had someone with you."

"Well I didn't, and this ex-policeman doesn't lie." No doubt he'd done all the training on spotting a liar at work and I hoped my expression and behaviour didn't give me away. Two can play at that game!

After a brief pause he grunted and started looking around my lounge.

"Would you have any objection to us borrowing your computer, y'know, taking it away so we can have a good look?" That sort of question represents a double-whammy. Hardly anyone is going to agree. And surely everyone says things like 'sorry, but there's lots of private and personal stuff on there'. More aggressively you might say 'not without a warrant' which just plays neatly into their hands. The reply to that is usually along the lines of 'maybe we'll get one'.

Following a brief hesitation I responded in a hopefully neutral way.

"Is it voluntary?"

"Yes, of course *sir.*"

"Then I'm afraid I have to decline." I was feeling shaky and I knew the colour had risen to my cheeks, and his smile acknowledged his victory. He didn't pursue it. I decided on one last and pointless throw of the dice.

"I will be keeping my solicitor in the picture, Sergeant."

"A very good idea, if I may say so, *sir.*" He rose and stretched to his full height which I estimated to be just over six feet in (or nearly two metres if you insist on using metric). DS Okafor exuded raw strength being muscular, trim and clearly very fit. Self-confident too. Very smartly dressed in a dark blue pin-stripe suit. I could appreciate him being readily attractive and desirable to the opposite sex.

Not allowed to think like that these days, Dave, I admonished myself silently. Let's just say attractive and desirable. Wonder what Laura would think?

We shook hands and I escorted him from the premises.

"Very nice bungalow, sir, well kept garden. Do you garden yourself?"

"Yes, but I'm at the bottom of my learning curve."

"You'd never know it. Looks good to me. Well done. Must be on my way and, as you'll remember from your days on the force, if you think of anything please give us a shout. Thanks for your time."

I muttered my goodbyes and watched him drive away. Flash white Audi, latest reg. Huh! Flash git, full stop.

It was time to brief Laura. I didn't want her confessing the truth if she was ever confronted with the opportunity, and I was counting on her own criminal past making her a convincing fibber.

Talk of the devil, the phone rang and it was Laura.

"Got loads of stuff for you. Come and buy some time with me and I'll tell all." She'd been researching murders in Devon and Suffolk. "Need a bit of dosh. Buy an hour of my time, and anything else we do is between consenting adults blah blah."

"I'll be over. How can you be short of money?"

"Laura is short. I'll explain when I see you. When you coming?"

"On my way. Lie down in the road and save me a parking space."

"Like the idea of you telling me to lie down..."

"I'm buying time only..."

"Says you."

"Says me. See you soon."

***

Across the other side of the country another private eye was being questioned by a police officer.

"Let me level with you, John. Here's a scenario. Nathan Kethnet employs you to spy on his wife and her lover. You learn the truth and present the details to Mr Kethnet. Either then, or as an unwritten part of the deal when you started, you kill off Edward Nobbs on Kethnet's orders, or, may I suggest? on his *implied* instructions. You can see my difficulty, can't you John?

"Now you're a good detective, good reputation and so on, honest, decent and law-abiding, so let's say you had nothing to do with Mr Nobbs being strangled. Even so it's possible Nathan did it himself. You two have to be prime suspects, John, there's no getting away from it, and you know I'm telling you more than I should."

John Wapernod listened carefully, aware he was being soft-soaped and trying to work out exactly what DS Geoff Alcock wanted. He had an alibi for the time of Nobbs's death. So too, for that matter, did Nathan Kethnet but, Wapernod reasoned, it was irrelevant if a hired killer was used.

Proceeding cautiously the private detective spoke after a short interval during which both men looked directly at each other unblinkingly.

"As Nathan and I have alibis, which you have checked out, then the only possible assumption you can make, Geoff, is that if Nathan wanted Nobbs dead he must've employed a hit man. On that basis I am out of the frame, wouldn't you say? Are there no other suspects, Geoff?"

The Sergeant studied his man. This conversation was going nowhere.

"I can't tell you that, John. And no, I don't think your alibi would stand up to intense scrutiny, so you're still in the running." Wapernod was not the sort of person to labour a point, and knowing his alibi would not prove to be weak even if he and the provider of his alibi were tortured mercilessly. If it's the truth you can only reveal the truth.

He had spent the night with a lady friend, a one-time customer, who had been interviewed but who was trying to stay in the background as she had a husband. So far she had kept the issue from him.

And in another part of the country a suspect in another murder was being interviewed yet again.

***

Daytime parking near Laura's was easy so I was only a few seconds walking to her flat where she was waiting at the door, bursting with enthusiasm.

"Got the gen on them murders, Moncks, and I found out where Devon and Suffolk are, and I know they're nowhere near Derbyshire, and Shel's asked me to go over tonight, can you give us a lift?"

All that before I crossed the threshold. I was marched in, ordered to sit, and offered a drink.

"Black coffee, please, and give me a chance to get in."

"Okay, okay. Anyways I've worked out how we can fit this all into our schedule and without me losing any time at me job, okay?" I was left to contemplate this data as she sped to the kitchen, and I began to wonder who was running this operation, and whether Top Bitch was actually supplanting me. She returned with two mugs.

For once she looked very basic, if you know what I mean. Hair unkempt as ever, no make-up, and she was wearing very old and unflattering clothes, namely baggy trousers and a voluminous top, all hideously complemented by large fluffy slippers and multi-coloured socks. What a picture!

And yet she ignited some fires inside me.

"Found this guy in Barnstaple, and I know where that is now, Edward Nobbs, strangled, and a woman in some village in Suffolk, can't remember where, but got it all written down, stabbed through the heart. Phyllis Downport, some bigwig, well, pots of money, that sort of thing. No murder weapons found.

"Edward Nobbs, nothing special about him. Now there's nothing else on the news about either of them, and that's what struck me as odd. Like, a bit of speculation but the police aren't saying much and maybe there's nowt to say. What I mean is, like our murder, Bourne-Lacey, there don't seem a lot to go on.

"Other thing is the dates are recent but sufficient time between them, y'know, for a killer to get around." I couldn't fault her eagerness or, for that matter, her attention to detail or her deductions. Beware Top Bitch, I told myself, she's really after my job!

"Three different MOs."

"What's medical officers got to do with it?"

"No, not that kind of MO. *Modus operandus*, method of operation, that sort of thing. Strangulation, stabbing and shooting. If it's one killer he might be widely experienced in using all three styles."

"He or she," Laura interrupted.

"Okay, he or she or whatever. Anyway, that could be deliberate to try and keep the police off the scent, you know, strangle one, stab the other and so on."

"Yeah, what's with the modus operandus thing, like? If it's method of operation why not say so? Seems daft to me using some foreign language to say something you can say in English just as well."

She had a good point. I decided against trying to explain.

***

Jayne-Marie Panahan was indignant.

DS Stephanie Broome believed indignation to be the prerogative of the guilty.

Ms Panahan (aka Mrs Bailey) was being interviewed for what she described as the 'umpteenth' time, although her calculations were well adrift by many 'umps', and was being quizzed as a result of the miniscule connection the Police thought might link three different murders.

Alibis were not the problem. Everyone had one including, Stephanie mused, the Chief Constable. If there was an association they would be looking at a professional killer, hired for the purpose, and the fact the assortment of prime suspects had alibis for the times of death would be of no consequence whatsoever.

So they needed to dig deeper.

On the face of it the private eyes were less likely to be guilty as there were three of them, and all possessed excellent reputations and track records of honesty. That didn't rule them out, just lessened the chances.

Also on the face of it the three 'wronged' spouses had most reason to want Nobbs, Bourne-Lacey and Downport dead, so that put them at the top of the list.

Then there were other potential suspects. The straying partners featured on this part of the list but were widely regarded as outsiders. Otherwise there was a collection of people who had relationships with the deceased that had displayed grounds for animosity for a variety of reasons. Normally these would be insufficient for murder motives but people had been slaughtered for less.

Thus it was that Jayne-Marie Panahan was facing another light grilling.

DC Grant Hadlesome was asking the questions, DS Broome was observing. This was an agreed tactical procedure and bore its origins in the concept that Ms Panahan did not like being interviewed by anyone of lowly station. If she was rankled it might loosen some tight bolts in her story.

And she was rankled. On this occasion her solicitor, the faithful Sumitra Bhatia, was not glued to her side, for which instance the police gave grateful thanks. But she had been summoned and Hadlesome and Broome knew they had to move quickly.

Hadlesome asked why her marriage to William Bailey had been kept quiet, and was there any question of him playing the field again, did she think. Her eyes were on stalks as she gave an Oscar-winning performance of a woman showing indignation and resultant anger.

"None of your business," she snapped. "My husband will not play the field again, as you so crudely put it, but none of it is any of your business." Grant pressed on regardless.

"It's our business in a murder inquiry. Has he been satisfactorily warned off, from your point of view and how much has he mourned the loss of his lover?" Broome smiled inwardly. Well done Grant. Touch paper well and truly lit. The explosion was not long coming and was accompanied by shrieks of 'get out of my house, get out'. Broome spoke, quietly and silkily.

"Well, keep your solicitor to hand, Ms Panahan. Our senior officers will now probably want to interview you formally at the station again." And she and Hadlesome turned and let themselves out just as Ms Bhatia was rushing up the drive.

In the car Stephanie Broome said Jayne-Marie's showing had sent her rating sky-high on her 'guilt-ometer'. Grant Hadlesome agreed.

"She didn't like those personal questions but reacted particularly to the prospect of William wandering again. No chance. Can she be sure, could anyone be sure? Unless he'd been told categorically that he'd suffer the same fate at Phyllis Downport if he did step out of line."

"Yes, I wondered that, Grant. Why mention that one aspect at all when she was so annoyed by the questions. Why not stick to 'none of your business'? That was a matter that was of overriding importance to her.

"Yep agreed, Steph. As in look what I've done to Phyllis and if you so much as look at another woman and you'll lose your vital equipment and then, while you're in agony, lose your life. That'd frighten me Steph." She chuckled.

"Value your own equipment, Grant, do you? That's some imagination you've got there, but seriously, I agree, she might've put the frighteners on him a bit like that. And that would also mean that she had Phyllis killed. Now just how did she arrange that?"

***

I rang Adam Pensfield and told him about the killing of Nobbs and Downport. After a sustained silence he said we needed to meet.

"There's two things, Dave, and my career is one of them. I don't want you saying or doing anything that shows you had inside info. But I'll have a pint and a chat with you. That's the second point; you don't ask any questions. Nothing comes back to land on my doorstep. I don't care if they attach electrodes to your bits and pieces, and subject you to a waterboarding, you keep mum."

The meeting was arranged for the following day at his home, with the usual provisos that work might keep him away. Tea or coffee would be our refreshments, the pints would have to wait for another day. Two conscientious drivers.

That evening I took Laura to Faversham.

The next day I drove over to Adam's and found him alone. We chatted about old times, as you do, then got down to brass tacks.

"Just listen, okay? Don't ask questions, you won't get replies." He looked and sounded very businesslike, and yet there was a weird wariness about him. If I hadn't known him better I'd have said he was afraid.

"No DNA, nothing forensic showing up. Looks professional. The only thing left behind was the bullet in your guy, Dave, and that's run-of-the-mill, pretty standard ammo. Barnstaple – Edward Nobbs – strangled, probably rope. Suffolk – Phyllis Downport – stabbed, possibly large kitchen carving knife.

"And the one thing that links the actual killings is that whoever it was left no trace. But is it mere coincidence that all three victims were having affairs with the spouses of rich people, and those rich people had employed guys like you to have their spouses followed?

"No leads, Dave, just motives. Watertight alibis for the rich people. One difference. Phyllis Downport, apart from being the only female victim so far, is that, unlike the other two, she was extremely wealthy herself. Very. It's obviously flagged up that you're ex-force and the opinion is that you're clean. However, some smart officer in Suffolk has suggested you might well have underworld connections, maybe even a revenge motive." I went to speak and he held his hands up to stop me.

"I know, I know, I know. But I thought it was important you knew; that's why I wanted to meet you. This can't get back, Dave, you know that. Generally, around the three forces involved, the agreement is that there's nothing more than coincidence. Just a nagging doubt and, as we are all good coppers, everything, *everything* has to be investigated.

"They've all got the gen on your career, the in-depth stuff. Just watch your back, Dave, that's all. Be aware and pay attention, and more than that keep your nose so clean in the meantime that it glows in the dark."

It felt a very lonely drive home, with only Adam's words and warning to keep my mind company. Fortunately, my mind had the traffic to contend with. And then the bloody Sheppey Crossing was shut. That added another thirty minutes to my anticipated arrival time in Minster. Turned out someone conked out just over the summit so they closed the whole bloody thing 'for safety reasons' and to recover the offending vehicle.

Everyone fights to get into one lane to use the old bridge. I'm courteous but I get fed up letting the pushy drivers in.

Once home I decided the priority was a drink, so poured myself a Pedigree and switched on my mobile. A text from you-know-who, a text that to my tired eyes and addled brain appeared to be comprised of abbreviated gobbledegook. Happily, she'd left a voicemail too, asking to see me.

I sent a clear text back. 'Come round if you want, but you have to walk home.' Dangerous territory, but one Pedigree just wasn't going to be enough. Her reply was instant. 'Jus lvng' which I took to mean she was setting out at once, a correct assessment.

\*\*\*

"Don't forget you're walking home," I reminded my guest.

"Get a taxi."

"No you won't. You need your money, *my* money, so don't waste it."

"Stay the night."

"Nope."

"Sleep on this reclining sofa..."

"No means no. You go home tonight.

"Read me a bedtime story before I go. Goldilocks and the three bears is my favourite."

Silence.

"Oh all right, you meanie, I'll go home, walking in the dark, taking me chances. If something happens to me you'd regret it forever."

"True. You can sleep on the sofa on the understanding that at no time do you venture up the hall, is that clear?" She giggled, snuggled up to me, planted a wet kiss on my cheek, then spoke.

"You're learning top dog, you're coming up with more and more of the right answers. Top bitch wins again." I had to agree she was right. "Now when we two off to Derbyshire, then?"

# Chapter Twelve
## Derby, Dinner and Detection

When the police are pursuing a wide range of enquiries into puzzling cases, and doing so diligently, thoroughly and effectively, they tend to suffer the odd smidge of annoyance at ill-informed press speculation.

Certain sections of the media had been busy with a capital B, and it soon emerged that there might be stark similarities in three murders in different places, and that the police might just be interested in a link. Of course, it hadn't been possible for media representatives to uncover too much background material but what they had was sufficient for a little speculative prodding.

For example, it was soon 'news' that three wealthy people had been interviewed in connection with the crimes, and then someone landed a scoop, thanks to an anonymous call, that Edward Nobbs was engaged in extra marital activities with the wife of Nathan Kethnet. That sent the scribes scurrying afresh around Kent and Suffolk, and by fair means or foul a reporter stumbled on the possibility that Phyllis Downport was a flame of one William Bailey, husband of Jayne-Marie Panahan. And the police had interviewed *her*.

By this medium her marriage to William became common knowledge. Unfortunately coverage in the press hindered the police, especially as there was the usual flurry of publicity seekers and those after earning a decent pay-off from the papers, ready to tell all in the hopes of achieving their targets. Now the police had to sort the wheat from the chaff, as much 'new' evidence turned out to be false.

Jayne-Marie decided it must've been hotel staff in Southwold that tipped off the journalist and told both Sumitra Bhatia and Yvonne Pratt she wanted the culprit hunted down and legal action taken.

Sumitra was told face to face, in fact, when her face was less than six inches from Jayne-Marie's. The solicitor decided it was raging paranoia and hoped it would die a natural death.

The private detective was told over the phone, and Ms Pratt took it in her stride, said 'yes ma'am' in all the right places, and started to consider the financial rewards *should* she succeed.

My former colleague Adam made it clear he would answer no questions from me, but he must've known who the other two private eyes were, and that was something I wanted to know too. I had mused on the point with Laura over a breakfast of tomatoes on toast. Not that I expected any bright ideas, it was just I needed to think out loud.

I hadn't slept well. She'd kept to the bargain and stayed in the lounge, but I repeatedly woke thinking I could hear footsteps getting ever nearer, and then laid awake waiting for sounds that never came. I know, you're going to ask me if, deep down, I was disappointed. And you want me to be truthful, don't you?

Well, the answer is that I don't actually know. My conscious self was far from upset and feeling let down. It had turned out precisely as I required, which was a relief, and yet there was a part of me that had, how can I put it, become Laura-fied if that makes sense. That bit was disappointed.

She shovelled away a slice of toast and marmalade.

"Pleased you don't like those healthy brekkies, Moncks. I'd leave you if you were a healthy food person."

"Ah, I see. Well, in that case I'm thinking of becoming a healthy eating freak...."

"Not so fast, buster. That means no dwinkies either," And with a twinkle in her eye she added "but lots and *lots* of healthy exercise! Know what I mean?" She sniggered into her half empty coffee mug and gurgled as she drank.

Just for the record I don't think Shel Crackby was going to clean up any time soon, despite Laura's best efforts, and I didn't feel justified in taking any more of Linnie's money. That left me with the Lorraine McCaffield file (a non-earner) and Laura reminded me more often of that than her desire to get me into bed.

The sooner we made some progress the sooner I could move onto other business.

\*\*\*

It wasn't long before the intrepid reporter who'd unearthed some of the truth behind the relationships of Jayne-Marie Panahan, William Bailey and Phyllis Downport, scratched a little bit harder and learned that a private detective had been interviewed. More media speculation.

A short step for such a news-hound led to Yvonne Pratt, who refused to comment on anything whatsoever. But Ms Pratt was now a private eye in the public eye, and so unsurprisingly she soon received contact from two fellow sleuths, one in Kent, one in Devon. She responded to neither fearing some sort of media stitch-up, but at the same time she herself started to research the other two murders.

It was all very intriguing and mystifying.

She contacted Steph Broome but drew a blank. She hadn't expected any other outcome. The police were not going to reveal their information. Then she decided on an interesting course of action. She emailed the private eyes in Kent and Devon with each other's contact details, and the words 'talk amongst yourselves, boys, and let me know if you find anything of value'.

This covered most eventualities. If Wapernod and Canbown were being 'used' by the press they'd be up a dead end, and if they were genuine some good might come of it. And Ms Pratt was being careful lest the police were watching what the three of them were up to. It pays to keep a healthy distance.

John Wapernod sent a simple message to Pratt and Canbown.

"Too many coincidences, and I don't believe in them. Right now it appears the biggest hurdle we three have is trust amongst ourselves. Any thoughts?"

*** 

I was the only one of the three not to have a website.

It was on the horizon, but I was leaving it until I decided that sleuthing was the career I now wanted to follow, and besides I didn't want too many personal details appearing online. Apart from that, an online search for detectives in Kent will find me, and I do pay to be in a couple of web directories.

Laura said I should be on Facebook and Twitter, and not to worry, she'd run it all for me!

The downside of having a website right this moment is that she wants to be on it. No, no, a thousand times no!

Yvonne responded to John (copied to me) that a meeting might be an answer. She had to go to Long Eaton for one of her cases, so how did Derby strike us?

Two birds, one stone. That was the way me and Laura were headed. John replied that it was an easy train journey for him, and yes, Derby suited him fine. He added free dates and between us we agreed on a particular night, electing to stay in the same Derby hotel. This arrangement was good for my purposes as it enabled me to book Laura somewhere else! Turning up with an assistant was not in the script and might look suspicious.

Try explaining that to Miss McCaffield.

She had two choices: come with me on that basis or don't come at all.

And so we went to Derby and Laura sulked.

I had no trouble finding John in the hotel bar as he looked exactly like his website photo. We ordered a couple of pints and retired to a table in what appeared to be a quiet spot. Well, anyway, it was only six-forty-five. Bound to be quiet.

Apparently Yvonne hadn't arrived yet but was expected within half an hour.

"Checked up on you, David," John began, "and you're ex-police, aren't you?" I nodded and he continued, "I also think I know why you left the force," and he tapped the side of his nose in the way people do when they want to indicate they've located something not in the realms of public knowledge, and wish to keep their source private.

"How do you get on with the guys in your old force, and how does your past impact on inquiries into Alistair Bourne-Lacey with the local lads?" Straight to the point, Mr Wapernod.

"I've one or two old friends, basically loyal, but you never really know. They were behind me at the time, y'know, full of support…"

"Behind you," John interrupted, "being the operative expression. Good friends, best of mates, but heads below the firing line." I couldn't help but think he was right, and here I was already beginning to doubt former colleagues like Adam Pensfield!

"I think there's some sort of resentment locally. A bit of sarcasm, you know how it is, and they've got me on the list of suspects for sure, not as the killer necessarily, but I'd guess as the hirer of the hit man or woman. Tell me about John Wapernod." I wanted this conversation to change direction and not be all about me.

"Ah, David, a slow, dull work in progress compared to you I dare say. Mostly worked for a local council, loved the endless paperwork, reports and so on, but dreaded the work itself. I worked out that only about forty percent of my time was directed to the job itself, the rest was being bound up in red tape, reports and meetings.

"It was a solicitor friend of mine who accidently got me into this. He knew how much I enjoyed research and I helped him out with looking into things he really didn't have the time for, and from there John Wapernod hit the ground running as a private eye. I don't have much contact with the local force so have cultivated no friendships there, but they've been pretty good over this murder.

"I reckon they must have similar suspicions to your lot when it comes to us private eyes, but I've found them courteous and appreciative, and to a degree respectful. So we'll see what Yvonne has to say in that direction."

He raised his glass and drained off half the pint with ease. He looked immaculate, one could almost say elegant, and was totally relaxed, calm and spoke the same way. A three piece suit complete with watch chain; you don't get many of those to the pound these days. So I couldn't help but look at his black shoes which unsurprisingly shone, just as I had expected them to.

John struck me as ideal civil servant material. Precise and paying attention to detail, the prerogative of anyone who loves research work, he exuded an air of accuracy and correctness that I felt must benefit his business. In fact, he was well suited to many aspects of private detective work, the aspects that required deep, methodical and patient digging.

"I'm forty-three, David, unmarried, and quietly happy and content." Indeed, so he must be I mused. "You David? Married? Children?"

"Divorced. No kids." I added no more and he didn't ask.

"My alibi for the murder of Edward Nobbs is a married lady. I'm trying to keep her out of it but the police seem to lack my sense of discretion." The slightest of grins had appeared on his face. "Anyone on your horizon, David?"

"No, and for the moment I'm happy like that." We both drank some more as my mind took me on a guided tour of my feelings for Laura. My words were true, but my mind doubted my commitment. Empty glasses saved the situation and I went to the bar for refills.

If John Wapernod had been easy to recognise Yvonne Pratt turned out to be the exact opposite, that is, nothing like her website picture.

The photo, although probably quite recent, had been taken at such an angle that her facial features belied their actual plumpness. Her hair had appeared dark black and shoulder length whereas it was now red and short. I didn't expect her to be chubby but as she introduced herself to John (he hadn't recognised her either) I also realised she was remarkably attractive. They shook hands and he sent her over to meet me.

"Drink Yvonne?"

"Yes please, David. I'll have a Scotch and American, please."

"Do you prefer a single malt or blended?"

"Tut-tut-tut. Blended please. What sort of person would desecrate a single malt?" And she roared with laughter. At that moment I could've fallen in lust with her, she looked not merely desirable but achingly needful and equally demanding, her carefree laughter and the sizzling sparkle it produced in her face proving passionately enticing.

As I followed her back to our table I have to say, to my shame, my eyes were glued to the swing of her hips and buttocks as they performed so fervently under her navy-blue pleated skirt. John opened the conversation, having first ascertained Ms Pratt had secured a trouble free drive from Needham Market.

"David and I had just been talking about the law, that is, the police, and how we've been treated with these murders. David's met some coldness and resentment, but I've been impressed. How have you got on?"

"I copped a packet, to use an expression, by not going to them in the first place, but I honestly didn't think there'd be any connection, and I had the disadvantage of having a very tough cookie as a customer." None of her terminology seemed to fit comfortably with my impressions of the mid-aged woman sitting next to me. She continued. "So how was it for you two guys?"

"I was contacted by the police but I certainly wasn't given a rocket. I've always found abject apologies, unconditional surrender if you like, puts your opponent at a disadvantage. What about you David?"

"Well, I'm the odd one out then. I went straight to the police when I heard about my murder."

"That's the ex-cop in you," commented Wapernod.

"Didn't know that, David," began Yvonne, "but I must admit I haven't researched either of you. Been doing this long?"

"No, not very, but I've notched up a handful of successes so I might try and make a go of it. Nothing else is on my radar career-wise right now. What about you Yvonne?"

"Bin doin' it years, m'boy! Well, since my husband died. Decided I wanted some adventure. Still, funny thing to do, I suppose. My kids thought so. Mum, they said, you're mad. And who was I to argue?"

With that the three of us talked briefly about our lives and backgrounds and so it was that my departure from the force was explained.

"Speaking as a woman," Yvonne piped up, "I'd be proud to shake the hand of an officer prepared to stand up for the victim. But the silk was only doing his job. Presumption of innocence the corner-stone of justice, ain't it? And if you accept everyone is entitled to legal representation then it's no good being resentful if the defence wins, especially as you said the prosecution wasn't well prepared and presented." She must've seen the look on my face and decided to change tack.

"Just out of curiosity, John," she asked, "where does your name come from?"

"I'm told it might have Flemish connections, but it's been loosely traced back to the Normans. More than that I do not know.

"I've never looked into mine. Pratt. Fear of what I might find." And again she rocked with laughter and this time we both joined in. It was good to lighten up a bit. Yvonne spoke.

"Brass tacks, lads. Let's talk about our cases. None of us likes coincidences like this, do we? Putting it bluntly if *we* didn't hire the killer or killers then my money's on the guys who hired us, the only ones with a real motive if, and it's a big if, this is to do with wandering spouses. And a bit more of my money is on one killer. Of course, it could be a firm that specialises in eliminating wicked people on behalf of offended husbands and wives." There was a murmur of a chuckle all round, quickly dispelled.

"Maybe not such a daft idea," John put forward. "Perhaps we need to get into the dark web. Anyway, let's put our cards on the table and see what else we've got."

"Right now I'm putting drinks on the table. So what you chaps having? How about we then have dinner accompanied by fine wine, retire to my room and discuss away from walls with ears?" Yvonne certainly didn't stand on ceremony.

John and I readily agreed to her idea and Ms Pratt swept up to the bar to get the drinks. Fine wine, I thought? We'll be too pickled to be sensible at this rate!

\*\*\*

A disgruntled Laura McCaffield was having dinner at another hotel having been chatted up by some ponce (her word) of an executive at the bar beforehand. She despatched Mr Ponce by the simple expedient of explaining she was gender fluid and had been wondering what to do with her cock at bedtime.

Two young marketing men, looking suave and overwhelmed by being God's gift to women, were at the next table making eyes at Laura and winking at each other. Laura asked the waiter to move her. As she left she told her admirers they'd make a perfect couple in bed together where they could hold hands or anything else that sprang to mind, and not be a menace to anyone else.

Can't I dress like a woman and be left alone, she pondered. I don't mind being admired but why is the rutting season twelve months long? Leave it out guys. Please. And with that she tucked into an egg mayonnaise (by any other name, and it usually had, as on this occasion, a fancy name on the menu) as a precursor to gammon steak (also wrapped in an alien name).

Fancy names were all that decorated the menu that three private detectives were studying not a million miles away from Laura. Yvonne Pratt was quite, quite at home, and discussed various dishes, perfectly pronouncing the French headings and describing the epicurean merits of each.

It was all French to me. John Wapernod seemed slightly bemused but was capable of making a fist of it. The pair of them wanted wine that complemented their main courses but all I wanted was dry white. I gave up and decided to demonstrate my culinary ignorance and my heathen views on wine, asking Yvonne to explain the menu and saying that I'd have whatever wine they wanted; they were the experts.

With Yvonne's guidance, which bordered on the contemptuous and patronising, I settled for the soup of the day and pan-seared chicken, and nodded agreement with the selection of Chablis (a wine I knew and liked). I unfolded my napkin and spread it over my lap while my two colleagues gave me looks of distaste and pity. I soon realised why; I should've stayed my hand and allowed the waiter to perform that simple act.

John and Yvonne, being to the manner born, took such attention in their stride, as a natural matter of course, and looked down upon my naivety and lack of breeding as if they felt truly sorry for me. Just get the knives and forks right, David, I told myself. Now, you work from the outside in, I believe. And at that second I wondered how Laura was doing. No worries, I thought, on two counts; she was in a less salubrious establishment, and she wouldn't care anyway!

I watched John taste the wine and I wondered why connoisseurs, and those who haven't a clue, go through this pantomime. He signalled his acceptance with the slightest nod and after the waiter had poured and departed said he considered it just marginally over-chilled.

Ye gods!

Yvonne suggested we each in turn tell all we knew about our own murders, uninterrupted, a course of action that met with unanimous agreement and with me going first. My tale comfortably occupied the dubious pleasure of the first course and I was grateful to have something to do as the soup tasted all but foul. I needed my mind removed from its vulgarity.

John Wapernod was a natural story-teller and he began the saga of Nathan and Kathy Kethnet and the late Edward Nobbs as the starter dishes were taken away by a trio of smartly dressed waitresses who performed their art swiftly, delicately and in an impressively unobtrusive manner. For a moment I could imagine the process set to music and the balletic servers dancing around us plates held high as they twirled and sprang on their pointes to beguile us.

We sipped our wine (not an occasion for guzzling) as the sorry affair of Kathy and Edward was laid bare before us. Shortly a plate the size of a lorry wheel arrived in front of me. Somewhere towards the centre, and almost lost in the vastness of the dish, was a small offering which I assumed must be the chicken. Yvonne's eyes sparkled brightly as a similar plate was softly, quietly disposed in front of her, and she clapped her hands together and gave the faintest squeal of delight upon seeing her main course.

It could not have been far off a culinary orgasm, an outrageous fling of exhilarating pleasure kept in check only by good manners, decency, and by virtue of being displayed in public where such a display would be considered below ones dignity. I couldn't see what the fuss was about.

John smiled, pausing temporarily from his discourse to take delivery of his own entree and express with a smile and a mmmmmmm.... his happiness and satisfaction. The waitresses danced out from the wings and set down the dishes of vegetables; small dishes, small vegetables, small quantities. Mr Wapernod continued his tale between devouring small mouthfuls of food and small mouthfuls of wine.

Incredibly he stage-managed it well, eating and drinking where natural punctuation occurred in his text, and proceeded steadily and with ever-increasing enthusiasm to the climax.

My dinner was uninteresting. The vegetables were, by my own standards, under-done, the way they do it these days, I reflected. And as for the chicken, well, it was disappointing, and might easily have been seared in a bucket over an open fire for all I knew. But then I didn't really know what pan-seared meant. That's the trouble with ignorance.

My two fellow hotel guests sat back in their chairs with their food despatched and drank some more wine as they sighed their satisfaction at a first class meal, and briefly discussed the merits of their respective dishes. John had finished his account of the demise of Mr Nobbs and turned to me.

"Your meal, David? You looked as if you were relishing it."

"Yes thank you, John, absolutely delicious," I lied.

"Marvellous. Yes a splendid meal. Now Yvonne, I think it's your turn." Ms Pratt seemed ready to start but she waited for the plates to be cleared before getting under way.

By and large her narrative was the most absorbing perhaps because it involved completely different angles and the victim was a woman. Also, of course, the victim was a woman of great wealth whereas the two men who had died were not. It was equally true that Yvonne Pratt turned out to be the best story-teller of the three, in my opinion, and held us spellbound throughout.

I felt quite deprived when the waiter arrived with the dessert menus and Yvonne imposed an interval on her telling while we all decided on our third courses, and John ordered another bottle of Chablis. It was akin to watching an entrancing programme on the TV to find it interrupted by advertisements at a crucial point. You know the form.

For once I was on safe ground, or so I reasoned, ordering cheese and biscuits. So inspired and inspiring was my choice that John followed by Yvonne changed their minds and cancelled their previous order. Cheese and bikkies all round then. In a weird sort of way I felt quite the hero and a warm glow flooded through my body. It was short lived.

Anticipating some harmless Cheddar, innocuous Edam and tasteless Brie, the cheeseboard when it came represented my worst fears compounded. But there was the companionship of the Chablis, always the Chablis, to offset such a poor encounter with cheese the like of which I had never witnessed before.

I pointed to the two items that I liked the look of, unable to identify either to the waitress. I was certain she was aware of my embarrassment and was thoroughly enjoying every second.

Cheese and biscuits gave us the opportunity to chatter to a greater degree and ask questions of one another. This was a good thing on two fronts; we learned a great deal and it took my mind off the vile substance that passed as cheese. The alcohol was taking its toll but thankfully on all three of us.

I was beginning to imagine us retiring to Yvonne's bedroom and getting up to all kinds of mischief, and in my tipsy state I found myself fancying Yvonne and wanting to undress her. My mind, hopelessly out of control, imagined John sitting there, taking notes and then describing the operation over another dinner at some later stage, entertaining his fellow diners with a host of juicy details. And it all just seemed funny. Wickedly funny.

Laura had concluded her meal with death by chocolate and was as sober as a judge. She decided she would now rectify the latter situation, travelling to the bar and ordering champagne. A table in a quiet area was located and the barman delivered the ice bucket resplendent with a bottle of Bollinger poking out the top. He expertly poured the first glass and left 'madam' to look after herself thereafter.

Madam did and madam enjoyed, but not without attracting the attention of hungry males. One or two chanced their arms and waltzed over for a chat. Laura sent them packing. It's a bloody jungle out here, she thought to herself. Moncks, where are you when I need you?

Moncks, in the company of John Wapernod and Yvonne Pratt, and having disposed of dessert and refused coffee, was heading in the direction of the latter's bedroom still fantasising about the unlikely delights to follow. Indeed, there were no delights as such.

***

It was back in Suffolk that the police were at their most suspicious, and that was primarily because Yvonne Pratt did not come forward at the time of death, combined with the love affair of the victim and William Bailey, the appreciable wealth of the deceased, and the fact Mr Bailey and his extremely rich wife had kept their marriage secret.

All the ingredients, they supposed, that might add up to a motive for murder.

They were not alone in being sceptical about the wafer-thin link between the three killings, but all three forces had to investigate the possibility. Should the link prove a positive one then solving the crimes might become easier, because in truth there was little hard evidence in any other direction. And, of course, that was another feature that offered a tenuous link between the three incidents.

DS Stephanie Broome, by virtue of thorough and diligent work or perhaps pure chance, discovered that the three private eyes were likely to be meeting Derby. They had individually left their contact arrangements with their local forces. Broome had taken the call from Ms Pratt who was, apparently, on her way to the midlands for a couple of days on a case, and she just happened to be discussing issues with DS Holton Okafor in Kent when he mentioned David Canbown was going to Derbyshire 'on a case'.

From there it was a simple step to speak to Devon and Cornwall and establish that Mr Wapernod had also been drawn to the same area. Broome rang Pratt.

"Are you meeting a John Wapernod and a David Canbown?" she enquired directly. Yvonne was nursing a particularly sore head after the previous evening in the bar and then the dining room at her hotel, and was taken by surprise but recovered her senses swiftly.

"Yes, met them last night and we're all staying at the same hotel."

"And you know about their involvement in two other murder cases?"

"Sure do. That's why we're here. Putting our heads together. You never know, Sergeant, we might come up with something we can pass on to you."

Broome sensed the sarcastic tone but chose to ignore it.

"We might've liked to be told about this meeting," she said in a dictatorial yet resigned manner.

"We might've liked to be told about each other."

"You know we can't do that."

"Yes Sergeant, but we're all private detectives, one's an ex-cop, so we know how and where to dig. Now, you're not going to be cross with us, are you?"

Stephanie Broome wanted to be very cross, very cross indeed. She wanted to clutch Ms Pratt by the throat and strangle her for her patronising sarcasm.

"No, but please keep me in the loop, especially if the three of you decide to take any investigative action that might get in our way or, worse still, put the killers on their guard."

"So you're not getting very far, then, beyond thinking that it's three murderers." Broome bit her lip. Whoops, she admonished herself, nearly gave too much away!

The conversation ended seconds afterwards, leaving Pratt to call Canbown and Wapernod and Broome to ring her colleagues in Kent and Devon.

Investigative action, unbeknown to the Suffolk force, was exactly what the gang of three had in mind.

# Chapter Thirteen
# A Dally in the Dales

Jayne-Marie Panahan did not like being the centre of attention. Not one bit. Not a jot. Not this sort of attention anyway. She was in the vanguard in matters of business, but this was very different.

She raged at her husband, her solicitor and anyone else she could lay her hands on, and threatened everyone from her husband, her solicitor, her private eye, newspapers, television companies with fierce retribution, primarily financial ruin.

William took the brunt. If he hadn't strayed Phyllis Downport might still be alive and Jayne-Marie might be in the shadows where she preferred to be. William's retort was unanswerable and within their relationship represented the equivalent of the president of the USA pressing the nuclear button.

"Jayne, there's been no suggestion Phyllis's murder had anything to do with our affair. Where did that come from?" Jayne-Marie looked as if she might raise enough steam to launch a trip to the moon, and she blushed to the roots and spluttered all kinds of weird and alien words while waving her arms in all directions. Suddenly she stopped, and took a deep breath.

"No William, you are quite right; we don't know that, do we? Pour me another drink and let's sit together and be calm about this." William knew better than to do anything else, but later that evening, when alone, he reconsidered Jayne-Marie's comments and found them disturbing. The question was, did she know something about the killing, and the thought worried him sorely.

He was not alone in his worry.

In North Devon Cathy Kethnet had been told to behave or else, her husband explained, she might be the next to die.

"Easy to arrange, *sweetheart*," he'd said, "and I am sure I've all the right discreet connections." Kathy was a woman afraid. Her husband had hired a private eye to discover her indiscretions so was he capable of hiring a killer? Had he already done so, of course?

***

Their meetings were deliberately all too rare.

And this one was going to be typically brief. They covered their tracks well leaving few if any traces. Messages, money, conversations, contacts, all kept to the minimum. Any physical traces destroyed, SIM cards torn asunder.

"The presence of innocent private eyes is an inspired touch, one of which I am inordinately proud. Spreads the whole area of guilt wide upon the ground." The speaker, looking immaculately smart as ever, did indeed sport a grin of pride and self-satisfaction. The voice was soft and crisp, the words enunciated with that clear, cool "home counties" roll that marked someone out as being of good breeding and upbringing. The listener was sure of that, and the listener was the opposite in so many respects.

Today the listener was not even in his customary brown suit, a well-worn and appreciably shiny piece of cheap tailorage. Today this tubby, sweaty, badly-shaven man was in jogging bottoms two sizes too big, and a white T-shirt wet in the armpits. Disgustingly wet. And he hadn't even been jogging. His voice grated and whined, like a moped motor struggling to drive its charge above 20 m.p.h.

It had been some while since their meeting in North Devon, and despite the chubby man's nervousness, business now seemed to be booming.

The trouble, to his way of thinking, is that already, and out of the blue, the police had made a link between the three killings, and at the sharper, wide-awake end of media journalism experienced reporters were sniffing in all the right places. Or so it seemed to him. Not to his handsome and unfretting companion.

"You worry too much," his companion soothed, "and you'll end up with a heart attack or a stroke. Or as another of my victims, of course!" Both smiled, the tubby man not certain his companion was joking. "Anyway, I'm taking the risks, I do the killings, so you chill, my friend. You're doing fine and we have much to look forward to. There is nothing to link you to me." A measure of Ardbeg ten year old single malt was sunk without trace. "I adore Islay malts, y'know, and yes please, I'll have another. And we can toast our next adventure. I haven't visited Bakewell for some time."

\*\*\*

DS Okafor, having a naturally suspicious nature, a rewarding feature in such a successful police officer, had with the agreement of fellow Sergeants Broome and Alcock contacted colleagues in Derbyshire apropos the meeting of the three private detectives on their doorstep. However, his approach was met with some disdain. No, he didn't want a tail put on all three and no, he didn't want them contacted. Not that such efforts were being seriously offered, even in the line of inter-force co-operation.

So inevitably, what did he want? As in, why have you bothered calling?

Okafor explained that it was more of a courtesy call to keep them in the loop and to prepare the ground lest there should be some development they all needed to know about. It was vital the local force knew how important it was, and was aware in advance in case the other three forces required something urgently, like yesterday. Because you never knew.

At last things happened and the matter was professionally resolved and records made.

Progress.

And at that stage none realised how soon they would need such co-operation.

***

"Laura, just listen please. I am going to explain the facts of life."

"Oh goody, you're going to take me to bed..."

"Just listen. Searching for your sister earns us no money whatsoever. Chasing around after killers earns us no money whatsoever. And we need an income. Understand?"

"What you gettin' at Moncks?"

"We can only spend a day or two up here and then we must sort out some business back home. I've had contact from two potential clients who require some sleuthing and I must get home asap and go and see these people. We need dosh Laura. Dosh. Comprende?"

"What, like you spent on that posh hotel, expensive drinks and gourmet dining?"

"That's different..."

"Yeah, guessed it would be. I hate it when blokes say *that's different* so they can do what they like and I have to do what I'm told; it's like, I'm wrong and you're right."

"Alright, have it your way. And, if it makes you feel better, I bet a pound to a penny you had a more enjoyable meal than I did."

"Yeah, proper grub! So why did your crap cost more than my lovely grub?"

"It's the way it is."

"Nope, it's the way pillocks like you get taken in and ripped off. Don't tell me, big plate, hardly anything on it, a few under-cooked veg, and a bill for hundreds of quid."

"This pillock knows when he's beaten. Okay, okay, you're right and I'm in the wrong. I know, okay?"

"Nope, want a penance paid. That's what they call it, ain't it?"

"And it wasn't hundreds of quid. But otherwise you're right. What penance do you want Top Bitch?"

"Kiss 'n' a cuddle. To start with."

"Tonight?"

"Yep, just before bedtime should get us underway. Now, where we going?"

"Matlock for starters. It's just up the road."

"Take me up the A6 wonderman."

"How d'you know it's the A6?"

"Watch me and learn brother Monks."

\*\*\*

Georgina Hayle had the glow of love in her eyes. Her eyes were afire with passion, and adoration shone forth like a bright star in the night sky. In this her eyes matched those of the woman looking directly at her. Desire overcame them as they stood embraced tightly in each others' arms and they kissed with all the warmth and fervour they could muster.

Leonora Cuthbert had worshipped Georgina since that day they had met at the gym those years ago. Worship turned easily to love in the weeks ahead and Leonora was surprised, astonished but overwhelmed with happiness to find her love returned. Mrs Hayle had the body of a goddess, the bearing of a princess and the manner of an angel, at least in Leonora's eyes.

And Miss Cuthbert could not believe, simply could not believe, that anyone so lovely, so fabulously beautiful, so enthrallingly desirable could possibly want to share love with such an ugly old cow as she thought she was. But Georgina had reassured her time and again that she was a lovely person, and the very dream she had longed for, hoped for, since she was a teenager. Certainly since she had married Jason.

Jason Hayle had started his career as a humble bank clerk. And that was the last time he was humble. He now had an executive position in a firm with a wide financial portfolio and had amassed a small fortune playing the markets and managing hedge funds. Utterly ruthless, he had taken the besotted Georgina, Georgie as he called her, as his wife for her beauty and sexuality and little else. He was envied by many men, especially his colleagues.

He gave his wife money, clothes, expensive holidays, a flash car and a mansion of a house in the Derbyshire Dales. And for this he expected fidelity. On one occasion when he suspected she had dallied with another man he beat her black and blue, but not where bruises would show, and hoped the warning would suffice. Innocent of the charge as she was, she acknowledged the warning and steered clear of men.

But then she met Leonora.

It was girlish friendship at first but Georgina pined for love and the desperate Miss Cuthbert provided it. Mrs Hayle was able to introduce Leonora to Mr Hayle as a friend and she came to stay with increasing frequency. It would never have occurred to Jason that the two women might be lovers.

When Jason was away the cat did play. Miss Cuthbert stayed and she and Georgina made love in so many wondrous ways. It was paradise. That is, until Jason Hayle had his suspicions aroused when, returning home unexpectedly, he found the pair of them in the summer house in the garden cuddling up together.

Georgina dismissed the incident, but for the first time Jason started to see the way they looked at each other and it made him nervous. So much so that he decided to hire a private detective to keep an eye on his wife. He wanted proof if there was any proof to be found.

Thus it was that Kenny Parrett, using a long range lens, was photographing the two women enjoying their lusty kisses in a quiet spot high above Matlock Bath some weeks ago.

\*\*\*

And it was through Matlock Bath that I was now driving with my trusty assistant who had insisted on imparting, like a tour guide, all the history she'd learned as we travelled. She explained about Richard Arkwright's water-powered mills and the role they played in starting the Industrial Revolution.

"Ordinary blokes, Moncks, come up with some great idea inspired by natural resources. Brilliant, ain't it?"

"And Arkwright was a bloke, not a bloke-ess, please note."

"Yeah, right, but bet his missus drove him on."

We followed the Derwent through the gorge as road and river twisted this way and that in the tightest of spaces, cliffs soaring sharply above us.

"What them cables, Moncks?"

"Cable car. Goes to the Heights of Abraham."

"Wow, can we have a ride?"

"Only if there's time, and there won't be."

"Know why it's called Matlock Bath?"

"Spa, I guess."

"Nearly. Goes back to the late seventeenth century when they discovered warm thermal springs, and built a bath house or something. People must've been clean in them days."

"They weren't. Quite the opposite, know-all. In Georgian times they thought it was bad to keep washing so they used a lot of powder and perfume."

"George has got a lot to answer for. Not washing. Ugg! So what they use a thermal bath for then, clever-clogs?"

"Thought it had curative properties, that sort of thing."

"Curative? What's that when it's home."

"Makes you feel better, makes you feel good."

"Like heroin today."

"No, not like heroin ever. Besides, in those days they smoked opium."

"Well, they're both opiates, sunshine. Here, changing the subject, look up there over the river, right on top of the hill. Riber Castle; it's a folly. Fancy having enough money to build a folly like that. Mock Gothic, bloke called Smedley built it like that in the nineteenth century, as his home. Just to have a view and to gloat over the plebs, I expect."

"According to you, Laura, it must've been what his wife wanted and pushed for."

"Sarky sod."

We were now in Matlock and I glad of what I hoped would be some relative peace and quiet. What I wasn't anticipating was an incredible shock.

***

Kenny Parrett ended his call and checked the credit left on his phone. £10.32. Must top up *toot-sweet* he concluded, and chuckled ruefully. It wasn't as if he was short of money. Time he had an account mobile, and one of those phones that does everything except make the tea!

By no means in the first flush of youth he'd been turned down twice by the police whereupon he'd given up hope and his childhood dream and spent some time in a branch of *McDonald's*. At least his spare time was all his own. He'd met Katherine there and they were married less than a year later.

Getting on the housing ladder hadn't been easy. For one thing, given their limited income and prospects, just finding the ladder would've been a start. Working on a zero hours basis now had an advantage for young Kenny. He started, almost as a hobby, *Parrett Enquiries*, and advertised his services as a private investigator in newsagents' windows and the like.

He found a missing cat, a missing daughter, but failed in two other searches. They lived at his parents' home in Upper Hackney, north of Matlock, and he and Katherine longed for their freedom.

In due course he left McDonald's and devoted himself to *Parrett Enquiries* as he was proving rather successful at it. He ran that from his parents' home too. Once he had ABI membership business took off and he needed help. Deserting fast food his wife joined him and they made enough money to add to their savings to put the deposit down on a small two-up-two-down terraced house nearby.

Two things happened as soon as they moved in: Katherine found herself to be expecting and Kenny landed a couple of major projects. His reputation expanded and business followed suit.

They now had two children, with Mrs Parrett managing to cope with admin and two youngsters with little difficulty. This evening Mr Parrett had prepared dinner and afterwards, once the children were abed, they discussed current cases and the news in general.

Both had been interested in the Suffolk murder of Phyllis Downport, but more especially as it now emerged a private eye was somehow caught up in the affair. It had been two weeks since he'd handed over his file to Jason Hayle and been paid handsomely. All the man wanted was proof, there being no question of divorce, but the matter had worried Kenny, and he'd fretted about how a hard man like Hayle might settle the score with his wife.

But right now a horrible thought was going through his mind. Were there any similarities to the Suffolk murder, and those other two, where were they? Ah yes, Kent and Devon. He had looked up the detective, Yvonne Pratt, and left a message on her mobile. His call hadn't been returned, so he sent an email. Again nothing. But he wasn't to know Yvonne was concerned about a press stitch-up in their lust for information.

*** 

First stop for me was the public convenience.

"You drink too much coffee, Moncks," Laura had admonished. We'd put our notes in some order in the car and it was wise to refresh our memories. We had both been busy carrying out initial research in the days before and I'd been keen to contact a local man, Kenny Parrett. But for mo he could wait.

We decided on our courses of action and had just parted when it happened.

I ran back and caught hold of her arm. Fearing she was being mugged she swung her handbag round violently and cuffed my right ear rather painfully before realising it was me. A middle aged woman, sensing she might be witnessing a handbag snatch, tried to intervene.

"It's alright love, I know him. He's with me, but thanks anyway. Thanks a lot." I nursed my throbbing ear as she explained her actions to the woman who looked far from convinced. A small crowd had gathered to watch but now started to disperse, no doubt disappointed.

Recovering my senses, and failing to obtain an apology, I pulled the photos out of my file.

"Your mother's photo. I can't swear to it, but I'm sure as can be I saw a dead-ringer just getting into a taxi." The excitement overwhelmed both of us and we hugged and swept each other around and around. Then common sense took over.

"Look, I could be mistaken. It might be coincidence. Let's be sensible..."

"No, let's be excitable. What do you always say? Because you never know. Because you never know. And there's an outside chance it was Lorraine."

"But a good chance it wasn't."

"Yeah, but, well, hey, what else have we got? Which direction, Moncks?"

"North..."

"Get the name of the taxi firm? Did you, did you?"

"Yes, and the registration. Let me write it down, give us y'pen and calm down."

"Here's my pen. Wonder-woman is always prepared and no, I will not calm down. You sound like one of them posters. You know, 'keep calm and find a missing sister'."

"Thank you, and would you mind addressing your sarcasm to my left ear since that's the only one I've got left that's still working."

"Ooooh ... alpha male is bear with sore head."

"Alpha male will give alpha female a sore bum in a mo."

"Promises, promises."

*** 

Eventually Yvonne Pratt honoured Kenny Parrett with an email:

*"If you are genuine, please forgive me. The media has been hounding me and if you are in their employ forget it, pal. I'm in Derby on business. Do you want to meet? I'm a good detective and I'll soon know if you're up to something. Please understand. But I am interested in your email content."*

And the reply:

*"Judge me when you meet me then. I'm near Matlock or I could come to Derby."*

This time Yvonne answered her phone to him and, after a tentative beginning when most words exchanged leaned towards the cautious, the pair decided to meet at the Heights of Abraham later that day.

In the meantime we were pursuing our enquiries into Gary and Lorraine Wimbush and getting nowhere, and I was discovering that the taxi firm was not going to play ball either. A dead end. Then it struck me that the local lad, Kenny Parrett, might have keys to doors I couldn't unlock so I gave him a call. His wife took the message and said he was out but she'd get him to ring me the moment he walked back in.

What to do now? Well, I couldn't magic Lorraine out of thin air so decided to earn some brownie points with Top Bitch.

"Right, how about a cable car ride, loyal assistant?"

"What you up to, Moncks? Men don't give in that easily unless they want something."

"Well, I don't and I genuinely thought you'd like a treat. You deserve it."

"Men only say a woman deserves something when *they* want something in return."

"Do you want a cable car ride or not?"

"Yeah, lead me to it, lead me to it."

128

# Chapter Fourteen
# Love, Lust and Lethal Injections

Video conferencing was a boon and a worry all at the same time.

With a telephone call you can't see the other persons face or, for that matter, what they're up to. There is an intriguing element of the unknown. But to be able to see those you speak with, to learn their facial expressions, their 'body language', is to open a potential Pandora's box of secrets.

It has led to a whole new industry of deceit. How to hide your feelings, how to exude confidence and ability you maybe don't possess.

Detective Sergeants Okafor, Broome and Alcock were currently engaged in such a conference at the request of their senior officers. Stephanie Broome jokingly asked if she could get the other two some coffee; Holton Okafor wondered if they were all in the same time zone; Geoff Alcock asked if either of them needed an interpreter. Gentle, polite chuckles all round. Humourless chuckles.

"The one thing that bothers me, guys, is that if there's a connection the killer may strike again. This could be just the start." Okafor was now serious and looking vexed.

"Yeah," began Broome, "and we could be looking at a serial killer to more than match the Yorkshire Ripper."

"Right," added Alcock, "and worse still this one might just be a bloody pro."

"Okay," intervened Okafor, "let's look at that possibility. The common factors: three wealthy people employ private investigators to confirm that their other halves are up to something, but not for divorce purposes. Interesting in itself. A little bit later three people are killed, different methods but no evidence, no DNA, no forensic. Too much of a coincidence."

"So here's a crazy idea," Broome interjected, "are we looking at some sort of organisation, a kind of business, that's started specialising in the murder of adulterous persons, and if so where do we find them?"

"The dark web," Alcock suggested, "or there's some sort of knowledge out there. From what I gather Neville Gradling and Nathan Kethnet have the sort of background that might have placed them in or close to the criminal underworld. But Panahan? What's y'thoughts, Stephanie?"

"Agree. Most unlikely. But the world of very wealthy people, is it a nice clean world guys?"

No words came in answer, but a nodding of heads confirmed. Okafor spoke.

"And talking of an unclean world, can we really be sure these seemingly unconnected private eyes had clean noses?" More nodding. "Especially as they have gathered in Derby."

Further nodding. Broome broke the spell.

"And if we're looking at an organisation, no matter how small, why specialise in the lovers of cheating spouses? Could it be someone with a grudge, someone who has suffered badly in such circumstances? You know, now mentally deranged and out to punish this type of wrongdoer?"

"I hate *mentally deranged* when it comes to the criminal." seethed Alcock in his otherwise lovely and warm west country delivery, "Enables people to get lenient sentences or get off altogether. Look, if we know right from wrong, if we know stabbing someone is wrong, why should your state of mind have any legal bearing? I mean, a drunk driver mows down a pedestrian and we don't excuse 'em cos they were drunk, do we?"

Another outbreak of nodding and this time it was Okafor who arrested it.

"Well, mentally unfit or not, that right now is not our problem, but take your point Geoff, no offence mate. I think the biggest issue facing us is this link. The last thing we need to do is head off on some pre-conceived notion. Right?" Concurrence was nodded. "Must keep an open mind. And let's say, for arguments sake, there is no connection and it's all mere coincidence. Okay, I don't believe it, but we have to look at every possibility. Now Geoff, you suggested the dark web. We've got some guys who can search that. Are you happy for me to organise that?"

As was now normal consensus was acknowledged with nods, this time a little more enthusiastically than before.

"We need to hit the underworld side of things. Any thoughts?"

"What about the Met, Holton? London, or any big city, might have better leads than any of us, although Kent's right on the doorstep, of course."

"Thanks Stephanie. Good idea, talking to the Met. We've all got contacts, so let's use them. I'll get in touch with the guys in the smoke. Either of you any big city contacts?"

"Suffolk's a bit short of big cities, thank God. But here's another idea. What about our intrepid three sleuths? If they're above board might we find a way of using them, you know, contacts and all that. And yours, Okafor, is an ex-cop." Okafor visibly bristled.

"Don't like getting involved with them. They're bad news. We ask them to help and they'll get ideas above their station and interfere with what we're doing." Geoff Alcock spoke at this point.

"Appreciate that, Holton, but mine, John Wapernod, he's got a first class reputation and I'm confident he'd know better than to get in our way. Very co-operative man. Does David Canbown strike you as being a loose cannon, Holton? Is he the bitter, resentful sort? You know, after taking his revenge on the force?"

"Don't think so Geoff, but I'm not up to taking that risk. He might think he's got nothing to lose. And Stephanie, yours, Yvonne Pratt, didn't exactly rush forward when Phyllis Downport was murdered."

"Good point Holton. Perhaps keep them out for the time being. Just one other matter. My murder is a bit different and not just because the victim's a woman. She left her vast wealth to William Bailey, her lover, which gives him a motive despite the fact he was rich anyway, and married to another wealthy woman. And nobody here rushed forward to help us when our body was discovered."

Now the nods were accompanied by a selection of words such as 'true' – 'good point' – 'that's right'. Broome continued.

"Except in Kent. Canbown came straight to you. But you're right, perhaps we should keep the private eyes at armslength for the time being."

But the private eyes were not for keeping at armslength as they soon discovered.

*** 

Georgina Hayle, having enjoyed a pleasant and stimulating half-hour in her hot tub, was relaxing on a 'helicopter' chair that was swinging gently in the breeze that barely rustled the leaves on the trees. With Jason away on a business trip to the States she was looking forward to the arrival of Leonora early evening and was already partaking champagne as a means to establishing an emotional, if metaphorical, bed of roses upon which to lay her heart.

Leonora would ignite the fires, take 'simmering' to 'boiling' and intensify Georgina's dreamy sensations as she always did. And Mrs Hayle could hardly wait. Her whole body tingled as the late afternoon sun provided the slightest touch of warmth and the champagne fizzed purposefully inside her. Imagination and longing did the rest.

She was alive. Vibrancy raced through her willing and receptive body. Less than an hour now.

Her maid was summoned and asked to ensure another bottle of Veuve Clicquot was chilling, and to be certain to direct Miss Cuthbert to the back garden as soon as she arrived. Surely Leonora must be feeling every bit as alive as she did, throbbing with anticipation and desire, yearning for their meeting, that first kiss, that exhilarating caress, that all-absorbing passion.

Surely she must feel just as alive.

***

Yvonne Pratt had no bother finding Kenny Parrett, who was taken by surprise.

"Didn't recognise you from your website photo," he said.

"It was taken by a top professional, and designed to achieve three things: to enhance my best features, to hide the worst, and most importantly make me look like a no-nonsense business-like woman of power and distinction." Kenny wasn't sure if there was any intended humour in her response and settled for the tiniest of grins, just in case. She glanced at him with a wicked look and her eyes burned with fun. He was stuffed and he knew it.

They bought coffees and sat together, discussed each other and then moved on to the reason Kenny had made contact. At this stage Yvonne didn't mention the meeting she'd had with John and David.

"Hope you now think I'm genuine, Yvonne, but either way I'm worried. Probably paranoid! There are such extraordinary similarities. I've been employed by a wealthy and powerful businessman to follow his wife and provide evidence of infidelity. Not for divorce. Just the evidence. I've done that and been paid. Now that must've been how it was for you, yes?"

At that moment and before she could reply she looked up and saw David Canbown and a young woman just feet away. He hadn't seen her.

"David, David," she called, "oh, sorry Kenny, I must introduce you. Sorry to interrupt." And called a startled David Canbown and his companion over.

***

The lawned garden, even with its planted treasures and intoxicating dalesland views, proved a poor venue for two lovers dying to sample the physical gifts they wished to share. Georgina and Leonora kissed the very second they met, embraced and kissed again, now with added vehemence and focus, and just about managed to gather up the ice bucket and glasses in their headlong rush indoors. Only the bedroom would now suffice.

Once there glasses of champagne were poured with a rapidity that produced more bubbles than drink and therefore a great deal of mirth, and both women collapsed on the bed, shrieking and giggling. The drink was quickly forgotten, as was the squealing and laughter, as passion took over and guided them to their earthly paradise.

Jason had never offered anything on this scale or with this depth. He usually satisfied himself, and with appreciable alacrity, and then laid back, a proud, exhausted but supremely happy man, leaving Georgina a lonely and sad figure. It was little wonder she had allowed herself to wander beyond the marriage, and poor little ugly, shapeless Leonora had been the answer.

The latter was desperate to be loved, the former found herself desperately in love. Love just happened. Lust came first but had never deserted them, especially now they were lost in the most beautiful of emotional loving mists. Georgina convinced herself nobody could love her as Leonora did.

And it was all so safe! Jason was happy Georgie had such a loyal female friend, and had become firm friends himself with Miss Cuthbert. There could be no hint of suspicion. She'd put on such a show when he discovered them cuddling in the summer house; just two girls being girls, darling, just two mates engrossed in girly-talk, all very silly darling, she'd explained.

He'd accepted it, forgotten it. Except that he hadn't. He'd seen the look of love as the two women glanced at each other, and had subsequently hired Kenny Parrett to obtain the evidence.

So where was the violent explosion when he confronted his wife? It never came because he didn't confront her. He had something much more explosive in mind.

*** 

Not so very far away a tall stranger had checked into a hotel. The receptionist was suitably impressed; handsome by any definition, superbly dressed, extremely well-spoken, exceedingly polite. She was impressed. She might have been less impressed had she known she was booking in a ruthless killer.

In the guest's room the murderer filled the kettle, placed a tea bag in a cup and started to unpack. A small case, just a few things. After all, it was a one night stay. The hypodermic syringe was checked and placed on the desk with the small jar of poison. A new method of despatch this time.

The victim, of course, would have to be rendered unconscious or better still tied up. What fun! The trouble with the latter is that it takes precious time and the poor sod might not be that keen on being co-operative. No, an unseen assailant whacking the unsuspecting person hard enough to knock them out, a swift injection, and away. Timing was everything.

Just imagine how heartbroken the victim's lover will be! And unable to share their grief with their spouse in their hour of need. That's what adds to the fun, knowing the straying spouse is really going to have to suffer. That'll teach 'em. And now for the cup that cheers.

The kettle had boiled and tea was made. The drinker smiled at the mirror and saw the smile reflected, a smile of satisfaction, the smile of the cunning, the smile of the pitiless, the smile of the shark!

***

I was too astonished at first to understand what I was looking at, or more particularly *who* was in my field of vision.

"Yvonne!" I cried at the approaching and unmistakable figure of Ms Pratt as realisation flooded my mind. "What are you doing here?"

"Never mind that, what are *you* doing here?" We both laughed and hugged like long lost friends.

Kenny and Laura stood back, not quite sure what to make of this. Yvonne took my arm and led me to her table.

"David, this is Kenny Parrett. He's one of us and this is his patch. Kenny, meet David, my fellow private investigator from Kent." We shook hands and I turned and beckoned Laura over.

"Folks, this is Laura, my assistant, and by coincidence also my current client." Kenny and Yvonne looked puzzled. After handshakes all round we sat down. Now Yvonne wanted to know more about Laura.

"We're looking for her sister," I offered, "and I've left a message with your wife, Kenny, as I thought a bit of local knowledge might help." He sat back and smiled. "And Yvonne, what's all this about then?" I said, keen to change the subject.

"I'll let Kenny tell you, but first I'll tell him about the three of us meeting in Derby yesterday."

As I had come to expect Yvonne related the story as if she was writing a book, adding edge and mystery in equal doses, and a touch of the melodramatic for good measure. She was a good story teller as I knew, and she had a way of presenting the most mundane of detail in a gripping manner. Kenny looked positively excited.

Then he gave us his own account, about Jason and Georgina Hayle and Leonora Cuthbert, and his worries about the similarities with the Suffolk murder. He didn't tell his tale as well as Yvonne might've handled it, but we got the picture, and we duly shared his concern.

"And now I'm more worried than ever," he added as he concluded his report, "so do I go to the police and do I say I've met you?"

"I say yes," Yvonne said decisively, "and mention us by all means. Agreed David?" I nodded. "But be prepared to be metaphorically laughed at." Kenny turned to me.

"Now, David what can I do for you?" I asked Laura to briefly explain the background but Laura is not always given to brevity and in that respect she didn't disappoint. A few minutes later I took up the story when she paused for breath.

"I think I may have seen Lorraine, in Matlock, earlier today. She was getting into a taxi; I got the firm and the reg but they won't play ball, needless to say."

"What firm?" he asked and I told him. "And the reg?" He took out a notebook and wrote down the information. "Time and place?" I told him. "I might be able to help there. Leave it with me and I'll get back asap."

It was an absolute shot in the dark, a chance in a million. But then Kenny's problem was also a shot in the dark. Plenty of private eyes follow errant spouses without anyone dying as a result. Of course, it could be simple coincidence, but then he'd be haunted forever if it turned out to be the next killing.

Although we didn't realise it we were just hours away from the horrible truth.

# Chapter Fifteen

# The Deadly Dales

John Holgarve didn't know what hit him. If he had he would've realised it was the spindle from a wooden balustrade (easily purchased from Homebase or Bunnings or whoever they are this week), typical of the surrounds of many garden patios.

It left him sufficiently dazed for his assailant to inject him with a deadly substance, and gradually he passed from daze to death without any real knowledge of what had befallen him. His body remained where it had been pushed until discovery much, much later.

Before this fatal occurrence Kenny Parrett had descended from the Heights of Abraham with a view to contacting the police, convinced now this was the right course of action. He knew one or two officers (of course he did) and hoped he would be taken seriously.

It had been a lively conversation above the Gorge between the four of us, and Laura had felt free to join in whensoever she pleased, which was often. He'd taken a copy of the photo of Laura's mother which he promised to return next time we met, and set off hot-foot on his mission. A woman's life might be at stake.

We lingered a little. I was amazed at how well Laura and Yvonne hit it off, even though I winced once or twice at Laura's phraseology. The pair seemed like chalk and cheese, but then people might've said that about *me* and Laura! Opposites attracting? Anyway, the time came for Yvonne to depart but not before she'd asked to be kept up to speed on the Lorraine McCaffield trail. This was promised.

Laura was longing for her cable car ride back down to Matlock Bath so we descended, regained our car and set off the short way to our B & B. She was disgusted we had separate rooms and kept niggling me about it, but it wasn't going to change anything. I was reminded, with depressing frequency, that I'd agreed to the penance of a kiss goodnight.

Meanwhile Mr Parrett had appraised the police and, although it wasn't mentioned to him at the time, a link was established and in due course DS Holton Okafor in Kent was notified. What immediately disturbed him was not simply the knowledge that the three private eyes were now four and the police were being advised of a likely fourth victim, it was that Canbown, Wapernod and Pratt (the gang of three) had all travelled to Derbyshire prior to this turn of events.

A huge question mark lay suspended in the ether near Okafor, and said question mark also found itself in the vicinity of Detective Sergeants Broome and Alcock. The 'gang of three' needed questioning, but for the moment the Derbyshire force was more concerned over whether they should be taking Parrett seriously amid fears that if he was right something should be done.

It would look very bad if they did nothing and Miss Cuthbert perished.

Okafor's opinion, supported by senior officers, was that the matter might have some weight but could all too easily be a non-runner. Private investigators have been hired probably thousands of times to check on straying spouses, possibly less so these days, and rarely did the activity end with someone's demise. So how much of all of this was coincidence? How much credence should be attached to Parrett's report? More to the point, what resources should be directed at it?

Before any decisions of note could be taken and actioned everyone was overtake by events.

***

Kenny Parrett, true to his word, called me later, related his visit to the police, and advised me the mystery woman had been taken to a hotel in Matlock Bath. He then went on to say he wasn't happy that the police didn't appear too worried, but what else could he do? He couldn't mount a guard for Leonora Cuthbert round the clock, and the police clearly weren't going to do it.

We agreed that, in all honesty, we couldn't expect otherwise. Once again the spectre of private eyes following adulterous other halves was the demon at our shoulder. Nothing new under the sun. And lovers were not being routinely executed, so really the police across the country could hardly be expected to follow up reports like Kenny's, unless there was evidence to go on. Adultery happened all too often.

I thanked him for his efforts, and he said he'd pursue the Lorraine Wimbush angle, thinking it unlikely that anyone who lived in the district would be staying at a hotel. Unless, he added, she was a 'working girl', that euphemism for a sex industry participant, but he would certainly be able to check up on that for me using the photo as a rough guide.

Laura was listening intently. If she had indeed been a dog she would've been panting furiously with anticipation, as dogs do.

Within minutes we were off to a neighbouring hotel, one that discreetly mentioned the word class without shouting it from the rooftops. The polite and otherwise helpful receptionist would not be drawn, quite rightly so, but did not prevent us from looking in at the restaurant and the bar.

My assistant bought herself a pint and me a lemonade and lime, and we waited hopefully but not patiently. Then Kenny rang again.

"Dave? Listen, this'll cost yer. Mate of mine can take that photo and do a 3D graphic, y'know, make her look her present age. He can make her thinner, fatter in the face, all the options. But it don't come cheap, buddy." An updated photo, why didn't I think of that?

"Okay, go for it Kenny."

"Cheers mate. Now can I get some details from Laura?" I passed the phone over and for once she was the soul of discretion, even going into the corridor and speaking softly. There really is no need for people to shout into mobile phones, unless they're showing off of course. She returned after a few moments and handed the phone back.

"Strange, ain't it? The possibility my sister's upstairs right now giving some bloke a good time! Hope she gets well paid. Talking of which, well a good time, not getting paid, don't forget you has your penance to pay at bedtime and who knows where it may lead."

"You to your bedroom, me to mine."

***

Job done, the killer was looking forward to a good night's sleep, an early breakfast, and up and away first thing. Pay the bill in cash, leave no obvious trace, disappear quietly, put some distance in. Make no contact with the chubby man. Not yet; the payment arrangements were clear to both parties.

***

We had to leave, but not before Miss McCaffield, having borrowed a tenner, had purchased another round of drinks.

So it was with a mixture of sadness, emptiness and raw elation that we headed back to our modest B & B. It was late although neither of us felt tired. An adrenalin rush? Maybe, but once in my room we talked endlessly about the day and the way things had turned out. Finally it was time for bed.

"Kissy kissy for missy missy," she squealed, squealed like a tiny mouse I thought. It was a lovely passionate kiss, but I was dreading what she might try next. I was in for a surprise. She gently undid our embrace, freed herself, said 'see you in the morning' and was gone.

What I didn't know was the next day was going to be full of more surprises. For the moment I snuggled up under the duvet, closed my eyes and found myself thinking about Lorraine. Late fifties now. Be interesting to see what Kenny's mate comes up with. Did she have children? If so, probably adults now. Was she still with Gary Wimbush?

If she was indeed the woman I'd seen, and the graphic would show that, where did she live and what had she done with her life? Why did I want to ask myself all these questions instead of getting to sleep? My mind changed its subject, and the new subject was Laura.

What a kiss! What a narrow escape!

\*\*\*

Mrs Holgarve called the police.

It was the early hours and John had never been this late in. Never. He often went to visit his old mate Barry (Baz as he called him). Joan Holgarve had her own friends and occasionally went out with them herself. She did all kinds of hours at a local supermarket.

They'd not had kids. She'd been for tests but he hadn't, so it was assumed the problem lay at his doorstep. At that point relationships between them began to sour. Even so, she loved him, or so she thought, and was genuinely concerned that he was missing. Joan usually had the car so she could get to and from work, and John would take the bus to and from his place of employment in Buxton.

Barry didn't live far away, walking distance, and she'd phoned him about 11 p.m. only to be told her husband had just left. It was now 1.30 a.m. Where was he? She called Barry again and not only awoke him from a deep sleep, but left him feeling almost frightened.

John's visits were a cover. Barry knew his friend was actually seeing a girl about whom he had kept very quiet. 'Best you don't know' John had advised, and Barry had agreed. The errant husband never took his mobile despite the fact his wife wished he did 'just in case'. His excuse was that he was going no distance at all, a five minute walk each way.

Now Barry Welahome was worried. What had happened to John, and if he'd disappeared how would he explain it to Joan, let alone the police if they were involved. Supposing he'd had an accident or been mugged and beaten up? Mr Welahome began to realise that he could be up to his eyes in muck, and in the way of the guilty wrung his hands together and squeaked and sighed as he screwed up his face and tried to cry tears that would not come.

The police took some details but gently advised it was a bit early to start a hunt; he might turn up any moment. This made Mrs Holgarve angry and frustrated. She was told there had been no reported accidents, emergencies or incidents in the Bakewell area. They took Barry's number and said they would call and that was the start of Mr Welahome's nightmare come true.

He was now confronted with a worse-case scenario, and decided to tell the truth. He was advised to call John's wife pronto before they got back to her. Obviously he could tell them nothing about the girl or where they met, and feeling a complete and wretched failure elected to walk round to Joan and face the music. He wished he was dead, little realising that the man he'd been covering for already was.

***

For the time being the police simply believed John Holgarve was overdoing some illicit passion with his girlfriend. It wasn't an unusual situation these days. But be sure your sins will find you out.

About the time Barry was ringing Joan's doorbell another woman, a good few miles away, was also having a sleepless night. In Rosie Pequeman's case it was simply because her evening had been so blissful even if deliriously exhausting, and she was reliving every intoxicating moment, every extraordinary thrill, every sizzling sensation, every second of unbridled, unlimited pleasure.

Rosie was a city girl and she loved the country because it was escape, or had been in those far off days. Escape from the noise, the muddled throng of people, the dirt and pollution, the urgency, the bad tempers, the impatience that marked any large city. She'd been brought up in Arnold in the north of Nottingham and after school had gone to art college.

She didn't last the course. It wasn't because she was lazy (by her own definition) but because she lacked application, this sounding marginally better. Rosie also lacked true ambition and a clear picture of what she wanted to do, so meeting upwardly-mobile Daryl Pequeman had given her ideas. He appealed for three main reasons.

Although her experience of men was narrow when compared to the experience of her friends, she believed Daryl to be God's gift to women, since he himself exuded that impression, being exceedingly good-looking, of a wonderfully athletic build, and possessing charm, a romantic heart, a decisive manner and the ability to please her. Under the latter heading was the ability to satisfy her demands utterly in matters of intimacy.

Secondly, he was already wealthy and worked as a commercial architect with boundless aspirations. Thirdly, he shared her passion for the countryside and her thirst for money.

Rosie had laboured in various jobs, none of which either paid well or lasted very long, and she reasoned Daryl might be her ticket to more than one heaven. For they also shared a desire to live in the country amidst the glorious scenery they adored, and be miles from anywhere.

They were often to be found walking in the Derbyshire Dales and the Monsal Trail was their favourite area. It was here they sat at Monsal Head, high above the Wye and the now defunct railway viaduct where they walked so frequently, and planned their future as couples so usually do.

Having married they bought a house in West Bridgford as it was close to Daryl's base near the city centre. It was intended as a temporary measure until their dream came true. They didn't have long to wait. Out of the blue a lonely farmhouse high on the hills not far from Monsal Dale came up for sale. Although the deserted building was in poor repair they fell in love with the remote spot and the incredible views and knew they wanted it more than anything. That night, their offer having been accepted, they enjoyed a bottle of wine and made love more excitedly than they had ever done before.

As an architect Daryl knew builders and his way around planning regulations, and was confident that he could renovate the farm house within conservation bounds and still make it a dream home. Meanwhile Rosie had found a small job that she could do from home. It kept her occupied because, although it was not difficult, she was deliberately slow.

After months and months of longing their new home was ready.

The day they moved in marked the start of the decline of Rosie Pequeman's life.

As city dwellers the countryside had a natural appeal, but there is a huge difference between visiting the loveliest of scenery and trying to live there. As Daryl achieved greatness at work so his employment took him away from home more frequently, and sometimes overseas into the bargain.

His wife continued her job at home and sank into friendless boredom. There were no friends to be had. The beautiful views took on the role of a bleak, windswept wilderness, with only the movement of sheep to break the monotony. She met John Holgarve by chance.

She was being bored in boring Bakewell, down by the boring river, and had sat down to revel in her boredom, a task in which she usually succeeded with honours. Just as she was light-heartedly contemplating throwing herself headlong into the Wye a man sat down beside her. It transpired he was on his lunch break and they soon got talking.

Friendship followed. Inevitably the friendship developed apace, as she found she liked this ordinary man, this unambitious yet thoroughly interesting ordinary man, and their relationship evolved until they were ready to try intimacy. John persuaded his close pal Barry to cover for him, in the manner hitherto related, and Rosie came to collect him from Bakewell, driving up through Ashford-in-the-water, past Monsal Head and on to the farmhouse.

It was now that she discovered that Daryl was not entirely God's gift to women, more of a kind of aperitif or stop-gap, and that she never really had been blessed with the presentation of any gifts truly worth cherishing. John wasn't God's gift to women, he was the Almighty's personal treasure trove bestowed solely upon Rosie Pequeman. How he lit her up, inflamed her passions, made her sizzle and how she responded, goodness how she responded!

And, of course, she wanted more. Much more. In her loneliness she became insatiable. John was Premier League, Daryl was in the relegation zone of League Two. She began to loathe being with her husband, and she made more and more arrangements to meet John whenever her husband was away. The farmhouse rocked and rolled any evening Rosie and John spent there.

Careful and discreet at first, her lust for forbidden fruits made her reckless, and Daryl was clever enough to pick up the signals, eventually finding a love note she had written but screwed up and discarded in the bin.

As he was due to go away to Dubai for a few days he enlisted the help of a private investigator to find the damning evidence. He explained all he wanted was irrefutable evidence, nothing more. There would be no divorce; just a one-off confrontation with his wife and her left in no doubt about her future conduct. He also planned to seek out the lover and warn him too. Nothing official for either of them. Just a warning.

*** 

The next day meant different things to different people.

After a long, peaceful, happy sleep Rosie Pequeman put on her walking boots and suitable clothing and, with a spring in her step and a smile on her face, set off for Monsal Dale. She stared over the top at the River Wye, coming from the north-west and swinging sharply south-westwards almost back on itself, under the famous railway viaduct, between steep green slopes on its way to Bakewell.

'Give my love to Johnny' she whispered, unaware he was beyond receipt of such heartfelt kindness. She strode briskly down the path towards the Monsal

Trail intent on a fine old ramble before going home to lunch. Or maybe she'd buy a meal at the Monsal Head Hotel. She was on cloud nine and nothing would be allowed to spoil this precious and vital freedom of spirit that thrust through her body, heart and mind today.

Save the one thing she didn't know about yet.

Kenny Parrett had gone spying. He knew where Leonora Cuthbert lived and he wanted to know she was safe. More importantly, and rather foolishly, he wanted to protect her, knowing full well if there was a professional killer out there the strike wouldn't be made if there was any chance of detection. Nor would he be aware of the day it might happen. Hopeless, pointless, but he wasted the morning with the effort prior to the sensible abandonment of the project.

DS Okafor was deep in thought. It was a chance in a million. He remained certain as certain can be that they weren't looking at coincidence, yet by what curiosity of purpose did the killer take out the lovers of straying partners when the latter were married to wealthy people?

Scenario one: the wealthy were paying for the exterminations, but how and through whom?

Scenario two: was it the same killer, but a killer who also dealt death to others, the current three simply highlighting one aspect? So did they have a far worse serial killer situation on their hands? And he shuddered.

Scenario three: coincidence, three separate killers. Unlikely. Very.

Scenario four: just how seriously did they take Kenny Parrett's report?

And then a thought struck him. First up, why not see if it was possible to easily and swiftly contact all private eyes to ascertain if similar work had been undertaken? Clients wanting proof of infidelity only, not to be used in any action such as divorce. All private eyes? If only it was that easy. Why doesn't the government licence them?

Would it merely reveal the numbers of people 'up to it' behind the back, or did people, even the rich, really bother having their partners followed these days unless, of course, divorce was the target?

In scenario one exploration of the dark web was proving a dead end, but even in that obscure field of operation perhaps they shouldn't be looking for the obvious.

Scenario two was a nightmare, hopefully without foundation, but let's check around the country on outstanding murders especially where a lack of evidence was involved.

It was possible to dismiss scenario three given the similarities of the killings.

The fourth scenario was today's problem, a matter of immediate anxiety, but maybe none at all. But it raised the interesting feature of four private eyes meeting in Derbyshire, three of them directly or indirectly caught up in recent murders.

Time to take the sum of his knowledge to the boss; let someone else make the decisions.

Laura and I had been back to the hotel early in case the woman was having breakfast, and all we learned was that she wasn't and we'd missed ours. By lunchtime we were driving north to meet up with Kenny Parrett, and he'd been busy on our behalf.

The photos were ready. "Wow" exclaimed my enthusiastic assistant. All of us were struck by the similarity of the woman to Laura, and I was now positive she was the woman getting into the taxi.

"Nothing on the working girl front." he informed us. "Sorry I had to suggest that about your sister..."

"No worries, mate," Laura interrupted, "been on the game meself. Maybe it runs in the blood." Kenny looked at me, clearly unsure if he'd heard correctly. We didn't pursue it.

"Gary Wimbush, left long ago, thought to have been heading to work in Cumbria somewhere. But can't find any trace of a wife or anyone called Lorraine associated with him. Sorry, all I could manage in the time but if anything else comes up I know where to find you." But we were both overwhelmingly grateful for what he had done, and as he was in a state about Leonora Cuthbert we thought it best not to hang about.

I paid what I owed and he wouldn't take a penny more, and then my phone rang. It was Okafor.

"Mr Canbown, in Derby with John Wapernod, Yvonne Pratt and now Kenny Parrett. A sleuths' convention? Trying to do the real police out of a job are we? What are you doing up there, Mr Canbown?"

"I think that's my business, Sergeant, and it's my business I'm pursuing. A missing person, that's all. I met John and Yvonne by prior arrangement as I was coming to Derbyshire as was Yvonne. As far as they're concerned you'll have to ask                                                                                                          them."
"Touchy today, Mr Canbown? Never mind, just like to know where our suspects, sorry, parties of interest are and what they're up to. And you've told me. By the way, what are your thoughts on Mr Parrett's revelations, assuming you've discussed them and he hasn't told you to mind your own business?"

"Officer, you know as much as I do about Mr Parrett's revelations as you call them. You have that info because a private investigator handed the matter to the real police, just as I voluntarily brought everything to you the minute I heard of Alistair Bourne-Lacey's murder."

There wasn't much more to the conversation. I'd put him on loudspeaker, or whatever it's called on a mobile, and Kenny and Laura had listened, chuckled quietly and applauded noiselessly when they thought I'd scored a point. Kenny shook his head afterwards.

"They don't like it up, Cap'n Mainwaring, do they?" he said, mimicking Corporal Jones in TVs *Dads Army*.

For Mrs Holgarve it was a day of frightening despair. But at least the police had given the matter of her missing husband every degree of urgency and importance. She'd kicked Barry Welahome out as soon as he'd told his story leaving her shocked and shaking, trembling with that unpleasant mixture of rage, sadness, heartbreak and worry.

By mid afternoon she knew the sorry truth.

It was mid evening before Rosie learned.

## Chapter Sixteen
# Variety the spice of Death

Laura couldn't or wouldn't understand why we had to leave and return home. There was the possibility her sister was in the Matlock area and she would've willingly stayed forever in the hope of meeting her.

I tried to reassure her that now there were photos which were every bit like the woman I'd seen Kenny would get copies distributed, perhaps in the local rag too, but we had to accept that, for whatever reason, Lorraine might not want to be found.

The journey home was quiet, which was something of a relief, but I found it heart-rending that she kept a copy of the picture in her lap and stared at it from time to time. I cannot imagine what it must be like to know you may have been that close to your long-lost sister and you're driving away instead of delving into every nook and cranny.

I've never liked the M1 or associated roads; going north it's always been the good old A1 for me, and now we were motoring across country to pick up the Great North near Grantham. The A1 isn't perfection but I view it as an old friend, a throwback to the glorious days of road travel, and it has a mysterious charm, an enticing force about it. In fact, it can be dreadful. It can be a rotten road. But it's still *my* A1 and to me it's the only way.

We sped past Peterborough on the wide, wide motorway section, one of the few pieces of road built for tomorrow. All too often where roads are concerned we solve yesterday's problem tomorrow with no future-proofing. So a new stretch of road just about copes when it opens and fails to cope a few years later. I swung gently round the arc that leads to the M11 while Laura informed me she wanted a wee-wee.

"Next services are off the A120 junction I think, near Stansted; can you wait?"

"Have to." More silence.

Later I drove into the service area and parked and Laura burst into spontaneous tears. I hugged her to me unable to find the right words, so kept quiet. She sobbed uncontrollably for a while then pulled out her hanky and started to compose herself.

"Sorry Moncks," she whispered through falling tears, "just something I needed to do."
"I know, Law, I know. It's okay, it really is, and we'll find her very soon. Promise."

"Yeah, but it's like you say, she may not like want to be found. That's what hurts."

"Well, after all these years Law, she may be pleased and relieved to be found, especially now you're on the right side of things."

"She still won't want me. But what the heck? Who cares? But I'd like her to tell me to me face, know how it is Dave?"

"Yep, guess I do."

"Right, well now I've started to wet me knickers, so let's get to the bog and then I'm ready for a nibble of something disgustingly unhealthy. There's one or two outlets here have just the sort of naughty rubbish I'm keen on."

***

During the journey, and unbeknown to us, a body had been found in Bakewell. After John Holgarve had been dropped off, as usual a safe distance from home, he made his way by a round-about route but one that he followed time after time. It was easy for the killer lying in wait. And the deed was done.

Joan Holgarve was informed of the find. The police had found John's wallet, driving licence, and other items such as his house keys on the body. It all but confirmed who he was. There was a slight wound and dried blood on the back of his head. The doctor, making a preliminary on-site examination, was confident he'd been hit with sufficient force to knock him out, but couldn't immediately say he was looking at a cause of death.

Maybe shock. Perhaps he'd then had a heart attack or stroke. There was work to be done once the body was back at the mortuary. What was certain was that foul play was involved, and Barry Welahome was carted off for questioning, his home and possessions searched.

Was Welahome having an affair with Joan Holgarve and the barrier to their happiness had to be removed? The fact Barry couldn't furnish any details of the other lady only seemed to add to his presumed guilt.

Later Joan carried out the identification and at once found herself at the centre of the investigation. They were kind and gentle but it was becoming increasingly obvious the suspicion she and Barry were lovers, and may have colluded in John's killing, was foremost in officers' minds. Of course, those minds were open and exploring all possibilities, not just the one plonked right in front of them, but Joan wasn't to know that.

Rosie had walked to Millers Dale and back, still on an emotional high, and had climbed back to Monsal Head and onwards to her home where she arrived tired, worn out but happy. It was to be a short-lived happiness. Her husband called from abroad and said he'd be home the day after tomorrow and she said she couldn't wait. He guessed it was an unconvincing lie, but let it pass.

She was once again in love with the expansive scenery that surrounded her home, a home she'd shared briefly with her lover last night. Looking out of the window to the south-east she revelled in the green of the grassy fields and knew afresh why she'd fallen in love with the place. As far as John was concerned, same time next week, for Daryl would be in Scotland.

Rosie truly could not wait for that. Sadly she would wait for eternity and never experience it again.

***

We arrived home mid-evening, my home that is, and I offered to rustle up a meal. Laura said she'd rather I rustled up a bed for the night and with me in it, but accepted the suggested food.

Soon we learned about the dead man in Bakewell. It seemed no more than coincidence then.

John Holgarve's face appeared on the TV just as it must've done at that lonely farmhouse in Derbyshire. We took little notice, but the reaction at that farmhouse was probably very different indeed. Kenny rang us with the news but was still worried that Leonora Cuthbert was in danger, not realising that she wasn't to be the victim after all. We all remained in ignorance that the Bakewell killing fitted the Devon, Suffolk and Kent pattern.

Nobody else realised that either, not just yet, but the next day a Mr Gordon Pembrake called the police.

He introduced himself as a private investigator working for the Manchester firm of Parrish, Lome and Hurdsley. Having seen the story of John Holgarve's demise he thought the police ought to be aware that the deceased had been the subject of an investigation they carried out on behalf of a Daryl Pequeman in Derbyshire, and it related to his wife, Rosie, and John Holgarve. Mr Pembrake believed officers ought to be conscious of the matter. Questioned, he replied that all Mr Pequeman wanted was irrefutable proof with which to challenge his wife. Evidence provided, Parrish, Lome and Hurdsley was paid off by the contracted amount. End of story.

His details were taken, he was thanked, and advised a statement would probably be needed, as would access to any files. He responded by saying he understood and that his company would be contacting their solicitor immediately for legal advice. There was the question of client confidentiality and they needed to maintain their integrity. For the moment the police officer let the matter rest.

Once more Laura had slept on the sofa without venturing any further than the bathroom. Now we were tucking into bacon rolls for breakfast. Proper bacon rolls; lots and lots of bacon with rashers hanging out the sides and butter dripping on our napkins. She was over the events of the previous day, had shed no more tears, and was more like her usual self.

It was time to get down to business, trade that might make us some money, and I was keen on two opportunities that now lay before us thanks to our (or rather *my*) ever improving reputation. Laura needed something to take her mind off Lorraine for the present and Shel Crackby provided that diversion.

I drove her to Faversham and came all the way back to Minster to revel in my own world, my own home, my everything, all of devoid of my assistant, and only then did I feel that I was missing her! Silly, isn't it?

\*\*\*

The doctor was a lady of few words.

"Injection site, Inspector, left arm. Some light bruising. The whack on the head wasn't the death blow, so this injection might've been. Plenty of tests to go. Not confirming any of this until I'm sure, but that's my initial analysis. Just don't quote me." The Inspector knew better than to quote her, but he relayed the information from his phone call to the waiting officers, then adding:

"Right guys. As you know we had a call from a Kenny Parrett regarding a possible target in the area, a target that matched up similar successful targets in Devon, Suffolk and Kent. We now get a call from a Manchester PI saying the departed, John Holgarve, had been watched by them in a similar situation. So while we look one way the killer strikes in another.

"We're wondering whether to look after a potential target. Then someone else, in much the same situation, gets topped. If this is a ruthless serial killer, and it's beginning to look more than coincidence now, we've got a serious problem and that's going to spell the National Crime guys.

"Let's see what we can do first, huh? We'll talk to Rosie Pequeman. She must know her lover's been done in by now. Unfortunately we have to make her day even more horrible. Let's get what we can out of the private investigator. And let's talk to Kenny Parrett. I also have to announce that the private eyes involved in the other three murders are all known to have been in Derbyshire this week, and have met our Kenny.

"Things in common, all four cases. Private eyes hired by jealous spouses ... do we use the word spouse any longer? .... anyway, they're all wealthy spouses. They all just want the evidence, nothing for divorce purposes, and then bingo, the lover gets the chop. No forensic, no DNA, nothing at all. Four different means of execution. This is some joker we've got.

"My money is on the wealthy spouses hiring a hit man. Sorry, should say hit-*person*, forgetting my political correctness again. Whatever came over me! Let's liaise with the other forces and get this show on the road. National media's got hold of it and they won't be letting go any time soon. Right, down to details, guys."

Past media speculation turned out to be the substance of mild patches rather than the blanket coverage the murders received now. And speculation was earning a new lease of life big time.

In Kent it was decided to turn Neville Gradling over and his home was raided, his computer seized and his business and bank records checked. It was to prove an utterly fruitless search and for the moment it put the other forces off. But it did succeed in making Neville an extremely angry man and that did not bode well for his wife Jacqueline.

The killer was well away from Derbyshire.

By arrangement the operation was going to vanish for the time being, allowing the dust to settle. No traces whatsoever. Providing nobody else perished for the foreseeable future and perhaps even longer then maybe the scheme could be resurrected at a later date, or reincarnate itself in some other way, different targets possibly.

There were always wicked sinners to be dealt with.

It had been good to redistribute wealth. Proper socialism that, the killer concluded. Those four had paid well over the top for a sound professional job that left them absolutely in the clear. They were paying for that level of service. Anybody can hire a hit man, but the police will always pick up on something, finding a lead that takes them to the malefactor.

No, those wealthy four are safely in the clear, no doubts whatsoever, and they know it. Very comfortable that, knowing you've got away with it with very clean hands. But then they've paid. Oh God, have they paid! Or rather, I should say, they are *going* to pay.

And of course while the little business sits on the back burner for long time a certain amount of blackmail can be indulged in. So they haven't finished paying yet, not by a long chalk. And pay they will! Odd expression that, the killer mused, by-a-long-chalk. Must Google it!

How wonderful it is to deal with adulterous lovers in a way that leaves grieving people in far more emotional agony than they otherwise would be! A lesson in life that. Don't do adultery and you won't suffer. Enough to put anyone off straying. The trouble is, these people don't realise the pain and anguish they cause their husbands and wives. It's not right.

At least I've been able to sort a few out. Let's hope with the publicity it puts others off.

However, back in Derbyshire another wronged husband was about to deliver his own solution to a problem of adultery.

***

It wasn't long before a news hound made contact. I played a straight bat, advising my business matters were not for discussion, that I had been interviewed by the police having voluntarily handed over my files, and that was that.

"Weren't you once a copper, Mr Canbown? Seem to recall you were mixed in something and had to resign." This one knew her onions and was throwing everything at it in pursuit of a story. I was fed up saying 'no comment' but I said it one more time.

"I'll take that as an okay," she decided, "and I expect it must be galling for you being on the receiving end of interminable questions after a career asking them." I bit my tongue and held fire, saying nothing at all. "Take my number, just in case you ever want a chat, y'know, off the record." I took her number.

I'd met my two new clients, one a middle-aged lady of considerable wealth and standing who wished to locate an old school chum, the other an older man looking for a particular pot lid that he'd given to a friend donkey's years ago. His friend had 'lost' it, probably sold it, but now my customer thought it might be far more valuable than hitherto considered, and anyway he wanted it back for sentimental reasons, these not disclosed.

Pot lids? Pot lids? A quick Googling revealed that they dated back to the mid-nineteenth century, although the idea of decorating pottery went back much further. Upon jars of snuff, cosmetics, and all kinds of popular substances, sat lids with a variety of artistic impressions appropriate to the contents.

A Mr Pratt (that name again) discovered a way of using emergent printing technology to decorate these lids on a commercial basis. Extraordinarily, they are now collectors' items and some rare examples are worth a great deal of money. Well, in doing this job my education was being improved.

Laura stayed over with Shel and Linnie and I wondered if I ought to be worried!

Would any good come of it? It was no longer an 'earner' but it kept my assistant occupied so maybe it was doing some good. And I was pleased to be doing anything other than looking for Lorraine and being up to my eyeballs in a murder that was none of my business.

*** 

John Holgarve's post mortem demonstrated that being hit on the head did not kill him. Further, tiny wood splinters and the shape of the impact wound suggested a thin piece of timber, cuboid, not treated, varnished or painted, had been used. The injection site revealed that the jab was given just prior to death, and since there was no syringe in the vicinity it was most unlikely he'd injected himself. Even less likely if he was unconscious, of course.

The pathologist concluded that whoever gave the shot knew what they were doing, up to a point (if you'll forgive the pun). That is, as far as its administration was concerned. Withdrawing the needle with care and cleaning the site didn't come into the equation as the killer was then more interested in getting away. So what was injected? That data were still to come.

Jason Hayle had arrived home and was pleased to see his wife Georgina with her friend Leonora. He wanted to talk to them. They chatted briefly about his business trip while the maid brought them tea and biscuits. Then they spoke of the hideous murder that had taken place under their noses. Having exhausted that topic and all of the biscuits Jason took the women by complete surprise.

"Now darling, and Leonora if you please, the fact is that I've paid a man to spy on you so I know you are lovers." Their jaws dropped open, their eyes bulged, and they both made to speak. Jason raised his right hand to stop them. "No, ladies, let me speak, you can talk later. Let's keep this civilised.

"First of all Georgina, do you want a divorce, yes or no?" She looked terribly flustered, her mouth made several movements suggesting words might be forming behind them, her head shook a little and the colour rose in her cheeks. This was the opposite of Leonora who sat stock still, shock etched in every part of her face from which all colour had drained completely. Before Georgina could reply Jason spoke again.

"I don't want one. As long as I have my beautiful wife and we continue to share a loving relationship the way we have always done, I am quite happy for you to enjoy the love of Miss Cuthbert, and the comfort of my money. In other words, everything just as it is now." His wife was horribly suspicious and looked it. "You just carry on living your life as you do with all the benefits of my money, and with Leo for company when I'm away." It was the first time he'd shortened

Leonora's name and such abbreviation did not meet with her approval. He guessed it wouldn't.

Georgina thought about the pre-nup agreement. Divorce would leave her with so little and perhaps the necessity of having to work. "I don't want a divorce, Jase," she finally said, but in a voice deprived of conviction and depth.

"Leonora, you have a choice of two options. You can abandon your affair with my wife and make sure you never come near us again, or you can agree to my terms and conditions." Miss Cuthbert managed to look as if she was dreading what was coming, and did so with with a mixture of disgust and distaste.

"You carry on now, with Georgina, just as you have been doing but free of worry, free of the thought of being caught and the consequences, because you can be lovers with my blessing. How does that sound?" He waited for no answer, ploughing straight ahead. "My conditions are, and don't forget if they are not acceptable you can end the relationship, that you and I meet from time to time for some pleasures of the flesh. I will expect you to allow me to do the things Georgina won't let me. Sorry and all that, but that's the price.

"Finally, just occasionally, and for my entertainment, I would like to watch you both together if you understand my meaning." He let the words sink in before continuing. "I'll pop out for a while and you can let me know your decision later. Have a good chat, ladies." And he was gone.

Both ladies found the contemplation of murder a companionable thought, once they had got over their initial revulsion and resultant nausea.

*** 

The Detective Inspector had expected Mr Pembrake to be either like his vision of a gum-chewing American private eye, or an immaculately dressed middle-aged gentleman, rather in the mould of the traditional image of a solicitor. He was neither.

Young, athletic looking, dressed smart-casual but in a style that made him look fit for purpose, ready for business, ready for anything. He spoke as a true Mancunian, 'clipped Lancashire' the DI called it, and was precise and positive. His eyes, which rarely left the officer, made the Inspector uncomfortable, and his manner made him feel as if it was *he* being interviewed and not the right way round.

Nonetheless, the DI made headway, receiving clear answers to his questions, but the man's firm, having sought legal advice, had told him not to reveal anything that might breach client confidentiality. This impasse led to some difficult moments, for Pembrake had volunteered to come forward and had already disclosed that he had been following Rosie and John, and who he was working for.

Having gone that far the DI felt it was reasonable for him to provide more details and in that Gordon Pembrake was becoming rather cagey. It wasn't an easy interview, and it didn't last long, the officer deciding he'd got enough, or as much as he was likely to get, and that someone else would have to decide how Pembrake was going to be opened up.

Back in Kent Laura was arranging professional help for Shel Crackby, a lengthy process in itself, and a road along which only Shel could travel. Laura and Linnie were there for moral support, allowing, as had to be the case, Shel to drive the issue forward. But at long last she was going to try and that was a whole herd of progress.

I was developing an interest in pot lids and in working alone again. The long-lost school friend, which would've been my first choice of business, was now on the back-burner if only temporarily. The pot lids had captured my imagination and, frankly, I was right off the idea of missing persons having worn myself out over Lorraine.

One of my contacts phoned saying no evidence of Gary and Lorraine divorcing, but no sign of where they might reside, together or apart.

It proved the great day of phone calls.

Adam Pensfield called next. He was giving nothing away but suggested another meeting. I said it was pointless unless he could tell me something I didn't know or that was of use to me.

"Let's meet and you can decide." I had to take him up on it. I just knew he wanted me to know something, and that it was vital I knew. Neither of us actually mentioned the murders because you can't be too careful and he's got more to lose than me. So I planned to go over to his drum the next day.

The next call was Kenny Parrett. He'd been circulating the picture and he'd got a lead. More than that, he'd learned that she'd been in Matlock some years back with husband Gary Wimbush, but she left him after she caught him with another woman. Rumour had it she'd set off north but Kenny's contact could offer no more. Did Gary follow Lorraine? Did he know where she'd gone?

We nattered about the fresh killing and he advised me on the QT that it might be a lethal injection. "Don't quote me mate, but it makes you wonder how he's going to kill the next one. Strangulation, stabbing, shooting, injection ..... fancy opening a book on the next method?" There was a chuckle. I said I'd call him back in a day or two as I was meeting an old friend, nudge-nudge, wink-wink, and I might have something to share. He took the hint, said he knew what I meant and looked forward to my call.

How does that boy do it? He seems remarkably well connected and picks up tidbits like nobody's business, as well as copping inside information denied others. A few of those media hacks would like to be in his position I guessed. But perhaps some of them were.

The national media might help me find Lorraine but that was a double-edged sword and I would be facing the most lethal side. If I could use a reporter with cunning and guile and that reporter did me a favour what could I lose? Slip her or him some bits and pieces in return for help in my search? No, it would never work. They'd see through me or I would be hung out to dry.

I didn't know any journalists. But wait a moment, Adam might! Yes, I'd ask and get his comments and advice at the same time.

And so, as the day drew to a close, many things moved on from where they had been, and the wheels of life turned and dragged some of those involved down dangerous roads. Progress could be achieved but at what price? And just how dangerous were those roads?

# Chapter Seventeen

# Laura Revealed

Adam Pensfield behaved differently from the way I had come to expect. I thought our meeting would, as before, be wracked with riddles and puzzles in which I would be required to not only read between the lines but fill in the gaping holes as well. I assumed that, once again, he would be cagey about what he told me and I wouldn't be able to ask questions.

How wrong can you be?

"Dave, you've seen the news. None of us likes coincidences, and they think this is a very professional killer on the loose. Two things: either someone is hiring this guy, for example the betrayed husbands and wives, and managing to avoid anything traceable. Or it's some crazy loony got it in for adulterous other halves. But then how would he be getting his info?

"Too many questions. Bakewell, lethal injection. If it's the same guy it's something different every time. Has he some kind of weird sense of humour?" I thought back to my chat with Kenny which I was keeping quiet about. "Anyway, there's real concern about you four investigators, worries you'll get stuck in and upset their own routes to solving this one or, worse still, that one or more of you might be the go-between.

"Some IT bod's come up with the idea your computers might've been hacked, so expect them to want to check it out. Advice Dave, don't rush home and delete things or move them to storage devices or up in the iCloud or whatever it's called. They can detect such activity. If you're in the clear you'll be okay. Yes, they'll get to see your own private stuff, maybe those porn pics you've been saving, but don't let it worry you." I giggled not sure if he was serious, about the porn that is. I don't have any porn on my computer. No, I really don't. Oh, well if you don't want to believe me there's not a lot I can do about that.

"Might be some mileage in inviting them to do it. Up to you. For what it's worth Kent are happy with you...."

"They don't give that impression."

"Don't blame 'em Dave, you were a copper, who did you ever trust? Anyway, look, there's a bit of doubt about that Parrett bloke, can't say more than that, but keep your wits about you. But the real worry is you lot joining forces and getting in the way. Don't sod up your business; put some distance in, that's my advice.

"You see, you've done all you can, full co-operation, so let nature take its course as it were. You've gone to Derby, met the others, leave it at that. Why get into this?"

"Because I'm ex-police and because my work may have led to man being killed."

"Don't start taking things personally, Dave. You're building up a business and you'll be looking for qualifications, ABI membership and that, so don't let this affair bung a dirty great cloud over your future." I nodded ruefully but had nothing to say.

"Talking of which, one other thing. I don't know how they know, and that Parrett bloke might be the source, I don't know, but they are aware you're going around with a woman with a record, and that could seriously damage you. Believe me Dave, keep her at armslength or you'll get hurt. What do you know about Laura McCaffield Dave? Are you an item or something?"

I tried to convince myself the police were simply being thorough but this news went through me like a knife. But it was a chance to learn about Laura's past without asking her.

"I know she's done time, been a druggie and a prozzie, but I'm helping a friend look for her sister and that's all. Truth. No relationship other than friendship."

"Dave, I've been a copper a long time. To use that cliché '*I didn't get where I am today... blah, blah*' believe me I know when I'm hearing porkies. Anyway, we've all done body language, you and me both, recognising facial expressions and all that nonsense, and you're telling porkies."

Of course I was, and I was probably trying to deceive myself into the bargain. I sighed and allowed surrender to rule my body language, facial expression et al.

"Yeah Adam, and you know me too well in any case. No, I'm not in love, there's been no sex or anything, but we do get on really well and I like her. But I've never asked what she went inside for although I know much about her past, and I know it's not pretty."

"Do you want to know her record?" After a minute or two of hesitation I nodded.

"First time, stealing a van..."

"She doesn't drive..."

"Yes she does, but lost her licence, drug-driving, never renewed it. She was under a suspended sentence for shoplifting so in she went. She and this bloke were caught repainting the van which they were going to use for drug runs. Not

157

been out long and gets done for possession with intent to supply. Not much stuff but the bloke she was with denied all knowledge so she took the rap as the Americans call it. Suspended sentence.

"Second time, procurement. Effectively getting bookings for girls and taking a bit of their dosh. You know how it works Dave. In she goes again. While inside she duffs up a male warder, nothing too bad, no serious injuries; he probably chanced his arm knowing she'd been on the game. Been in the clear since getting out."

"You do pick 'em Dave. Laura McCaffield and Kenny Parrett. In your shoes I'd leave both alone, they're bad news me old mate, bad news." He got up and poured me a small brandy. I was driving. The shock must've manifested itself in every aspect of body language you could imagine, not least the fact all colour had vanished from my face and a small tear had escaped down my left cheek.

It felt as if not only the carpet and the floor underneath but the whole planet had been pulled from under me. Where's a nice bush you can curl up under and hide away when you want one? I felt used and dirty, silly and foolish, thick and dumb, a mug and a complete twit, and that's putting it politely. How could I have let it happen?

I wanted to believe in Laura, believe in the reformed criminal, believe that she wanted to better herself. Adam was still speaking, as if he hadn't said enough.

"Final point, and I've saved the worst till last. The press. Nosey bastards. Now this is all front page stuff some nosey git is going to find out a respectable private eye, a former cop, mixed up in the Bourne-Lacey murder, has an ex-con as a mate, an ex-con with some nasty form, me old son."

I was the definition of stunned and shocked, yet my emotions took me to all four corners of human suffering and half a mile further on. How could Laura do that to me? Was it just to get me onside over her sister? Was I being used and had I been recruited in a vile, cunning way? I hated her, yes I hated her.

But hadn't she fallen for the wrong guy, been pressed into his service through the drugs, and been raped, beaten up and forced into crime, a basic scenario of drug dependency that I'd seen acted out time and again while on the force. Didn't she deserve my pity and better still my help?

Wasn't she the epitome of my creed about the 'sinner who repenteth' and was thus deserving of another chance? As a human being I wanted to aid her on the difficult path back.

Love her, hate her. The cement mixer that was my mind was churning all the facts, all the evidence, and making a horrible concoction out of the ingredients. I wanted to scream, I wanted to confront her and throw her out of my life, I wanted to hold her tight, I wanted to kiss her and make it all better. In the midst of all this I hadn't realised I'd been crying freely and the tears, having run down my face, were soaking my cheeks.

Adam isn't the sort to offer a hug, and quite honestly I was pleased about that.

"Have another brandy, a decent one this time, and stay the night. Angie won't mind. You're an old mate, we can share a few bevies once I know I won't be called out." I was beyond the simple task of nodding or speaking, but he could see the affirmative answer in my face and poured me a sizeable brandy.

"Good for shock," he commented in a knowing sort of way.

***

Getting a text from Laura had always been some kind of odd pleasure, mainly because it gave me the opportunity to come up with a witty retort to which I would receive an often salty response, occasionally demonstrating a ready wit of her own.

Now I looked at her text with disgust. Thank God I'd never been to bed with her. If all I had left was that little consolation it would have to do and be to my eternal credit.

No point asking Adam about the media. He'd hit that on the head before I'd mentioned it.

Angie had come home from her job during the afternoon, I'd had a nap in an armchair, taken a shower and was now ready for a pleasant evening with a good friend. I'd been astonished how open Adam had been, but I reasoned he was really feeling it for a mate in trouble, and deep down he must've known I wouldn't betray him.

I could see why Angie appealed. She was full of life, full of fun, and dressed to thrill. I just knew the three of us would spend the evening together, and yet I didn't mind. Her conversation was easy, I hesitate to use the word 'simple', and I felt relaxed in her company.

If Adam was called out it was at the stage where they could either send a car or he'd get a cab.

So Angie prepared a simple meal which I assumed was continental or at least Greek in origin, and which did nothing for my appetite whatsoever, and as I slowly chewed my way through the revolting result watched Adam devour his with gusto. A cheap and nasty white wine was supplied, neither chilled as it deserved nor possessing any exciting palatable attractions.

Then we retired to the lounge and Adam's classic collection of beer. I opted for a harmless bottle of Pedigree, Adam attacked a Ruddles and Angie sank a Doombar without trace. Glasses were refilled instantly. This was going to be a drinkers' night and Mrs Pensfield was definitely one of us!

The media were digging with all the enthusiasm of prospectors knowing gold might be only inches away, and some journalists must've had shovels the size of mechanical diggers. The involvement of the Manchester-based firm of Parrish, Lome and Hurdsley was unearthed with comparative ease despite the role of Gordon Pembrake, as a private investigator, having not been disclosed by the police.

It was obvious to editors and reporters alike that if a private eye was involved the victim was up to no good and they wanted to know who he was being up to no good with. And that's where the trail ran cold. They needed inside info and none was forthcoming. Non-police contacts had nothing to say. However, the work of Wapernod, Pratt and Canbown was entering the public realm and it was as plain to the media as it was to the police that someone with inside knowledge was selling it to those who wanted to know.

In Kent, having turned over Neville Gradling without success, police attention did indeed focus on David Canbown. If they could see that his computer had been hacked it might well provide the key to a very important lock they wanted opened. In the process that might also put the private eye in the clear.

In Derbyshire Rosie Pequeman was occupying a dark place. Her husband had returned home and had remarked on the murder in Bakewell, just a few passing comments as anyone might make when confronted by such a heinous crime almost on their doorstep. Somehow, *somehow* she had to hold it all together and she was barely in touch with the reality of being with Daryl in their beloved farmhouse, surrounded by countryside she had all but danced in a day ago.

The house took on a hideous shape with blackness even where there was bright light. In her mind the place shook violently and closed its walls in tight around her, closing ever nearer and stifling the life out of her. She wanted to scream, but mostly she wanted to rush to Monsal Dale to escape the pain and the fear dragging her into a dreadful chasm of suffering. And she knew there was no escape. If the police learned the truth they would come a-calling and she would also have to face Daryl. But then she might be a suspect, and the unbearable haunting that was crushing her head would take on a new and vicious dimension.

If the killer had known the killer would've been well satisfied. This wasn't about taking a life, it was about making someone pay for adultery, breaking one of the Ten Commandments, and it was important that the suffering should be overpowering agony, overwhelming misery, and be capable of wrecking the sufferer's heart and mind.

Another Commandment says 'thou shalt not kill'. That didn't worry the murderer. Killing was only a means to an end. Rosie wasn't coping with the retribution and this time there would be a sad and terrible turn of events. She knew now she had loved John Holgarve, loved him with all her heart, and would've thrown away everything just to be with him. Too late now.

Not far away from where Rosie was paying for her crime Georgina and Leonora were facing up to retribution of a different kind. They wanted each other but knew they could not meet behind Jason Hayle's back; he would be onto them in a flash. So there was his suggestion. But how could they accept such a disgusting arrangement? Georgina loathed her husband, every last vestige of love having drained from her heart, but how could she live with him now, and how could she cope with his filthy, perverted idea of pleasure?

Well away from Mr Hayle his wife and her lover clung to each other, weeping, kissing with frenzy, desperate not to lose this one precious thing they shared. Georgina was not simply wed to Jason, she was wed to his money, she knew that, and there was too much to lose. The pre-nuptial agreement would see to that, as would Jason's solicitor!

Elsewhere the media representatives were making a nuisance of themselves with the three private eyes, even turning up on their doorsteps.

Jayne-Marie Panahan came to Yvonne Pratt's rescue by launching her own solicitor at the issue.

Bhatia Sumitra welcomed having something delicious to get her legal teeth into as it gave her a break from pursuing those who had betrayed her client. She was grateful and then some. And she got results meaning that gradually Yvonne was left alone. All incoming phone calls were intercepted, and there were no more personal visits to Ms Pratt's home or office.

Grayden Optics and associated companies often ran advertising campaigns with the nationals, and a veiled threat, whilst making no difference whatsoever to keen editors determined to find the truth, or something reasonably similar, hung over the newspaper industry. It may have had some effect, it may not. Ms Panahan was not a woman without influence. She certainly had a Rottweiler for a solicitor, a young woman set to earn her spurs and totally focused on a career that was not merely going to take off, it was ready to flourish and explode all over planet Earth with shattering outcome.

The principal players in this whole drama needed a diversion for the press that would give them some respite. And Rosie Pequeman tragically provided it.

***

Rosie seemed to be the only lover of a victim truly in love.

For Jacqueline Gradling the late Alistair Bourne-Lacey had been an athletic alternative to the intimate routine shared with her husband, a means to lustful events blessed with a wealth of variety. She was relieved that her affair had not seriously damaged her marriage and her lifestyle; there was much to be thankful for.

In Devon Cathy Kethnet reflected on the incredible love life of the dear departed Edward Nobbs. She knew she was only one on his list, but he had a list because he could make a woman feel alive, and she'd appreciated that and taken full advantage when she could.

In Suffolk William Bailey believed his affair had, indirectly, given him some brownie points. Phyllis Downport had left her fortune to him and in his contrition he had presented it to his wife. He tried to suggest that he'd only bedded Phyllis in order to receive such a bequest but he realised at once he was batting on a sticky wicket and reversed his revelation. He was forgiven for his transgression but, Jayne-Marie assured him, his error (as she called it) would never be forgotten.

Bailey already knew the truth of that, for periodic references were made to his folly, and he recognised he would suffer that way forever. There was a happy outcome in some respects as his wife set about improving their love life to the extent that he would never wish to stray again or, if he did, render him too exhausted to make hay in any meaningful way.

Jayne-Marie Panahan had the money, the power, the position. A woman dominating business, men, and William in particular, and she smiled with satisfaction. She could do as she pleased and nobody dare stand in her way. Very satisfying. And in the process she had tamed her man to the point where he was utterly subservient in all things. A proud woman, proud to be a woman, proud to be a women ruling with such unquestioned autonomy.

But in Derbyshire nothing could console the victim's lover. Her lovely and beautiful Mr Ordinary, who was so romantic, so gentle and kind, so sweet and yet so strong and decisive, he was gone, his spirit borne away on the winds that flooded across this land, and she hoped his spirit would return to love her yet thought it impossible. She must follow that spirit. In her devastation she knew it was the only way.

The police, acting on information provided by Gordon Pembrake, arrived to question her and so it was that the manifestation of an even more wretched nightmare was visited upon her. She admitted to her affair, admitted she had

162

driven to Bakewell the fatal night, brought John back to her home and then delivered back to the town.

She was taken for questioning and subjected to all kinds of unpleasant tortures, and a torrid period of fear and panic. Her husband hired a solicitor for her but otherwise all he was thinking about was she was being taught a lesson and would never cuckold him again. He enjoyed using the word 'cuckold' – old fashioned yet somehow apt, just as the word 'adulteress' appealed to him. She was the lowest of the low, a dirty little bitch. Yet he would love her again.

There was no denying she had a beauty that made him the envy of so many, and had a body moulded just for the pleasure of man. John Holgarvc had appreciated that much too closely; he had to go. Daryl would be kindness itself; he would nurse her back to health and happiness, and show he loved her in so many ways. And all the time he would be educating her (educating, yes he liked that word too; educating, as in brain-washing) until she was completely in his control.

And then he'd enjoy her as he would, and she'd do as she was told.

\*\*\*

The killer was revelling in the newspaper reports, and had started a book of cuttings.

*"They seek him here, they seek him there, those Police seek him everywhere, is he in heaven or is he in hell, that damned elusive ......."* The quote remained incomplete as a hearty laugh roared up from the throat and echoed round the room. "No elusive pimpernel, pimpernel indeed! Not me. More of a venus fly-trap, a prickly cactus, or a whole dark forest of doom. And the police literally haven't a clue! I am invincible, unbeatable. Elusive forever."

\*\*\*

Finding old school friends and mislaid pot lids. That's more like it! Why did I bother with anything more complicated? It's only led to grief, and trouble for me. And I should've left Laura in that shelter at Sheerness without exchanging any details. Now I'd be able to relax and use my skills to track down someone's lost school chum and some silly sod's pot lid, and do so in relative peace.

I phoned Okafor on my return to Sheppey and explained my theory that perhaps my computer had been hacked and would he want to check it. Since I already knew he had that in mind I can only blame myself for thinking he sounded suspicious! Of course it was *their* theory and not mine, but who's counting. Anyway, he sent a colleague round to collect said object and on the basis that I would like it back reasonably pronto.

Keeping a safe distance between me and Laura was nigh impossible. But I was seeing her in such a different light that she quickly picked up on my coldness, and kept asking what was wrong, what had she done that was so amiss.

Eventually I decided that honesty was the best policy.

"Laura, I'm going to be blunt. A mate of mine in the force has warned me off you. And the reason for that is the police know you're tied up with me and that's making them suspicious. And nervous. They've taken my computer away for analysis. They've done Gradling up like a kipper, searched his home top to bottom, gone through his accounts, his computer, everything, and I may be next. Nothing's come to light, but they know there's a clue out there somewhere and they have to stop at nothing to find it.

"Your record, and you've never told me about the details, does not stand you in good stead. Chances are you'll be questioned, and the last thing I need is the press crawling all over this making my relationship with you front page news. That's why I'm a bit cold. I'm sorry, but you asked and I've told you. Sorry."

"An' your mate, told you all about me record, did he? Or *she*? So what, I've never lied to you. You've never asked and I'd have told you if you had. I told you from day one I'd been inside twice, and I told you why. I'd have been killed if I hadn't done what I was told. I was drug dependant, and I couldn't risk losing me supply.

"I've made mistakes, sunshine, but I've paid for them, a million times over. And now I'm going straight trying to make something of my life before I die. And ... and ... I thought you were sympathetic, and wanted to help. You bastard, you're just the same as all of 'em. God I could hate you if I didn't love you....."

She pulled up and stared at me. I was probably staring back at her. Neither of us moved or spoke for a while.

"Listen Moncks, you knew what you were getting with me, I couldn't have made it plainer. I been inside, I done drugs, I been a prozzie, but I'm different now. Okay, so you don't want me around right now. Some fair-weather friend; you're afraid of a few drops of rain. Afraid of yer own shadow, more like. Kill off your business will I? Just by being yer mate and helping you out a bit? Is that it? I'm worth sod-all and you can just throw me away, is that what you think?"

She had torn me to pieces, and I felt wretched. The new improved me was desolate, ruined and I was kicking myself as I pitifully examined the wreckage. Yes, looks like I'm a bastard after all, just like the rest of them. Yes, you're correct. Now, how do I put it right?

"No good looking sorry for y'self, Moncks. I'm bad for business and that's all that matters, all that comes first. Don't worry pal, I've been there before. I'm just something people flush down the loo. Listen, I'm history. I'll get out of your life and your precious business so you can be Mr Wonderful again. You'll like that. Top Dog and nobody to tell you you're not. 'Cos you ain't you know. You're not top anything, but being a man you think you are.

"Hope looking after little ol' Law made you feel all virtuous and public spirited, isn't that what they call it? Giving some rotten kid a chance? Well, I'm a living breathing human being with real bloody feelings, and after you've done your good deed you can dump me and go back to being the prize twat you are, and you can ignore what you've really done to this real person. 'Cos you done your bit, ain't you, and I don't count any more."

She was shaking and staring hard at me and making me feel so tiny I felt like a minus figure. It wasn't any good saying sorry, or anything very much. There was nothing worth saying. I was finished, but I had to try something.

"You're right about everything, Laura, and I'm just a pig, not a man. But what I've tried to be isn't a facade, it's the real me fighting to get out. Yes, I've messed up. I'm not feeling sorry for myself, I'm sorry for the distress I've caused you. You wanted a second chance in life and now I'm asking for a second chance with you.

"Yes, damn them all. Damn the police and damn the papers. If I can't go on as private eye I'll find something else to do. But I won't sacrifice you on the altar of my vanity. If we end up on the front pages together let the world see us together." The shaking had stopped and the anger had gone from her eyes, to be replaced by wariness.

"You don't half do talking good, Moncks, but it takes more than words." I nodded agreement. "A lot more action than words."

"You got it."

"Time will tell, won't it? No good making promises your vanity and manliness can't keep. Don't make me promises then you can't break them, can you?" There was a genuine softness in her voice, and her expression had melted into a kind of affection. I recalled her words 'I could hate you if I didn't love you' and knew the truth was there.

We both stood and slowly moved together, arms outstretched, embracing and then kissing, kissing the most enchanting of kisses, kisses that united our very souls. There was nothing feverish or passionate for these were the kisses of reconciliation and affirmation. She leaned back in my arms and whispered.

"You and me's *Cagney and Lacey*. We's partners. In for the long haul." And we kissed again. Probably not the best time to ask whether I was Cagney or Lacey......

## Chapter Eighteen

# Rosie

When the mind is enclosed in a strait-jacket that is tightening its grip, and the pain increases with every second and there is no way to scream or cry out, when the body thrashes about wildly to vainly try and relieve the agony, then merciful release is impossible within this worldly compass.

It is in this period of perpetual bleak, black darkness, this period without a future, without promise, without hope, the miserable sufferer, complete in their worthlessness, sees one route and one route only. To free the spirit.

To free the spirit. To leave the eternal weariness and despair behind.

\*\*\*

They found Rosie Pequeman's body beneath the viaduct. It had been a terrible death.

In the night she must've walked to Monsal Head, stumbling across countryside that, like John Holgarve, had once stolen her heart, and down onto the famous viaduct where she had stood so many times before setting off on the Monsal trail. She was lying on the track below, adjacent to the river which had taken no notice of the falling figure and carried on meandering at its own sedate pace.

The doctor said that, although her injuries were probably fatal, she may have remained alive for hours prior to her death and discovery. What final suffering she may have gone through will never be known, but the killer had inadvertently claimed another victim, with untold anguish and unimaginable pain delivered through such vile punishment.

Her husband, playing the concerned and forgiving soul he now wanted to appear, had furnished her with a torch when she insisted on a late evening walk. She just wanted some air, and wouldn't be long. Just some air. Her ordeal at the police station had been dreadful even with a good and sympathetic solicitor for some degree of comfort. She just had to get some air and walk about in the cool night air.

It wasn't until the early hours that Daryl reported her missing. The sun wasn't yet up but the day was brightening when she was spotted.

Daryl blamed the police and wanted to sue everyone in sight, and in his rage completely forgot to be a grieving husband. That did not go unnoticed. What he wasn't told straightaway was that Rosie had a note on her, one she must've scribbled once she'd decided on her irreversible course of action.

***

My computer was returned. No evidence of hacking, but Okafor, in a phone call, said they'd be asking the other tecs to be just as co-operative. He was loving it, but I wondered if maybe I'd come over like that when I was serving, and would I behave like that now in his place? The answer was yes, possibly. So no hard feelings, and in any case I was beginning to ease up on all fronts.

The confrontation with Laura had taught me some important things about David Canbown and it was time to become more tolerant and considerate, and to stop and think instead of being instantly judgemental.

An interesting thought had lodged in my mind. I wasn't buying into the theory Adam had propounded about the killings being the work of a sort of religious maniac, or at least someone with a very serious mental health issue. The work was too well planned, too cunning, and far too professional, carried out with ice cool precision.

My thoughts had turned to the prospect of the person being very much in the know, possessing inside information or some knowledge of police investigations. Actually a person who might be extremely clever (there'd been no evidence of consequence left at any of the scenes, Adam confirmed that), and who was capable of meticulous planning, leaving no stone unturned.

Progressing that, I considered whether the fact a connection was now established between four crimes and national publicity was widespread might've put a spanner in the killer's works. Did the killer feel safe all the time the operation stayed below the radar? Had these developments brought a premature end to the sad business?

In other words was the killer now sailing close to the wind by virtue of the newspaper coverage and advancement in the police investigation? Would the killer pull back and bide their time? If we were looking at an intelligent person that might well be the correct strategy for them to adopt. My thoughts rolled on again.

If the murders were carried out to order, and someone was paying, the payments could be very substantial. Perhaps they were on-going, you know, so much up-front, the balance on completion. But the police would be watching and they would surely notice, for example, any unusual movements in Neville Gradling's fortune.

But if folk like Gradling, Kethnet and Panahan had paid for the murders then our killer also had the whip hand. Blackmail could follow. Good point, David, I told myself.

Of course, this would all go out the window if nobody paid and the killer was a total maniac, out of his or her mind, and just doing it for whatever reason such as punishing the adulterous. But seriously, how could some mentally ill soul find out who was up to mischief and design and carry out seemingly perfect crimes? That wouldn't make sense so, no, I wasn't buying into it.

A sane person. Very clever. Nothing religious or anything like that involved. Here was a vulgar individual making money and loads of it. He or she must have intelligence. Had they simply been entrepreneurial enough to create a market? But, ye gods, how did they advertise it?

How were payments made? How were orders passed? Could it be that somewhere along the line the role of private investigators was important? And there my mind hit a brick wall. Back to pot lids and missing persons.

Wait a mo. Could we be looking at an ex-cop, an ex-cop with some kind of grudge? Possibly. And once again my mind refused to move on. Yes, it was truly time for that pot lid hunt and, yes, I knew my mind wouldn't let go of the problem because my mind was like that, and why I was good cop. And although I didn't know it at the time I was already on the right track.

\*\*\*

Back in Derbyshire the police were studying the note Rosie left. It was scrawled, scribbled yet quite readable.

*The lovely Derby Dales can have my life. My life will live here but not in the flesh. At least I will be free. I loved John with all the love in my heart and would've given up everything for a new life with him and I think he would've left his wife. She didn't care. I've been a prisoner for too long and now my head's done in, my heart's shattered. I dropped my heart's desire back in Bakewell. I didn't kill him. If I wanted to kill anyone it would be my husband. Please find John's killer and bring him to justice. By the time you read this my pain will be over and my soul will be united with John's.*

Of course it didn't clear Rosie but it certainly made it less likely she'd murdered John. With that in mind the investigation looked further afield especially as the event tied in with the style of the three other killings. Kenny Parrett was interviewed again. In Suffolk as in Devon Yvonne Pratt and John Wapernod gave up their computers for detailed scrutiny. People with nothing to fear.

The concept of raiding Jayne-Marie Panahan in her own right (William Bailey having been searched) without a half decent excuse was not the kind of programme any sensible officer would contemplate, regardless of the input of the solicitor from hell. Knowing Kent had drawn a blank with both Neville Gradling and David Canbown reluctance was the order of the day. But in Devon there was a surprise when Nathan Kethnet offered a thorough search of his home, his business interests, and his computer. Naturally, there was also suspicion.

If he was up to no good he'd found a way of hiding what the police would be looking for!

Nevertheless his kind and generous offer was accepted with gusto and no time was wasted implementing the search. If they found so much as a hair out of place, metaphorically speaking, with either Nathan or John it would give Suffolk a stronger lever with Jayne-Marie.

No details of Rosie's suicide note had been disclosed but the death of a suspect diverted the media circus from the straight and narrow it had been following. Here now was another angle on the murders. Somehow they'd found out about Gordon Pembrake's role, about the suspicious husband, and the adulterous behaviour of Mrs Pequeman and Mr Holgarve. And Rosie was found dead at a beauty spot.

One police expert wondered if her note could be interpreted as the confession it appeared not to be, as in, John wouldn't leave his wife so Rosie killed him then committed suicide so their spirits could be together. As a Detective Inspector remarked 'Do me a favour, that sounds like the script for a movie.'

The media speculated that Rosie was John's murderer, and one or two went so far as to suggest that it had nothing to do with the three other killings. In fact, that was a good point, except that the police tended to believe the contents of the suicide note.

In the meantime the general viewpoint of the investigating officers was that Kenny Parrett was hiding something, though whether it had anything to do with the latest crime was open to conjecture. They had certainly lost interest in the report he brought them relating to Georgina Hayle and Leonora Cuthbert, apart from wondering whether he was creating a diversion.

The two ladies were currently plotting although mercifully not murder.

They had gone, with Jason's kind and condescending permission, to Leonora's in order to examine the situation and evaluate the solutions. Given their options were precious few, and one seemed to be as unacceptable as it was stomach-churning, they were faced with losing each other or the choice Miss Cuthbert was explaining.

This involved Mrs Hayle leaving Mr Hayle, who would presumably divorce her, and setting up home with her lover and very little else. Georgina would lose just about everything and that was a prospect that sore tested her true feelings for Leonora.

The concept of working for a living was anathema for Georgina, a horrid, nasty thing to be avoided at all costs. Having a wealthy husband who gave her money and all the delightful material things a girl could possibly want had its advantages, particularly as he was prepared to let the arrangement continue. And he hadn't beaten her up this time. Well, not yet.

Leonora did not enjoy the sort of employment to support a lover better suited to doing just as she pleased, or an income to support her lover's lust for the good things in life, e.g. top of the range car, designer clothes, expensive holidays, etc.

But what troubled Georgina was that she actually loved Leonora passionately, with a depth she had never known before and had never possessed for Jason. That gave her a dilemma, for she found she liked the idea of deserting the runt and joining her true love for a trip along life's highway. It was simply the practicalities that were defeating her.

It was at times like these that the slaughter of Jason Hayle appealed, but then she didn't know what was in his will, and she might well be outside it now.

***

Finding my client's old school friend proved quite easy having employed my contacts usefully.

I poured boiling water into the large mug that contained one of my treasured coffee bags and allowed time for it to infuse properly. These bags, although referred to as 'treasured' are not expensive and are easy to find, it's just that I keep them for special occasions. They smell good, the coffee is gorgeous (if you don't wreck it with milk or cream or sugar or whisky), and I find them relaxing in a way I cannot readily describe.

Sinking into the sofa in the lounge, mug loaded and only a few inches from my lips, I looked back over a job well done, despite the fact it hadn't taken much. I almost, *almost* felt guilty about billing my modest fee, but pulled myself together in the nick of time.

Locating a missing pot lid may not sound much of an adventure and certainly not the sort of problem to tax Rebus, Poirot, Morse, Holmes or Barnaby, so it is no surprise that such a matter had rarely featured in crime novels, let alone TV crime series. I consoled myself with the thought that Agatha Christie would've risen to the challenge, and probably written an absorbing murder mystery surrounding said pot lid. No doubt one for Miss Marple.

Come to think of it Ellis Peters might've put a small trinket at the centre of a story for Brother Cadfael to unravel, and I'm quite sure, thinking back over those exquisite novels, that she did. I've only been to Shrewsbury once, but I love Shropshire generally, Ludlow being my favourite town. There's Ironbridge Gorge and some magnificent scenery, and if I remember rightly the county is one of the least populated in the country.

Continuing my wallow into fictional crime I was conscious of the fact some of my most enjoyed novels were written by women. Frances Brody's Kate Shackleton stories are so well formed and delightfully told (Kate is a private eye, by the way). Gillian Galbraith and Alex Gray have written works based in Scotland to rival anything the grand master, Ian Rankin, has produced.

But I digress. However, it does show that I'm relaxed. Mmmm .... the coffee is better than I anticipated. This is good with a capital G.

Needless the say all this proved a false dawn where relaxation was concerned. Kenny phoned, Laura phoned, Yvonne phoned, and all of a sudden I'm on edge again!

*** 

I'd spoken to Neville Gradling once and that was just after the police raided him. He was much calmer than I expected and was wondering, if that was the right word, what I might have told the police that led them to his door.

I assured him that it was nothing to do with me. He said he was pleased to hear it but did so in a very menacing manner. I had the distinct feeling that the phone could've burst into flames and melted such was the seething threat his words veiled. No question, he didn't really believe me and he was making certain that I knew he wouldn't tolerate any action that might implicate him.

No words to that effect, just pure menace in his voice.

Now I called him and asked to see him. Something I didn't want to talk about on the phone, such devices, like walls, having ears. That approach did the trick, but he wanted to meet on neutral ground and suggested a point on the A2 near Faversham from whence we could go wherever we chose at the time. Can't be too careful.

We ended up at the Chequers in Doddington for lunch. He wasn't known there (neither was I) and we enjoyed an excellent meal accompanied by wine of which he drank most. He also put away a pre-lunch pint and a brandy afterwards without a thought for the fact he was driving, whereas I made do with a pint and one glass of an excellent dry white, the name of which escapes me.

He was a no-nonsense suspicious character with the sort of build that would deter most people from picking an argument. He wasn't pleasant company by any means but we managed to chat quite amicably and I'd like to think he'd warmed to me by the time we parted.

"Phones to silent running, preferably off altogether," he ordered as we sat down, with me selecting the off-altogether option for my mobile. He did the same. "Shove your phone in your handbag," he instructed, noticing I had a small briefcase with me. He made a show of putting his own mobile in a leather case, and the case into his trouser pocket. He didn't trust anybody but then I didn't trust him.

There's something about a person who goes through all that nonsense as if to demonstrate that his phone isn't recording or transmitting, but what I had to say wasn't private enough to worry about the police or an eager solicitor eavesdropping. He didn't have a 'handbag' so presumably, by placing the mobile in his trouser pocket, he was showing that the device was too far away and too concealed now to be able to listen in.

I did muse on what sounds a listening device might pick up located where it was! And I knew that it was possible for a mike to collect a conversation even hidden away like that. But no matter, it didn't bother me either way.

Neville insisted on paying. "It's all on me, boy. You did a great job so let's say this is a thank-you meal instead of a nice, pretty card." I hate being called 'boy' or 'son'. He went on.

"Jack's alright," he advised, talking about Jacqueline, the object of my surveillance. "She's fine now. Don't worry, no violence involved. But she won't do it again. She certainly won't do it with that son of a bitch Bourne-Lacey, will she?" And he laughed heartily at his own joke and then sought to drown it with his beer. I smiled and sipped at mine.

He tackled his starter like a man who hasn't eaten for weeks, was finished in no time and as I munched mine he continued talking. Clearly he liked having the floor, liked being the man doing the talking, and appeared to have an enormous capacity to hold centre stage and to fight off all who might seek to slip a word in edgeways.

The weather, the news, Brexit, the NHS and the government were despatched swiftly and with the ease with which he'd devoured his tomato and basil bruschetta, at the same time ensuring I had no opportunity to comment on any of his topics.

For the mains I'd selected honey roasted ham, egg and chips, Neville choosing the award-winning (so the menu proclaimed) sausages with creamy mashed potato, red onion gravy and petit pois. This was a delicious pub lunch and no mistake. Like a ventriloquist he managed to eat and talk, the latter quiet coherently, without spraying his food around.

Eventually, quite out of the blue, and when I had just placed a noticeably large amount of food in my mouth, ready for mastication, he looked me in the eyes as he leaned forward and said:

"Right, what did you want to talk about, son?" There it was again, 'son' this time. Oh it does get up my nose!

I collected my thoughts, which at that point were inconveniently scattered all over my mind, and reminded him I was an ex-cop who left the force under a cloud. Maybe I had a grudge, that was for him to judge. I meant to infer that I'd come by inside information and in my opinion he took the hint. I didn't actually say it, just inferred it, and that was the idea.

He was informed succinctly about the details and theories I was prepared to share with him but placed particular emphasis on the possibility of blackmail. I could see that hit home and was relevant to him. In that moment I knew he'd ordered Bourne-Lacey's death. It was written in his face and the way he reacted.

Needless to say I kept some information back; my purpose was to make him fret, if indeed he had ordered Alistair's execution, and worry that the killer might be coming back to him. I'm sure I achieved my aim, but he regained his confidence and after a little spluttering asked why on earth he should be worried about blackmail. He added:

"Look son, I had nothing to do with the murder, whatever the fuzz think. So I've nothing to worry about, have I?"

"No Mr Gradling you haven't, but I thought you might like to be appraised as to what I think the police might be up to."

"I see. So you can earn some more of my money?"

"No. I don't want any more of your money. But I've been implicated in this particular murder just as you have, and I'd like to feel we're therefore the same side of the fence. If anything comes to light that you think I might be interested in I'd like to hear. That's my only price, and if you don't pay, well you don't pay. No obligation either way."

"I can't imagine, son, what information you think I might come by. I'm innocent, no sweat. I haven't paid an assassin so I won't be blackmailed. No problem. But I'll bear in mind what you've said, Mr Canbown, and I appreciate you calling me and this meeting. Hope you enjoyed the meal."

I had and I thanked him. I left first just as he finished his brandy and after we'd exchanged some general conversation. I rather suspected he would have another brandy.

Rescuing and checking my phone the inevitable text from you-know-who was there.

*** 

In Derbyshire the police were preparing to accept Rosie's suicide note at face value. There was no evidence of any sort to associate John's wife Joan, or his friend Barry, with the murder. The contents of the injected fluid was now known, and it was a toxic cocktail by any stretch of the imagination. The guy at the lab said that, correctly injected, death would be obtained in seconds rather than minutes. To the post mortem team the injection was indeed 'correct' suggesting that the killer was quite an expert, maybe someone with medical training, but perhaps a drug user.

If this was the same criminal and four different methods had been employed then not only was he or she a very clever person but someone adept at killing with whatever came to hand. So was there a military connection or possibly even secret service? As one Detective Sergeant asked 'are we looking for James Bond or Blofeld?'.

But the point was made. This was one multi-skilled operative and one that emerged suddenly onto the scene. Why? And with that even the question of terrorism reared its ugly head, although that was more easily dismissed. Police top brass raised the secret service and terrorism angles at the highest and most confidential level, but produced a negative response which put those aspects more or less out of the picture.

Detective Sergeant Okafor pondered each killing. Strangled with rope; would need some strength, but relatively easy and effective. Stabbed; sudden but deadly if the knife was aimed right, and it had been. Shot; almost point blank, centre forehead, again perfect aim, totally lethal. Injection; victim had to be stunned first but then if you knew what you were doing the jab would induce death nothing far short of instantly.

Which one presented most risk to the killer, Okafor wondered. The stabbing? Possibly the only one in which the victim might have been able to try and get away or fight back. Strangulation? The victim would struggle, might scratch and get some DNA, perhaps under the fingernails. But it didn't happen.

Shooting, no. A whack on the back of the head followed by the syringe, no. There'd be no chance to struggle, fight or try and get away.

Just no clues whatsoever. Nowt, he concluded.

Detective Sergeant Broome was thinking almost incessantly about the end of Phyllis Downport, the only female victim that they knew of. Stabbed with great accuracy right through the heart. Stephanie Broome was coincidently considering the force needed and the strength the killer must possess. It had been such a firm, direct plunge into the heart. No chance of a near miss. Strangulation requires brute force, she decided, if it's to be quick, effective and a show-stopper. Not so good if the victim, for example, knows the art of self-defence, or just simply has the might to take on their attacker.

Or was it actually four different killers? Could it be so?

Both she and Holton Okafor were chancing upon the same line of reasoning. So many different avenues, so many possibilities. Incredible.

But things weren't going to get better any time soon.

# Chapter Nineteen
## Afterthoughts and After Effects

I had kippers for breakfast, Young's kippers. I used to pick at kippers until I learned the art of boiling them and then removing the black skin underneath, finally subjecting them to a quick burst in the microwave. Result? I just cut a chunk at a time and eat it whole without having to worry about the bits I don't want. I treat myself to a slice of white bread and butter, this being about the only time I have white.

I've really gone a bundle on Warburton's seeded batch (makes gorgeous toast for my homemade marmalade), but we also have a great bakers on the island (Boyce's) and their bread is first class.

Preceded by a yoghurt, kippers followed by toast, coffee au lait, a breakfast any man could be proud of and enjoy! Especially if he can enjoy it alone and in peace, and for once I was doing just that.

Well, one case solved, the pot lid still to be located, and another enquiry pending. That's not including Lorraine. I wondered what I didn't know about Kenny Parrett. Adam wouldn't be drawn but he was considered unreliable to the point of being suspicious. What could it mean?

He'd phoned just to say no updates on Lorraine and we agreed that if local people didn't recognise the picture then she hadn't been in the area for some time, and the woman I saw was only visiting.

I didn't expect to hear from Neville Gradling but it had been a useful exercise, and who can say what may happen in the future? He might end up needing my help if he doesn't want the police involved, so let's wait and see.

Yvonne Pratt was quite chatty when she phoned, but I feel she was relieved that Ms Panahan was onside and keeping the baying hounds, if not the police, at a comfortable distance. We both pondered that it might be in Jayne-Marie's own interests, if she was in any way complicit in Phyllis Downport's demise, to show every support for her private eye who might then support her. Yvonne thought that nailing the person or persons who'd spilled the beans to the press might improve her credit rating with the woman.

I washed up and put my things away, a place for everything and everything in its place. Not that I was always this methodical. My wife could never understand (or appreciate) that I was so hideously untidy at home yet appeared to be the complete opposite at work. Frankly, neither could I!

I peeled an orange, a very juicy one, ate the contents thereof, and cut the peel into thin strips and small pieces ready for the next time I made marmalade, which wouldn't be long now. I put little vac, as I called it, round and ran the duster over where necessary. My 'big vac' is one of those that is so powerful it eats the carpet and tries to pull up the floorboards! So I have a handy small vacuum for quick flits.

Unfortunately it is not always possible to revel in all this domestication, and today was going to be typical for Laura called up just as I put little vac away. Lorraine, Lorraine, morning, noon and night. For the umpteenth time I explained we had to make some money or we couldn't afford to go chasing after her. Then I had a bright idea.

Research Kenny Parrett. I hadn't mentioned what I'd been told. He had a website, was on Facebook and Twitter, and Laura could demonstrate her investigative prowess by looking into him.

"Whad y'wanna know, like?"

"Everything you can find out right down to what day he changes his bedclothes. Everything and anything, Law."

"Jeez. But why? He's a tec like you and me. What's this about Moncks?"

"Intuition," I lied. "Let's say I didn't leave my copper's nose at HQ when I left. I don't want him to know, but I would like you to dig deep, show me just how good you are. If you'll do this for me then I will factor in some time to devote to your sister and see if there are any other contacts I haven't thought of. But I need peace and quiet."

I got peace and quiet. She hung up.

But she texted later to say she was on his case. In the meantime I landed the 'pending' job which related largely to fraud. A partner in a business was worried his mate was siphoning off trade perhaps with a view to splitting the partnership and running off with the lion's share. There was also the question that he might be diddling HMRC. Heaven forbid.....

In Derbyshire Leonora Cuthbert faced the most awful time of her life. No way would she let Jason Hayle anywhere near her and that was final. Happily, Georgina Hayle was in agreement, not wanting her lover defiled that way. Sadly, the alternative was to call time on their relationship.

Mrs Hayle was between a rock and a hard place. Give up a life of idle luxury to be with Leonora or say goodbye to her forever. This was real pain. Total agony. And she wasn't equipped to cope with, never mind sort out, such a difficulty. Then she had a strange thought. Jason had hired a private eye to obtain proof of her infidelity. She was sure he was a good deal less than a legitimate businessman.

Dealing with financial matters that were beyond his wife, matters that often got a bad press, for example those hedge fund thingies, he might well have a dark past. Maybe a dark current too!

What was good for the gander might now be good for the goose. If she could obtain evidence by using a private eye she might be able to confront him and come out of it well. Threatening him would do no good; he would almost certainly beat her up as he had done before.

She was back in a quandary. What would she actually want to achieve with her evidence? Divorce with a good few bob? Maybe. Better than divorce with no bob whatsoever! She now realised that she wanted Leonora more than ever, but she also wanted money to start her new life.

Right now she had plenty of money, but not enough to fund a fresh start. But enough to hire a private eye? Time to make enquiries, but better to steer well clear of that Kenny Parrett and anyone locally he might know. Now, where to start?

\*\*\*

The killer always knew where to start. A thriving business was on hold. Time to diversify. All good entrepreneurs diversify. Re-invest capital in another project, create a new market demand, or perhaps simply milk your rich former customers!

And, indeed, the killer knew exactly how to start, from strategic planning right through to execution, although in this case nobody need die. Nobody *needs* to, but if they don't pay up then a little death in the family might provide the right prompt.

"Don't like the word blackmail. Sounds dark, dirty and criminal. Enforced payments perhaps? How about a Death Tax? No, the bloody government's cornered the market on that! I've got it; a Solutions Tax. I sort your problem, for which you pay, and then I charge you a Tax. Sounds official too. My own kind of VAT; very awful tax!"

And laughter rolled around the small, brightly lit room with its old-fashioned furniture and peeling, stained wallpaper.

\*\*\*

DS Stephanie Broome knew that all it takes is for a criminal to get careless and make one mistake, sometimes just a small one. Neither she nor the killer knew that the latter's diversification plans would provide a weakness that would lead to such an error. But Stephanie hoped that a mistake would come in an otherwise faultless display of horror; perhaps the mistake had already been made but not yet been picked up.

So keep on searching. And that is what they did. But the priority was to try and prevent further deaths although catching the guy would achieve that aim. He must make a mistake somewhere, she knew, for it has all gone so well for him, no traces, no clues, and that sort of success must lead to complacency.

She knew they weren't looking at random killings. There was more than just a pattern. A paid assassin would need some good money, and four 'innocent' spouses were rich, well rich, and that did seem to suggest they had to be in the frame. That being so how could payments have been made? Okafor in Kent had reported they had found nothing suspicious going through Neville Gradling's accounts and nothing flashing a red warning light on his home or business computers.

No big cash withdrawals. No payments that didn't tie up. But then business people like him would be into all kinds of things, probably legitimate tax avoidance, and the illegal sort too, and have a hundred and one ways of 'losing' a couple of thousand here and there. Yes, that was true of Gradling, Kethnet and now Pequeman. But Ms Panahan? Wealthy indeed, yet in this muddle she stood alone, and not because she was a woman, the victim a woman.

She didn't appear to be like the other three. Her business interests were right there in y'face. Grayden Optics for example, large factory unit, exporters, a major name in the UK. She was the boss, and made no attempt to hide from the public. The three men were nameless, faceless fronts for all kinds of operations. Jacqueline Gradling and Cathy Kethnet each had a business in their own name, obviously a tax fiddle and a means of reducing debt responsibility. And the latest guy, Daryl Pequeman, architect. Quite out of keeping with the other three: plenty of money but no millionaire.

The three men kept their personal distance. Anonymous by and large. Jayne-Marie was right out there leading from the front. Did it mean anything? Was it important? Stephanie didn't know. But the more she thought about it the more it frustrated her and the more her instinct told her Ms Panahan's case was different and therefore might hold an important clue.

\*\*\*

I'd been relying my instinct, and I was as sure as sure can be that Neville Gradling was responsible for Bourne-Lacey's death. And that could only mean that he'd paid. But where would he have found the killer? Then the next question had to be *how* did he pay? Obviously the police weren't going to tell me the nuts and bolts of what they'd discovered in their search, but from all I could pick up it had been precious little. So no large withdrawals of readies, or transfers of large sums to dubious destinations. But the extraordinary fact remains that, assuming Gradling did hire the person responsible for pulling the trigger, three other people managed to locate the same service. The dark web? Surely the police had looked into that.

Money. Naturally, having money means that you can ask questions in the right places and find goods and services denied to ordinary folk. And that thought gave me an idea.

Before I could do anything else Yvonne phoned. And talked without drawing breath.

"Thought you'd be interested in this, David. Had a client enquiry from a woman in Derbyshire who wants to find proof that her husband is up to no good in his business dealings, even if it's only defrauding the tax man, did you ever! She says she's worried and would like to confront him and to try and prevent him getting into trouble. I expect you believe that, David, as much as I did.

"Well, anyway, her name's Georgina Hayle. Ring any bells? Yes, it's the woman Kenny Parrett tailed on behalf of Mr Hayle. She didn't know where to look for a private investigator, no of course not, and got my name from the newspapers. Thought she'd call me as I seemed to have the right qualifications, having checked my website, and was a woman. She prefers to deal with a woman. Anyway, I didn't mention Kenny or anything else for that matter, and certainly not that he'd reported the matter to the police on the grounds that her lover, one Leonora Cuthbert you'll remember, might be the next victim of the phantom score-settler.

"My guess is Mr Jason Hayle has had it out with her, perhaps ordered her off Ms Cuthbert or else, and she wants to get even or, how about this, wants to be allowed to continue her affair."

There was silence and I wondered if I'd gone deaf. But I hadn't.

"So what do you make of that, David? Trouble is I'm a bit tied up, because I'd love, absolutely love to do it, and that's why I'm calling, well, another reason I'm calling. Just wondered how busy you were and if you had some time I could sub-contract, in a manner of speaking, some of the early investigative work, you know, things you could do from a distance without going to Derbyshire or anywhere for that matter."

I'd never known her so garrulous. Or so breathless with excitement. This was a new side to Yvonne Pratt but one I found I quite liked for some reason. And, of course, I was sore tempted; so much so that I agreed at once, providing she emailed all the info I'd require to get started. I said I could make no promises, and asked about remuneration.

"No idea, old fruit," *Old fruit?* Well it was better than 'son' or 'boy'. "But we can come to some arrangement. I won't do you or see you out of pocket, you know that."

"I know that, of course I know that. Yes, I'm game. Count me in."

I wasn't actually short of work but I was just too tempted. I didn't mention my doubts about Kenny or my suspicions about Gradling as I wanted to progress both before I involved anyone else. We chatted in general terms for a few minutes and then said goodbye, leaving my ears with a chance of recovery.

My phone gets *no* chance for recovery. The next call was Laura but for once I was interested in what she had to say.

***

Jayne-Marie Panahan was a happy bunny.

She had husband William where she wanted him. In order to preserve his beneficial marriage he'd handed over his bequest from the late Phyllis Downport and was now acting even more subservient than ever. Jayne-Marie would never let William forget his 'stupidity', as she called it, and would remind him of his folly as often as was seemly, and a more often than that if need be.

And how he'd suffered! She didn't believe he loved Phyllis, not in the accepted sense of the word, but he was definitely in lust with her and had to hide his heartbreak. He'd been known to slip quietly into the bathroom to cry his eyes out while, unbeknown to him, Jayne-Marie would creep up to the door and laugh to herself. Oh, how she was enjoying his grief and his penitence!

There was the bonus that Phyllis was dead and, as she'd hoped, stabbed right through the heart that had betrayed her with William. A fitting end. Engaging Yvonne Pratt had turned out to be an inspired move. It was Yvonne who hinted at such an apt means of death, punishment indeed for Phyllis, and a lifetime of regret for William. He'd never stray again.

Clever move Yvonne, she thought to herself, arranging to meet those other private eyes, private dicks if you ask me, and giving the police more headaches. Spreads the load of suspicion! And that guy in Kent, an ex-cop, bound to have old friends in the force, sure to find out what's going on. Then he passes it on to Yvonne and we all keep one step ahead. Classic stuff.

I give Sumitra short shrift but it keeps her on her toes. She'll go far, that one, and she's a gem for me. Not that I'd ever tell her. But she's erected a barrier here with the police; I don't think they dare organise a search, not like they've done in Kent and, where was it, oh yes, Devon. Not that they'd find anything untoward; they're not that clever, and I'm too good for them.

Once I know the coast's finally clear then I can pay Yvonne her bonus. I know these people don't like being kept waiting for their money and I don't want to end up dead, least of all now I have everything to live for. A loyal loving husband, thriving businesses, power and influence, and more money than, what's that expression they use, ah yes, more money than you could shake a stick at. Funny, the expressions ordinary people use. Still if they're daft enough to vote for Brexit then they must be pretty stupid to start with.

I never realised William was so good in bed. No wonder deprived, frustrated Phyllis fancied him. But at least he gives his all in pursuit of my pleasure and mine alone these days.

\*\*\*

Daryl Pequeman wasn't sure how to grieve and made a poor show, doing it all wrong, but then his heart wasn't in it. After a decent interval he could put himself about again and, who knows, he might find another bitch willing to do his bidding in all respects in order to enjoy an elaborate lifestyle in return.

Rosie's family were more than distressed and grossly upset at Daryl's crocodile tears. Her parents were desperately upset at the national newspaper coverage, especially the revelations about their daughter and John Holgarve, and the manner of her suicide which had been given far too much attention in their eyes.

Joan Holgarve was full of anger. Angry at her departed husband, angry at Rosie, furious with Barry because his involvement indirectly led to John's death. Angry with Mr Pequeman because his poor relationship with Rosie led her to John's arms. Angry with the police for being suspicious about her, searching her and her belongings, interviewing her for hours. Angry with the police for not yet catching the killer.

Her anger was the manifestation of the most dreadful feelings of despair, the wretched product of a heart torn to shreds and trampled into the ground, the pain and frustration of knowing she'd never see John again, the unbearable pain and frustration. The neighbours were growing used to the screams and shrieks when the agony overtook her and reduced her to a heap of indescribable human suffering.

Then came the moment when all good reason and sense deserted her. Breaking point.

Rage off the scale, her head throbbing with a wildness she had never known in her life and borne on the wind of fury, she dashed to the garden shed and equipped herself with a large and particularly vicious looking axe, and marched down the path by the side of the house.

Out into the road, swearing the most obnoxious and unpleasant oaths, stormed Joan, a creature possessed. Along the main road and up towards the place where Barry Welahome dwelled. Whether he was for the chop has never been related, but Joan's first port of call was his car and then his house.

With a swing of the axe she caved in the car's windscreen, and badly dented the bonnet with the next. Using all her might, and strength she would not have known she had, she swung decisively at the wooden gateposts, demolishing both and leaving the gate to choose between standing by itself or falling down.

Thrusting her way along the main road she had, by sheer good fortune as it turned out, been passed by a police patrol car. One of the officers recognised her and suddenly realised what could easily be termed an offensive weapon was in her hands. They thought they ought to check it out.

They arrived outside Barry's just as Joan was setting about the front door. The two officers, with great skill and presence of mind, to say nothing of immense bravery, caught hold of Joan and the axe swinging arm at the same time and managed to prevent further damage.

Once restrained Joan broke down completely, dropping the axe and squealing and sobbing torrents of tears.

It made the news. It was a diversion the police could well have done without.

It was a diversion that pleased the killer. More muddle, more confusion. Ideal.

Poor Joan had nothing left to give and pleaded with officers to let her die. Hospital was her immediate destination where she was checked over and sedated while her mother and sister were called in. Another victim of the killer of John Holgarve.

Barry Welahome sedated himself with gin and not much orange, and surveyed the scene before him. His blood ran cold just thinking about Bakewell's mad axe-woman coming to settle a score. His Vauxhall Corsa, already past its use-by date, might be a write-off. His gateposts certainly were. Thank God the police arrived in time.

\*\*\*

"What you know about this Parrett bloke, Moncks?"

"Very little. Only what's on his website. That's why I wanted you to search."

"How much I get paid? Used a lot of me time..."

"Laura, Laura, listen. You're the one who says we're partners. You get to share the winnings, that's all."

"Okay ...... okay. So you're admitting we're partners, that's good enough for me. McCaffield and Canbown. Would look good on our website."

"Would you mind telling me why you rang, apart from wanting to annoy me?"

"Not revealing my sources, okay, but did you know Mr Parrett was turned down by the police. Not uno but twice. Don't know why. Man with a grudge methinks. There, came upon the word 'methinks' – Googled it, and I rather like it .... methinks."

"Is this straight up, partner?"

"Wow, wowee. You called me partner. I'm in like...."

"Yes, yes, yes. Now can we get on with this?"

"Sure. So do you like my news and do you want me to dig some more?"

"Yes please, but just make sure what I hear is the indisputable truth, savvy?"

"Indisputable truth. Gotcha partner, methinks."

Irrepressible. Now where had she chanced upon that little nugget? She'd been busy and it had kept her out of my hair, but I knew it came at a price, and the price was more Lorraine searching.

But I did need help, and I arranged to meet her later as I finally conceded she could be useful to me, if only in record keeping (she was good at that).

Kenny, turned down twice by the police. Could be anything. Not easy to join up, not as easy as some people think. Oh why couldn't Adam have been more open? He'd told me so much, especially about Laura, and told me both she and Kenny were bad news. Just another little hint would've been helpful, was that too much to ask? Guess so.

I felt I wanted to tell Yvonne about Kenny but something was dragging me back. I was a mass of confused thoughts, and then I heard about Joan Holgarve's exploits in Bakewell.

***

Yvonne was not alone in enjoying the latest news from Derbyshire. Her employer was equally pleased. Ms Panahan was delighted with every little interference into the police investigations as it deflected attention.

Not a million miles away DS Stephanie Broome was plotting against both Jayne-Marie and Yvonne, so convinced was she they had something to hide.

In her desperation, and with permission from her senior officer, she rang DS Holton Okafor in Kent and threw all her thoughts and feelings into the ring.

"What's to stop you raiding JMP?" he asked.

"Influential woman, Holton. Wealthy, powerful, you have to be so sure before you go in."

"Ask JMP directly."

"We have. No way. It's all tread with care, tiptoe around, and I'm certain there's got to be a clue there. Look Holton, she's got money coming out of her ears, and she's so keen to keep us out of the way, and out of the way of that private eye of hers, I just know there's something. And it's driving me wild."

"Got an idea, Steph. I'm really warming to David Canbown, our private eye on the ABL case. I think he's as straight as a dye. Not that I'd let him know it! If you like I'll have a private chat with him, get him onside, and you never know what we might learn. I genuinely think it's worth a try. He may have left the force under a cloud, but what that guy did, y'know, sacrificing his career because of what he believed in, that counts huge in my book."

"Yes Holton, know what you mean. And he did it for all the right reasons. Okay, I'm with you. Let's give him benefit of the doubt for now. You'll soon suss him out if he's not on the level."

"Okay Steph. I'll let you know as soon as I've seen him."

Chapter Twenty

# Home Truths

Right out of the blue John Wapernod phoned.

"I don't know how it was done, David, but I'm putting all my money on the four wronged spouses. I realise this latest one, Daryl Pequeman, doesn't fit the stereotype of the other three, but he's in the money, and by all accounts he's something of a catch. Highly regarded architect, well sought after, and that sets him apart from your man, Gradling, and mine, Nathan Kethnet. Jayne-Marie Panahan is in my mix, even though there are some differences, simply because she's rolling in it.

"She's the face of her businesses and being influential she's kept the police from raiding her. But otherwise nothing to separate her from Gradling and Kethnet as an assassin hirer. Those two are, shall we say 'nouveau entrepreneurs' and yours, like mine, have got fingers in all kinds of pies, and have put businesses in their wives' names for all the usual reasons. We can file them under the heading 'fiddles'.

"Now they've gone through my computer with a fine tooth comb I've been able to access the dark web, but even so I don't actually know what I'm looking for. Any thoughts, David?"

"Well John, I reckon the police have hit the dark web, and they'll be looking at the criminal underworld too. They'll be speaking to their contacts, digging deep."

"Ah yes, the benefits of being an ex-officer, David. You'd know what they'd be up to."

"And John they are not going to share their results with us!" We both chuckled. "Have you heard from Yvonne at all?"

"Once. She was interested in what the police were doing down my way. Of course, they didn't turn up anything in their search of Kethnet's empire, and I think Yvonne was pleased about that from the point of view that Suffolk would be less likely to raid Panahan. What do you think?"

"They'll raid if they get so much as a sniff that the answer might be hidden there. But you're right. Powerful woman. They won't move until they can cover their backs. The fact the police have drawn blanks in Devon and Kent would hold them back for the mo. But if you're sure she and our two ordered the killings how do you feel about that? Surely the police wouldn't find anything raiding Ms Panahan's world anyway."

"I know, David. I want them to turn her over, but you're right; they won't find anything." Given my suspicions about Neville Gradling, which I wasn't going to reveal to John, least of all over the phone, I respected John Wapernod and therefore respected his opinion. He must have reasons for suspecting Nathan Kethnet just as I had about Gradling. "Shall we talk to Yvonne, see how she feels about Ms Panahan, and if she's going down my path of reasoning."

"No John, I'd leave it for the time being. I don't even know why I'm saying that, but I think we should keep her at armslength. Don't ask me to explain, I can't."

"So you're worried about Ms Pratt. Funny you should say that, but enough said for now. Walls have ears." Indeed they do although I worried we were getting a little paranoid about being snooped on.

After our call, which raised more questions than answers, DS Okafor was the next to warm my phone.

"Mr Canbown, can we meet? Just the two of us and away from eyes and ears."

"Sergeant, that's just about the worst way an officer could approach an ex-officer. Now why don't we start again?" I swear there was a muffled laugh. "We'd be so wary of each other the meeting would be pointless, a waste of time."

"Okay, okay, it's a fair cop, you got me bang to rights! Seriously, I want a chat and I hope you do too. Off the record, so I won't be wired for sound." More muffled laughter. "Straight up, Mr Canbown, I really am being open and honest about this, about my motives. I'll explain when I see you. I'm not going to ask you to trust me. You haven't got anything to lose, have you? Let's just try this one get-together eh? My name's Holton, okay."

"I'm David. No, you're right, I've got nothing to lose because I'm going to make sure it stays that way. Where and when?"

"You choose. Anywhere, anytime."

"Okay. Queendown Warren, south of the A2 off Hartlip. Small car park. We can walk in the open spaces with only the birds and bees to hear us. If we see anyone we'll be unlucky."

"Never heard of it...."

"I'll send you OS map co-ordinates, will that work on your Satnav?"

"Better than that. Know an officer who lives in Hartlip, she can direct me."

We sorted out day and time and concluded our odd little conversation. Now, what could he possibly want? I know, I know, if you can't trust a policeman blah,

blah. Still, if I kept my wits about me I might be able to learn something, although he was unlikely to share information not in the public realm.

∗∗∗

Yvonne Pratt had been delving in Southwold to no avail. She couldn't unearth anyone at the hotel who might have revealed the secret affair of William Bailey and Phyllis Downport. That is, she couldn't locate anyone willing to speak, for she was quietly confident now that was where the leak emanated. Even posing as a journalist when she arrived in person failed to loosen tongues that had already been loosened by financial gain from a real reporter.

"If we try harder," she reported to Jayne-Marie, "the police may get involved if someone complains and frankly it's better not to rouse them from their slumbers. We've got the cops where we want them, so let's keep 'em there. Please can we let sleeping dogs lie? It's for the best, that's my professional recommendation. Besides, with the papers sniffing around it could always lead to more publicity. Stay out of the limelight, ma'am."

With regret and poorly concealed annoyance Ms Panahan accepted the advice and gave Yvonne leave to drop the case. William Bailey was present at their meeting and he heaved an inaudible sigh of relief conceiving he had just been granted another step out of the woods. Needless to say he was no more out of the woods than he had been at the outset, but for all the intelligence, brainpower and ability he possessed he was unaware that he, like the police, was exactly where Jayne-Marie wanted him. A man totally controlled by a woman, and done so brilliantly he believed he was in charge, an assumption she had encouraged for her own gain.

In Manchester Gordon Pembrake had a pre-arranged visit from Daryl Pequeman. The grieving widower was learning the trade and arrived red-eyed and looked set to cry at any given moment. His acting skills would be capable of providing him with another career should architecture let him down at any time. He could not, for the life of him, understand why he wasn't truly heartbroken about Rosie's death.

He had loved her, loved her dearly, so he thought. When did he stop loving her? Was it when Mr Pembrake presented him with the irrefutable evidence of her affair, complete with those photos, those horrid photos? He was so confused. He'd given Pembrake keys to his house and the private eye, with Daryl's permission, had set up two hidden cameras, one in the bedroom. They recorded video pictures from which the stills had been taken.

In a fit of rage and anger he'd asked Pembrake for the moving pictures. The man was reluctant and advised against it, but Daryl insisted. Then there was that terrible day when Rosie was out that he loaded the DVD on the large screen TV, poured himself a vodka and Red Bull, a large one, and sat back and watched.

The tears rolled unchecked down his cheeks as he watched his wife and this other man cavorting on the bed, the bed of love he'd shared with her in their dream home here in the stark yet astonishingly beautiful Derby Dales they both adored. His own Rosie, his own dear Rosie. On the big screen, like a porno movie, in glorious Technicolor. Was that the day he stopped loving her? Or was that the day he decided to win her back?

The organisation he'd contacted had told him to hire a private eye to gather evidence. His initial reaction to Pembrake's written report (no pictures included) was to take a step back. Of course, as a husband betrayed by his wife, and with a real nobody, he wanted revenge and could cheerfully have strangled John Holgarve with his bare hands. But that wasn't right.

He'd been led by that organisation, whoever they were, who said that the problem would be sorted for all time. Mr Holgarve would be dead. Rosie would have no lover. Mr Pequeman could reclaim her. For a while he accepted that, revenge still throbbing in his mind with over-riding supremacy in all his thoughts, but gradually common sense wheedled its way back into his thinking and he began to regret his pact with the devil. Murder is wrong, he'd told himself, and bloody illegal. He wanted to back out.

But as he saw dear, sweet Rosie, naked on that bed, John helping himself to every gift that was offered, his resolve hardened and once again he wanted him dead. Dead. Dead. He stood up and shouted at the screen 'kill, kill, kill, kill, kill, kill' until out of breath and exhausted he collapsed on the floor squealing in agony. But he would have his Rosie back, make no mistake about that.

Was that really the day he stopped loving her?

He now sat in Pembrake's office, settling his final account, convinced he didn't love the girl he was pretending to grieve over, and asking all the questions he'd planned, questions that were designed to learn how much he'd told the police and how much they'd told him.

That organisation, or whatever they were, had promised discretion, secrecy, and an assurance that no blame would ever attach to him. He would be innocent of John Holgarve's blood. But even now the pressure hammered at him. Would he be found out? After they had all his money would they sell him out? He'd had no idea at the time that they were completing other 'contracts' that would suddenly become front page news. Now he was, if anything, frightened. Nervous and frightened.

And nervous people make mistakes. DS Stephanie Broome knew that. She knew it only took one weak link to destroy the chain. That weak link must be out there somewhere.

It was about this time that yet another theory nested in her mind where it was to be nourished and brought to adulthood. Four different means of despatch, victims respectively strangled, stabbed, shot and injected. But supposing that was not just the killer demonstrating their hideous array of villainous activities, their dexterous and expert touch with various weapons. Supposing each type of killing was symbolic in some way? Supposing the hirer, assuming there were hirers, could choose the method? Supposing there was something symbolic to the hirer?

Supposing. Just supposing.

***

I had pulled together a few basics on Jason Hayle and there wasn't much more to discover. Laura had exhausted every avenue on Kenny Parrett, so it was back to pot lids for me. I'd explained to my partner (might as well call her that now) all about pot lids, not that she'd shown any interest, but she had been making up computer records (which she is good at) at my humble abode when Kenny phoned.

His call changed the picture.

He had an address for Gary Wimbush in Barrow-in-Furness, Walney Island to be precise. Laura wanted to leave right away. How to calm her down without throwing a bucket of cold water over her? I thanked Kenny and told him to email his bill, and returned to the nigh impossible task of keeping Laura under basic control, if that were ever possible.

"It was years ago. We don't know he's there now. Not on the electoral roll last three years so we don't know. But I have contacts who may be able to give us more info. Law, we have to let them look into this before we set off. For pities sake do it my way. We have other work, jobs that pay real money, that we must, *must* attend to. Please understand that. You're my business partner, so please understand we must do work for *money*. Both of us.

"Lorraine wasn't on the electoral roll, so she may have left him as we've been told. Let me contact my guys and see what they can find out, and in the meantime let's throw ourselves into our current money-earning cases."

"Cobblers. We find Gary, talk to him, and maybe find out where she might be now."

"If my contacts can find him first, nail him down to an address, we'll go straightaway. Promise."

"Cobblers. I wanna go now."

"Then we aren't partners. You clear off and good luck. I'm staying here. Work to be done."

"Can I take the car?"

"No, you haven't got a licence now anyway, and I'll shop you if you nick it."

"You mean, crummy bastard, Moncks. Something else your mate told you I suppose. Yes, I got banned. Look buster, I done all me time, give me a break. Get off that high horse of yours."

And her words softened as her face creased and the tears came. I was a beaten man again, forced into taking her in my arms and providing comfort. But she'd surrendered. To my surprise she agreed to my suggestion and she said she'd help tackle our cases again.

"Tell me about this pot lid," she whimpered and sobbed as I cradled her gently, "and pour me a drinky."

Normality and sense restored.

***

I have to hand it to Laura, it was down to her record-keeping and alertness that we spotted a surprise connection. You'll remember I had a new case involving two business partners, one suspecting the other was about to stitch him up, not to say he wasn't fiddling the books as well.

The one I was looking into was Peter Hettisham and lo and behold he was listed as a director of an enterprise in which Jason Hayle was the chairman. I can't say I understand these things but it looked like a financial operation, possibly the front for a kind of pyramid scheme but based loosely on a sort of franchise arrangement. In itself it was unlikely to be illegal, but if it was all about get-rich-quick then Hayle's involvement would be explained, especially if he had launched it.

But if it was a pyramid then those in at the start will be the ones to benefit, whereas later investors would be the ones to lose their money when it crashed down as pyramids do. That's the whole idea; persuade people to invest on the promise of swift and large returns, but as more and more are recruited, and their money goes to the previous investors, it becomes increasingly impossible to claw in more cash.

When that happens there is no income with which to pay earlier investors, so it falls down in a heap, some lucky sods walking away with a mint. Most lose their money. If the operation is set up in a legitimate fashion then it is like any business failing when it goes to the wall. Nasty.

I had no qualms about passing my information to Yvonne. Let her delve more closely. Now, Mr Hettisham was a director so he must've been an early recruit. The franchise element was loosely connected with the manufacturing concern he ran with his business partner, Shane Fulknam, the man who had hired me. Would the collapse of Hayle's scheme in any way impact on Hettisham and Fulknam's business?

That could be the answer. Hettisham ruins the partnership but walks away with the profits made from Hayle's operation. Very nasty indeed. I don't know enough about partnerships from a legal standpoint but I always thought they worked like sole traders, in that the owners were responsible for the debts. That's unlike a company where the shareholders own the firm but aren't held liable for the debts if it fails.

This being more complex than anything I would normally deal with I advised Shane Fulknam of my findings, apologised for the fact I wasn't able to research any further and suggested he take some legal advice, possibly alert his accountant. He was very grateful for my efforts, said he would take my advice instantly, and promptly settled my account.

I love the BACS scheme especially when, as was the situation in this case, provider and client are with the same bank. Instantaneous transfer! Luverly jubberly.

Dosh in the bank! Laura given her cut. Happy David, happy Laura. But I asked Yvonne to keep me in the loop as I would most interested in any other data I could pass on to Fulknam, and besides, I was interested in how the Jason Hayle affair was going to pan out. Quite apart from that I had an excuse to keep in touch with Ms Pratt, which pleased me as something was rankling, like an itch you can't scratch, but definitely something about the woman.

Back to pot lids.

Thanks to my client, who gave me all the clues, I tracked down the daughter of the friend he'd given the pot lid to. Frankly, my client gave it away in the first place thinking it worthless, and simply because his friend liked it. To want it back now because it was worth a great deal more seemed a bit hard-hearted and mean.

He went to the funeral of his friend three years ago, but lost contact with the family. Before said gentleman died he apparently confessed he'd lost the wretched lid, not that it bothered anyone then. It might have been thrown away, there was no knowing.

Visiting the daughter in Redhill I learned that the missing lid had never been lost, it had been auctioned, but she understood why her father might want to keep it a secret from someone who had given it as a gift. On the other hand maybe he discovered its true worth and decided to cash in!

I found the auctioneers but they were bound by client confidentiality. The woman I spoke to did manage (accidently or on purpose) to let it slip that the new owner *might* live in Loughborough.

With my client's permission, as he'd be paying, I advertised in the local paper. Right now that was about it.

One of my contacts came up with an address for Gary Wimbush in Kent's Bank, close to Grange-Over-Sands. Two people appeared on the electoral roll, Victoria and Sian Wollardson. Mother and daughter? His new love? There appeared to be no trace of divorce from Lorraine. The next piece of news threw some light on the arrangements.

Victoria Wollardson owned the property, so he must've moved in with her. It helps to have contacts that can reveal information like this. They could be putting their jobs on the line just to help me, but I suppose it's a mark of the respect they have for me as a friend that they know I won't jeopardise them.

Now, there were other ways of playing this, not least contacting a private investigator up there to search further, perhaps call on Gary. We were looking for Lorraine, not Gary, he being merely a means to an end. If he had no idea where she was that would be that. But I had a partner who was becoming so excitable and frustrated that the simplest thing to do, all matters considered, was to go there. Easier life for me all round.

With the pot lid on the back burner, and the weekend upon us, we packed for an early departure the next morning. By early I mean around 2.30 a.m. Get past the Dartford Crossing, round the M25 and up the M11 and the A1 as far as possible before breakfast. But first, this Friday afternoon I had my get-together with Holton Okafor, and that turned out to be not at all what I expected.

***

DS Broome could appreciate why you would want your partner's lover stabbed clean through the heart. Complete de-activation, she thought crudely. The heart would never love again, regardless of the fact the owner would be dead. Symbolic. The heart that took your partner's heart. Wrecked.

Symbolic.

And she emailed her thoughts to Kent, Devon and Derbyshire. Okafor leapt into action and quickly discovered Alistair Bourne-Lacey was an expert pistol shot. Shot dead with a bullet between the eyes. Symbolic or what?

That left strangulation and lethal injection. How could a lethal injection be in any way symbolic? Might they be about to find out? But would any of this lead them any closer to their quarry? Senior officers were sceptical but they were short of anything that could be remotely identified as a lead, and one thing could always take you to another. Never dismiss anything until you've examined it.

Sometimes police detection work is all about painstaking detail, about a slow drudge, about putting pieces in a jigsaw one piece at a time. TV crime shows can be largely action but real life isn't quite like that.

When it came to paying attention, *meticulous* attention to minute details, nobody was doing it better than the killer. But the killer had hitherto dealt with ruthless self-made people who were not above bending the law. Daryl Pequeman, although coming over as a man without a conscience, a cold-hearted individual, was anything but.

He was actually coming apart at the seams. After a sustained show of brashness, befitting the man, his heart was beginning to ache for Rosie. From there it was a short step to conscious realisation about what had happened, that he had never stopped loving his wife, that he wanted her back, desperately wanted her back. And the next step beyond that, as the pain dragged him to hell, was that he regretted his role in John Holgarve's death.

The killer had already become over-confident in taking Daryl as a client. Thinking you're invincible can produce errors of judgement, lax moments, loss of concentration and mistakes. Sitting comfortably in your niche market is one thing, diversifying into a completely new realm can have drawbacks, not least a serious threat to your perceived invincibility.

Blackmail, by whatever name the killer wanted to give it, was a journey into the unknown. Murder was the specialist subject, but this was a new ball game and perhaps the killer didn't understand or want to accept all the rules of engagement.

Slowly the tide was turning. The police didn't know it yet, but then neither did the killer.

***

There was a small red car in one corner of the car park plus the unmistakeable presence of Holton Okafor's impressive motor. He was standing beside it and he and the car looked as if they had been made for each other. Together they looked as if they had arrived straight from a TV commercial for the model, he in a snazzy, dark blue suit with matching tie, and non-matching dark glasses.

It's a small car park but, if everyone parks considerately, which is rare, it can probably take ten vehicles at a push, not that I've ever seen it that busy. I reversed my shabby, unclean Fiesta next to his monster feeling ashamed of my transport yet pleased that I'd dressed smartly and had a very good shave.

"Cool spot, David," he announced as I slipped out from behind the wheel. Cool, as in not so warm, or cool, as in this is the place to be? I guessed the latter.

"Love it here, Holton. It's one of the places I come to escape. During the week it's usually fairly quiet." I pressed the central locking button and then checked both the driver's and the rear passenger doors.

"Great the way people do that, y'know, lock up then go back and try the doors." He was smiling warmly, which was a warning sign in itself. "Now my mean machine, soon as it locks the door mirrors close in, so a quick glance tells me all I need to know."

"*I've* got a proper spare wheel," I boasted, and he laughed freely as he held out his hand.

"Let's call it a draw, David. Pleased to meet you in these circumstances."

"And what might these circumstances be? But pleased to see you again, nevertheless."

"Hey, leave the caution to the real police!" We shook hands and at last there did seem to be some genuine sincerity. It's always odd when two people trained in the art of reading body language meet, especially if they are analysing each others' voices too. A nod from both sides showed that we appreciated what we were subconsciously doing!

And then we laughed at ourselves.

"Right, you know the place, David, lead on." I headed for the gate.

"We can walk across here, plenty of open space, enjoy the views, and talk knowing there's only our ears. Unless, of course, you've got a cunningly concealed drone ready to fly nearby."

"My Inspector drones. That's as close as I'm going to get to something like that!"

Yes, that's right, tell me a joke about your Inspector just to show how matey you want to be. In my time on the force I tried that a few times but nobody was fooled.

The path forms a narrow ridge on the sloping hillside that drops down to where a car can just be glimpsed driving along the lane at the foot. The land rises smartly over the other side where there's a large house, presumably a farm, and one or two other buildings. This is rural Kent. Mostly you're looking at a green landscape, trees, hedgerows, fields, and inevitably sheep, although they tend to be white.

The Warren is a conservation area. Thank heavens somebody cares. There are trees and shrubs here too, but much open space, and the chance to feel that you're a million miles from what passes for civilisation, and from reality as well.

Coming towards us is a Weimaraner taking its owner for a walk. I hope the dog's cleared up after her! What a beautiful animal, the loveliest of well-groomed grey dogs, and I can sense Holton is as impressed as me, even though he thinks it's a Labrador. I put him right. The owner is a small middle-aged lady, well wrapped against a coldness that hasn't manifested itself this bright autumn day.

We meet and pass what is proverbially known as 'the time of day', pat and cuddle the hound, who is extremely appreciative of the attention, utter the time-honoured words such as 'You're a fine dog' and 'what's his name then?' We are told she's a bitch. Yes, we should've looked first! Then we go our separate ways, me and Holton, the lady and Sheba.

There has to be time to take in this breathtaking spot, simple in its rural charm, complex in its nature, this enchanting vista of true rolling English countryside, and we stand side by side in silence absorbed and temporarily lost in the glory of the beauteousness of this natural creation.

Okafor nods.

"David, this is so cool. A taste of paradise on earth. What a view! Majestic, lovely, yet no high mountains, no meandering flowing river, just unabashed countryside, yearning to be admired.

And so many sheep!"

"It's really kind of stunned you, Holton, hasn't it? You should get out more. Maybe relax more."

"Yeah, I know what you mean. Almost a shame to spoil it with business."

"You can't spoil it with talk. That's not the way your wreck our countryside. By the way, where do *you* live, where do you come from?"

"Me? I'm a man of Kent. Born and bred Folkestone. Third generation of an immigrant family. And I now live outside Canterbury with my girlfriend, and we have no plans to spoil it all by getting married. You married?"

"Divorced."

"Anyone on the go?" A curious way of asking if I had a special girlfriend.

"Not at present."

"Where does Laura McCaffield fit in then?" So that was where this meeting was heading. Did everybody know about my friendship with the fair Laura?

"She doesn't fit in at all. Now what did you want to see me about?"

I could tell from his glance that he knew he'd chosen just the right moment to hit me the hardest and I was angry that I'd reacted, visually and verbally, with such irritation. He would see it for what it was, and his single nod and the way he looked away told me I'd scored an own goal. Damn and blast!

"Sorry David. No offence, but you know she's got form, including drugs, and that means there's a warning light flashing over in the corner of this police investigation. I'll explain. My colleague in Suffolk wonders if the method of killing is more allied to the victim, rather than the assassin showing off his or her range of expertise. Bit like mail order, if you get me. You choose who you want done in and you select the means, appropriate in some way to the misdemeanour being punished.

"Like Phyllis Downport. Stole the heart of the man Jayne-Marie Panahan loved, so she was stabbed through her own heart. Jackie Gradling met Alistair Bourne-Lacey through their love of sport, the gym and all that. ABL was a renowned pistol shot. Did you know that? Anyway, he gets shot in the head. See my direction of travel, David?" My turn to nod.

"Now, John Holgarve, Bakewell. Turns out he was a pusher, or had been, according to his wife. Got Rosie Pequeman started. The PI, Gordon Pembrake put cctv in her house with the husband's permission. Adultery in the style of a wild, vivid porn movie. Destroyed the husband, so I'm told. But he barely noticed what they were smoking yet he did see John injecting his wife.

"So when his time came John died by lethal injection, a horrible cocktail of all the nasty substances you can imagine. On the subject of drugs that other PI, Kenneth Parrett, tried to join the force but one of the problems was the concern he might be a user, so I understand. He was turned down, mainly for lack of aptitude, so it was recorded.

"And then you and Miss McCaffield, ex-druggie, turn up in Derby around the time it's about to go tits up for John Holgarve. I'm telling you all this for your own sake, because I believe in you, I seriously do David, and I know as the good copper you were, the good PI you are, you won't breathe a word of this to anyone. I haven't misjudged you have I?"

I stood looking across the valley but with eyes that didn't see. After a pause I turned to face him.

"No you haven't Holton. But are you suggesting someone thinks Laura was involved in Holgarve's death, because I know she wasn't." He put both hands up in mock surrender.

"No I'm not, and nobody else is, but some people wonder what you're doing with a girl like her."

"She's a friend and helper. There's no relationship."

"Okay, change of subject. Any theories then on why Edward Nobbs was strangled with rope, if my colleague's idea holds true?"

"Bondage? Maybe he used to tie Cathy Kethnet up for their combined pleasure."

"David, David, my boy, that's a very good answer. You may have hit the nail on the head."

"I don't like being called 'boy' or 'son' – it's akin to a hate crime in my eyes." He roared with laughter taking a young woman by surprise. We'd been so wrapped up in our conversation we hadn't noticed her approaching along the same path we had trodden. Okafor apologised at once and set about making a fuss of the obligatory dog held on a short lead by the lady in question.

Getting the sex right this time we said farewell to the woman and to Lucy, a King Charles Spaniel.

"David, I just want us to be talking. That's all. Nothing sinister. Sharing info, stuff like that. Believe me." He looked so earnest and almost desperate. It must difficult when your investigations have stalled for a lack of evidence and a lack of leads, and your only hope is to become best chums with a private eye. "Sorry about the 'boy' – bloody rude of me. Sorry."

And he so obviously meant all of it. I was sure he wasn't putting it on. I offered the hand of friendship which was accepted with relish.

"Holton, you don't expect me to mention what you've told me. So that applies the other direction, right?"

"You got it. Goes without saying."

"Okay. This is a policeman's intuition, nothing more. A copper's nose. I can't say more because I don't know any more, and that's the truth. Neville Gradling, I'd put my pension on him having hired the killer. You've searched him, checked his computer. You're no nearer than I am. But it's a gut feeling. The answer's there *somewhere*." Okafor stood and stared at me. His lips made a pretence of trying to mould into the right shape to say something but nothing materialised at once and I had to wait a full minute before he spoke.

"Okay David, I got you." He looked away, no doubt, like me, observing this wonderful view, this glorious piece of Kentish countryside, this peace and tranquillity, this beauty, this dream, and not able to comprehend in that second that we had been discussing something so hideous as pre-meditated murder, slaughter, death. It was incongruous on this sloping green bank, under a lovely blue sky that was bothered only by a few light clouds here and there, that two people could so desecrate nature in such a dreadful way.

And yet both felt we had soiled the land upon which we walked, soiled the scenery, soiled the gentleness and pleasure to be enjoyed here. I realised that we were as one in this matter, and it hurt us both. Yet we had done nothing wrong. We weren't planning a housing estate here; that would be desecration!

"I'll come here again," he declared, "and bring Gilly, and we'll enjoy it as it should be enjoyed. But for now it's about business. I'm grateful to you, David. We understand each other, agreed?"

"Yes, but I hope this spirit of co-operation continues."

"It will, but it's also up to you, y'know that." More nodding.

We parted, each having so much to think about now, but knowing that we could count on each other. He'd broken the rules, he was that anxious to solve these crimes and, more importantly, prevent further killings. I respected him for that; I'd risked it myself as an officer. Sometimes you just have to do it, because it can bring results.

In silence we strolled back to our cars and shook hands one final time today. No words; none were necessary. There was much thinking to do. I watched him drive away and knew how much he would love to bring Gilly to this spot, and in happier circumstances. I wondered if it would ever be the same again for me.

# Chapter Twenty One
# **Various nets close in**

Yvonne Pratt was revelling in her position of power. She was given to occasional and tuneless bursts of song and had even whistled briefly at odd times. She was basking in a lovely glow of self-satisfaction, the warmth of feeling completely in control, the thrill of success married to utter achievement, and enjoying the light-headed sensation of being beyond question or challenge.

Ms Panahan was now, so she reasoned, firmly in her pocket. Her 'bonus' had been paid and had set Yvonne dreaming of how life might be when all the fuss died down, as it was sure to do. The operation could be resurrected in a different format at some later stage, but for now enough money had changed hands and both she and killer could relax and appreciate their substantial ill-gotten gains.

Of course, the killer took the lion's share and that was only fair. But now Ms Pratt considered that she was taking a risk every bit as great as that of executioner, and surely she was entitled to ask for a larger percentage than hitherto awarded on that basis?

After all, the police had interviewed her, searched her records, a pleasure denied the killer. Happily, from her point of view, Yvonne kept the illegal business records elsewhere.

She had set that bunch of idiots, those so-called private eyes, on wild goose chases so that she could keep in touch, especially so that ex-cop. He was bound to have contacts on the force, and inside information was always useful. Only this morning she'd phoned John Wapernod to say she'd had a tip-off the police were checking out Kenny Parrett. Very real suspicions.

Play them off against each other. Make mischief. Create suspicion.

There, that should keep 'em busy. A woman in charge of men, pure minions of no consequence, singing her tune. The thought amused her.

So Yvonne Pratt was less than happy when the killer made a brief call on the mobile she kept hidden. It was buried in her garden and, by agreement, brought out at certain times only.

"Good-day," the voice intoned, "and have you got my money?"

"Yes, but there's something to be discussed about that."

"Oh really? I don't think so. I've posted the forwarding details. Nothing to discuss. Now, I have another plan and it's ready to be actioned, so we need a meeting as you'll be, how shall we say, helping me again."

"A new idea? So soon? I thought we were going to lie low."

"Did you? What a shame. You got that wrong. Now, I'm going to blackmail our clients. Obviously they have pots of money and being a socialist I believe in the redistribution of wealth. I thought we might start with Jayne-Marie Panahan as you and she are so cosy. Let me know what you think when we meet. Time and place in my letter; it had better be convenient. Because if your involvement ever becomes inconvenient there will be only one way of dissolving the partnership.

Bye for now."

Yvonne sat and stared at the phone. It was all very wrong because everything had gone so well and the arrangement was that the whole matter be allowed to lie dormant until it was reasoned it was safe to press on. With a rueful grin and a tiny smirk Yvonne found herself pleased that she hadn't raised the question of a bigger cut of the winnings!

From there it was but a short journey to considering that she could earn more money anyway. Nobody who had bought into their prestigious, luxury service was going to report the issue of blackmail to the police! Yes, it *was* a five-star service, wasn't it? And she could be proud of being part of it. Panahan would indeed be a good place to start, for hadn't she just come into a fabulous fortune to add to her own wealth. That dimbo Bailey! Men are such fools, but aren't we the grateful ones when we use them so well, for they always come up trumps. And William Bailey did. Yes, Mrs Bailey, as I shall soon call you, much to your annoyance, you have stacks of money and you wouldn't begrudge some of it going to a good home, would you?

\*\*\*

John Wapernod stood in a particularly lonely part of Exmoor, over the border in Somerset, and was alone with his thoughts. He loved a walk here when the rare opportunity presented itself. In thinking terms it was his equivalent of a lie down in a dark room. Here he could think untroubled by humans. No phone. Just this delightful wilderness for company.

He thought of *Lorna Doone*. It was a natural progression to think of the four appalling murders that all began with the strangulation of Edward Nobbs. Wapernod was not the sort of person to hate another, and Nathan Kethnet had been most generous, but he did not like the man one little bit and was fretting at the notion Kethnet had indeed ordered up the slaying of Nobbs.

While the sun favoured the east of the country, where Canbown and Okafor were meeting at Queen Down Warren, it was submerged behind scurrying clouds that threatened rain and nothing of pleasure. He must get back soon.

His thoughts were plagued by unease over Yvonne Pratt that had been fuelled by David Canbown whose intuition, like his own, was giving rise to disquiet. And now she had called to cast the hand of suspicion on Kenny Parrett. Whatever could she be up to? But as the weather looked as if it might finally become unhealthy he decided to call it a day and head home, for he knew these lands well and knew of the trouble the unwary and unprepared could land in.

John had something to look forward to. He would be seeing his lady-friend tonight. And then, as dreams of a most exciting and uplifting evening waltzed before him he was seized by a terrible thought. If her husband behaved like Kethnet it was he who would be in the firing line! And his pace involuntarily quickened as he hurried back to his car.

***

Planning on leaving this Saturday morning at 2.30 a.m. it had been necessary for Laura to stay over, she on the settee (it was her turn) and me in the bed. We'd had an early night with everything packed and ready for departure before we retired.

Quietly we locked up, crept to the car and set off. Over the bridge, onto the M2, the A2 and finally up to the Dartford Crossing. M25, M11, our progress only hindered by overnight roadworks and mind-numbing fifty mile an hour speed limits on deserted highways. On through Cambridgeshire as the first signs of dawn, very dim signs, appeared on the eastern horizon. On the A1 motorway we sped past Peterborough and were soon in Lincolnshire skirting Grantham.

Dawn was increasingly upon us but we still needed lights. Traffic was building. The overnight lorries were joined by cars and vans and motorcycles as the world came to life. With no serious delays we were passing Doncaster. It had been a quiet ride, motormouth being fast asleep since Essex, but now she woke as we crossed the Don.

"Where we, Moncks?"

"Just past Doncaster." She got the book of maps out.

"Right, then York, Northallerton, I see. And we join the A66 at Scotch Corner."

"That's it, but brekky first at a Little Chef. We can feed and water the horses at the same time. Once we're on the sixty-six I'm going to pull in for a power nap."

"Pleased you mentioned brekky cos I'm starving. Little Chef eh? Yeah, heard they do terrific breakfasts. Can I have what I want?"

"Yes."

That did the trick; silence was resumed for a while.

After general chit chat as I negotiated heavier traffic than expected we arrived at Skeeby and the first shock of the day. The Little Chef was permanently closed. I felt like I'd lost an old friend. So it was up the road the Scotch Corner services with one belly-aching woman for company!

"You'll get your breakfast, promise, now give me a break and save your jaw for chewing."

Bull. Red rag shown to. Lift off. David Canbown in the doghouse forever and a day, or at least until just after our meal.

Breakfast taken it was round the roundabout and across the Pennines, getting our kicks on route sixty-six. This is a spectacular ride, over the so-called Backbone of England, and we were refreshed and ready to take in the ever-changing scenery. It was Laura's first time and, having got over the business of food and my rudeness, she was wow-ing every new vista. It didn't last.

I pulled into a lay-by for my rest and, as she'd slept for over four hours during our journey north, displayed her displeasure by rabbiting without taking breath until I was snoring. Well, I assumed she stopped when I fell asleep, for I had no way of knowing, but she may have continued unabated. I'd got myself comfy using my coat as a headrest against the window; it wasn't the finest position for posture as I was curled up under the steering wheel with my top half contorted so that my head was where I wanted it to be.

But when you've woken early, driven wide-awake for nearly five hours (we arrived at Scotch Corner soon after seven) sleep comes easily.

I suppose I enjoyed about forty minutes repose but at least woke in silence. I actually felt very comfortable and closed my eyes with the intention of drifting into the arms of Morpheus again, but failed in the task, despite my companion keeping the peace. Soon we were under way again.

Now we crossed the highest part and the views were magnificent. Laura was beside herself.

"Never seen anything like this, Moncks. Wowee!" I smiled and drove on pleased that she was enjoying herself and, I have to admit, pleased with myself for giving her this simple pleasure. As there was little point arriving on Gary's doorstep first thing on a Saturday morning I was taking the A66 to Penrith and was going to treat Laura to a drive alongside Ullswater and across the Kirkstone Pass.

From Windermere we'd be heading south, ultimately towards Kent's Bank.

Ullswater thrilled her to pieces. She squealed and wriggled in her seat as she gazed across the water to the mountains beyond. She'd never witnessed anything like it in the flesh. Yes, she'd found photos online when I told her which route we'd take, but they couldn't have prepared her for the real thing.

Much as I love the Lake District I'd forgotten how to be amazed by its splendorous beauty, familiarity breeding contempt. It's too easy to take something for granted, and Laura was teaching me look again at something I adored and appreciate it afresh and all the more.

We paused for coffee at Glenridding and she pleaded to be brought here for a holiday.

Suddenly I felt so sad. Deep down inside I knew she wasn't the right girl for me, and knew only too well she wasn't going to be good for business. And I felt sorry for her. But perhaps we could come here for a vacation as friends, maybe our last time together. And that thought made me sadder still. Was I guilty of leading her on, of giving her false hope?

I knew my own feelings but perhaps I was doing a bad job of relaying them. Or could she possibly 'read' my *real* feelings and that was where her hope stemmed from? I was subdued as we headed up to the Kirkstone Pass. Laura made up for it by being over-enthusiastic enough for two of us.

As we started the descent the 'wow' factor went into over-drive and I thought for a moment she was having an orgasm. I pointed out the 'Struggle' – the steep road down to Ambleside, and further on the mountainous 'High Street' ridge. I couldn't resist a little jest.

"And the only Boots and Woollies you'll see up there on this High Street will be on the walkers."

She giggled and gurgled and laughed till the tears ran down her cheeks.

"Oh Moncks, you got a sense of humour after all!" So it came to pass that my spirits were restored, despite a private admonishment for amusing her. My man-training reminded me girls like a man who can make them laugh, so I'd been told. I re-admonished myself for thinking such a stereotypical thing; not in keeping with the new me.

But she was awash with happiness, and loving the views as we gently weaved our way down the narrow winding road, possibly the worst part of the pass for a driver. With stone walls both sides you can't afford to pull over too far when negotiating oncoming traffic. And then it was over, Laura close to relaxing after her exertions, as we swept down to Windermere, through the town and away to the south.

Needless to say, picturesque as the scenery was, especially one view right across the lake itself, this wasn't in the same category as the Kirkstone Pass, and Laura settled for gentle sighs rather than more agitated exclamations.

And thus it was that we came upon Grange-over-Sands and Kent's Bank beyond, and hopefully a date with destiny.

In the same way music can stir the emotions clearly scenery can too, and such emotions can all too easily become entangled in personal matters such as fondness and affection and turn them into something all too engulfing. And my emotions were getting tangled, believe me!

*  *  *

DS Alcock, having heard from DS Broome, who in turn had been alerted by DS Okafor, called on Mrs Kethnet while her husband was out. This was a private matter, and Alcock was conscious of the delicacy of the issue he was pursuing.

"Mrs Kethnet, I wanted to see you alone as there is something I must ask, and which you may not want your husband to hear. I am very sorry indeed, but I must ask, and I apologise for any embarrassment. But we are trying to unravel a mystery and are piecing together all manner of clues." She beckoned to him to sit, and sat herself, her face now showing all the signs of worry and fear.

For his own part Geoff Alcock was nervous. These weren't the sort of things a man should be asking a woman, but he had to accept that police work involved all kinds of nasty matters, and that sometimes distasteful subjects had to be raised, regardless of personal feelings. To Alcock, having a rather old-fashioned outlook, it was anathema that Cathy Kethnet should've been frolicking with Edward Nobbs behind her husband's back in the first place, but now the possibility it might have been frolicking with kinky additives had reared its ugly head.

"Mrs Kethnet, did you and Mr Nobbs engage in acts of bondage at any time?" Both parties blushed. Alcock had spoken to Wapernod who had never seen anything to suggest they did, and the Sergeant was comfortable asking the private eye, and doing so over the phone. This was different, quizzing a real, live woman face-to-face.

"Sergeant," she began, her head slowly lowering, her eyes closed, her hands held tightly in her lap, "please tell me why you want to know." He knew she was weeping, very tenderly in his opinion, no heaving shoulders and few tears, no sounds, but enough to convince him that weeping is what she was about. A very feminine sobbing, he thought. Undemonstrative but effective, for it made him miserable and rendered him unable to put a cold face on it. He actually wanted to hug her, apologise again for his vile question, and make good his escape without waiting for an answer, sparing her blushes.

But as a policeman he couldn't do it. Must be hard-hearted Geoff, he told himself. Now, how much can I tell her?

"Mrs Kethnet, I'm sure you are aware from the news that we believe there are similarities between this case and others, and we are anxious to apprehend the villain and prevent further atrocities. We don't have one murder weapon to hand; we need all the help we can get. I can't tell you more but it's important you answer my question. I really am so very sorry." She looked up, her faced etched with despair and resignation, pain and anguish.

"Sergeant, Edward and I had a very full sex life. He was extremely experienced and found so many wonderful ways to please me. He was so kind and loving, please understand that, but he probed my feelings and discovered ways in which he could enhance my pleasures." Alcock knew he had gone bright red. He wanted a simple answer, yes or no would've sufficed, but he was being given an enormous amount of background material that troubled him as a police officer as well as a conventional human being.

"He introduced me to ideas that I barely knew about." Alcock's face had passed red and was now maroon, and he was dreading what was coming next. "For example I learned that I liked being spanked, so it was quite a natural progression for him to suggest I might like to be tied up helpless beforehand. And it did, oh it did, Sergeant. You can't imagine how it increased my sensations. That's what I mean about Edward being an experienced lover. He researched me, I suppose you could say, found out what was good for me and made it better."

Alcock was ready to turn and run. This is disgusting, he thought. The answer to my question was one word and, it now transpires, that one word was 'yes'. Why couldn't she just say 'yes'?

Unsurprisingly the meeting ended seconds later. Alcock threw in one last question.

"Rope?" and received, at long last, a one word answer.

"Yes." With that he thanked Mrs Kethnet and was through the door, out of the house and into the fresh air (and pouring rain, which he didn't care about right then) before you could say Jack Robinson.

Returning to his car and taking some deep breaths, during which time he found himself regretting joining the force, he phoned DS Broome.

There was still the question of how anyone else knew. Wapernod hadn't come across it during his covert surveillance, and obviously Nathan Kethnet wasn't aware. Or *was* he? Perhaps, Stephanie Broome mused, Cathy took her new ideas home with her and practised them with her husband!

However, no way was Geoff Alcock going to ask Nathan about that!

***

Leaving Laura in the car as agreed I wandered up to the house and knocked.

A young woman answered. There was a towel wrapped turban-style around her head, her T-shirt hung loose about her torso in complete contrast to her jeans which clung tight to her wafer-thin legs. The jeans had the obligatory cuts and tears. The T-shirt bore the words 'A meal without wine is called breakfast'. In my one glance I also took in the sunken cheeks and the lifeless look in her eyes, and the lack of make-up, the latter confirming my obvious view she had washed her hair. Obviously.

I couldn't have guessed her age but I reckoned she was younger than she appeared. My opinion, which was also founded in the aroma emanating from the hall, was that of a woman ravaged by drug abuse.

"Is Gary at home?" I enquired.

"Gary who?"

"Gary Wimbush."

"Who wants him?"

"Calling on behalf of a friend. Actually we're looking for someone else and Gary can probably point us in the right direction."

"Well, bloke called Gary left here a year ago, so I've been told. So you don't know as much as you think you do, do you?" She made to close the door. I produced a card.

"I've written my mobile on here. My name's Dave. My friend is looking for Lorraine. If he should drop by please ask him to ring if he's got any info at all, anything at all on Lorraine. He knows who I mean." And I turned and left without being invited to do so. She stood on the doorstep for some seconds before closing the door.

She was lying alright. Gary might even have been there. I relayed this to Laura who wanted to know what we were going to do next.

"I'll go up there, knock and enter and I'll search the bloody place," she added, suitably enraged.

"No you won't."

"Watch me..." She grabbed the door handle and I grabbed her.

"Let go or I'll scream." I didn't release her.

"Listen to me then you can scream if you want. And if you scream and the police get called that's it, over and out, and a wasted trip."

"You got ten seconds, buster."

"If he's there, or even if he isn't right now, he must be able to tell us something about your sister. So let it ride for the time being. He might ring and give me a mouthful, or simply say he's never heard of her. Or he might ring with information. Or he might invite me back for a chat, then you can come with me. Whatever happens, if I don't hear we can both call next time. Let it lie for the while, Law, let it be. Wait and see; believe me, that'll make them more nervous than trying to barge in and being in the wrong."

Laura sat back and pondered my words.

"Okay, you get one chance. Don't sod me about, David Canbown, or you'll regret it, pal."

"Right, let's drive down the front and look across Morecambe Bay."

"What the muck for?"

"Because it's next to the station and I like trains."

"Drive on and enjoy your last moments alive." She was sneering and looking everywhere but at me, yet I had won this round and I breathed a sigh of relief.

We parked at the station and used the level crossing to reach the marshland beyond. Tyre tracks seemed to reach down the slope and out into the distant sea.

"With the local guide, and not without, you can walk right across the Bay from here."

"Yeah, I know. When I looked it all up it was suddenly in my bucket list somewhere  near the top. I think you can go with the guide on a tractor or something."

"Yes, I think you're right. I certainly wouldn't do it without the guide. People have died out there. Look at it, miles away to the other side. A fast inrushing tide and if you're caught it's curtains."

"Be curtains for you if you've messed up with Gary...."

Her warm, friendly words were cut short as the phone rang. No caller ID.

"You after Lorraine mate?"

"Yes."

"I don't know you and you don't know me. We leave it like that?"

"If whatever you have to tell me proves valid. Otherwise you'll be pleased to know I don't give up."

"Carlisle. Don't know where. Using the name Lucy Kenyon." The call ended and I put Laura in the picture. She threw her arms around my neck and kissed me passionately as an elderly couple tutted as they passed. It was altogether an odd event to occur in the middle of a level crossing.

"Right, let's go to Carlisle and find somewhere to stay."

"Double room?"

"You'll be lucky if we're in the same place after the way you spoke to me. And listen up. He could be selling us a bum-steer just to get us away from here."

"What else can we do?"

"Tell you what, let's do a spot of surveillance close to the house. Someone may be going out."

"Yeah, now you're talking my kind of language. And I'm sorry about what I said. You was right, Moncks, you was well right."

***

A generous measure of *Bruichladdich* sat as yet untouched on a small table in the compact lounge. However, it was the second sitting since the drinker had just despatched the predecessor and re-filled. The killer was celebrating diversity.

I think, in all seriousness, I should be able to blackmail Jayne-Marie Panahan for about three quarters of a million. That would nett me about six hundred thousand, as I need to keep Pratt on board. She's very useful and I'm pleased with her so a hundred and fifty thousand should do for her.

The killer needed the trusted associates and knew they had to be treated well. Making sure Yvonne Pratt was rewarded and happy was essential.

Now, I think I'll tackle Neville Gradling at the same time, then if I have to fire a warning shot I'll only need to take out one person. The news will travel. Seeing off someone close to Neville, for example, will also serve as a cautionary note to Ms Panahan, not just our Nev.

Gradling, Gradling ... now let me see. Not in the same class as Jayne-Marie so might have to settle for, say, five hundred thousand, fifty thousand of which to Mr Pickles, my own dear Mr Pickles. Oh he does get in a sweat over things. He could do with losing weight and having a bath! I'll get in touch and get him started on Neville. That'll make him sweat alright!

# Chapter Twenty Two

# Lorraine

I'm a shareholder in Carlisle Cathedral. Years ago I sponsored a brick in the wall as part of a money raising scheme, and have a photo showing my brick, yes *my* brick, as proof of ownership.

Nothing else happened at Kents Bank so we drove up to the Cumbrian city and found a decent city-centre hotel where we could get a night. But we would have to share a twin, that being the only room left. You cannot imagine Miss McCaffield's excitement. Well, perhaps you could.

The meandering journey northwards to Carlisle was a moving and captivating experience for the untraveled Laura who sat spellbound for mile after mile, almost incapable of taking in the beauty she was witnessing for the first time, unable to absorb the expansive loveliness spreading out and ever changing before her.

Our southbound journey, over the Kirkstone Pass, had stunned her beyond comprehension, but now she was realising there was a constantly varied spectacular panorama that attracted and thrilled millions of visitors to the region, which is why it is so popular.

Newby Bridge, at the southern end of Windermere, to Bowness was just the start, the aperitif to an astonishing series of revelations of scenery. Yes, she had seen some of the Derbyshire Dales and Peak District, and thought nothing could outdo such memories.

The gorge at Matlock Bath, where the Derwent charged between steep, soaring cliffs, twisting and turning, unwilling to check itself, in too much of a hurry to lap up the views, had found itself firmly imprinted on Laura's mind. Now she was in for a shock.

Ambleside, alive and crawling with bustling tourists, waited at the head of the lake that she had glimpsed from the road as it ran along the eastern shore of Windermere. And then she and David were past, and headed for Rydal Water. The scenery had changed again. David gave a brief account of his knowledge of Wordsworth, it being brief because, in all honesty, it was limited and he was unable to recount any verses. Nonetheless he regaled his companion with some pointless information relating to William Wordsworth and his sister Dorothy and the poet Samuel Taylor Coleridge, who often roamed these parts together.

Laura decided the word enchanting didn't do it justice when it came to our drive past Rydal Water but struggled to find better descriptions.

"It's like someone painted a picture of paradise from their imagination, like, then nature built the real thing taking the artist's picture as a guide." I had to admit Wordsworth might've had trouble putting it better than that. Nice one, Laura.

When Wordsworth left Dove Cottage Thomas Quincey, another poet, moved in. Laura was fascinated to hear that Quincey loved opium.

"Wow, did they have drugs then?"

"There have always, always been drugs Laura," David explained. "Nothing new under the sun."

Past Grasmere itself and a short diversion through the charming village and up to Dunmail Raise. Not a dramatic place. Nothing here to match the Kirkstone, Honister or Newlands Passes. Gentle slopes either side of the road gradually reared up and became mountains down which cascaded streams which, I explained to my companion, could be like torrents and waterfalls in winter or at any time after rain.

"There's a grade two listed building on your right," I pointed out.

"What, back there, the house?"

"No, there now, on your right."

"Give over, there's no building."

"Look again, what do you see?"

"Only an old AA phone box."

"You got it. A listed building."

"Wow. Does Dr Who come this way?"

Across the brow Thirlmere came into sight.

"Man-made, this one, a reservoir for Manchester. When they wanted to flood the valley there were protests and that led, indirectly, to the formation of the National Trust."

"Thirlmere ... Thirlmere ... let me think. Hey that's at the foot of Helvellyn, ain't it? And you can walk up there and land a plane there if I remember right."

"Something like that," I added with a smile.

Along the delightful St John's-in-the-Vale and right onto the A66, with me pointing out Skiddaw, Ol' Skidder as it's known, and Saddleback, named for obvious reasons, among the mountains in front of us. East towards Penrith and the M6 to Carlisle.

I'd phoned my contacts but knew nothing could be looked into until the next working day. This being Monday I resigned myself to enjoying Sunday in the Lake District and doing so with Lovely Lady Laura. She was overjoyed.

I said we would dress and undress in the bathroom.

"Not a lot of room for two people in there, Moncks."

"One at the time, Laura."

We rested and then washed and changed, ready for dinner. I was reading the paper when she emerged from the bathroom. She was wearing two tiny pieces of material that I was given to understand were called a bra and knickers. Gawd, how I wanted her!

She held up a bright dark blue dress in one hand, and a conservative blouse and navy skirt in the other.

"Which one you fancy, Moncks?"

"Skirt and blouse."

"Spoilsport."

"Okay, wear the dress. Why bother asking?"

"Hoped you get the right answer, and you didn't." And she was gone, back to the bathroom.

A vision of loveliness emerged. I was shocked for I had never seen her looking so beautiful, so alluring. I wanted to kneel before her and worship at her feet. I did the next best thing, so I thought, and praised her to the heavens. She looked so gorgeous, so desirable, so demure.

We enjoyed a fabulous dinner, with drinks beforehand, wine during, and liqueurs after. And thus stunned by a combination of beauty and alcohol I surrendered completely to that which must be. Unfortunately, from Laura's point of view, the latter sent me into a deep sleep, much to my partner's chagrin, and although only one bed was used, it was used for sleep. Miss McCaffield soon dropped off anyway, despite her disappointment.

In the morning I checked my phone and there was a text giving an address in Carlisle, and that put paid to any hopes of romance and/or passion before breakfast. Laura's desire to find Lorraine now overrode every other consideration. She was too excited to enjoy her breakfast but I had my money's worth. Yes sirree! At least we'd given up the nonsense about avoiding nakedness in front of each other.

"God, you're all man, Moncks. Can't wait till we're sober."

"Law, you're all woman, and I can't wait either, God save me."

What changed the picture was a call from Neville Gradling.

\*\*\*

Georgina Hayle couldn't bear it any longer. She wanted to see Leonora and Jason could go to hell.

Yvonne had submitted information to date, together with her bill, and a recommendation that Mrs Hayle terminate her appointment. In her email Ms Pratt apologised but said that she had unearthed very little that could be reasonably unchallenged by Mr Hayle, and that therefore he was covering his tracks too well if he was up to mischief (not her actual words).

It was hopeless. There was nothing in Yvonne's email that she could approach her husband with that would make any difference to the situation. In a moment of recklessness Georgina decided to tell the private eye the truth, and did so in the briefest of emails, adding this at the foot:

*I could kill him for his filthy, disgusting suggestion. Where's a serial killer when you want one? Missed my chance with that latest murder just down the road! Still, that isn't funny, I know. Please forgive.*

*Georgie*

Ms Pratt read the contents with interest and amusement. There wouldn't be any money to be made there even if Georgie, as she'd styled herself, was serious. The message confirmed payment by BACS and the termination of the appointment, and Yvonne sighed happily. Must remember, she thought, to send a few bob to David.

She sat back in her chair and studied the ceiling in the way of someone deep in thought, tapping her fingertips together as if trying to conjure up a magic genie. Let's look at this the other way round, she decided. Jason Hayle is rolling in it and despite my best efforts to uncover wrongdoing is keeping himself marginally legal in appearances. Yet he must be dealing in underhand operations.

He has offered a most intriguing and exciting solution to his wife's extra-marital shenanigans. Trust a man to want to watch two women. But that does suggest that Mr Hayle, as a very typical male, might be indulging himself with other ladies, especially as we wants to bed Miss Cuthbert as well as his wife.

And the more she considered it the more she sensed that money could be made by some means or other. Time to chat with Kenny Parrett; just conversation mind, but draw him a little on his investigations into Georgina and Leonora. Yes, that should do nicely.

*** 

Laura found the address on the device that I would've called a mobile phone. Perhaps I ought to have one of those. I checked the street map with the road atlas and we were there; who needs Satnav?

Pleasant enough; residential terraced, as I would call it, complete with small front gardens, but few properties with off-road parking. Being Sunday morning parking was, similar to that near Laura's flat, almost impossible, but we checked into a recently vacated spot a couple of minutes walk away. Once again I had to convince madam to stay put.

She was like a cat on a hot tin roof. I wondered how I would handle it if this was all nonsense or the wrong person. I rang the doorbell; it had an ear-piercing clang that could've woken the whole street. Minutes later a woman opened the door on the security chain, so I couldn't see her face.

"I'm looking for Lucy Kenyon."

"Who are you?" I knew that was coming and hadn't thought of any sensible answer in time.

"My name's David Canbown and here with Laura McCaffield, looking for her sister Lorraine." Yes, it was all or nothing, and I knew that this time there'd be no holding Laura back if I returned to say the door had been closed on me. But it wasn't.

"Laura? Here?"

"Yes, in the car."

"Bring her here and I'll let you in." That is what I did. Lucy, or rather Lorraine was waiting by the front room window. No mistake, the girls recognised each other and Lorraine spun round and came to the front door. She couldn't get the chain off fast enough, fumbled the door open and Laura was in. They hugged each other silly, crying and kissing, caressing wildly. I felt like a spare fart in a thunderstorm. I closed the door behind me.

"Would you like me to go for a walk?" I whispered. Both girls spoke at once.

"No, no, come in, come in," they urged with all earnestness, parting from their embrace and wiping their cheeks and noses. Lorraine pointed to the lounge which is where we sat, she next to her long lost sister.

My bill's in the post, I thought rather wickedly. Job done. Lorraine spoke first.

"This your bloke, sis?"

"Naw, but I'm working on him. Without him we wouldn't be here. Ace detectives we are, love."

"Oh Law, Law, I'm so pleased to see you, you can't imagine. Of all the people to turn up on my doorstep you are the one I could've most done with. Bless you, bless you."

"Why ain't you tried to find me, Lor?"

"Didn't think you'd want anything to do with me after I deserted you, Law."

"You silly sod. Come 'ere, you duffer." And they hugged with vigour afresh.

Lorraine looked like the photo we had and she was a dead ringer for the woman I saw in Matlock. It was quickly established she was living alone and renting, and working at a nearby petrol station. With equal alacrity it was disclosed that Laura was now a private eye, and it wasn't the time for me to be pedantic about the technicalities. Lorraine, red-eyed but exuding gladness in a most pretty way, was for a split second very obviously Laura's sister. Then the similarity vanished as rapidly as it had advanced.

I was struck by her simple attractiveness; taller than sis, she looked neat and tidy in a rather old-fashioned blouse and cardigan set, with a reddish tartan skirt. Thick brown tights and flat shoes completed the picture, dress-wise. The impression of neatness and cleanliness extended right down to her brown shoes that were highly polished; perhaps an odd thing to notice but I did.

Like Laura she had a round, likeable face that could change easily to reflect sadness or joy according to her mood. When cheerful her face lit up and her eyes shone and I could see they were sisters, two peas in a pod.

After a mish-mash of conversation between them Lorraine went to the kitchen to rescue a bottle of red she'd been keeping for a special occasion, and been keeping for over two years she said. I was given the task of working the corkscrew which I tried to master in the true style of an alpha male and got into real difficulties, cutting my finger into the bargain. I tried to hide my wound and my dented pride.

Laura rescued me and opened the bottle with ease and a look that said 'you big nelly, can't even open a bottle of wine unless it's a screw-top'. They wanted to tell each other their life histories and, in their eagerness, do so at the same time. Quickly they sorted themselves out and Laura went first. You more or less know her story, so here is Lorraine's which followed, and in her own words, initially told between sniffles and nose-blowings.

"I was goody-two-shoes, wasn't I? Did everything right by mum and dad. Got what I wanted and I often got you into trouble, didn't I?" Laura smiled, almost sadly as the memories returned. "Did well at school, remember that? The sun shone didn't it, little sis?

"You got into serious trouble almost as soon as you were out of your pram, Law, and you got into them drugs and things. Mum and dad loved you, never stopped loving you, just hated you for what you became. And like you know when they died the house got left to me, cos they knew you'd waste any money you came into. And they weren't wrong, were they pet?" Laura's facial expression didn't change one iota, and she made no sound, no movement, nothing to show agreement or otherwise.

"I bet you hated me, getting all the dosh from the sale. It won't make you feel any better but I wasted most of it too. Because, you know what Law, I got into trouble big time. You were attracted to money, I was attractive because of it. Like you, in so many ways, I got in with the wrong bloke, well, blokes. Guys who knew I'd got money.

"You might remember Terry, my first real love. Got a lovely home together, planned a family, but it didn't happen. Then we went for tests and it turned out to be me. It was me, I couldn't have kids, couldn't have the children and family I'd yearned for. And you know what that bastard did?

"Told me if I couldn't have a baby I was no use to him and packed me in. Where'd love come into that? Tell me that, where'd love come into it? I pleaded with him, because I thought I loved him, said we could apply to adopt and he said he wasn't having no other sod's unwanted child. It was then that I realised how awful he truly was. Anyways, I'm pleased I never married him.

"There wasn't a lot of money in our home. Mostly mortgage. I hadn't come into the lolly then. But it was split when the place was sold and I rented a flat. Thought I might buy me own place outright, and then decided I wanted to get right away, be shot of Kent, make a fresh start. The firm I worked for had a branch at a place called Hemel Hempstead, you heard of it?" Laura gave the faintest of nods, a tiny gesture.

"So I got me a transfer and rented a flat for the time being, y'know, until I could be sure I wanted to settle there. Met this guy, Robbie, bit persistent he was, but all romantic, but I was so wary after Terry I suppose I mucked up and he packed me in. My fault. Knew I was going to have to get over the business about Terry and not being able to have kids. Ali came along, and he was real nice. Took his time wooing me, very gentle, no rush like.

"He moved in with me then the fun started. I thought I'd found someone I could share my heart with but he used me. Then the rough stuff started, you know, when he couldn't get his own way. I came to the conclusion all men were like this, and I'd just got to put up with it, probably like all women have to, I don't know. Turned out he was a crook. He tried to get me on the drugs, Law, but no way, not for me. I wanted to throw him out of my flat but didn't know how.

"If I'd threatened him he'd have walloped me good and proper." Laura had barely moved and her expression hadn't changed, but the first sign of tears had appeared and the first drop made good its escape and trickled slowly down her right cheek. She was sharing her sister's pain, not just in the telling of the story, but in knowing what it is like to be in thrall to a violent man.

"He started getting me to do things, like shoplifting to start with. He called me his artful dodger, the bastard. Eventually I got caught but got a caution, but it frightened the life out of me. Didn't want to go to prison, Law. That night I told him it was over and to go, so he gave me a beating, raped me, and beat me again, just to make sure.

"But at least he stopped getting me involved in his crimes, and a couple of days later I met Gary, Gary Wimbush. He was so kind, but it seems to me they all are when they want you. We got on so well and eventually I told him everything. That night he threw Ali out for me. There was a real fight. I was afraid cos Ali looked a bruiser, so big and strong, but Gary took him on, had a few good moves on him, and battered Ali to the floor. Knew what he was doing, like.

"Think Gary knew self-defence, but he knew what he was about. Ali never stood a chance.

"For a moment I felt like a princess, being fought over like, and my knight in shining armour had come to my rescue. So then Gary moved in, and he was really okay. Cut a long story short we got married and bought a tiny house nearby. He wasn't worried about not having kids, said he felt sorry for me, but he loved me just as I was and all that.

"I found out by accident he was into crime too, been stealing cars to order for some gang. When I challenged him he said just to keep out of it, if I don't know anything like, I'd be alright with the law. I pleaded with him to pack it in. He said he would if I'd finance a business he wanted to start. I still had some money left, you see, cos we'd bought the house with a small mortgage on top of what I put in up front.

"But when he told me everything it turned out he wanted to buy an existing business in Barrow-in-Furness. I ask you! I had to look it up on the map. Never heard of it. Told him he'd got to be joking, but he was very persuasive in that lovely kind way of his. He was never violent with words or fists, I'll say that for him. I wrestled with me thoughts for days and then agreed; another fresh start, and at least I had me a husband. Just hoped I'd get a job up there.

"So we sold up, bought a place there and he started his business. Oh sis I can't tell you how happy I was. But happiness don't last in life, does it? He started seeing other women, broke my heart it did. Then right out of the blue he said he was leaving me for some bitch in Grange-over-Sands or somewhere. He sold his business but I didn't get a penny. The divorce was bad and the money got split pretty much equal.

"That was me money gone up in smoke. Not got enough to buy a place now and never will have.

"Came up here cos I thought it was best place to find a job. Had a few, but this one up the garage suits me. All kinds of hours, not overnight though, the gaffer won't let a woman be there overnight, and I'm well liked and enjoy it. Often work with another girl, Suzy, and we've become best mates. Both been treated bad by blokes, and you have too Law.

"Not a day goes by I don't think about you, but never dared dream you'd ever want to see me again......" And the words tailed away as the sisters embraced once more, heartily, lovingly, tearfully. The sobbing became louder, the embracing more intense, and I crept quietly from the room, for this was a private grief and a very private time.

I went and made myself a cup of coffee and sat in the small kitchen. The house interior, I'd noticed, was in poor repair with wallpaper starting to peel on the lounge walls, the paper itself sporting the odd stain. Lorraine kept the kitchen clean and tidy but it was in need of some decent maintenance. She was doing her best, but she had a disinterested landlord. I did notice there was a crucifix on one lounge wall and another on the wall in the kitchen. Curious. It didn't mean anything then, but it stuck in my mind for future reference.

Looking out the back window I just happened to notice the glass recycling bin and to my surprise two empty whisky bottles. Not any old Scotch mind. Ardbeg and Laphroaig. 10-year-old single malts. Lorraine's tipple? Expensive tastes for a garage forecourt assistant! Did it point to a hitherto unmentioned boyfriend? From what she'd been saying a boyfriend seemed unlikely. This was a bit baffling. Like the crucifixes it stayed locked in my mind.

I checked my phone and had a voicemail from Gradling. He sounded agitated. I'd spoken to him and he's asked me to call on him as soon as I was back in Kent. As if to try and hurry me along he said he'd re-hire me at whatever rate I wanted, but he needed help. Now he'd left a further message and this was bordering on despair. Were the police on his case again? I phoned back.

"David, thank God it's you. Look, I know I'm a nuisance, but something's come up and I need you because you'll have the right answers. I can't go to the police. I've got to take you into my confidence, get your advice. Can't do this on the phone."

"Mr Gradling ....."

"It's Neville, or call me Nev, whatever."

"Neville, sorry if this is blunt but you're wasting your time with me if this is anything less than legal, I'm not interested. I'm an ex-cop and I still uphold the law. If you're going to tell me something....."

"No, no, no, nothing like that. Look, let's start with a one-off consultation. I just want to put something hypothetical to you, understand? That's all. Just give me some advice, some information."

"Right Neville, a one-off. Seventy-five pounds cash on the day. I'll be there tomorrow evening. Is that okay, and is anytime fine, for example late evening?"

"Yeah whatever you say, David. Just give me some warning that's all I ask, a bit of notice. Use the intercom on the gate when you get here, park behind the Lotus."

"Thanks. But first mention of anything illegal and I'm off. Got it?"

"Yeah whatever you say. Safe journey." And he rang off.

I didn't like this one little bit, but I could pick up seventy-five quid cash in hand simply for paying him a visit. Of course there was something illegal behind it! This was Neville Gradling. Park to the rear of the Lotus, yes of course, I'll leave my Roller right there!

"Moncks, Lorraine and I want to be alone please. Thanks for going out when you did, but would you mind leaving us be for a while, go get something to eat? We'll have a bite here. Perhaps you could bring some more wine back?" Laura's head had appeared around the kitchen door. I made a suggestion:

"How about champagne? There's something to celebrate." Her eyes lit up.

"Jeez Moncks! Yes please. Wow."

"Okay, I'll go and find some lunch. I've got my phone if you need me and I won't be far away, but any idea what time you'd like me back?"

"Early afternoon if you're bringing dwinkies!"

"Whatever you want to do is okay by me, but I've got to be back in Kent tomorrow and I'll be leaving after breakfast. If you want to stay here overnight I'll pick you up in the morning."

"Yay, sounds good to me. But you'll have to sleep alone at the hotel."

"I'll get over it. And anyway I can't drink and drive can I?"

"Nope, so all the dwink for me and sis, huh?"

Yes, very true. At least I might get a quiet pint or two tonight.

# Chapter Twenty Three
# Destiny Beckons

Daryl Pequeman was struggling to come to terms with the loss of his wife and succeeding in the pursuit of becoming alcohol dependent.

It wasn't supposed to be like this. Once John Holgarve was dead he would win his beloved Rosie back for sure. He would forgive her with kisses and kindness, and help her to share love with him again, allowing her time to grieve and time to rebuild their relationship. It had been Gordon Pembrake's disgusting movie that had turned him into a rabid, hate-filled moron, he knew that now.

So overcome with loathing for dear Rosie and her lover, when he now realised he had loved her all the time, he had grown obsessed with the idea of a world without John Holgarve. He had discovered that money, a great deal of it, could be used in an underhand way to achieve that aim.

They'd promised him his involvement would be untraceable.

His hatred for Rosie was a facade, born of anger, blind rage, grief and emotional agony. He knew that too well now, when it was too late. How he loved her, wanted her back.

It wasn't supposed to be like this.

He poured another whisky and sent it packing, down in one, and re-filled his glass. Again. His vision was beginning to swim, his mind was an equivalent blur. In his anguish he wanted to confess all, go to the police and give himself up, pay the price.

It was only the thought of spending the rest of his life in prison that stopped him.

No such worries clouded the mind of Nathan Kethnet in north Devon. For one thing his wife was still alive. No question of suicide for Cathy who had far too much to live for. Besides Edward Nobbs was loved only in so far as he provided an exciting diversion from the one-dimensional Nathan. His loss was not worth grieving over, although tears had been shed, more for the loss of an intoxicating paramour than her heart.

Jayne-Marie Panahan too had nothing to reproach herself for. Her love rival's heart had been brutally pierced and killed off, and she had William exactly where she wanted him, where he was pleased to be, pleased he had 'got away with one'. Certainly not a potential suicide victim!

In Kent Neville Gradling had been smiling contentedly with the success of his mission, but suddenly he'd been faced with a horror he didn't need and hadn't anticipated. He knew what he must do; talk to that private eye he'd employed, just for advice, that was all. It was unlikely self-righteous David Canbown would want to get mixed up in it, but he might. After all, everyone has their price! Money can buy people, money can buy results.

And in Suffolk the time was approaching when Jayne-Marie was going to be beset by a similar problem. Or perhaps that should be nightmare?

***

I spent the afternoon with the sisters, who nattered interminably, sobbed and cuddled occasionally, and drank champagne freely as in my generosity two bottles had been supplied. Then I drove back to the hotel. With Laura staying on I was going to pick her up in the morning, so I had the task of packing her things, quite an illuminating task. Something was niggling. What was it? Nothing to do with Laura's possessions.

It was over cheese and biscuits in the restaurant later, and while I was devouring a particularly tasty piece of Shropshire Blue, that it hit me. No mention of Matlock. Lorraine's story didn't include Derbyshire and neither I nor my buddy remembered it and asked. She said they high-tailed it straight from Hemel Hempstead to Barrow, and yet we had information she and Gary lived in the area with her leaving him then because of his wanderings.

Curious and worrying. It wasn't a slight error or a question of misunderstanding what had been said. A whole chapter was missing. Lorraine clearly said Gary had pushed off to live with another woman and divorce followed, yet my contacts found no record of them having been divorced.

Now she was living as Lucy Kenyon, which she admitted to, in order to keep a safe distance from her past. Puzzling.

Maybe the subject came up last night. Surely Laura would've told her all about our coming to Matlock, and indeed about how we'd tracked her down. So perhaps she asked. I'd tackle her on the way home.

Jaw, jaw, jaw. It was hard to get Laura away but once in the car there was non-stop one-way dialogue about their evening, their lives and just about everything you could think of. I had to negotiate about sixteen miles on the M6, and if that's all I ever have to drive on the wretched motorway before I die that will have been sixteen miles too many. Mind you, it's not a bad stretch, but when you're getting earache it seems like a hundred miles.

Onto the A66 at Penrith she finally paused for breath and I took my chance and jumped in.

"Lorraine didn't mention Matlock, did she? Only when she told us her story it jumped from Hemel Hempstead to Barrow. And is she actually divorced?"

"You suspicious brat! That's my sister you're talking about. She ain't a liar. Just an oversight, I expect...."

"Big oversight, forgetting a whole chapter of your life. Don't forget Kenny told us she left Gary for his philandering, so he'd heard, while still in Derbyshire."

"You having a go because we didn't sleep together last night and you were looking forward to your big chance? You *have* got the rats, going on about my poor sister like that."

"Well, I was just asking. I thought that maybe it was something private and you got round to discussing it while I wasn't there. You know, perhaps it was embarrassing for her, or she wanted to tell you about something so bad she didn't want me to know. That's fair enough. The only reason I was asking." I stopped asking, Laura stopped talking, and I carried on driving.

We went into Brough for a paper and a comfort stop, then over the Pennines and down to Scotch Corner. Over coffee she apologised profusely.

"Look, I'm sorry Moncks. It's bin an emotional time for me. Big emotions, and I'm dying to see her again. It was me what got the rats because I knew in me heart of hearts you was right. And no, we didn't talk about it, and I'd forgotten about it."

"Didn't you tell her how we'd traced her, y'know, even been to Matlock looking for her?"

"Yeah, told her a bit about our search, but we had so much else to chat about, and we got drunk anyway. Tell the truth she looked very alarmed when I said you thought you'd seen in her in Matlock, y'know, I said, same time as that bloke got murdered. She said it couldn't have been her, she wasn't there. But her living there, no never came up."

South the A1 and Laura locates a radio station broadcasting ear-shattering thump-thump music which even she doesn't like but doesn't re-tune, just turns the sound down.

"Want me to ask her, Moncks?"

"What about?"

"Blimey, Matlock of course."

"If you want. If you're as curious as I am. Leave it up to you."

225

"Spose it's not very important, is it?"

"Good job you're not driving having got drunk. Does Lorraine drive?"

"Yeah, but her motor's poorly, off the road at the mo. Still, says she don't go out much, gets a lot of basic stuff from her garage, y'know, there's like a mini-market. She runs that too when she's on duty. There's some serious traffic here, babycakes. We could've gone straight down the M6 according to my map."

"I know, but this is better and don't think the M6 is quieter than this. It's Monday and everybody and his brother is on the road."

"Yeah, and everybody and her sister...."

We lunched at services, Laura having to subsequently buy some beer to drink on the move, there being no alcohol available in the self-service restaurant. Then she dozed peacefully and I surreptitiously turned off the radio.

As fate would have it we hit the M25 and the Dartford Crossing right at the evening peak, the perfect end to a delightful weekend in the Lake District. So it was very much later, having dropped my companion off, that I reached Chez Gradling.

I parked behind the Lotus and found Neville waiting at the front door. It was a bit like being escorted through a security check; cameras everywhere, outer and inner front doors, both heavy duty by the look of them, and I even felt conscious that he could be visually checking me for concealed weapons!

Jackie waltzed by in something vaguely similar to a negligee but a great deal smaller in all dimensions. Neville was watching me though whether it was because he wanted to know I appreciated his wife for her very obvious feminine charms, or as a warning not to look at all I couldn't say. I guessed the latter and kept my eyes glued to his.

In the lounge .... sorry, in *one* of the lounges he bade me sit in an all-enveloping armchair that I sank helplessly into. It was so comfortable that after all the rigours of the drive I could've dropped straight off to sleep.

"Drink?" I declined. He poured a large brandy and settled down opposite me.

"I expect you're wondering why I've asked you to call." Oh God, the clichés, I thought. Of course I'm bloody wondering why you've got me in, you dollop. I nodded my reply and waited while he sipped a good mouthful of his drink. It was then I noticed what a large brandy he had.

"Right, nothing illegal, okay. Look, we're men of the world, you know how it is. I'm wealthy and got to be wealthy and stay wealthy by looking after my money properly. Now this guy, guy I've trusted before, finds a handy way to ensure I pay less tax. Him and me both. Now there's nothing illegal about not paying over the top to HMRC, is there?" Before I could comment he continued.

"So I've done really well thanks to him. But now he's trying to blackmail me. Says he'll go to the police if I don't pay up, and he wants more than I saved on tax, a whole lot more and then the rest, if you know what I mean. Should I pay up?" I looked straight at him and instantly knew this was nothing about tax, so could it be to do with the murder of Bourne-Lacey?

"I'll tell you this, Neville, pay up and your guy will be back for more. That's usually the way blackmailers work. You said this guy benefited from the scheme as well?"

"Right."

"Well then, there's nothing to stop you shopping him is there? Try that. If he ditches you in it say you'll stitch him up too."

"Problem with that, David, is that he's threatening violence and not against me, against a family member. Nobody specified."

"You just said he'd go to the police if you don't pay, and there'd be no point doing that if he was going to hurt a loved one. Doesn't make sense." I watched him so closely that I was convinced by the way he appeared that this was the killer blackmailing him, or trying to.

I was right. He'd hired an assassin to take out Bourne-Lacey and the killer wanted some more money, quite possibly tens of thousands. HMRC was going to be the least of his problems! The police had searched his world top to bottom and found nothing significant, so there were two unsolved mysteries. How was the enquiry and 'booking' made, and how was payment achieved?

"Look David, I hear what you're saying, but I'm a worried man."

"You've got an impossible choice, Neville. Go to the police, in which case your activities will have to come out, pay up and wait for the next demand and the one after, or use your contacts and arrange for the proverbial 'boys' to make him a visit." He smiled. Then he laughed quietly.

"Yes, I could always do that. Trouble is, he could put his own 'boys' onto my family. Anyway, that's helpful enough for now, but hope I can call on you if I need any more, shall we say 'advice'?" He stood and I made three valiant attempts to follow suit but the armchair was not giving me up so easily. Neville was right by me when I finally made it upright. He held out some notes. "Hundred, David. For now." I ignored the proffered money and his comment.

"You've qualified for a freebie on our frequent flyer programme, Neville. Have this one on me. No offence. I'm happy; sadly I can't give you any other advice right now. If you try and call his bluff, as I hope you'll do, let me what happens by all means."

He showed me out without another word, not even goodbye. Yet I knew I'd hear from him again. So much for a consultation over a hypothetical situation. This was real.

I also knew only too well I'd got to tell Okafor something, *something*.

***

"Sorry, Mrs Bailey, but that's the way the cookie crumbles, as they say."

In deepest Suffolk a startled and stunned Jayne-Marie Panahan was also facing up to the prospect of being blackmailed. She was so staggered by what she'd just heard that she didn't even realise Yvonne Pratt had called her by her married name.

"I'll let you know payment arrangements and, as you can probably guess, I can always let the police know what we both know. Or alternatively my colleague can stab someone else through the heart. No, not you, my dear Jayne-Marie, just someone you love, that sort of thing." And she was gone leaving Ms Panahan, as she preferred to be called, open mouthed and speechless.

In Devon, and having researched his subject exhaustively, as was his wont, John Wapernod decided to abandon being suspicious about Kenny Parrett and moved on to being suspicious about Yvonne Pratt.

A man built for intricate examinations of tiny details he delved into all he could lay his hands on regarding the redoubtable Yvonne. He studied her website photo, according to her professionally taken to hide physical defects and to enhance the appearance of a no-nonsense, efficient private investigator. Yes, it was her, and the camera, which supposedly cannot lie, had done the required job he had to admit.

But it was also a facade. An impression. Yes, she came over as a woman of mental strength and appreciable attractiveness, but the real Yvonne was missing. By that he meant that the camera had told porkies in relation to the actual person. The more he thought about it the more it became an enigma, the more he found it impossible to explain.

He looked at his own photo, very matter of fact by comparison. A good picture, yes, and he thought modestly it showed honesty and integrity, as well as a man of good and strong character. He would be instantly recognisable, and that was the difference between his photo and Yvonne's.

Would a private eye really want to make herself unrecognisable? Possibly, for it would ensure anonymity when working. Leaving aside the websites John embarked on more searching through the computer. She was on Facebook and Twitter, but nothing obvious there. It was later in the day that, acting on impulse, he tried to find her elsewhere, for he knew where and how to look, and thus he made a most interesting discovery. One to be relayed to David Canbown urgently.

But could even he be trusted?

***

"So Steph, we now know Nobbs was strangled with rope because he was into bondage, and that wraps it all up, if you'll forgive my sense of humour, as far as weapons are concerned. What warped people we're dealing with."

"I know Holton; it frightens me. But now it's all out in the open, national publicity and all, I still reckon the killer will lie low for a while. It doesn't help solve the crimes but it buys us time before another victim dies. Anyway, have you spoken to Canbown yet?"

"Yeah, but no joy there; waste of time. Changing the subject, give me your home email then I'll send those holiday snaps I promised."

DS Broome realised immediately what Okafor was up to, what he really meant, and reeled off her private email. What DS Holton Okafor had to say regarding Canbown was off the record in every sense. They discussed other details and Broome agreed to keep Geoff Alcock in Devon, and their colleagues in Derbyshire, in the loop.

It was Derbyshire that provided a nugget of information about the same time.

Detective Inspector Ray Drunbolt was on the receiving end of Stephanie Broome's call. He listened to the update although he was already familiar with the position from the system. This was a properly co-ordinated effort. Then he spoke.

"Stephanie, let's recap. Kethnet, Gradling and Panahan fit the bill as wealthy self-made people of power and influence. With the exception of yours, Panahan, they've been searched and interrogated with nothing short of lighted matches under the fingernails. And even Panahan's had a good grilling. They're holding up, perhaps unsurprisingly. That means they think they're in the clear and we can't touch 'em. You said yourself you dare not go and search your woman.

"The odd-man-out is our guy, Daryl Pequeman. Yes, successful architect, plenty of money, but not in the same class as the other three. Not the same type of person at all. He's the only one to lose his spouse in the immediate aftermath,

229

right? I've chatted to him, questioned him at the outset, and I think he's heading for a breakdown.

"He's a completely different animal from the other three. I've just got this funny feeling that he's a few short steps from confessing. The trouble is we don't know how to push him down those steps, and we've got to keep one eye on his mental health at the same time. It could be that Rosie committing suicide will mean we'll get a breakthrough.

"Not everyone here agrees with me. Call it intuition, but I think Daryl will break, but it could backfire in court."

"Don't I know it, Ray ... sorry ... sir." He laughed.

"It's Ray. We're all in this together. Just call me Ray"

"Thanks. You're right though. Every step we take we're checking that we're doing it by the book."

"You're telling me. But if I can get through to this joker I will. We're pulling in some consultant, psychologist whatever, to advise the way forward. Give me a trusty truncheon any day." It was Stephanie's turn to laugh.

"Okay Ray, good luck, and let me know." And Ray Drunbolt set off to follow his intuition and with a consultant in tow.

Good coppers know when they're on to something.

***

I slept like a log, had a refreshing shower, prepared breakfast and sang while I did so, and sat down to enjoy my tomatoes on toast. The sun was shining and I knew it was about time I did plenty in the garden. But first work.

On the pot lid front I'd had a response from a lady in Loughborough who claimed to possess the missing article, and what was I prepared to pay for it?

I rang one of my contacts on the force who I knew would access some data from the DVLA for me. I was curious about Lorraine and wanted to know about her licence, and also if she was the registered keeper of a vehicle. When you are using contacts like this you are putting their jobs at risk, so I always tell them not to do anything they don't want to do, I'll quite understand.

Basically they'll only do what they know they can get away with, and only tell me what they feel justified in doing. They generally will not tell me things that they consider should remain outside my knowledge. Adam had been different on that one occasion, and I put that down to genuine friendship and the certain surety that I would not breathe a word of it to anyone, and never say where such intelligence came from. He was also concerned for me.

There was another job enquiry to be followed up, something to do with a missing person, and I didn't want to miss out. Lorraine, as a non-earning case, had eaten up resources including some of my savings, and it was high time for some financial input. I wanted to kick myself for refusing Gradling's hundred quid, but that was a point of principle and my principles need a good kicking!

A text arrived from the inevitable quarter, asking when we were next on the job and I had no trouble ignoring it. I've found your sister, now leave me alone, I wanted to reply, but I didn't.

The odd thing was that we'd slept together for one night. And sleep was all we did, snuggled up together in a single bed, with me admitting to myself that it had been a magical experience, the warmth, having someone to cuddle, feeling a body next to mine. All the little things that make the sun shine in your life, put a smile on your face, and make you feel good about yourself, about the world and everything in it.

And I wanted to experience it again. But not from lust. Simply because I wanted to be snuggled up tight to Laura again, warm, happy, content. Could life ever be that wonderful? Probably not. Reality lies waiting and my rented garden lay waiting too.

I mowed the lawn, trimmed the edges, did some dead-heading and went back inside for coffee and chaos. To be in the garden may be a sojourn in a small piece of paradise, but to return to the office is to find Hades.

Two voicemail's from Laura, one from John Wapernod, another from Holton Okafor and an email from my potential client spelled trouble all round. And I wasn't far wrong.

*** 

Stephanie Broome was positively living for the investigation. Was it wrong to feel elation and the throb of the adrenalin boost over such appalling crimes? Surely not, not if you joined the force for the right reasons. She'd looked in the mirror in the bathroom that morning and decided the work had put colour in her cheeks. She'd never felt better, healthier and fitter, and it was the thought of solving these hideous murders that had provided the basis for this progress in life.

Mentally she was right on the button. Four killings had done that. No, of course it didn't seem right and proper, not right to feel the exhilaration of knowing you may be closing in for an arrest, not right to feel on top of the world because you were near to outwitting a master criminal. Deep down inside she knew that they weren't reaching that point just yet, but her intuition, her female intuition, her police officer's intuition, all told her it was nigh.

She refused to let disappointment and frustration make her feel down. Nothing must be allowed to dent and smother these delicious sensations. She must ride on them until the killer was behind bars. That's why she became an officer and why she was now a rising detective, ready for the next climb up the promotion ladder. Stephanie Broome was made for leadership and longed to hold a rank that put her in charge. Depression wasn't in her vocabulary.

In the same way her job ruled her private life and nothing would ever stand in its way. Yes, there had been boyfriends, but nothing serious. Stephanie was convinced that no long term relationship would ever happen and that allied itself comfortably to her desire to avoid children. She was not the sort of woman who believed you could combine a top post with a family, and that did not upset her in any way. The 'side' wasn't being let down; it was her choice, nothing more. Children simply didn't figure in the Sergeant's long term plan.

Her bosses had marked her out for high station and were giving her every support. It didn't bother her that others might solve this nasty rash of murders; as long as she was actively involved, perhaps even provided vital clues, that was good enough for her. Not for a moment did she consider personal success as the proverbial 'feather in the cap'. Police work was about team work, but every team has a leader, and that was the place she wished to inhabit.

Right now a vital clue was about to land her lap and it was all down to persistence. By coincidence she chose to call on Ms Panahan shortly after the woman had received her blackmail notification.

I won't let her go, she thought, as she drove out to Grayden's Optics. I know she doesn't want to see me, and I've got to come up with a good excuse for this visit, but if she hired a killer then I want to keep at her. Phoning for the appointment she'd mentioned only that additional information was needed, and as it related to her husband she might prefer a one-to-one. She'd managed to make it sound as if she was doing Jayne-Marie a favour. Jayne-Marie surrendered and said she'd spare Broome five minutes only.

All I need, Stephanie agreed with herself, as she charged out of the building and into her car. Just want to keep the pressure up. The Suffolk countryside, more used to farming and attracting tourists, sped by unnoticed. Pigs in a field paid no more attention to her than she did to them; both continued on their respective life paths.

Onward to destiny.

## Chapter Twenty Four
# The Quiet before the Storm

"Had to search, David, and I'm not saying how I came by all this but it's on the top line I can assure you."

It's difficult to tell over the phone but I sensed John Wapernod was nervous, probably worried that he might be sharing his findings with the wrong person.

"If you'd rather not tell me I won't be offended, because I think there's some real worries out there. So please don't fret over it, John, I really won't be offended."

"No, I think you're okay, maybe about as much as you feel I'm okay."

"I know what you mean. Don't you just get the idea that someone's watching over us, and I'm not talking about the police. Well, I hope I'm not!"

"Somewhere along the line we have to take a chance, don't we David? So here goes."

John's voice rarely betrayed any emotion and today was no different.

"Couple of little snippets apropos Yvonne Pratt. Years ago, before she became a private eye, she was arrested at a demonstration that turned violent, in the Midlands. Public order offence, conditional discharge. It was a womens' rights march. Then, not so very long ago, she may have had a page on her website relating to womens' rights issues, and stating that she could look into any aspects that required investigation.

"Page no longer there, but you can find a search engine reference to it, details as I've explained, but you can't get any further. So it's reasonable to assume Ms Pratt has a cause to support, and nothing wrong with that. But I've been delving into things not everyone can.

"And I believe I may have found a dark side to our Yvonne. I can't say for sure but a few things tie up, not least the similarity between one of her website pictures and one on another site. A hidden site. At first you might be forgiven for thinking she's a prostitute, but why hide away? Surely you'd want business?

"I am unable to dig deeper, nature of the operation if you follow me. But it looks sinister, unpleasant. I came across the line '*Let me lure you to … your death? … your endless pleasure!*' and I remembered I was reading about a respected private investigator, if it's her. The name of this lady, her stage name of course, was Eve Parr. Not a million miles from Yvonne Pratt."

"So, John, you could be telling me in order to spread misinformation."

"Indeed I could. Trust has become a horrible word in all this. Everybody's unhappy about everyone else, and I share your misgivings. You have to decide whether to *trust* me." He spoke the word 'trust' very slowly and emphasised it in a particular manner, a manner that suggested a lack of suspicion on his part. I had to take it at face value.

"Anything on Parrett?"

"Not a sausage, David. So I turned my attention to a potential *femme fatale*, if you'll forgive the expression. By the way, have you checked me out?"

"No John, not felt the need."

"I've dug into you, David, which is why I'm sharing these tidbits. Hope you're not offended?"

"I'd have been surprised if you hadn't."

"So why haven't you looked into me?"

"Call it a copper's nose, but maybe I will now. No, as you said, trust is a difficult thing, but trust has to start somewhere and you've never done anything suspicious. Until now!"

"Understand, understand. You're right. We have to start somewhere."

"Will you be looking at Yvonne further?"

"Possibly, but I must get on with some money-making work now."

"Yes, me too. Thanks John. Catch you soon; and I'll call if I learn anything."

We said our goodbyes. So Yvonne was into womens' rights, no problem there, but how would that square with her operating in a field you wouldn't normally associate with a womens' rights activist? Now that really would be a puzzle. Maybe John had the wrong woman; he wasn't totally sure.

Then there was John himself. Could he have made it up to see who I would share it with, perhaps Yvonne herself? Worrying times, but I did need to press on. The missing person first, because business takes pride of place right this minute.

Ye gods! It transpired I'd be looking for a woman's missing sister. Aarghh! But I said I'd be pleased to act, was told my fees were reasonable, and that my potential client would like to meet me before proceeding. Later in the day at her home in Minnis Bay, north Kent, was agreed.

Before that there was more to be done. No doubt Holton Okafor would be after a meeting in some remote part of the planet, but that might be to my advantage of course. No doubt Laura McCaffield would be after a meeting in a remote part of her bed!

Otherwise it was to prove a day of revelations and discoveries. John's news was just the start.

***

I have only one regret, the killer concluded, that I couldn't slay that Bailey chap instead of his mistress. Jayne-Marie doesn't deserve a rat like him. Men are such filthy animals, disgusting creatures. Sad about Rosie, but then she was committing adultery. Yet is it not the fault of their husbands that they fall prey to nasty beings? John charmed his way into her bed and then made her a slave with his drugs, vile bastard, but he could only achieve that because she wasn't happy with hubby.

Strange about the Panahan woman. It was the other way round, but there again we are talking about two very busy, very successful business people, both wealthy in their own right. So in a way I can't understand how he found time for Phyllis! I'd like to think he led Ms Downport a right old dance, probably an ace conman, just one more horrid male specimen, for he certainly worked his magic when it came to her will!

There, Jayne-Marie gets her man back and a heap of cash to boot, as they used to say. I feel perfectly justified in having a share since I made it all possible. And that's where I shall concentrate my efforts for the time being; leave murder on the back burner. Now, come to think of it, it's about time I heard from dear Mr Pickles. I do hope he's not experiencing trouble with Neville bloody Gradling.

***

Ms Panahan made it only too obvious she was extremely busy, the police had interviewed her time and again, surely they had all they wanted, and they should now leave her alone. Her solicitor would be in touch, they could be sure of that.

In fact, to Stephanie Broome she appeared every inch a guilty party.

"Why did you choose Ms Pratt as your private eye?" The question was flung at JMP with lightning speed and it took her by surprise. She was so bound up in making protest that she barely saw any significance in the enquiry. This eliminated any thinking time, so determined was she to answer swiftly and be rid of her visitor.

"She's a woman for one thing and we share similar beliefs when it comes to the obnoxious nature of the opposite sex," she blurted out before her brain caught up with her mouth.

"Is Mr Bailey obnoxious by that reckoning, ma'am?"

"How dare you, get out this minute....."

"How did you know you shared similar beliefs before you approached her?" Stephanie's voice was deliberately soft, the words carefully and gently enunciated. Jayne-Marie Panahan, eyes glowering, cheeks reddening, fists clenching by her side, once more ordered Broome out.

"You'll hear more of this my girl," she stormed, her voice almost a shriek.

"You mean, ma'am, you'll get one of my useless male bosses to tear this woman off a strip?" JMP looked like a rabbit caught in a car's headlights, and just about as motionless and stupefied.

She slumped down in her chair, much to Broome's surprise. Her eyes were still wide open, but now with shock not anger. But the greater shock was to be the Sergeant's, for Ms Panahan suddenly shook and started to cry, except there were few tears, just a horrible kind of wailing noise as she buried her face in her hands.

"Go now, go now," she whimpered through her fingers as she made a weird show of sobbing, but Broome wasn't finished.

"You knew Yvonne before you booked her, you knew her in some other way, there's another connection." Jayne-Marie looked up sharply, screwed her now tear-stained face into one displaying rage, and roared at the Sergeant:

"Yes, we were friends, and that's all. Now clear out." Stephanie Broome left the room and was almost smiling as she made her way downstairs and back to Reception. She might not have won much on her lottery, but she had a small prize and she treasured that, something more to look into especially if she was right that JMP hired the assassin.

As far as the assassin was concerned a wee problem had arisen. Mr Pickles reported back that Neville Gradling was in fighting mode. He wasn't paying but he was ready to shop the guilty if any further action was taken against him or his family. This was not music to the killer's ears, but there was greater concern that Mr Pickles, rather than use any skill he might possess to sort the matter out, was making too much contact. That wouldn't do at all, not at all.

Mr Pickles had not enjoyed his meeting with Mr Gradling.

Full of water Faversham Creek, and its immediate environs, has a quirky picturesque appearance, bordering on the quaint at the town end. When the tide is out it takes on a strangely odd look, more akin to Faversham Mud Squelch. Modern properties have sprung up and these are regarded as tasteful by the developers and planners.

Neville sat impassively while Mr Pickles wandered up and down in front of him. Had it been very dark Neville might have considered throwing the corpulent Pickles into the mud where he was sure to sink and perish. Bedecked in a tight, ill-fitting suit, in places shining from wear, Mr Pickles dabbed at his moist forehead with a hanky.

"Mr Gradling, Mr Gradling, this is no good. I dare not report back, I dare not."

"Do you repeat everything you say Mr Pickles, Mr Pickles?" His comment was ignored, as was Gradling's equally sarcastic smile.

"You're a wealthy man, Mr Gradling. You can afford it."

"I'm not paying it. I've paid now for the service I arranged, every last penny. The contract is complete. End of story."

"No it isn't, no it isn't. A few more pounds ensures no unpleasantness and nobody need bother the police."
"Mr Pickles, frankly I won't be bothering the police. Not yet anyway. Any harm comes to me and mine or my property and it'll be me and my associates you'll have to deal with. I'm as big a crook as you are, you fat pig."

"I don't doubt it, I don't doubt it Mr Gradling. But you won't find us, that I promise you."

"I've had enough of this, Pickles, run home to mummy or whoever it is and tell the glad tidings. No more money. Finish. I'm off." And he strolled away leaving his companion to rest on the vacated seat and to contemplate breaking the news to the killer.

***

"Look Moncks, I been thinking about all this. We've had loads of fun but you've never been into having me along, have you? I mean we've found sis, bless you for that, but that's it as far as I'm concerned isn't it? We might as well call it a day. You were bloody embarrassed in that hotel room and if we hadn't both had too much to drink we'd have had separate beds. Now, you know that's true. You never fancied going to bed with me. As I said long ago, you don't know where I been, and isn't that the truth?"

It was a phone call I could do without. I decided to shoot from the hip.

"You stupid cow. We're business partners and I need you. Don't talk utter nonsense. Are you working tomorrow or can I bring you back here to do some work? And if you want to stay over we can discuss your comments over a bottle in the evening."

"Same bed?"

"Yes."

"And because you want to?"

"Yes."

"Will you call me a stupid cow again?"

"Not if I'm sensible."

"You ain't sensible, Moncks."

"Agreed. Pick you up at 9.30?"

"Can I come for brekky?"

"Okay, make it 9. Do you want cooked, because I'll need to defrost the bacon, etc?"

"Course I want cooked. You really gonna treat me like a partner?"

"Didn't I just say that?"

"Yeah, but a real partner?"

"A business partner, yes."

"Knew there'd be a catch."

"See you in the morning."

"Shall I bring a nightie?"

"You do usually."

"I know but maybe this is different and I won't need one."

"Bring one in case there's a fire."

"Better be a fire in your heart, Moncks. Just better be."

"Let's find out together."

"You've no idea how lovely that sounds. You beautiful romantic man, you. Bye"

*** 

Georgina Hayle had learned something about herself. She had everything a girl could want in a material sense. Money, luxury home, luxury car, fabulous clothes, no necessity to go to work and glorious holidays with her husband. That was just for starters. There was also security and a secure lifestyle.

And today none of that meant a jot. For she had come to realise that true love must be valued above all else, that all the material benefits she had were of nought compared to being swamped by the bliss of love so pure, so tender, so deep-rooted that it could not be challenged.

She was leaving Jason for Leonora. That would mean divorce and coming out of it with nothing of value, and she did not care. With Jason away Georgina and Leonora were packing the few clothes she wanted, mainly underwear and the practical everyday things, a few shoes and coats, and other personal items that she didn't think her husband would deny her.

Standing back in the walk-in wardrobe she glanced around the multitude of designer dresses, skirts, tops and trousers and then yelled "To hell with the lot of it." Leonora smiled, knowing she had won her great love, and what great love it was to behold. Georgina danced around and sang a tuneless, wordless ditty.

The arrangement was she would see Jason tonight, explain what she was going to do, hand over all the keys including those to her car, and leave a forwarding address, her new home with the only person who mattered right now. She'd already given instructions for her post to be re-directed but that would take a while to kick in, she'd been told.

How would he take all this? It might mean violence but she was ready for that. Would he be reasonable? Probably not. She was also ready for that. Not that it made any difference by being prepared, for he could still strike her down, still give her a hundred and one reasons not to leave, still make it clear she wasn't going anywhere.

But she'd get up and go, and that was the idea of taking all her personal possessions now. At Leonora's suggestion she'd copied all her personal stuff on the computer to a memory stick and forthwith deleted it on the machine. She wasn't taking her i-pad or her smartphone and therefore checked those instruments for anything that required removing. Get a new phone, use Leonora's computer, this was a new life and it meant new beginnings.

The two women, taking coffee on the lawn, even found time to laugh at the absurdity of Jason's suggestions for continuing both marriage and affair. This was no longer an affair and, quite apart from the fact Leonora did not want Jason anywhere near her, his wife didn't want him pawing her love, her darling. For that matter she no longer wanted him near her either.

Would he try for one last act of sexual gratification? He'd get a knee for his trouble. She was resolved and her resolution made her strong. A weak, puny excuse for a man. Let him use his fists, let him lay down the law, let him try and take her. She would accept what she could not avoid and be on her way. Would his temper boil over? Hopefully not, but a poor apology for a man, when scorned and defeated might well throw his toys out of the pram.

Men could be like that. The old saying went *'hell hath no fury like a woman scorned'* but there was no such analogy for a male of the species thus disparaged. Leonora suggested *'hell hath no fury like a man put in his place by a woman'* and with that they went indoors to finish packing, the smiles of freedom decorating their faces.

"Well, Mrs Hayle, we shall have something to celebrate later tonight so why not take a bottle or two of Mr Hayle's finest champagne with us?" Both laughed, agreement was instantly reached and Georgina helped herself to three champagne bottles, one of Southern Comfort and one of gin to 'make up the weight' as she put it.

However, the evening was not going to go to plan.

***

Oare Gunpowder Works seemed like an apt place to see Holton Okafor as the meeting was bound to be explosive in content. There are pleasant woodland walks around the now defunct site, and we strolled at leisure as if we had all the time in the world and were the best of long-term friends.

"First up, Holton, I need to know this'll never come back to haunt me. Let's put it down to my intuition or whatever you want to call it. The source vanishes from your mind forever."

"David, I know what you mean. That's our two-way agreement. I want this investigation moving and producing a result."

"Then there's two things. Payments. I'm guessing but it could be, after a moderate deposit, there's a huge balance to be paid after the killing and after the initial police searches. I'm convinced Neville Gradling organised an assassin to take out Bourne-Lacey, and the killer now wants a whole lot more dosh. You've searched him inside out but I reckon he's either only just paid or he's yet to do so.

"Second. Savage Yvonne Pratt. No need to risk doing that Panahan woman yet if she's too influential. Hit the dark web. Look for Eve Parr, possibly a nom-de-sex if you get my drift." Okafor laughed out loud but I could see from his expression he understood only too well.

"Search her background, search her, search her accounts. If you find enough you'll be able to go and do the same to Ms Panahan, or rather Suffolk will." The Detective Sergeant looked serious.

"Your intuition, David, is far reaching and could end my career while you walk away scot free."

"That's right. It's up to you."

"I know, but if you were on the strength what would you do if some guy came up with this fantastic theory?

"If I trusted him I'd go for it. One other thing. Gradling would like to involve me in some way. I'm keeping the distance so far. But if you'd like to enlist me, well, I'm not an undercover cop, so it can't come back on you, but I could get in deeper for you, and it might just lead us you-know-where."

"Mmmm .... I don't know my bosses would wear that. But we ought to explore the concept. If you're close enough to Gradling and he trusts you, hell David, it's an opportunity too good to miss. Are you really up for it, man?"

"Yes. I'm the only hope you've got Holton. Bust Gradling and the connection's broken. He doesn't have to give anything away and you might not be able to prove a thing. And he can afford a pretty decent lawyer. He's looking for advice on dealing with a blackmailer. If I played my cards right I might just land a link to our killer. You'll never do it.

"He's offered me cash that I refused but I'm working on the basis he'll try again. Every man has his price, and if I act the bitter ex-cop this may just work."

"Jeez, David. I don't know. It won't be up to me. Can I get back to you?"

"Sure. But do Pratt first. If you find anything out of place, and I bet you will, you'll know I'm on the level over this."

"Yeah, but how to I tell my people when I've got to explain these meetings away?"

"You're a clever cop, Holton. You think of something. After all, if it all comes together you'll get a lot of credit."

"And if it fails I'll be covered in muck, head to foot, with career out the door."

"Think positive mate. You'll win because you're good at your job."

We walked on in silence back to the car park then shook hands.

"I'll be in touch David."

"Just remember Holton, this is a two-way road. You keep me in the loop. That's our agreement."

"Rely on me. I'm relying on you David. And what you've suggested could put your life on the line, which is why I don't think they'll buy into it. But then it's up to how I sell it." And a smile stretched across his face as he released my grip.

He was up for this, and I knew ambition would drive him on. I knew it would happen.

\*\*\*

Later one of my contacts provided me with two snippets of information relating to Lorraine, and a dark cloud descended over the ecstasy of finding her.

Her driving licence, for the address in Carlisle, was in the name of Lorraine Wimbush, suggesting no divorce had taken place. Secondly, she was the registered keeper of a four month old BMW, and not at the less expensive end of their market either. Where did she keep that little monster?

No wonder she said her car was poorly. It was unlikely to be parked in the street outside, but it may have been. Where on earth did she get the money for that? I went cold. There was something suspicious about this woman, this woman who didn't mention an entire episode in her life when telling her sister everything that had happened. I found myself hoping that Laura tackled her on the subject, they were bound to speak on the phone.

Isn't it funny how you can feel so full of doubts all of a sudden? On the way home Laura had told me how anti-men Lorraine was, but more importantly that she believed those who broke their marriage vows should be held to greater account. Gary had broken those vows but, according to Laura, Lorraine held the women responsible. They had provided temptation and Gary, being a typical weak man, had given in to his impulses.

I saw a confused mind. It had obviously hit Lorraine very hard, but according to the information I had Gary had wandered off the straight and narrow in Matlock, *before* they ended up in Barrow. It didn't add up and as a former policeman I didn't like it when two and two ceased to make four. And, of course, there were other things bothering me about Lorraine especially as I now had the car to add to the mix.

Meanwhile, having left Holton Okafor at Faversham, I'd driven on to Minnis Bay, one of my favourite spots for parking and having seafront walks. Along the wall to the west a four mile trek to Reculver. I'd done that a few times. In the other direction you're heading towards Westgate and Margate via a series of small, sweeping bays such St. Mildreds and Epple Bay. Cliffs, sand and seaweed.

But no walk today. I still parked on the front as my destination wasn't far away. Mrs Carter opened the front door before I could ring the bell and guided me to her living room where I was invited to sit. Her armchair, I noted, was not as physically absorbing as Neville's, and more comfortable for it.

She was straight down to business, asking me to relate my most recent experience of tracking a missing person. I could tell she had some sort of mental check list and I was conscious that she nodded to mark each occasion upon which I ticked an imaginary box. There being plenty of nods I assumed I was doing okay.

I simply related, in précis form, omitting the less savoury features, how I found Laura's sister and had just returned from uniting them in Carlisle. Mrs Carter was clearly impressed and I guessed I'd ticked several boxes at once. Her words confirmed that.

"Goodness me, Mr Canbown, I didn't realise your work was so extensive and included personally pursuing the person. I'd always assumed you people worked from offices, perhaps did a bit of tailing, I think that's the word isn't it, but to go to the lengths you've just been to ... well, I can only imagine you must be very expensive, and I presume you charge your expenses as a separate issue?"

I'm not judge of age but I reckoned Mrs Carter was in her fifties. She was conservatively dressed, had a good figure and an angular face which thoroughly suited her short, very curly ginger hair. There was a little make-up but expertly applied to enhance her natural features. A very attractive woman.

I noticed there were no family photos in the room. It was cosy there, nothing extravagant in furnishings, but everything neat and tidy and it looked like home. Tastefully decorated in soft pastel shades, the room had a modern feel to it and certainly the sofa and the chairs were unworn and matched their surroundings. Now I came to look again there was no television, no radio or CD player, but maybe they didn't 'live' in the living room. It was a small house but perhaps there was another lounge.

"Mrs Carter, my basic fees are reasonable, or so I believe, and I will carry out some research first to get a feel for the direction the hunt will take us. I will then advise you and you will be able to choose whether you wish to employ me further, but at every stage I will keep you in the picture and let you know before I accrue any additional expenses. That enables you to say yes or no.

"Further, if I make a recommendation of that nature that you accept, and it proves to be a dead end I will not make any charge for those expenses. The ball really is in your court, Mrs Carter."

"Please call me Daphne."

"And I'm David."

"Right David, thank you, I'm quite happy with that, but first your *reasonable* fees?"

I explained my rates and I could tell she was pleased.

"But obviously we have to start with a mutual agreement. If you are interested in hiring me then I'd need to know more before I can consent to taking the case."

"I'm very interested David. Your last case sounds extremely interesting and it was successful. Tell me, do you get a thrill out of actually tracking someone down? And I expect your client must've been so excited to find her sister. You were there, you say, and I assume it was a very emotional moment. Do you feel that emotion yourself, in a way?"

"Well, yes, I suppose it is the thrill of the chase, so to speak, but success brings its own rewards and that's my main driver. Yes, my client was beside herself, but I left them together for a while because the moment belonged to them, so I witnessed very little. But you're right, it was a very emotionally charged meeting and I do confess to having been swept up in it."

Daphne was smiling, her eyes aglow, and I guessed she was trying to imagine what it would be like to meet her sister. She looked very happy and I suffered a pang of doubt. Had I misled her as to my skills and left her to believe I would definitely find her sibling?

"The only thing I can't actually guarantee is success," I added hastily, going on to explain. "There is also the possibility that your sister does not want to be found, indeed may refuse to see you, if you understand me." Daphne's expression of pleasure did not change.

"I've taken that into account, David, and I'm prepared for the worst. Now, if you have the time today I will outline the case as you call it, and give you brief details. Please ask any questions you wish. If not convenient now please arrange to see me again, for I've decided on you. You're just the man I need."

"Thank you Daphne, and my time is yours right now."

"Good, then would you like a cup of tea, or something stronger? I have some French Fancies I could try and tempt you with unless you'd like some plain biscuits."

There was now such a look in her eyes that I began to worry. If I hadn't known better I'd have said her face was full of mischief.

"Thanks Daphne. Tea and Fancies sounds good."

"Right, I'll put the kettle on, it'll only be a couple of minutes, I got everything ready for your visit. Would you like to look at the paper while I'm gone?" She waved a copy of the *Daily Express* in front of me.

"Yes please, thank you."

I flicked through, read a couple of small articles and before I knew where I was Daphne was back with a tray bedecked with a teapot, tea-strainer, cups, saucers and plates, and of course the small iced cakes. At her direction I rose and collected a coffee table from next to her armchair and placed it in the middle of the floor equidistant from our seats. In this fairly confined room the table was actually less than two feet from either chair.

"I'll be mother," she said with a wink that in other circumstances I'd have considered naughty.

Tea poured, cakes distributed, napkins provided, she regained her chair and set about her Fancy in a most seductive way. I felt the sap rising, for she was making a first class job of it and I suddenly realised she was flirting and I didn't mind a bit. It drove the next question from my lips.

"Mr Carter at work?"

"I am divorced, David. What's your position since you appear to want to check out mine?" She giggled and I knew she had my number.

"Divorced." She smirked and ate another Fancy in the sauciest way a woman could manage.

She talked about her sister and I decided that I would take the assignment if required, convinced that Daphne was merely testing her flirting skills without any real intent, and had found those skills to be in perfect working order. I was pleased I was able to provide proof that she still had what it takes, and even more pleased when I was appointed to handle the case.

"Do I get a case number?" she asked in her best little-girl voice.

"No Daphne, I could never think of you as just a number. You will always be Daphne to me." Well, if she could flirt freely I was entitled to add some spice to an otherwise bald and uninteresting text. We both laughed, amused by the facade and by what lay behind.

Driving away from Minnis Bay I realised that not all the days in my current profession need be bleak, cold, raw and depressing. That meeting with Daphne Carter had been fun and a pleasure to be involved in, and I was sure that she had no real interest in me as a man, but then, as Laura had observed, I'm not always sensible.

Heading home I was aware that I was leaving my idea of fun behind and driving towards just more of that same bleak, cold, raw, depressing work that was now my lot. I'd offered to help the police in a serious crime investigation in a way that might put my life on the line, there were concerns about Lorraine, about Yvonne, and just about everybody within my immediate compass.

No, there wouldn't be much fun.

But it was certainly about to become very hot. Very, very hot.

And that was without locating a sought-after and valuable pot-lid!

# Chapter Twenty Five

# Wages of Sin

Ray Drunbolt had mainly listened there being little else to do.

Daryl Pequeman rumbled on listlessly sharing his sorrow with his audience, the Inspector and the police consultant. Drunbolt wanted to press on relentlessly but his companion had warned against it. Let Daryl believe they were on his side, were sympathetic and, most importantly, there to help him.

The consultant appeared far more interested in what Daryl was saying whereas he was watching closely, watching the signs, categorising behaviour and manner, and listening out for anything that might concern Drunbolt. The Inspector was bored. Assuming the man had hired a killer he had only himself to blame for the sorry loss of his wife. Had he loved her more, Drunbolt thought, she might not have strayed, and John Holgarve would be alive.

Served him right having to watch those porn movies of his beloved Rosie! That and Rosie's suicide had driven him to the brink of collapse, and absolute breakdown. The consultant wanted to avoid pushing him too far, Drunbolt wanted to beat the truth out of him.

But it was the consultant who spotted something in Daryl's wailing discourse and, when opportunity presented itself, asked some questions that demonstrated his empathy with and concern for the widower. There was however purpose, as he deliberately spoke with calmness and the sort of voice a kindly grandfather might show a small grandson.

Pequeman rang his hands continuously as he had done throughout this queer interview, he cried tears that mostly would not come, and his face was squashed into a mish-mash of horrible expressions to illustrate his grief and anguish. Each question tormented him and pain filled his voice as he stuttered through his responses.

"Daryl, you regret being a poor husband."

"Yes I do, I do, I do," came the whimpered comment, accompanied by despairing nods and shakes of the head.

"Daryl, you regret everything that's happened, don't you?"

"Everything, it's all my fault, all my fault."

"Daryl, you regret allowing Mr Pembrake to film Rosie, don't you?"

"Yes, yes, yes, yes."

"Daryl, you regret forcing yourself to see those films, don't you?"

"Yes," and a forlorn nod of the head as the whispered answer fell from his lips.

"Daryl, you regret everything, don't you?"

"Please help me, please help."

"I'm here to help, believe that. You said if it hadn't been for you John would still be alive and therefore Rosie would be to. Do you believe that?"

"Yes of course I do," and a further shower of real tears shot down his cheeks.

"You believe it's your fault Rosie died."

"Oh God, yes I do."

"You believe it's your fault John died."

"It is my fault."

"But you didn't kill him Daryl."

"No, of course I didn't."

"But you paid someone to do it, Daryl. Do you regret that as you regret everything else?"

"Yes, of course I regret it .... I mean no, no I didn't pay someone. What's this, what's going on?"

He raised his voice but Drunbolt's ears had already pricked up. Were they on the verge of a breakthrough?

***

DS Stephanie Broome gaped open mouthed as she read the two emails from DS Holton Okafor which he'd sent to her private address. They outlined the meetings with David Canbown, and there was a shake of the head as she recognised the dangerous territory Okafor was marching through. For he must remain impotent in terms of action, the result of the deal struck with the private eye.

But he could and would instigate anything that was reasonable and that he might validate as being of his own creation. His backroom team, as he called them, had been set to work on Yvonne Pratt and the mysterious Eve Parr. He hoped Stephanie in particular and Suffolk in general would not mind.

No, thought Stephanie, I don't mind, speaking for myself, because if you come up with an excuse to bulldoze that Pratt woman and the outcome helps solve these terrible crimes it won't matter at all.

Of course, she knew it would matter. It always did. But hadn't these investigations been designated a combined operation? Needless to say, various forces duplicating work did not represent best use of resources, and all must be co-ordinated correctly. Yet nobody else was investigating Ms Pratt. Somehow she must make this official with her bosses.

She possessed a modicum of tact and diplomacy, necessary if she was to get on in the force, but had a blunt streak that all too often had provided the impetus for getting the job done in the past. It had also put her into trouble once or twice, and she had managed to extricate herself by virtue of the success that went hand-in-hand with her efforts. Play it by the book, and if you can't do that, keep as close to the pages as you can.

Stephanie did not believe in sailing close to the wind and knew she would not have gone to David Canbown in the way Okafor did, let alone make some private pact with a person who had valuable information. And the thought of arranging Canbown's involvement in a police operation would've been out of the question, as Holton Okafor was discovering.

He had a quiet word with his Inspector projecting an hypothesis in which a member of the public, with his or her full agreement and co-operation, was used as bait in some way or other, luring the killer out of the shadows. Without saying so, the Inspector knew the Sergeant was not speaking hypothetically at all, and there was someone in his mind for what might be a dangerous role. And the Inspector was reluctant to support the concept, telling Okafor that 'upstairs' wouldn't go for it.

\*\*\*

Kenny Parrett's call added another dimension to the mystery that was Lorraine.

The case had got the better of him and he was only too pleased to help, he assured me, and was delighted to hear that the two girls had been re-united.

"Well, that's that, David. Case closed. Enjoyed the thrill of the chase as it were; nice to have been a little part of it and no, you don't owe me anything. Been a good exercise. I rang just to say that I'd unearthed some gen on Gary Wimbush. Did you know he'd been in the services, the army, way back when?"

"No Kenny, I didn't."

"Probably no relevance because that must've been before he married Lorraine. Odd there's no sign of a divorce if she reckons there's been one. Still, plenty of women retain their married name after the break-up, so maybe no puzzle."

I thanked him profusely. It was even now at the back of my mind that Adam warned against him, but frankly he'd done alright by me and I hadn't fed him any of my private information relating to the killings. I did ask him if he'd heard from John or Yvonne.

"Not last few days or anything, nothing of note, nothing serious. Did try talking to that Gordon Pembrake guy in Manchester but he wasn't much interested, so I left it at that. You had any contact Dave?"

"Only from John," which was true, "and it was just a catch-up really."

The conversation didn't proceed much further and upon termination I treated myself to an ice-cold San Miguel which I was determined to savour. Laura didn't like me savouring anything that wasn't Laura herself, although she can hardly have known I was imbibing a drink with such relish and satisfaction at that moment. But that didn't stop her phoning.

"Been chatting to Lor, and we wanna meet up again soon, but neither of us got much money. Do I get paid soon?"

"I expect so, but my client, that Miss McCaffield, hasn't paid a penny...."

"Yeah, yeah, yeah ... blah, blah. Anyway, you got any to spare?"

"I'll think of something. I've taken on a new case today and I'll need your help I daresay, and I've got a lead on the missing pot lid. Tell you all tomorrow. Oh and did you ask Lorraine about Matlock?"

"Yeah. Funny that. I mentioned it all casual like, full of tact me, y'know, said we'd been up there, and she sounded really, really surprised. Then she says, like, what did we find out while we were there, as if she was really concerned. So I asked why she didn't mention it when she was telling us all about the life and times of Lorraine Wimbush nee McCaffield and she got all shirty. Said they were only there briefly and then got the rats asking me why it was so important, and I had to tell her to calm down, only asking, no reason. She said you couldn't have seen her in Matlock cos she wasn't there when we was."

"Okay, we'll chat about that as well tomorrow. Any ideas about where you two would like to meet?"

"Yep, I said I'd have to go by train and she said she could do the same, she's only got an old banger and it's off the road, so we reckoned perhaps a weekend in Birmingham, sort of halfway, well in railway terms. Go shopping and clubbing together..."

"And the money is coming from?"

"Trust you to think of that. Did wonder if you could treat us to a hotel with one of those magic credit cards you got, and if you could give me some wages in advance, and if you wouldn't mind getting the train tickets sorted out on one of your cards...."

"Okay, okay, okay, we'll discuss it tomorrow."

"Yay, and have you defrosted my bacon, Mr Canbown?"

"Be ready for the morning. Collect you at nine."

"Great, and tomorrow night I hope you'll defrost something of mine..."

"That's enough of that. Now clear off. Goodnight, goodnight," and I hung up before she could respond.

It's not everyone who would call an expensive BMW an old banger. And she was angry when Laura tried to ask about Matlock. Curious, very curious.

I studied the response I'd had from the Loughborough area as the last drop of lager made its way down my throat and I returned the glass to the beer mat on the small table. Somebody unmistakably realised that they could be on to a good thing, a nice little earner. How much is your client prepared to pay? I read the words again. Not 'I would like x pounds for it'.

It would be my job I suppose to advise my client as to the best course of action, which would include verification of the pot lid and a valuation. I decided to ring straight away and hear the immediate response.

Just about then something caught my eye in an open file on the table.

***

Georgina was lying perfectly still apart from when she winced as Leonora bathed her wounds.

But at least she was free of that monster. He listened quietly as she explained what she was going to do, giving no hint, visually or verbally, of the tempest to come. The shaking her body was experiencing was present in her voice as she made it clear that there was no going back.

He wasn't in a rage. He simply came to her side, then moved in front of her while she shook, and placed his hands on her arms. But she knew that look in his eyes.

"Not a sound. Understand? Not a sound." His voice was whispered and ice cold. Then he ripped at her clothes, threw her to the floor, tearing her dress and underwear to shreds, and started biting, clawing, thumping, everywhere the marks would not show. In her terror she was grateful he was leaving her face alone. She thought it was all over as he stopped the beating and stood up, but it was only to get an ornamental brass poker from the fireside.

Georgina closed her eyes and hoped. He held her face down and thrashed her with it while she bit into the carpet to stifle the screams. And then it was all over at last.

"Go and get washed up, put some clothes on and I'll drop you at that bitch's place." She obeyed without comment, fleeing to the bathroom. There were no tears, even for the pain, the tears had dried up months ago, there was nothing left to cry. All she wanted was to be free of him.

Leonora was a good nurse, but much more than that she was a concerned lover, and in front of her was the beaten woman she loved so dearly. Leonora had tears aplenty and they flowed profusely as she tended her heart's delight. Georgina was free. Both women knew the significance of that, and were glad that they were now together forever, never to be parted.

And through all the agony Georgina wanted to shout her happiness at the top of her voice. The wounds would heal. Both knew only too well that all too many women suffer such treatment and either have nobody to turn to or are frightened to seek help. Or believe their role is to take that which is given and just carry on as if nothing had occurred.

It is a strange love that can apply such vicious and merciless beatings, yet a stranger love still that can accept them, tolerate them, forgive and move on. Of course, for those like the young Laura McCaffield a problem such as drug addiction can result in dependency on a violent human being. Love does not come into it.

Georgina simply wanted her freedom and her Leonora; the past is gone, look to the future. The beating is over. True love lies ahead. There was no question of revenge in the minds of the two, they just wanted to start their new life.

At that precise moment Jason could've cheerfully killed Leonora, the woman who stole his wife from him.

***

I'm not sure how it got into one of my files.

I probably picked it off the doormat and had intended to throw it straight in the recycling bag, but had instead swept it into an open file.

No matter. There it was, one of those leaflets various religious sects put through the door from time to time, or offer you in the street or on your doorstep. It was headed *The Wages of Sin* and its content was aimed at early repentance in order to save ones soul. 'It's never too late to repent and turn to God' it proclaimed.

There was a reminder about the Ten Commandments and mention of the principle of 'an eye for an eye and a tooth for a tooth'. I wondered how that squared with the Ten Commandments, for example, thou shalt not kill. On that basis if you kill then someone has the right to kill *you*? Sounds like an argument for capital punishment.

Taking that a logical step further I considered what a fitting punishment for committing adultery would be? How would you apply 'an eye for an eye' to that? My quirky line of reasoning took me in the direction of the killer, for had not this person used an 'appropriate' method to despatch his or her victims, all of whom had committed adultery?

And I just began to speculate if this person was a religious crank that had gone out of their mind, maybe because they themselves had suffered betrayal by a loved one. For a reason I couldn't fathom I felt I needed to know more about Gary Wimbush; there was something circulating in my brain that had allied itself to the religious leaflet, or rather its message, and the enigma of Lorraine.

She'd been let down by Gary, allegedly, who had enjoyed the company of other women, gone off with one and by nefarious means deprived Lorraine of most of her money. Nice one: use your wife's money to go into business, sell the business as a going concern and pocket the winnings.

I was surprised by my own reckoning, for it was as if I saw Lorraine as the betrayed and ruined woman, driven mad by the way her life had been wrecked.

That's the trouble with being an ex-cop; you never let go of the suspicion that anyone and everyone is up to no good! And the memory of Lorraine's crucifixes surfaced unbidden.

Yes, it was time to look into Gary. Mr Parrett had been pretty good tracking him and Lorraine down; I didn't know if I could trust him, even with this assignment, but it was surely a fairly safe road to tread. I emailed him, said I'd employ him, that this was a professional enquiry, and that I would pay his fees. Urgency was the order of the day. His agreement arrived in minutes.

He said he'd start with the Kents Bank address in Cumbria, so did I want to cover his expenses if I sanctioned a trip there? After a second's hesitation I mailed back 'Yes, go ahead.' It was a fairly reckless thing to do especially knowing Laura was after serious money, but tomorrow I would get her to work her socks off immersed in my office work and any other issues I could get her involved in. My gut feeling was that she would throw herself into it if she thought she would get the rewards she wanted, so I would make the most of her.

Jayne-Marie Panahan had been giving the matter much thought and had come to a conclusion. She would pay up and be done with it. Thanks to William's inheritance she had access to a fortune and the amount required, although large by any stretch of the imagination, was a drop in the ocean.

The BACS payment went straight to Yvonne Pratt's account, the process being followed by a short email advising that the deed was done. A delighted Ms Pratt sent a thank-you message and Ms Panahan assumed that would be that.

The killer found a coded message on a Facebook page, a page that looked innocent in every other respect, a page belonging to a person who didn't exist. There were very few details on the page and it was only used for the receipt of secret communications, these being deleted quite quickly.

One person had coughed up their additional 'tax' and that just left Neville Gradling, and he wasn't going to be allowed to get away with it. After all, tax evasion is a serious matter! The problem facing the killer wasn't Gradling but sheer greed. Even now, with JMP paying-up and the coffers swollen, a halt could've been called and all might have been well.

But the ease with which Ms Panahan, or Mrs Bailey as Yvonne delighted in calling her, had sorted out her 'tax' and settled the account excited the killer. It was worth going back again for some more. Perhaps later on, perhaps right away. It was a glorious conundrum to have to work out!

In the meantime DS Stephanie Broome was dreaming of the day they raided the Panahan woman and realising reality did not come within a million miles of her dreams. However, in Kent DS Holton Okafor was about to discover something of immense interest that might just tip the scales in Stephanie's favour. And that was before he heard from David Canbown about another issue.

"Holton, an idea. Shoot me down in flames ... blah, blah, but I was glancing at one of those leaflets the religious zealots put through your door, and I wondered if our killer is hiding behind a perfectly legitimate front, well, that is, not necessarily legit but one you might not think of looking behind. A religious group. The leaflet got me thinking, y'know, the wages of sin, thou shalt not commit adultery; what if you're after a religious fanatic, someone who's been stuffed by their partner, and has gone ever-so-slightly nutty as a result?"

"David, may the Lord bless you! I hear what you're saying, now I don't want to hear any more. Leave it to me, and you can count on me getting back to you. Amen."

"Thanks Holton. Sounds like you should be taking more water with it."

"David, if anything comes of this you and me is going to get plastered! Now, may peace be with you."

"Peace off, Holton. Hear from you soon."

Tomorrow for David Canbown was going to be anything but boring administrative drudgery.

***

Having retracted his hasty 'confession' and blamed the consultant for putting words in his mouth when he was clearly distressed, unwell, and grieving, Pequeman was temporarily released while Drunbolt seethed. But the interview was a start, nothing had been wasted, and Drunbolt knew he'd got his man, it was just a case of getting something from the man that would stick, and indeed, stand up in court.

And the news was relayed to the other forces involved.

# Chapter Twenty Six

# The Book of Revelations

In Derbyshire the consultant had been explaining mental health issues to DI Ray Drunbolt who could not have been less engrossed. Drunbolt felt obliged to listen. He credited the man with taking Daryl Pequeman to the brink of confession and knew he could scarcely have done better himself. But there the two methods parted company.

The consultant had quietened Daryl down and spoken with great sympathy and understanding, whereas Drunbolt would've pressed home the advantage there and then, for such a technique had worked before and was standard issue for the Drunbolts of this world.

Now together in the Inspector's office Drunbolt was being forced to come to terms with the fact Daryl Pequeman was as close to a breakdown as you can get without actually having one, and that he need to be gently coaxed into submission. However, the consultant was wholly confident a confession would follow, sure as he was of the man's guilt, and that it just needed time.

"Sir, another murder could take place while we give Pequeman time."

"I understand that, Inspector, but this is not a day and age for putting people on the proverbial rack. Such concepts no longer stand up in court, as I'm certain you're aware. I'm not telling you your job, and I'm not being patronising. We both know why I'm here; those that must be obeyed want this done by the book because otherwise a well-drilled barrister will tear you to shreds. The other side of this coin is, Inspector, that if we set about Daryl he may clam up, you'll never get your confession, let alone a lead to the killer, and the medical profession will close ranks around him."

Drunbolt knew when he was beaten, knew that the words he'd heard were the truth, godammit, and that he had no option but to wait patiently, and the terms 'wait' and 'patient' had never been in his vocabulary. In the meantime he'd get an update on the system, which in return had updates for him. If things had come to a halt in his neck of the woods, there were developments elsewhere and he would have to make do with that for now.

In Suffolk at her home Stephanie Broome looked again at Holton Okafor's email sent, as usual now, to her private address. It was headed:

*The wages of sin is ... DEATH!*

And below he spelled out David Canbown's theory without giving the private eye any credit for its birth in his mind. Stephanie was amazed and excited all at once and she typed a brief reply of acknowledgement as fast as her fingers would go. Okafor's people were going to look into that aspect, searching the net for anything remotely allied to the delivery of death as a punishment.

Time ticked by, the night wore on, and the principal characters turned in and slept, and the morning slowly came into view. Another day.

***

I was up early, prepared breakfast, and drove over to Sheerness where Laura was waiting at the roadside. There are times when it is hard to stop her talking and today was one of them. Enthusiastic about working on cases with me when she thought it might have been all over, she gabbled at length, asked me questions I said I would answer later, and mixed it all up with comments about her sister.

I couldn't tell her about Lorraine's BMW but I desperately wanted to, and a part of me felt it was necessary to do so. But that would lead to confrontation and I didn't want to come between sisters. I'd save it.

Before setting out I'd emailed Adam Pensfield to say I was aware of substantial developments, was it worth another meeting? That should be enough to prompt him if he had anything more to tell me, that is, anything more he felt able to tell me. I guessed Holton Okafor would be moving as fast at the system would allow him, but he would have one hand tied behind his back unless he sold me down the river. There was always that chance.

"Did you speak to Lor last night?" We were both in the kitchen, Laura doing her best to get in my way without actually trying to help, so I thought I might start the ball rolling.

"Yeah, she's cool. Hoping we're gonna meet up again soon, like I suggested to you, boss-man."

"Boss-man will not work with me. You're not getting round me. We will discuss all aspects of your proposed trip and the financial arrangement appertaining thereto, and we can kick off by abandoning the idea of going clubbing. Agreed?"

"Nope, but I'll work on you in the hours ahead."

"Your sister? Last night? Telephone call?" I was trying to change the subject.

"Yeah, she didn't mention anything. We didn't go back over Matlock cos that caused grief last time. She said that her car looks like being off the road for some time, and I suppose that happens with old bangers, maybe it'll happen to your old crate."

"You are talking about my beloved Fiesta, the girl I love, so be respectful."

"Yay, she did get us to Lorraine, didn't she? So okay, I'll be kind next time."

"Would you put the toast in the toaster, please, and boil the kettle and make the coffee?"

"Yessir, yes indeedee," and she saluted as she set about her relatively easy tasks. The other ingredients were coming along nicely under my control and there was a delicious aroma of cooked breakfast, principally bacon, wafting around the room.

Shortly we took our trays to the dining room, which doubles as my office, and tucked into our largely unhealthy spread.

There was little conversation so absorbed were we in scoffing my tasty cooked treats, but over toast and marmalade I asked again about Lorraine in tones I hoped might raise some doubts in her mind. I definitely didn't want to alienate her or make her suspicious about her sister; I just wanted her to see her in a different light and maybe probe deeper into her past. Lorraine wanted Matlock kept quiet; now why might that be?

"What sort of business did Gary have then?"

"Not sure. She didn't want to talk about him, the bastard. Have a feeling he did repairs, y'know, lawn mowers, all that sort of thing. Very good with mechanical things apparently, very good with his fingers. Very good with other women."

"If he already had a record in that direction when they were at Matlock why did she stick with him, do you suppose, and move away, sinking her money into his scheme?"

"No idea Moncks. Love's a strange thing, ain't it? Makes people do things they wouldn't normally do. Love makes people stick together when perhaps they shouldn't."

I've never really liked the concept of working breakfasts. The idea is that it saves busy people time, but as a food lover I've tended to put my desires to the fore, and I do have an aversion to people spitting and spluttering food and drink over the table as they struggle to get their two-penneth into the conversation. But it wasn't me speaking when I spluttered into my coffee; it was Laura taking me by surprise.

"Tell you what Moncks...." she started, pausing to chew a chunk of toast heavily buttered and liberally spread marmalade, "I think she's got religion or something. She reckons the way she's been treated by men, and what with Gary going off with some old tart, his word, is wicked and against all God's teachings. You know, not doing adultery and that, and she reckons Gary'll reap his reward if not in this life then the one after.

"She really believes the heaven and hell thing. Thinks people should be punished for being wicked, and that ..." pause for more mastication, "and that if it means death so be it. Why you looking at me like that Moncks? Only telling you what she says; not into it meself."

"I know, but you've shocked me, that's all. How does that thinking reconcile itself with your sorry past then? Does she think you should be punished in any way?"

"She didn't talk about it much, just said that I'd kind of repented, so I should be in the clear."

Another half slice of white toast made its way to her plate where it was attended to with gusto, receiving a more than ample covering of butter, well, a healthier spread actually, and then a generous dollop of marmalade.

"Love yer home-made marmalade, Moncks." I ignored her praise and pressed on.

"Has she committed no wicked sins that she might need punishing for?"

"Sarky, sarky. I expect so, but nothing serious, and if she's repented then that's fine, ain't it?"

"Is lying to you a sin?"

"What? She ain't lied. Well, didn't want to talk about Matlock, a bit of an oversight not mentioning it in the first place, but if something bad happened round that time maybe she doesn't want reminding, like, and don't want to talk about it. People are like that, y'know, want to push bad memories out of their minds. She hasn't lied to me. Where'd that come from?"

I had to think quick. Her attitude suggested that she was going on the defensive because she thought her sister had not told the truth. Did I stay on the attack or change direction and retreat? Saved by the bell! The phone rang and I left her to enjoy the last part of her repast.

"David, it's Nev. They're coming on strong. I need help and I'll be dead straight with you. Can you come here in the morning? Name your price."

"Telling me to name my price let's everything down, Neville. Telling me you'll be dead straight with me puts me on my guard. So cut the nonsense, eh? How about 10 a.m?"

"Good with me. I'll tell you everything and you can judge. I'm just asking that if you don't want to get involved you walk away and not a word to anyone."

"If you're going to reveal something illegal, and I mean something that's against the law even if you think it shouldn't be, I am not going to guarantee my silence."

There was a long pause. Laura had appeared in the doorway, cup of coffee in her hand, and she was wearing a puzzled look and a sideways smile. I don't know why but in that moment she turned me on. I wanted to remember her look forever. Neville broke into my reverie.

"Okay. Look David, come over and let's talk. I won't try and buy your silence, but please let me plead for it. Can we agree on that?"

"I can't see us agreeing on much Neville, but let me see the real you, if that's possible. For a few minutes chuck away the poor-guy-done-well facade and come out of hiding. I'm not impressed with your wealth and that foul desecration of the countryside you call home, with its massive gates, cctv cameras, and expensive motors. And I daresay I can't like the way you've made your money if I did but know."

"Phorr, cut it out, Dave, give a bloke a break. That's me told. Okay, okay, we know where we stand with each other. See you in the morning." Laura looked even more puzzled.

We cleared up as I told her all I wanted her to know about Neville Gradling and his problem. I prefer to wash so threw Laura the teacloth as she listened without comment. Our labours took only a few moments and then it was back to the dining room which was transformed instantly into my office, with the exception of the gorgeous smell of breakfast bacon.

I went into the computer while she sat at the desk and made herself look business-like.

"What you want me to do first?" she enquired. I filled her in on the missing pot lid and said we needed to contact the person in Loughborough and ask for verification and a valuation which our client would pay for.

"Once I've checked the emails you can sit here and send the message, okay?"

"You got it!"

I went straight to the email from Kenny; he had info and wanted to leave for the Lake District at once. He said, without explaining, that he needed to move fast, and I decided it had to be worthwhile. But in my response something made me add 'take it you're going to Kents Bank and not Carlisle'. His reply was simple. 'South Cumbria only. Lorraine's all yours, and I take it that's what you're referring to. I won't be in contact. On my way. Cheers buddy.'

Cheers buddy. Jeez, I detest all these things. And I was having pangs of concern; Adam had told me he wasn't to be trusted and I was only a few steps away from having palpitations about Lorraine and the wages of sin. And I was authorising his visit up north. I would need to be on my guard and then some!

Email from Adam: 'Nothing to add but call me at home tomorrow night'. That was ambiguous and contrary all in one hit. He was probably being cautious but at least he wasn't ringing alarm bells, for there was no sense of urgency in his words and I knew he wouldn't divulge sensitive data over the phone.

With that we got down to the sheer bliss of good old-fashioned office work and I have to admit she worked like a Trojan, competently, swiftly, accurately and much to my liking, all of which left me with a feeling of glorious self-satisfaction. This comfortable sensation was derailed before I could really enjoy it, for all of a sudden she asked me a question I hoped would never be asked.

"No idea what sort of banger me sister's got. You can't remember her saying, can you? Wondered if it's a Fiesta like ours."

"It's my Fiesta and it's not an old banger."

"Silly me, just recalled you don't like your little jam-jar maligned, do you my little sweetie-weetie?"

"No, and I don't remember her saying."

"Mmmm ... any ideas? I mean, you've met Lor, any idea what sort of banger she might drive?"

Now did I lie or tell the truth and ruin a perfect day, and probably my whole life? It was now or never; she'd backed me into a corner. I turned and looked her in the face and tried to sound more confident than I felt.

"Laura, I've got a contact at the DVLA. She's got an almost brand new mid-range BMW." I waited for whatever terrible retribution would be heaped upon me, and waited in vain. Her eyes started to water and she spoke in a very soft, quiet voice.

"That's why you said she was lying. Cos you knew. You should've told me sooner. I guessed you checked as part of our search for her," I didn't disillusion her, "and you were probably surprised when she said about her banger, and didn't want to hurt my feelings or anything."

I was getting away with one, I knew that, and it made me feel rotten to the core, but at least there had been no storm, almost as if Laura had some belief, deep down inside, that her sister was not right on the top line. Of course, we'd taken Lorraine by surprise and presented her with a huge emotional upheaval, so maybe she did get in a muddle, perhaps memories of Matlock were painful, but still no excuse for the car. Unless she was embarrassed by it and chose to keep it under lock and key as it were.

Perfectly rational explanations? Could be, and in a way I wanted to believe that was the case, if only for Laura's sake. Small tear droplets had slipped down her cheeks but she wasn't sobbing.

"Can we get back to work Moncks? I was so enjoying my day with you. Can we forget this for now? When the time's right I'll ask her more about the car if you like. She could be saving it as a surprise, y'know, an expensive set of wheels, me turning up in an old Fiesta, she might've been embarrassed." Laura was thinking along my lines, but I knew I'd planted seeds of doubt and maybe that was no bad thing.

"Of course. Sorry it came out like that..."

"No, no, no, you were okay Moncks. Best way to do it."

"Right, well if you're ready let's update all our files, and I'll see if I can set you to work on our new job, a missing sister." She laughed.

"Yeah, I'm real good at that. Sorry David, meant to say *we're* real good at that." And so we resumed our day in the office with at least one unpleasant hurdle out of the way.

I just had a feeling other hurdles were about to be placed on the course.

***

The ubiquitous Mr Pickles was keen to set sail for the west country and had hoped to sort Neville Gradling out before it was time to go. Nathan Kethnet had some extra 'tax' to pay. The difficulty facing Pickles was that it was desirable that all contact should be kept to the absolute minimum and minimised in every way possible. That would diminish the chance of detection, and avoid any clues being left behind.

He was full of admiration for his boss, the killer, and agreed with himself that they had done pretty well up to now. It had all gone so smoothly and the police, who had been responsible for putting his dear sweet mother away, had been left baffled and trailing in their wake. What was disturbing Pickles right this moment was that, in his eyes, sleeping dogs should be left to lie, and after an enormously successful run of slayings they should lie low and enjoy their financial gains.

Blackmail was greedy and unnecessary, and the killer had not anticipated anyone cutting up rough, Mr Gradling not playing ball at all. This bothered Mr Pickles and made him sweat more than usual.

The killer has not entirely happy either. Gradling needed to be taught a lesson, and word on the ground suggested Daryl Pequeman, long before he was approached for more money, might go to pieces and confess. Suddenly the watertight scheme had sprung leaks, the masterpiece of strategic planning and execution was shown to have flaws, and there was too much contact being made between the various parties for the killer's liking.

In contrast Yvonne Pratt was enjoying a new lease of life blissfully unaware a dark side of her existence was about to be uncovered, and that it might lead to unpleasant contact with the police.

DS Okafor put the phone down and waited while the message from his colleague uploaded on the screen before his very eyes. Eve Parr was a dominatrix, as was Evida Prada and both appeared on closer inspection to be the same woman, so Okafor's colleague suggested. There were no clear pictures, no real facials, but the department had done a good job illustrating with all their graphic design skills how close the pictures were to the one on Yvonne Pratt's website.

Evida Prada? His lips curled into an odd kind grimace as he smirked at the name. Not a stone's throw from Eve Parr and Yvonne Pratt, and he could understand why using the name Pratt might have a negative effect on business!

All he had been able to learn about Ms Pratt suggested she was a feminist with extreme views and this new development slotted neatly into place. Men paying to be humiliated and beaten. Men surrendering to whatsoever a woman might want to do to them, and pay for the privilege! Both ladies possessed a well-equipped dungeon, Eve in west Suffolk, Evida in east Suffolk, but both were willing to travel any distance if the payment was right. Well, well, well.

Both women advertised on an adult site that anyone could find if their parental controls were off. And he smirked again, this time more openly. There it was, right in front of them; not hidden at all. The site took enquirers who were members (you had to join first) to more detailed pages and straight away he noticed a curious and almost sinister item relating to Evida Prada.

Fortunately his colleague had been authorised to sign up and he'd thus been able to access the information, copy and paste to internal documents, and forward the whole stinking lot to Okafor.

He read carefully:

*I provide various other services for clients. I am a problem solver and if I cannot solve your problem myself I have a handy range of contacts to carry out the work for me on your behalf. No job too small, no job too big as they say! You might be astonished to learn what I can arrange for you. You will probably visit a dominatrix for punishment, but there are all kinds of punishments available for wicked people. Perhaps someone you know and love needs punishment. Let's discuss it soon; I'm ever-so keen! And please remember my services are available to all regardless of sex, although I personally enjoy dealing with wicked men.*

He sat back aghast. It did stink. This whole horrible thing stank. He believed he was beyond being shocked, and goodness me, he'd seen and heard of some things in his job, but he knew he was stunned by the entire morass of depravity. What made it worse was the 'problem solving' footnote. And he shuddered and found himself cold. Almost unnerved.

Now he had to send this on to Stephanie, but first he needed permission and he knew he would have to justify it, and do so without implicating Canbown.

David Canbown was pressing on with work in his office, and doing so with great help from Laura who was proving an excellent secretary, coffee maker, researcher, go-fer and do-fer, and deep thinker, the latter being a surprise but welcome revelation.

The pot-lid owner in Loughborough was having none of it. Verification and valuation indeed! Did Canbown's client want it or not, and if he did then how much was on the table? This was relayed to the client who replied in amazing fashion with an offer of three hundred pounds. Not enough, said Loughborough. Four hundred? You must be joking. Five hundred? You're getting warm. And there the exchange ground to a halt with Canbown's client saying he'd get back asap.

The private eye decided this was a strange affair. The pot-lid might well be worth a lot of money, but this wasn't the right way to go about buying and selling. And five hundred pounds for something of obscure sentimental value? It didn't fit.

After a very busy day in which Laura excelled herself in all departments, the pair closed down the office and looked forward to a relaxing evening together, with the phone off. Their day may have been over, with pleasure beckoning, but others were hard at work and a great deal of activity was about to be unleashed with varying degrees of success. And Kenny Parrett was on the verge of an astonishing eye-opener about Gary Wimbush.

# Chapter Twenty Seven
## Some Enchanted Evening

Neither of us is that keen on television largely because, from our perspective, there is so little to watch that we would enjoy, so after dinner we decided on a DVD, Laura choosing *Persuasion*.

She said she was in a loving, cuddly mood and fancied something romantic to add passion to the evening, and a Jane Austen adaptation was just the ticket especially as this one is of about ninety minutes duration. I'd left her to read the paper while I prepared dinner, steak and chips with mushrooms, tomatoes, peas and carrots, something we'd decided on in advance. In fact I'd prepared it before going to collect Laura in the morning.

Furnished with a bottle of *Whitstable Bay*, preparatory to tackling the *Sancerre* over the meal, she looked quite at home and I even caught her doing the Daily Mail quick crossword, much to my chagrin. That is sacred territory!

We took our meals on trays to the dining room. One thing I'll say about that girl is that she was out to the kitchen like lightning when there was washing up to be done while I served up. Less to do afterwards that way, and we wanted the evening to be special. I had a glass of wine at the cooker; I didn't want to be seen to be falling behind.

The food looked wonderful and appetising and we toasted each other before tucking in. We chatted about this and that and in no time the steak was no more. With, by agreement, no dessert, we returned to the kitchen to finish clearing up and thence to the lounge and subdued lighting. The film was launched as our wine glasses were re-filled, and we snuggled up together on the settee to enjoy both. It was that sort of evening. Cosy.

The only Austen I've read is *Sense and Sensibility* so I have no idea how faithful the adaptation of *Persuasion* is, but such a delightful presentation just after a delicious steak meal, aided and abetted by *Sancerre,* and an extremely comfortable sofa, led us into a magical fantasy world.

We snuggled closer revelling in the film and the wine and by the end we were in danger of becoming quite emotional.

As we watched the heroine pursuing the man of her dreams on foot through the streets of Bath, I could've been Captain Frederick Wentworth, Laura as Anne Elliot. The two finally stood face to face as the chemistry between them, at a level to dissolve the toughest metal, drew their longing, quivering lips closer and closer, and we were shouting 'Kiss, kiss' at the screen! And so they did. We felt as emotionally charged as they were and as soon as the film was over Laura demanded we re-enact the scene.

We stood together, our lips closing in for the kill, when we spontaneously burst into laughter. But it wasn't long before we shared an Anne and Frederick kiss. I held her tight in my arms and wanted her, ached for her, and she was like a creature possessed, arms around me furiously caressing me as our passions exploded in that one symbolic kiss.

Exhausted we flopped back into the settee, our laughter and gaiety and happiness enveloping our whole world.

"Shall we open another bottle Moncks?"

"Why not?"

"Fine, and do you know what? I'd love to just sit here awhile just jawing and drinking with you. That'd be so nice, really would." And she so obviously meant it that I couldn't help but agree. Off to the kitchen I went, back with the opened bottle.

"Chilled Moncks?"

"Chilled, Top Bitch." I poured two glasses. "Cheers Lovely Lady Laura."

"Cheers David, my top dog. 'Ere, give us a kiss." And we shared a brief encounter of the sort one might experience under the mistletoe at Christmas, then snuggled up once more, relaxed and content, a million miles away from our work and our problems. It was certainly a diversion I needed.

*** 

"Y'know David, this feels like it's always been like this, like I've never been away if you know what I mean, like this has always been my life."

"I'll tell you what's strange, you calling me David. Almost sounds formal. I've come to quite like the way you call me Moncks."

"Moncks it is then. Hey, you haven't got a pet name for me, have you?"

"No. Suppose I could call you Mac but that doesn't sound luvvy-duvvy."

"Nope, and if you once referred to me as Big Mac I wouldn't be responsible for my actions! Don't you like Law then? You often call me Law."

"Yep, but your sister's Lor as well, bit confusing that, and it's really only shortening your name, not a pet name."

"We're gonna have to think about it. Now Moncks, you liked that movie, unusual for a bloke to be into all that romantic stuff, but I like you for it, shows you got feeling like."

"I *am* romantic, just a realist too. F'rinstance, in true love, real love, I think there's a place for tender romance as there's a place for all-out lust. But it's not the bedrock upon which a proper loving relationship should be based."

We sat quietly for a while, sipping our drinks, hugging and letting the sides of our heads come gently into contact with each other as she mulled over my thoughts.

"I've never known real love Moncks. Sad innit? I mean, I always used to dream of being a princess and marrying a handsome prince, like so many little girls do, and I took the same sort of dream into adolescence, so I was easy prey for the wrong kind of bloke, know what I mean? I thought I'd found love but of course I never had.

"Never lost me romantic streak, but never found love. Don't think I've ever actually given my heart to anyone, maybe because I knew deep down they didn't deserve it. You must've been in love with your wife, Moncks."

"Yes, and it went deep, and it was beautiful. It was all about caring, being tolerant, being forgiving, about wanting to please and remembering your partner is a human being and has frailties just as you have. Neither of us was perfect but that didn't matter. We often knew what the other was thinking, we were that close. It was about knowing that love is always there no matter what. You don't forget it when you're busy, that's just the lovely reassuring thing about that kind of relationship. It might be out of mind but it's always, always there."

"Where'd it go wrong then Moncks?"

"I was a dedicated policeman, Laura. Married to the job I loved. Penny was always so understanding, so supportive, but I suppose I forgot all about being supportive to her. I don't know. At first she was good about leave being cancelled at the last moment, about me working all hours, about never knowing what time I was coming home. But it had an impact. If cases were getting on top of me I used to get the rats, would be grumpy for no good reason, and then Penny would say things like 'don't take it out on me' and so on. Finally we talked about it like sensible adults.

"We decided to go our separate ways. We'd wanted a family but Penny didn't want to be left to bring the kids up by herself. It was all so sad. It wasn't love that died. Difficult to explain. Once we'd agreed to split she did wonderful, loving things like teaching me to cook, wash and iron clothes and that. That's what love's about, Laura. Even when it's gone hopelessly wrong you just can't kill it off like that. How did you feel when that guy was putting you in hospital?"

267

"I didn't feel love, that's for sure, not like you've just described love. I needed him for me stuff, you know that. I blamed meself, Moncks, cos it was my fault he attacked me and I just resolved to mend my ways, I spose."

"How do you see making love, y'know, intimacy? To me there's having sex and there's making love, and they're not necessarily the same. Two people truly in love 'make love' and embark on an enchanting voyage of exploration and discovery, demonstrating their love for each other by the way they attend to each others' needs, and are driven by the desire to please. The experience is exhilarating, rewarding and totally satisfying. Having sex isn't making love."

"Wow, you talk nice Moncks, you got me all warm and excited."

"So, if you'll pardon the expression, how was it for you?"

"Never satisfying. If I wanted good feelings I took care of myself, if you follow me! Blokes just used me, so it was easy to go on the game. Look after 'em, give 'em what they want, enjoy a few bob in yer pocket. It gets to the stage when you don't care if you never have another bloke near yer privates. I could cheerfully have said I don't want sex ever again, and meant it. Just finished up a meaningless act for me."

I refilled the glasses, more for her, I had to remember I was driving in the morning, and we partook of a short, sensitive kiss, exchanging deep, wondrous glances before imbibing again.

"Tell me, Law, why have you appeared so keen to get me into bed?"

"Don't know really. Experience has taught me it's what men want. I thought you were playing hard to get so I tried harder knowing you wouldn't give in till you were ready. I know different now. You'd like sex, same as the next man, but you wanted it to be special with me, didn't you?"

"You've caught me on the hop, Law. You may be right but in my own mind I really don't know. What I do know is that I wanted to get to know you better before we went to bed, and perhaps that means that I wanted to see if any, well, y'know, feelings developed between us. I didn't want it to be a service provider and client relationship. I guessed you saw it that way at first. Am I right?"

"You sure is Moncks. And I'm pleased it's turned out the way it has. That was a lovely cuddle we had in bed, and I'm pleased we didn't go any further."

"We were incapable of going further!" We both chuckled at the memory.

"Moncks, can I ask you something?"

"Yes, of course."

"Would you mind if we just chatted like this for a while, then went to bed and just cuddled all night, y'know, don't make love? It's peculiar, but please try and understand, I just feel in my strange feminine way, whatever, that sex would spoil it. Can you see what I'm driving at? Please don't lets lose this wonderful moment, this wonderful evening. Oh God, I'm explaining this all wrong. I don't mean it would spoil it ..... oh flip, just can't find the words. You've spoken so beautiful about love and that, Moncks, please try and understand."

We were looking directly at each other.

"Laura, I've never been so happy, and believe it or not I know exactly what you mean. If it's any consolation I wouldn't find the words either! Forget words, they only get in the way. Nothing would make me happier than doing just as you've said. Chat away, then go to bed for a great big huggledy-cuddly-snuggly." A small tear departed her left eye, and a tiny smile appeared on her lips, and then we kissed again. In her eyes I could see her heart and I knew mine was exposed to her gaze as well. Our eyes were as locked together as our lips had been, and I knew she was going to steal the heart she had within her grasp.

Would I steal hers? Yes, I knew I would.

\*\*\*

It was very dark. I've no idea what the time was.

I have a piece of thick material I call my blackout curtain which I put up on the inside of my bedroom bay window. Before I invented that I was forever being disturbed by security lights on neighbouring properties going on-off-on-off-on-off at the slightest provocation, as well as the annoying habit Geoff over the road had of reversing up his drive late at night, headlights full on. My bedroom was fully illuminated. Now I sleep untroubled.

It was very quiet.

Laura was asleep in my arms, her close company everything I could desire. We were wrapped up under the duvet, warm, cosy, entwined, her soft, rhythmic breathing the faintest of sounds and the most exquisite of sounds. We had enjoyed a glorious freedom; there had, by arrangement, been no expectations beyond conversation that appealed to both of us, and we were the better for it, our cuddles appreciated all the more.

There were periods when we didn't speak at all. We weren't searching for something to say, we weren't concerned that there was nothing to be spoken of. Our happiness superseded every other consideration and we lived for those simply idyllic and harmonious times when all we needed was each other, and the feel of our bodies enfolded as one. The darkness and the silence brought us together and nurtured our feelings for one another.

When we spoke it was with a quietness and effortlessness, usually about life in general, about love and contentment, about being together. It was that easy. Her last whispered words before she committed herself to the arms of Morpheus echoed peacefully and angelically around in my mind.

"I love you Moncks." And she was gone, overtaken by sleep in a private world of joy.

I was still listening to those words when I too fell asleep.

## Chapter Twenty Eight
# .... **Some Disenchanted Day**

After showering and a breakfast of porridge, followed by toast and marmalade, I took Laura to work as she still had her part-time job and the income was important especially, as I'd stressed, if she wanted her weekend with Lorraine.

Yes, I'd agreed to that, but with conditions attached that I appreciated could easily become *de*tached. Sitting in my office I did begin to wonder if I'd been sucked in by one clever lady, but time would tell. At long last I gave some thought to my forthcoming meeting with Neville Gradling.

I drove over in an apprehensive state and parked behind an enormous white Mercedes battle-wagon; no sign of the Lotus. Jacqueline showed me in and led me to another of the lounges where Neville was waiting and wearing a look of impatience, despite my early arrival. Jackie looked smart and was wearing noticeably more than the last time, but still managed to appear 'scantily clad'. She was the indirect, if far from innocent, cause of the trouble and it didn't seem to worry her a jot.

Having offered me a drink (politely refused) she left. Before her husband could speak I threw my cards on the table.

"Neville, if you're recording this meeting in any form, shut it off now. If I feel uncomfortable I'm off. One chance – don't waste it." I felt like a TV cop, all mouth and trousers! He held one hand up and nodded once.

"No recording Dave. Besides if anything fell into the wrong hands, and that includes the police, it incriminates me as well, doesn't it? So, nothing doing. No recording."

"Incriminates you? Does that mean you're going to be talking about something illegal?"

He sat down opposite me, laid back and crossed his legs trying to look as nonchalant as he could and probably aware he was failing.

"Dave, the whole story, the whole truth. I love my wife. I wouldn't do anything to hurt her, no violence, nothing like that, but I had to do something when I suspected her of seeing that Bourne-Lacey guy. It occurred to me the best thing was to hire a private eye to confirm my suspicions, present Jackie with the evidence, and let something unpleasant happen to the other geezer.

"Not that I don't trust Jackie but, you know what I mean, remove the source of temptation and she can't, well, be tempted can she? So I reckoned Bourne-

Lacey needed to be on the wrong end of an accident. Nothing too serious, just a good beating he'd soon get over, so he'd lay off my wife, if you get the picture.

"Arranged that with someone. I didn't arrange to have him shot dead, but nobody's going to believe that, so I might be in the frame for murder, or manslaughter. It's all gone wrong and I'm to blame. Now I'm being really open with you, Dave." And to emphasise the point he leaned forward in an earnest gesture, which I presumed he'd learned along the way somewhere. There was something 'corporate' about it. "It was a good arrangement; small deposit up front, nothing traceable, balance *way, way* after the event. Trusting people, you understand. It was for my benefit, I was told, so if the police turned me over they'd find nowt, no big cash withdrawals or anything like that.

"As you know they did search me and found nothing. Then, of course, they wanted paying when they thought the coast was clear. I told them they'd gone too far and they kind of said well, what the heck, pay up anyway or else. Now they want more dosh and you're right, it'll go on forever. But the worst of it is that they'll hurt one of my family, not necessarily Jackie and the kids, but anyone, like mum and dad and so on. I can't protect everyone and neither can the police.

"That's why I'm in a dilemma, Dave. I can't get involved with the police."

"You must know something about them Neville? A contact, anything. And how did you pay the deposit and how will you pay the rest? You've got to tell me everything."

I still had this weird death wish about going undercover for the police and leading them to the killer, so I was determined to play Gradling along, taking care not to overcook it. His statements so far appeared to lack that vital ingredient of truth he'd promised me, and were comprised of contrary comments and dubious revelations, and a hash of nonsense. For example, I liked the line about ABL getting a good beating he'd soon get over! And Neville doing shady and illegitimate business with 'trusting people'? Yes, I believe you, Nev!

"Dave, I don't know how much to tell you. I'm in your hands. You'll tell me to go to the police and confess all this, but then one of my family will get hurt, maybe killed. Perhaps you'll go to the police. I expect you still know lots of them. So I'm up the creek, so give me a break. Please try and help me, but don't let me tell you anymore unless you're going to give me that break. Please."

He was twixt a rock and a hard place. Good. I gave reply:

"Okay, I'm going to tell you to go to the police. But only you can decide if you're going to tell me anything else, and if it's nasty then yes, I may go straight to the cops. I can't make up my mind if I want to help you or shop you. Convince me as to my best course of action, Neville."

He poured himself a large Scotch, offered me the same (I declined), and sat down again having bought a little time to consider his predicament. I continued:

"What do you actually want to achieve? A killer brought to justice? The chance to put the frighteners on your blackmailer? Revenge? *What?*"

"Look, it's like this, I don't *know* what I want, I just don't want to go to prison and I don't want to keep paying, and I don't want my family targeted."

"So if I can help find the killer, technically speaking on my own initiative, without any obvious input from you e.g. this meeting, can turn them in to the police to face justice without them knowing you had anything to do with it, you'll be happy in inverted commas."

"Yeah, that's the level of it."

"And you get off Scot free?"

"Yep, unless the killer brings me down for good measure anyway, and I'm going to have to take a chance on that. Your nose stays clean with the cops because you've led them to a serial murderer."

In some respects this conversation was going the way I hoped it would, but I would still be faced with the moral quandary of whether or not to go to the police straightaway. I just had to get some contact details out of him.

"Well, I can't do anything without any contact info, can I?"

"Look, how about I pay up and you follow the cash? Got to take you to the top man, the killer, hasn't it? Now are you a good tec or not, Dave?"

"Tell me more about it. And Neville please, just cut out the lies and embellishments and give me the real nuts and bolts." There was a long pause again, and this was followed by the provision of another long shot of whisky. He regained his seat and took a decent mouthful, swirled the remainder around in the glass and allowed the drink he had taken to leave his mouth and burn a path down his throat.

"Dave, it's like this. A fat guy called Pickles will arrange a time and place. You follow him."

"Any photos, Neville? Caught him on your cctv?"

"No, never been here. He makes sure it's somewhere there's no cameras. I've never seen a car and he's been nowhere near my dashcam. So yes, I've tried, but he's shrewder than you might think."

"If he's that good I might have trouble following him. And it's possible the cash might change hands once or twice en route to its final destination. Tricky, very tricky and no guarantee of success. And if I'm observed one of your family might suffer a 'warning', have you thought of that?"

"I think you're first rate tec and you won't get noticed. You must've trained in the real police to avoid being seen."

There followed what I believe is called a pregnant pause. His suggestion was identical, except in fine detail, to my own plan of action, the main difference being that I wanted to track down not only an assassin but also those, like Gradling, who paid for vile, cold-blooded murders, and make sure the police landed them all.

I had no idea how I was going to take all this to Okafor, never mind the way I might present it, and having shown my hand what the outcome would be. Sadly, it would be all too easy for the police to set about Gradling without getting anywhere; he'd deny it all, and there'd be no hard evidence. I'd be driving directly into a brick wall.

It was go-it-alone time, with the ex-cop in me calling me back to common sense, sound reasoning, and the right way to do something, while the adventurer in me wanted to try it my way and hang the consequences. With the latter I knew I could not afford to fail, and failure would be all too easy.

Unknown to me at the time DS Stephanie Broome was presenting a case to senior officers in Suffolk, a case for a surprise raid on Yvonne Pratt and her aliases. There was nervousness about dealing with someone so close to influential Jayne-Marie Panahan, but the concept of a raid on a leading businesswoman of her standing had already been thrown out the window. Yvonne Pratt was Stephanie's only chance.

Her superiors were rightly concerned about where the inside information had come from and it couldn't simply be dismissed as emanating from Kent. Okafor's advice was to say that it arose in an off-the-record conversation between an officer and a known informer.

They were going to have to 'sleep on it' and Stephanie Broome was not by nature a very patient person. But there was no choice. She'd done her best and she knew her Inspector supported her and had backed her judgement. One officer queried the relationship with Okafor and with Kent in general. It had been easily dismissed but of course something like that can sow seeds of doubt in the subconscious. Kent wasn't setting Suffolk up, but there is wise and natural caution when another force is leading you towards action that can backfire, and that's right and proper, even in a joint investigation. One force comes up with a bright idea, and another has to take the risks.

Yvonne Pratt and Jayne-Marie Panahan were in Stephanie's domain, and she was confident Okafor was on to something having had to make the initial judgement and deliver her verdict based on the data she'd received from him.

Elsewhere the killer was growing impatient.

Mr Pickles should've been on his way to the West Country and he was still in Kent, arguing the toss with Gradling who was determined to make some sort of silly stand, the sort of macho demonstration of impotence so typical of his sex. And there wasn't really time for the killer to drive to the south-east in order to inflict a warning against prevarication. But if it had to be done then so be it. The target was already chosen as was the punishment, and it was time Mr Pickles told Gradling retribution was imminent.

Why couldn't everyone be reasonable like Ms Panahan? She had plenty of money, was easily parted from it, and could see what was good for her. But she shouldn't have to bear the brunt of this new tax. A good tax is a fair tax, the killer recalled, and it's only fair if everybody pays their share. Trust a woman to pay up!

And then there's that dreadful Pequeman chappie. It's just possible, the killer felt, that I might have to sort him out on the way home from Kent should I have to go to the garden of England. It's all a rather grim nuisance, not at all the way it should've been. But I'll kill him if I have to rather than see him have a breakdown and enter confessional mode. The poor man's suffering and I should put him out of my misery.

***

Neville, in a rush over something or other, left his wife to show me out which she managed to achieve with a saucy grin and mischievous wink to set me on my way. You haven't learned your lesson, have you? But I kept silent on the subject.

I drove home in a confused state, or perhaps that should be 'befuddled'. Maybe the same thing anyway. I was perplexed about where my responsibilities lay, for I so surely should be going to the police and I knew Holton Okafor wasn't about to agree to any plan I might have. No way would he get permission for my escapade, and in fact it was more likely they would descend on Gradling and deal with him without making further progress. My efforts might be in vain.

The arrangement was that Neville would get in touch with me the next time he heard from Pickles and that he was going to pay up, so it was down to me whether I wanted in or not, assuming I didn't shop him in the meantime.

Was there something inside me that wanted me to be a crazy kind of hero? Or was I wildly reckless and beyond caring? No, never reckless. I couldn't hope to follow my plan through if I was in any way reckless or careless, and I knew I needed help into the bargain. Right now I just about trusted John Wapernod but he was miles away in Devon. I'd have liked to trust Kenny Parrett but Adam had warned me off, but without saying why.

There was a message on my phone to ring Kenny. He was full of bounce and excitement.

"Listen up, David. Two things: Gary Wimbush hasn't been seen for months. Doesn't mean he doesn't exist, just that he could now be anywhere. Second, the business he had in Barrow was in his wife's name. Lorraine Wimbush. Usual sort of arrangement, possible tax fiddle, that kind of thing. But when it was sold she must've got the money."

This was disturbing news and I was afeared for Laura. It was increasingly obvious her sister was a sinister character, untruthful even with Laura, a lady with secrets, some of which (for example the BMW) suggesting a curious state of affairs quite probably in the realms of the illegal. But just how bad was it?

I thanked Kenny, asked him, on his advice, to pursue his enquiries a little further, and said I'd like him to have another rummage into the life and times of Mrs Wimbush. I said she worked at a garage near where she lived. If he was up that way perhaps a look in? He was happy with that and also confirmed he was boarded in a rough old B&B in order to save me money.

"Kenny, your reward will be in heaven."

"Better not be, mate!" We both laughed. On the spur of the moment I elected to challenge him on Adam's warning.

"Kenny, a friend in my old force had warned me off you. No details, nothing at all. He won't say, but any reason, anything I need to know about?"

"God David, no. No idea. I got turned down for the force, wrong aptitude, meaning I wasn't bright enough I suppose. I still think there was concern about drug usage in my past. Well in my youth I liked a bit of weed now and then, it was about being big and one of the gang, but it never went any further and I grew up."

"I really don't think my contact, and he's a very good friend, would bother warning me about anything like that."

"Wait David. One other thing. Long time ago now, but I stuck my private investigator's nose into a police case, found them a vital clue and they were able to make an arrest, the villain being sent to prison. Well, this DS hated me on two counts and told me so. For interfering in the first place, especially after he'd told me to butt out, and for solving it for them!"

"I got wind of the fact he'd put a rumour about in the force that I'd been having an officer's wife away, and I suspect he hoped his colleagues would keep an eye out for me in anticipation of me breaking the law. Even a minor infringement might have done, he was that angry about me. But I thought nobody had taken it seriously and I've never heard another word. Don't suppose your mate has found that stale old rumour floating in the ether somewhere, do you?"

"Maybe. And were you carrying on with this woman?"

"No, definitely not. And that's the daft part, for neither she nor the officer were ever specified, never named. Still, I just can't think that's the reason for your mate's warning, because surely he'd tell you that? Not a state secret is it?"

"No Kenny, it's not, and I think you're right. But that therefore leaves me worrying about you, doesn't it?"

"I wouldn't be here working for you if you were that unsure about me."

"Good point. Anyway, good hunting, thanks for the gen, and keep me in the picture at every turn. You're right Kenny, I trust you and you've done well for me up to the present."

"Thanks David. Call you tomorrow or sooner if I discover anything."

And he was about to do just that.

***

When I phoned Okafor I decided to lie. I said my information was that payment for the assassinations was to be made a long while after the work was completed, allowing time for police investigations to die down.

"I don't know why but I think Neville Gradling hasn't paid a penny yet and won't for a long time. That's the deal, but that's only me putting two and two together and making five. After all, whoever heard of a hit man giving credit on such a scale." He chuckled. I continued. "Holton this is just my policeman's intuition, nothing more...."

"David, you're a terrible liar, but I believe you, I believe you," he interrupted, giggling some more.

"Can we meet?" I asked.

"You mean you have more lies for me? Yes okay David. I'll call on you mid-afternoon if that's okay with you and you haven't got your recording equipment on." He was still laughing.

"Fine Holton. Just text if you can't make it. And every camera here will be on you, I promise."

He cackled again, said goodbye and hung up. How much could I trust him? About as much as he trusted me, and I knew that he wouldn't hesitate to sink me in it and give the game away for kudos in his chosen profession. For all I knew his bosses had been fully informed of our meetings and approved of his tactics. I didn't feel I had a friend in the world. Then Laura phoned.

"Hey Moncks, great news. Lor wants to come to Kent and stay with me a couple of days. How's that, my old monkey? Says she's got a couple of old friends to look up, so she'll have to go out but that's wonderful. She wondered, well, actually I wondered if you could cough up the train fare."

"Yes, I'll reimburse her, or if she gives me the details I'll order the ticket online and have it posted to her. I take it an advance ticket will do."

"Cheapest Moncks, cheapest. She's not proud. Don't want first class."

"Tell her okay, make the arrangements and just let me know."

"Yaaaa-hoooo ... you're an angel of the highest order, and do you know, I might just go to bed with you again. Here, can the three of us go out for a meal?"

"Cheaper if I cook for us here. If you both stay over we can all have a glass of wine or three."

"Brilliant, and I thought I was the brains in this outfit."

"Must dash, pet. Speak tonight."

"First time you called me pet. That's made me go all wishy-washy inside. Love you lots. Bye."

Perhaps I did have a friend in the world. Or maybe not. And my one friend had a dodgy sister. Oh for heaven's sake, this ain't fair!

***

When it came to crime I didn't much believe in coincidences but here was one I'd rather not had to contemplate. Lorraine denying she was in Matlock the same time as us, and trying to keep the whole thing quiet, and by coincidence staying there when John Holgarve was slain.

No, it had to be mere coincidence. How could I think otherwise? The bastard in me, I suppose. Of course there could be no connection. This was Laura's sister I was thinking about. Of course it was coincidence.

So why was I starting to fret? The detective in me was driving my mind down a cul-de-sac. It was as if I was seeing things, imagining the worst, and yet it was my intuition that was playing merry hell with my thoughts. Why on earth did I want to think it was anything other than coincidence?

And the more I thought about it the more suspicious I became.

\*\*\*

DS Okafor was straight on the phone to DS Broome with my latest disclosure. There was caution. If they raided Ms Pratt (or rather her alter egos) too soon there would be no sign of the large movement of money, and absolutely no chance of going back for another raid. JMP's solicitor would see to that. Stephanie Broome was frustrated and annoyed and realised she could show neither emotion to her seniors. And there was always the chance David Canbown was selling them a bum steer, although Holton Okafor seemed to think not.

But salvation was at hand.

Her bosses authorised a thorough check on Evida Prada, and this began with a trained officer making an appointment at her dungeon, an act that produced all types of humour and filthy banter, laced with some genuine wit. One detective suggested they have a whip round for the man. And so it went on until it was unceremoniously put a stop to.

The killer was also deciding to unceremoniously put a stop to a couple of things. A visit to Kent, return via Derbyshire, and now there was an excellent excuse. No need to book into a hotel and attract attention; this might well be the perfect solution after all. Just need somewhere to hide the car. The railway line ran into Sheerness, so somewhere along the route? The wheels might look a bit out of place in the wrong area, so it could be a good idea to research Sittingbourne, that being the start of the branch line. Big town, plenty of top notch motors.

Mr Pickles could have one last chance to collect from Gradling, and if the guy paid up so much the better; the killer could take the money home. Yes, this might, on reflection, be the best answer.

The diversification into blackmail had not gone well, but of equal concern was Daryl Pequeman. Should never have accepted the booking from such a man, the murderer concluded, not the sort of person I normally deal with, but I had no idea his wife would commit suicide and Daryl would lose it completely. I'll have to kill him; he could so easily confess.

And Daryl was indeed close to confessing.

In his state of mental illness he wanted to be rid of all blame and guilt and the police consultant knew it was close. Ray Drunbolt, like Stephanie Broome, did not suffer patience as a virtue, believing it simply got in the way of getting the job done. But the consultant had assured him the break*through* was coming, and ahead of the break*down*, and Drunbolt's seniors had backed the consultant as might be expected.

"I hate waiting," he told one of his sergeants, and spoke with such venom that the sergeant feared that she was about to be visited with one of Drunbolt's infamous diatribes on inefficiency, these being unpleasant and largely unnecessary.

***

In a moment of folly, for such I thought it to be, I phoned John Wapernod and told him everything.

"Right David. I've nothing pressing at the mo, how about I drive to Kent for moral if not practical support? I'll sort my own accommodation out and won't get in your way. If you're really planning to follow Gradling's cash you'll need more than yourself."

"John, I just don't know who to trust. I don't know I can trust you."

"Correct. But we're both private eyes and we need each other. Have you spoken to Kenny about this?"

"No, I've just engaged him to find out about Gary Wimbush and his wife. He's had nothing more from me."

"Good. I don't know what to make of his situation."

"Have you heard from Yvonne?"

"No I haven't David. And I'm not making contact, least of all after what you've told me."

"Thanks John. Please come over, if you don't mind. I feel isolated and worried sick that I can't trust anybody. Sorry that includes you."

"No offence taken. I don't trust you. So what have we got to lose?"

Probably everything, I decided!

***

"Okay David, you reckon payments are made a long time after the services have been provided. What makes you think that, precisely?"

"Intuition, Holton."

280

"Bollocks, David."

"Probably, but that's how I'm explaining it."

"So the truth is that you *know* payments are made on a credit basis, and as you've said we're going to have trouble believing that. Criminals do not routinely go out and kill people on tick.

"And is Gradling going to pay up?"

"My intuition says he's thinking about it. A demand for more money might come with a threat. Let's face it, as far as we know, this person can kill at will, so can almost certainly hurt someone if they chose to do so."

"You're assuming we, the professionals, are not on top of things. You know there's matters I can't discuss with you, much as I'd like to, but I will say progress is being made and a great deal of work is under way out of the public eye. You know how it all fits together. We're not going to be shouting from the rooftops yet, and you're going to have to accept that we are, in every sense, on the case."

"I don't doubt it. But I did hope we would exchange info. Any progress on the story so far in relation to what I've told you?"

"David, there is progress and there is progress. But there is nothing to share at this time."

DS Okafor sat back on the settee, twisted his mouth slightly, the gesture of 'pick the bones out of that', and then took a final mouthful of coffee, waiting for me to speak. He'd arrived full of bonhomie but I guessed it was probably a front, and his attitude, as our meeting developed, led me to believe he had either been warned off or had allowed second thoughts to overtake his earlier cavalier approach.

There wasn't going to be any more co-operation so I abandoned any idea of putting forward my plan of action under any guise whatsoever. Had he already surrendered to the fact he was first and foremost a serving officer and had possibly put his cards on the table with the bosses?

He wasn't going to fill me in on the outcome of information I'd supplied. This was a pointless meeting now and I was fretting about him organising another raid on Gradling. That could already be at an advanced planning stage.

Later that evening I called Adam Pensfield and put my new knowledge of Kenny Parrett to him, hoping to coax him out on the subject. There was a long silence. Long silences are tactics, for quite often the other person will feel compelled to speak, whereas I was an old hand at this game and kept quiet.

"You're still there?" he eventually queried.

"Yes," my simple reply. More silence.

"No, it was none of those reasons. You know this is top secret and the penalty for ever breathing a word in the wrong place is death?"

"Just tell me, Adam."

"Okay. He investigated a fraud case for a private client and just happened to chance on something worse. He presented his findings to the police who took the evidence at face value. Innocent man was arrested, his home searched, his reputation shattered. Child porn, David. Parrett's excuse was that it was up to the police to check his information. Turned out the investigating officer was a real zealot when it came to child porn and was too keen to nail this guy. Got a reprimand that damaged his career and he left the force soon after, a good man lost overboard. Lot of resentment over Parrett, and a red light ever since on anything he brings to the cops."

"But why was his info so bad? Was there any truth, was there another villain?"

"History does not record what happened, but there were no further arrests. The innocent man sued and settled out of court."

"So in truth, Adam, the officer acted indefensibly. He should've gone into it more."

"Yes, but he made the mistake of trusting Kenny Parrett in the first place, and just because he was a highly regarded private eye."

"Do you think Kenny intended to ruin an innocent man, perhaps over something else?"

"It's a possibility, isn't it David? But I'm not privy to any details and I'm sorry but that's the truth."

"Anything you can tell me on the murder enquiries?"

"No. And that's a 'no' I can't tell you."

"Meaning yes there is and no you can't tell me."

"Have it your way, pal."

"Okay Adam, let's not make this personal. Sorry, just seem to be a bit touchy right now. And for the record I'm seeing plenty of Laura." And I told him about finding her sister. He had some uncomplicated advice for me:

"David, keep your eye on her, that's all I ask. I don't want to see you hurt or worse still find yourself in trouble with the law." Our conversation continued for a while in more general terms before we said our goodbyes. Then Kenny rang, talk of the devil.

"Wow, David, have you got some kitten-cat here."

"Go on, tell me then."

"Found Lorraine's garage. She wasn't working. Round the back I saw this gorgeous heap of pure BMW, a lovely monster. So I said to the girl in the shop, owner must be doing alright having a motor like that, and she says it's not the owners, belongs to one of her colleagues, she parks it there for security, 24-hour place, cameras, you know the form. So I took a chance and said, oh yes that'll be Lucy Kenyon, hoping her alias was right, and she said yes, did I know her?

"I had to think quick and I said yes, but not personally, through a mate of mine, Gary Wimbush. And she says, Gary? Have you seen him recently because Lucy's been looking for him. Lucy says she hasn't seen him for ages. The girl wondered if he was the boyfriend or husband, you know, walked out on her maybe. Well, she was obviously fishing, David, talking to a complete stranger like that. So I said no more. Hope I did right."

"You did Kenny, that's a great piece of work. I think you can leave now, well in the morning of course, and if there's nothing else to do email me your bill. Now, have you got anything else on your plate right now?"

"Nope, nothing that couldn't wait a day or two. What's on your mind?"

"John Wapernod's driving up and I was wondering if you could make it to Kent as well. Very good reason but we need to talk away from eyes and ears if you understand me."

"Gotcha. Yes, I'm game. I'll pop in home on the way tomorrow, so email me directions and any other gen."

That was about the sum of our call. I would tackle him over the innocent man face to face, and if I felt I could trust him I'd want him in on my scheme. He has a remarkable ability to dig deep in the right places and I bet he's A1 when it comes to covert tailing, and just about everything else. But trust would be the thing.

I was starting to speculate whether I trusted myself anymore, for I was only too conscious that those I could bank on in this business amounted to a big zero, Laura included. Was I inviting two vipers to my bosom? In a way I was pleased to lose faith in Okafor, not as a competent officer, but because if we were no longer in each others' confidence that suited me better now.

Who could I rely on? It would be good if I could say Laura was my best bet but the thing that worried me most now was Lorraine; where would Laura's loyalties lie if she was faced with a shocking truth, a truth I dared not try and contemplate yet knew I had to.

It appeared that this deadly drama could be entering its final act, with the finale the most potentially dangerous part of all.

In the next couple of days things were going to come to a head more dramatically than I could ever have imagined.

## Chapter Twenty Nine
# Time Waits for No Man

Woodbridge is a well known and attractive town on the River Deben in east Suffolk, possessing a reasonable share of old and historic buildings, and the air of an artists' quarter equally accentuated by the riverside setting.

Boat building, rope and sail making here date back to the Middle Ages. Much of the area was granted to the powerful Bigod family who erected the fearsome looking castle at nearby Framlingham. Woodbridge oozes class and has a reputation for seafood fully justified. So unsurprisingly it attracts many visitors from all over.

Depending on your point of view then, it is either an entirely appropriate or rather weird place to find a practising dominatrix and a fully equipped dungeon, admittedly located on the outskirts and in a cellar under a terraced house. A completely soundproofed cellar, of course. Down here, one might say, nobody will hear you scream.

The detective sent on an extraordinary mission to the establishment was being shown around the dungeon preparatory to his next visit, supposedly for a 'session' amongst the most evil looking of gadgets. This was part of the deal. Evida Prada was expensive, very expensive, and the man wanted to be sure that the surroundings lent themselves to the full enjoyment of the occasion.

Photos of Evida, in various poses, decorated the walls, but not one was a full facial. The woman escorting him on the guided tour was not Evida but he was aware she was summing him up. Probably, he believed, can smell a plain clothes cop at ten paces. The game may already be up.

He was wrong. The woman was quite happy he was above board, had he but known it, and even offered him a brief warm-up right away, a free sample if he was interested. He declined. Her job was to chat to him, find out exactly what he required, and ensure Evida was properly briefed so that she was ready in the right clothes and with all the right gear prepared.

She made copious notes and the booking was made for the following night, a deposit of thirty pounds being requested. Yes, they took card payments and the deposit was settled by the contactless arrangement. Very different, he knew, from a quickie up a dark alley somewhere, a place where thirty pounds could buy you a few minutes pleasure, if you could call it that, with the chance of catching a nasty dose of something anti-social thrown in as bonus.

Once Evida made an appearance, and he was in no doubt he was facing Yvonne Pratt, he would send a signal on a concealed radio and a raid would ensue with Stephanie Broome in the vanguard. It was to be hoped they'd arrive before he was required to participate in any fun activities. If it wasn't Yvonne he was, to use an expression, to make his excuses and leave.

***

If trust was becoming a difficult animal to tame and a rarity of high magnitude, suspicion was falling all around, well beyond the parameters of the police investigation.

William Bailey had noted only too well how distressed his wife had become of late, how easily she angered, how off-hand she could be, and it wasn't the woman he'd married. Already worried she might have hired a killer, he was more concerned than ever that it might be the sad and terrible truth of the matter, and he fretted and wrestled with his conscience.

If Bailey was a troubled man then Cathy Kethnet was a frightened woman. Her husband had told her quite clearly that killers could be hired and she had no doubt he would have the contacts. It made her agonize over whether he had arranged Edward's murder, and as time went by that appalling thought riddled her senses to the point where she found she could believe it.

What was going to exacerbate her disquiet on the subject was going to be the rotund, sweating visitor Nathan Kethnet was shortly to meet.

And in Kent a private investigator was sweating about the possibility his girl-friend's sister was closer to the murders than it might be hoped. He wanted to be wrong but being an ex-cop his natural instinct was to think the worst and actually set about proving it or, in this case, proving it wasn't so. He really wanted to find out he was wrong, for Laura's sake.

A man in a remote part of Derbyshire, a man whose mind was shot to pieces and incapable of rational thought, was on the verge of deciding life wasn't worth living and that he might either confess or join his beloved Rosie in the afterlife. He could go the same way as her, off the famous viaduct at Monsal Dale. He could achieve both ends by writing a confession and leaving it as a suicide note.

Even when the mind is torn asunder that final act can focus the attention of the brain, and Daryl Pequeman suddenly discovered that he was thinking more clearly and precisely than for a long time. His sister and mother were staying with him and trying to persuade him to see a doctor, for they recognised his illness for what it was. He would have to give them the slip. Not for one moment did his mind allow him to consider the pain his death would bring to them.

If dark clouds hung over part of Derbyshire the sun was shining elsewhere. Georgina and Leonora were celebrating being themselves and the beautiful people they were, and making the most of the first tentative steps on this new road and revelling in the joy it brought them. Georgina was free at last and despite the previously disagreeable thoughts about things like getting a job, having to make her own bed and drive around in a small six year old car, she was positively looking forward to the prospect.

Leonora could barely believe she had won her great love but wallowed in the gladness of her success and rejoiced in their togetherness. She would make her new partner the happiest woman in the world and had dedicated her heart to achieving that aim.

Far from being happy, beautiful people, Jayne-Marie Panahan and William Bailey were sharing a currently strained relationship and it was about to get a whole lot worse. Bailey decided to take his life in his hands and confront his wife.

It had been a long, stressful day for both of them in their business world and he reasoned there had to be something serious bothering Jayne-Marie, dreading that the problem was possibly the murders, particularly the despatch of Phyllis Downport. It was mid-evening and they were relaxing in the small lounge, the snug as they called it, and attacking a bottle of a pleasing *Furleigh Estate Dorset Coast Special Reserve*, when William threw his live hand grenade into the arena.

"Jay, you hired a hit man to deal with Phyllis, didn't you? Don't bother denying it. The fact is I love you and I'm not going to shop you to the police or anything like that. She got what, in your eyes, she deserved, and I got mine as well. It's in the past. I've got over her, and we've both benefited from my inheritance, you and me, and we're a great couple and we're going places and I don't mean prison.

"But if your conscience is getting the better of you let's talk about it. I'm a good listener, and we can ride this out together. We've got such a fabulous future nothing, *nothing* must be allowed to spoil it. I'm on your side and I want to help, believe me I do. Let me in, let me help. I love you Jay, and I'd do anything to pull you through. Let me be your rock; lean on me. Share your troubles. We can overcome them together."

Ms Panahan was wearing such a look of shock that her husband was temporarily frightened she'd had some sort of attack. He was genuinely afraid of the backlash should he be wrong or should she propagate the lie, always assuming, of course, that she was actually guilty. Then she spoke.

"I'm being blackmailed Will, and the money won't last long. Please help me....." And the words dissolved into tears. This was an unusual event and William did not know how to handle it. Jayne-Marie was not a cry-baby, and rarely showed such emotions, yet now he could see the real pain rise to the surface and knew he was right. For a second the realisation his wife had indeed hired a murderer turned his mind and his heart into a morass of hatred, revulsion and anger.

She'd paid to have Phyllis stabbed through the heart, the woman he had laid with, the woman whose companionship and sense of physical adventure had lured him from Jayne-Marie's bed. Then, in the twinkling of an eye, the nastiness passed and he looked at the stricken woman he truly loved, and dashed to her side to comfort her. She was all he had, he did love her, and she had the keys to the money and their lifestyle, so he swiftly persuaded himself that he did not loathe her and wanted this difficulty to be sorted in their favour.

After sundry hugs and many her tears William returned to the matter in hand, feeling a safe period of comforting had passed and his wife was ready to open up.

"Blackmailed Jay? Tell me, please tell me." And she told him and he was horrified, but even more horrified to learn that Yvonne Pratt was the go-between with the assassin.

"I'll go and see Yvonne," he volunteered, "and see what I can do. That okay?" She nodded her acquiescence while he returned to comforting her. His mind was all over the place. His original intention had been to challenge her, discover the truth, and hate for her it, perhaps to the extent of going to the police, but now he knew he could never do that. Solve the current problem and they could still be the happy, loving couple they had been and would be again.

It was a future worth fighting for. Yvonne was his next port of call. That woman had a lot to answer for and William Bailey was not a man to be easily deflected from his purpose. It could be a deadly business.

\*\*\*

And so time moved on, not that it had ever stood still, and with it time swept along the many varied facets of the chronicle of deceit, betrayal, death and love in all its glories that events had opened up. If there was a tangled web, with all too many cross-threads, there were also calmer waters being sailed upon where there was clarity and purposeful design, Georgina and Leonora being prime examples of a better, simpler life. They had carved that life from the solid rock of a marriage founded on poor principles that had trapped Georgina by her own hand. Leonora had the strength to pull her away.

But elsewhere the wider issue was riddled with pain, anguish and despair, just as it was laden with mystery, complexity and deviousness.

And further complexity was soon to be added when Kenny Parrett arrived in Kent.

But my first visitor was John Wapernod.

I'd set my assistant the task of finding out how Yvonne Pratt's husband died and she busied herself in my dining room on the computer; it saved her going to the library and sending me nuisance texts every now and then.

John was fascinated by my small garden and wondered how I ever found the time to tend it.

"Frankly John, I don't know! I put a bit of effort in now and again, perhaps more than I realise. But it is relaxing, and I do some of my best thinking out here." We strolled around the lawn, which I have to admit was looking deliciously green thanks to my weed and feed programme, and admired the plants still in bloom. John was obviously a gardener himself as he was able to identify some which I could not. "Do you garden?" I asked.

"Yes, I'm quite pleased this year, but it is time consuming and often it involves time I haven't got. Does Laura give you a hand?"

"No, she likes the garden alright, but she's not actually often here."

"Oh I see. But you're both very much in love, if I may say so, and I thought you were living together."

"Perish the thought, and no, I'm not in love."

"Ah yes, song by 10 c.c. if I remember! And don't kid yourself David; you're in love. In fact I wondered if I'd be hearing wedding bells by now, or maybe you're not into marriage."

"John, I think you're reading me all wrong! Tell me about you. Ever come close to marriage?"

"No, and if you'll pardon my corny expression, that's because I haven't found the man of my dreams." He saw my uncontrolled startled look and smiled. "Yes, I'm gay David, or probably bi. You see, I like some romantic female company from time to time, and intimacy is rather different, but I much prefer my own sex. You know where you are with a man. Shocked David?"

"Not at all, just surprised after you said your alibi for Edward Nobbs's murder was a woman. I think it would be wonderful if we could scrap all the labels and just be ourselves, you know, be true to our real selves. Get on and enjoy life freely. It therefore follows that in my reasoning we should be free to love whomsoever we please."

"Do you mean that David, or are you saying the right things as you see them?"

"I mean it. Comes from the heart as well as the mind."

"Good, because they're my thoughts entirely."

We returned indoors and Miss McCaffield was making coffee.

"I have news. Can I speak in front of John?"

"Yes of course."

"Mr Pratt died in a car crash some years ago. I've got all the details when you want them. He was drunk and initially there was concern the car had been tampered with, as it seems the accelerator stuck. But that was ruled out eventually after more detailed scrutiny of the wreckage. Isn't Google fantastic for unearthing all kinds of things?" John spoke first.

"Well done Laura. Mmmm .... more and more interesting by the minute."

"Agreed. Let's have that drink in the lounge and a chat."

"Me invited?"

"Yes Laura, you're invited."

"What I told you is true," John whispered to me as we walked to the lounge, and he was sporting a most lecherous grin as he said it.

Daryl Pequeman was making his final plans. He'd written his confession, printed it, and intended to post it to his sister at his address where she should receive it the morning of his suicide. He was astonished how clearly he was now thinking driven, as he was, by the desire to be re-united with Rosie in the afterlife. It was the only way out of the eternal anguish that preoccupied him, the only escape from the pain and regret that nothing would ever make better.

But even the best laid plans can go astray.

Whereas Ms Panahan paid up instantly Neville Gradling was now the fly in the ointment for the killer. The faithful Pickles had been relieved of his duties in Kent and sent to Devon to tackle Nathan Kethnet. The killer had a good reason to visit Kent, an all important alibi, and would deal with Gradling. Oh, how the best laid plans can go astray, but sort out the wretched Neville and eliminate Pequeman on the way home and things might get back on track.

Why couldn't they all be like Jayne-Marie? Mr Pickles was dreading Nathan Kethnet cutting up rough; it just wouldn't do, wouldn't do at all. He had his fingers crossed. He was pondering why his boss had decided to pursue this blackmail business and created chaos out of good order. Of course, he loved bewildering the police, but he didn't think so much of tempting providence.

Poor mummy, he mused, as he drove west on the A303. Not a man for motorways, Mr Pickles, and this run was truly scenic compared with the M4 and M5. Poor mummy, in that secure unit just because she stabbed nasty daddy to death. She had suffered so badly with him running off with that barmaid. Yes, a barmaid of all people; not someone of quality and breeding, a shocking tart, all tits and bum. Horrible. Mum was heartbroken, and if she hadn't dealt with dad I would've had to, he concluded.

***

In the afternoon I drove Laura to work, her other employment and the one that earned money with guaranteed frequency, showed John around Sheerness and found Kenny Parrett waiting for us on our return.

"This is interesting," he announced as we settled in the lounge, "just look at this. Found this photo in a newspaper. It's a womens' rights rally. Two ladies, arms linked in the front there. Now here's what my mate in Graphic Design made of it." He produced a blown up picture but all the features of the two women were clearly in perspective. I saw it at once.

"Lorraine and Yvonne," I exclaimed. "How old is this Kenny?" He showed me the date printed at the bottom. Very thorough, our Kenny. "How on earth do you come by all this, mate?"

"Good at the job," he replied with more modesty than his words might've appeared. And I began to consider that I might never be up to it, that I was pursuing the wrong career, that I could never match his ability. There were doubts about Mr Parrett, granted, but we can't all be perfect and maybe you can be better at this job if you have grey areas. I still had to tackle him about the other matter, but not in front of John.

Right now we were interrupted by a call from Neville.

"Dave, had a call, from a woman, she wants the money in a couple of days or one of the family's going to be hurt. It's got to be cash, in a suitcase. Help!"

"Okay Neville, this is what we're going to do." I was speaking in front of John and Kenny whose assistance I was going to need and I wanted them to hear. "You get the money and do as you're told. Let me know. I'm going to tail whoever does the pick-up. Don't worry, I've got professional help to hand. You won't see us and neither will the other person. A suitcase eh? How very quaint. A classic job if ever there was one.

"Now, you've asked for my help, and you want the police kept out of it, so no arguments, no negotiations, just do as I say."

"Right, in your hands then Dave, just don't foul up. And I don't want them coming back for more, understand? And if a loved one gets hurt so do you." I just ignored him. His day will come very soon.

"A suitcase full of used notes," John remarked once the call had ended, "how very novel, how delightfully old-fashioned. That'll be one for my autobiography. Wonder when that was last done in real life?" We all laughed. "How do you know this is all going to happen, David? You seem very sure, and obviously you didn't ask us here simply to admire your garden."

I explained my theory. John was agog, but Kenny had a knowing look about him. It had been arranged that Lorraine was coming by train, would arrange her own ticket and I would reimburse her. I still hoped that I was wrong, but having put my views to John and Kenny found eager agreement that it was a nasty possibility.

There was the photo we now had of Lorraine and Yvonne and that added fuel to the fire.

"I think we can say we know why Yvonne's website picture is so different from the real thing. Not only harmful to trade as a private eye if anyone associated Eve Parr, sex worker, with her, but also a blind to anyone watching her womens' rights involvement." John continued. "The missing link is not that Lorraine and Yvonne obviously know each other but what the association might be.

"Another missing link, guys, is that we don't know what the police are doing. They may be closer to this than we can imagine." There was one other problem. "And what if we've got Lorraine all wrong and it's not her? I think she'll drive down in her very distinctive BMW. If she collects then we have a clear path, and I'll explain what that is. But if it's someone else then we have to be prepared to tail and do it properly."

"I'm up for it either way," Kenny interjected, "we've got to get this to the stage where we've got something concrete to hand to the police. But Dave, Dave, what about Neville? He'll be after you if he thinks you've double-crossed him."

"I've thought of that. He'll never know because I may get his money back anyway, job done, box ticked, and I reckon once the police set about Yvonne and the Panahan woman they'll find the evidence they need to raid Gradling."

"Forgive me, gentlemen," John commented, "but we do have to contemplate failure. Not a pretty picture. And we have to allow for danger. This *person* knows how to kill."

"Being afraid sharpens your mind, your reactions, helps you focus. It's natural," Kenny offered.

"Another thing David," John queried, "you're talking about Laura's sister. Could Laura trip us up, tip off Lorraine?"

"I'm not going to tell her until the time's right, and it won't be right until I know for sure, absolutely certain. And only then if it's in our interests."

"You're talking about the girl you love David. This might be the end of a lovely relationship." John had his head down and was looking over the top of imaginary spectacles.

"Thanks for your sarcasm, Mr Wapernod, but I'll take that chance."

Later John went to his car to deal with two phone calls of a private nature, business he assured us, and I took the opportunity to challenge Kenny.

"That," he responded, "*That?* No idea why that should put me in the black books of the boys in blue. I carried out some private work relating to someone defrauding the firm he worked for. He was falsifying expense claims, and that's what I was primarily checking up on. He was a top manager, a mason, well known in town, that sort of thing, big at the golf-club, you know the form.

"The CEO wangled me access to his private pages on the computer system, and there I found them. Images of child porn. I threw up Dave. That's beyond bad, should be a hanging offence in my book. Must be in yours Dave. I tipped off this copper I knew, bloke who hates the bastards as much as I do.

"Instead of getting a warrant for the firm and getting into those computer pages he goes round this guy's house, arrests him, searches the place top to bottom, takes his own computer away, well, you know what happens Dave. Someone at the firm must've got wind of it because when the law got a warrant for access to their computer system, no images.

"Not my fault. I've never thought anymore about it. And you reckon they hold it against me? Copper did it all wrong, but that's his fault, not mine." I knew Kenny was right and I hoped his version was the correct one. It was almost as if he was being smeared, and for the first time I began to wonder if there was an officer somewhere in this terrible mix that was helping the killer keep one step ahead.

I relayed my new worries to Kenny. He looked aghast.

"Yeah, not thought of that. Jeez, we could end up right in a ditch on this." John returned and we gave him the new gen.

"Don't frighten me anymore," he exclaimed in mock horror, "but you gentlemen may have a point. Or are we just becoming paranoid? By the way, changing the subject, I'm staying at Hempstead House, the other side of Sittingbourne, where are you Kenny?"

"Blimey, hadn't thought of that...."

"Let's ring and see if they can fit you in. Let's get organised. My advice is let's calm down and start to think everything through logically, make notes, whatever. Let's be thoroughly professional."

"Me?" said Kenny, "I'd rather be reckless! No, I'm joking. Hey, we're some gang of three here. We're all quite different from each other. This could be the start of something big." I thought with mild amusement that Kenny was unaware of one of the differences John represented, but we were indeed an intriguing set of ingredients as private investigators, and those ingredients could make a very successful banquet of success in this case. For the moment we laughed at the concept and embroidered it with salty witticisms.

And so time continued to move on, just as before, just as ever, and in our part of the world the heat was turning up to full volume. And time was waiting for nobody.

# Chapter Thirty
# The Die is Cast

The day before D-day, as we three amigos called it, the day before Lorraine was due in Kent, she'd actually set off intending to spend the night in the Sittingbourne area instead of coming down by train the next morning. Laura expected the latter whereas I was confident she was driving down earlier, as proved to be the case.

Lorraine collected her car from the garage and drove into the city, first stop the station to buy the train tickets. That was part of the cover. Then the sleek BMW headed for the M6 and the south.

She'd researched the best place to park and decided on Sittingbourne where the branch line runs to Sheerness. David and Laura said they'd pick her up at Sittingbourne station so she'd need to be parked a safe distance away, not the Sheppey side of town, and get to the rendezvous point in plenty of time. Using *Streetmap.com* she'd selected some likely roads, reasoning parking near the station was going to be nigh on impossible, noting importantly that suburban roads extended beyond her chosen streets. If you can't get parked on plan A you need plan B ready!

At least she wouldn't have to worry about going on the branch. An unnecessary waste of time. Sittingbourne would do very nicely. She had a mapping system on her computer and had printed out various relevant pages apropos a transfer point for Neville's suitcase. There were no chances to be taken; he must be made very clear that a most painful and unpleasant attack would be made on one of the family if he went to the police or did anything else foolish. At this stage Neville assumed the killer to be male and the woman who had contacted him now was a go-between.

If he got it all wrong then for all he knew the killer would be elsewhere watching one of his family. No, Neville would be a good boy, that was for sure.

The mapping system had also produced details of the precise whereabouts of Daryl's cottage, but Lorraine had not yet decided how to lure him to his death. What she didn't realise was that she wouldn't get the chance to get near him.

In Kent David Canbown was getting in a state about Laura, or more particularly the prospect that her sister could be a ruthless assassin. In the middle of all this the day job loomed large, Daphne Carter phoning from Minnis Bay regarding her missing sister.

I decided that, as I was in the company of two super sleuths, John and Kenny could make themselves useful if they so wished.

And they went-to with gusto, Kenny glued to my computer, John with his laptop in the lounge, nobody making any promises. I had re-assured Daphne there was progress and I was using excellent contacts in my search, which pleased her no end to the point where she invited me and my 'team' for tea any afternoon that might suit. Hmph!

Looking back I am not sure where October went. We were enjoying a late summer well into September but now the nights were drawing in, the clocks had gone back, and there was coldness in the air. I'd spent whatever chance there'd been attending to my very small but perfectly formed rented rear garden, preparing it for winter and for next summer, and it was true what I had said to John, namely that gardening was hard work but a scene of relaxation.

Next up was November. These last few weeks had flown by in a flurry of murder, of investigations, and all the palaver of locating Lorraine as well as meeting my business commitments. The pot-lid hunt had come to a grinding halt. The Loughborough owner declined to have their lid valued and my client had given up. I suspect he'd hoped to get it back cheaply knowing full well it was worth a large amount.

Kenny Parrett, for all the question marks over his head, was an ace and now I doubted whether being a private eye was what I was cut out for. I didn't think I would make the grade, mainly because I had scruples and a conscience, and evidently Kenny did not. In his eyes the end justified the means providing they were almost legal, regardless of whether or not they were morally right. John was an equal expert and I deemed him to be successful because of his thoroughness and attention to detail, whereas it had become patently certain that he too possessed a willingness to dig where he shouldn't.

Yes, I could do it, but it worried me, the result of an over-active conscience. So maybe I needed to consider what else I could do. I was also thinking about what would happen to Laura. There was a good chance she and I might suffer a dreadful fall-out over Lorraine.

She might be entirely innocent so what would Laura think of me then for daring to believe she was a mass-murderer? And if she was guilty Laura might still blame me and hate me. Either way I could see our friendship ending, probably acrimoniously, and love would not come into it.

My mind roamed back to her own criminal record, not one to be envied, but as it stood no way could she have been in league with Lorraine. The search had been too genuine and wouldn't have been necessary if the two were in contact. Did they both own criminal mentalities, capable of being unleashed in the wrong circumstances, and that being so did I want to be involved with someone of such a nature?

John might've perceived love in our eyes but my heart told me it must be very superficial. Yes, Laura could think she loves me and I suppose I would look on her with a degree of warmth, and that might induce an appearance of love in our glances, enough to alert Mr Wapernod. But *real* love? Deep and true? No, it could never be so, and the present situation precluded any advance in my feelings.

Laura had never known real love beyond that furnished by her parents, certainly not the beautiful love that I once shared with Penny before the job came between us, so it was always likely that she merely *thought* she was in love with me. That kind of love is easier to get over when heartbreak comes, easier for both of us. There was definitely no solid bond between us, no unbreakable ties that could withstand an awful battering, no unmovable foundations that would not shake to destruction when put to the test.

But would any of this occur?

***

The deed was done.

Daryl put his letter in an envelope, stuck a first class stamp on the front and put it in his jacket pocket. He would find an excuse to go down the road later and post it, and that night he would find another excuse to go out for a walk by himself.

I'm coming Rosie, my Rosie, he said to himself, I'm coming. Soon my love, soon now.

The deed was done.

Neville had found an old suitcase and had arranged for a large cash withdrawal from his bank, not an unusual event for the Gradlings of this world, and one the banks accepted at face value. Five hundred thousand pounds in used twenties with a few fifties for good measure. As he checked the money he smiled at the thought this task would've been purgatory with the new plastic fives and tens! He hated them.

Of course the banks ran their own checks. Money laundering was a concern. Although Neville's was used to his ways of dealing with cash the withdrawal of half a million, placed in a suitcase which he then wheeled from the premises without any obvious guard, did more than raise eyebrows.

For fairly large amounts Neville usually employed a security firm, but not this time. The bank was aware that Gradling had been the subject of a police investigation which had involved going through his various accounts with a fine tooth comb. Alarm bells started to jangle.

The deed was done.

Lorraine had given Laura details of her journey tomorrow so we knew what time to be at Sittingbourne station in the afternoon. I made a special note because I wanted to follow her progress or rather the progress of the trains she was supposed to be on. The arrangement was that she would ring on arrival at Euston before walking to St Pancras and catching the high-speed service to Kent.

I found myself shaking inside. Laura was like a dog with two tails, so authentically excited and so unaware that I knew something about Lorraine she didn't, something that was souring my attitude towards her. I couldn't help it; it was as if I was preparing myself for the Armageddon that must surely come one way or the other.

If her sister was guilty and I had helped bring about her downfall how would she take it? If she learned I'd known for some time and hadn't disclosed my knowledge? Might she, as the frightful horror manifested itself, turn to me for comfort and support? And would my conscience allow me to give it?

I couldn't begin to imagine how she'd feel. A lifetime separated from her sibling, a joyful reunion, and just as quickly Nemesis, the whole world falling in on her. It might be incomprehensible, unbearably painful, intolerably raw and shattering. She might never recover, it was bound to be that devastating.

Oh please, please, let me be wrong about this, and let Laura never find out. Let her be ecstatically happy and overjoyed to revel in the company of long lost Lorraine. Yes, I wanted her happiness, wanted that more than anything, and knew all I might deliver was sadness and fury. It might break her completely and I felt the first pangs of my own guilt as this dark, black cloud smothered my thoughts.

No, it did more than that, it enveloped my heart, and it was in that period of turmoil that I realised that maybe I did love her. This was going to be so horrible. And there was no escape.

***

Somewhere in Suffolk someone got cold feet.

What would be achieved by revealing Evida Prada was none other than Yvonne Pratt? It wouldn't be an excuse for another raid as Jayne-Marie Panahan's legal team, which extended its cover to the private eye, would pounce like a tiger on its prey and all would be lost. At best Yvonne might have to cease to be a private investigator and a great deal of lurid publicity might follow the revelations which in turn might damage the police inquiry.

Taking the whole and arriving at a well balanced conclusion it was the verdict that more harm than good might come of it, and since JMP was the real target it would move the investigation no nearer, possibly halt it in its tracks. Now this was not at all to DS Broome's liking and she sought solace in a phone call to DS Okafor.

"Trouble is Steph, my contact down here's gone quiet and that means he's up to something. I will give him a call anyway, but I'm not hopeful. From what I've been told we need to see if Gradling's made any large unexplained payments or withdrawals, but we haven't any fresh evidence. My guys won't wear it, so I'm in the same boat as you, if that's any consolation."

"None whatsoever! The worst of it is Holton, that we both know they're right. I just know we are so close. The real bother here is Panahan's legal support; they're watching us like hawks, and we dare not sneeze in the wrong place."

"Same here. Gradling's got a legal eagle on our case." He sighed mightily. "If we get one move wrong where these dudes are concerned that puts it all back decades, if you see what I mean. We won't be able to even think about taking pro-active measures."

"What d'you reckon it was like in the old days, I mean the *old* days?"

"Wade in, truncheons waving, and hang the consequences!"

"I'm going to have a chat with Geoff in Devon, Holton, no harm done, see if he's any sort of update other than the official channels."

"Okay Steph, and give us a call, eh?"

"Will do; bye for now Holton."

***

Nathan Kethnet was not a man for being disturbed by a surprise visitor, and his first reaction to hearing that a Mr Pickles wanted to see him urgently was to tell his secretary to make it absolutely clear that Pickles was unwelcome and would not be seen. And no, he couldn't make an appointment.

Whatever could the wretched man want? Nathan had just paid up, game over. He was still curious, so that when his secretary said that Mr Pickles would not go away and was now demanding access to her boss, he relented and gave him three minutes of his valuable time.

Having listened to Pickles Nathan burst out laughing; not a real laugh, one of those manufactured roaring laughs that sound more like a heavy smoker trying in vain the clear their throat.

"Go away, you fat animal. Nothing doing. If anything happens to one of my family I'll hunt you down, believe me I will. My private eye is the tops. Between us we'll find you."

"I don't think you understand, Mr Kethnet," a startled, sweating Mr Pickles replied, "but we are all in this together. We can't shop each other for obvious reasons, so these disputes have to be settled out of court as it were."

"And listen up, matey. I'll settle out of court alright. You won't blackmail me, that's for sure. Any trouble and you'll get trouble alright. Clear? You understand? Good, now, to put it politely, why don't you go elsewhere and urinate? Get out of my sight, you horrible pile of fat."

And Mr Pickles found himself outside Nathan's office and covered in bewilderment, rage and despair. Whatever would his manager say? She had enough on her plate going to Kent to sort Neville Gradling out and wouldn't want another problem. He hadn't handled it well, it would be all his fault, and he might end up on the wrong end of the killer's objectionable skills. Why couldn't they all be like Jayne-Marie Panahan and just be good people and pay up?

Back in Suffolk William Bailey had arrived in Needham Market ready for words with Yvonne Pratt.

"Yvonne, this nonsense stops now. No more money. Jayne-Marie's told me everything including your involvement in the killing. You've had plenty of money, now back off....."

"William, you are now truly implicated. Had you gone straight to the police instead of to me you might have saved yourself. Yes, you'd have seen Jayne-Marie arrested, me too, and where would that have got you? Now tell your wife to pay, there's a good chap, and no harm will come to anyone."

"Wrong. Harm will come to *you*. There's no more money. Enjoy what you've had. Matter closed. None of us gets arrested, life goes on, and you get to keep the money. Leave us alone...."

"The service provider will not leave you alone. Mmmm ... service provider. Sounds much nicer than hired killer."

"Understand me well, any action taken against us and you will have a very nauseating accident, a very severe and painful accident. I'm not talking about finding the killer. The bloody police can't do that, so I'm not going to be able to, but I will take it out on you, so help me God."

"God won't help you. Nobody will. Now just do as you're told..."

"No. No, there's no more. The job's complete, payment made in full. You've all got away with murder, let's leave well alone. Tell whoever it's the end of the road." And he stormed from the building.

Oh dear, Yvonne said to herself, Lorraine isn't going to like this one little bit.

***

Enter Lionel Boldfield.

Lionel Boldfield, resident of Lancaster, was about to play an otherwise anonymous but vital role in proceedings. Lionel had nothing whatsoever to do with any aspect of the murders or any other issue hitherto described. He lived to tell the tale largely thanks to a railway employee with CPR skills, and never ever came to know how important his contribution to the search for and unmasking of the killer was.

Lorraine's train was due at Euston just after twelve noon, but as she was actually driving she arrived in Kent the night before and booked into a Premier Inn on the outskirts of Sittingbourne. She went into town to check out her parking spot and found exactly what she was looking for, although admittedly a decent walk away. No problem, however.

The next morning she checked online and found that her train, or rather the one she should've been on, had left Carlisle on time. Satisfied all was well she wandered over to the adjacent *Brewers Fayre* pub for breakfast and, after the morning peak, drove through the town and out into the countryside to the east, her plan being to suss out the ideal transfer point for Neville's suitcase. For this purpose she had her maps.

Meanwhile Mr Boldfield of Lancaster took his place centre stage unbeknown to Laura's sister.

He too was planning a journey to London and intended to board Lorraine's service. And board it he nearly did. He stepped back to allow a young lady onto the train, went to follow, whereupon he suffered a heart attack, and collapsed between the step and the platform, more on the train than off. Two things happened.

It was quite impossible for the train to move anyway, a crucial development in the great scheme of things for Lorraine, and Mr Boldfield needed attention promptly. The latter was immediately forthcoming when a woman in the employ of the train company dashed to help and quickly ascertained what had most likely occurred. At her instructions two men assisted her in moving Lionel to a better position in the carriage's vestibule, as they tend to be called on trains, enabling her to administer CPR to the stricken passenger. He was no longer breathing.

Her immediate and skilful application of CPR saved Mr Boldfield's life, and he was back in the land of the living when the paramedics arrived at the station.

A consequence of the delay was that the service was nearly two hours late into London, pulling into the platform at almost two o'clock. At ten past twelve Lorraine (actually near Lenham in Kent) had phoned Laura to say she was on time at Euston.

***

The previous evening Lorraine had enjoyed a light meal and white wine spritzer in the pub, drinking no more, anxious to keep a clear head for the next day, and thinking about her life. She might've been wishing it had all been so different but she was not the sort of person to dwell on those thoughts. That line of address can lead to regrets and she never wanted to consider she had any.

Where would she be without adultery? She'd never tried it herself because she didn't believe it was the right and proper thing to do, and the notion filled her with nauseous feelings and revulsion. She'd suffered the after effects of another's rash, foolish ventures into such sin. Lorraine was immensely proud that she'd forgiven Gary; she adopted a holier-than-thou attitude that gave her the moral high ground and enabled her to persuade him to carry out an act of vengeance for a friend.

She'd met Yvonne years back when they were fighting for womens' rights. It was an era at odds with the present day, although both women accepted there was still a long, long way to go. A very long way. Back then the road was longer still and there was public animosity. They became good friends, united in desire and belief, united in their militancy. Both thought they had met, loved and married the ideal man, men who shared their commitment to the cause and supported them in a manner unlikely to endear themselves to the male of the species. Not in those days.

But Mr Pratt couldn't keep his hands and other parts of his anatomy to himself, and wandered freely amongst the rich pastures of those seeking extra-marital adventure. Yvonne was stunned at the sheer numerical scope of his conquests. It was the shock of her life; it drove her to depression, pills, alcohol and a near-breakdown.

About the same time Gary Wimbush strayed, and did so only once, but he was discovered and forgiven with great generosity, for Lorraine's religious beliefs encouraged forgiveness. It was through her friendship with Yvonne that she met Malcolm Dartmend whom Gary described as a crank, a religious fanatic. But Lorraine found something very precious through Malcolm and came to love God and God's teachings.

There was a row when Gary learned she'd been giving Malcolm's sect money, and it may have been his wife's new life of holiness was too much to bear. Their house became a shrine and Gary was angry to realise God had supplanted him to the strange point where love-making was occasional and achieved in front of an altar lit with two candles, and after prayers had been offered up. Lorraine explained that love was God's gift, and that they made love only with God's blessing, and should therefore carry it before him.

This was too much for Mr Wimbush, and what put paid to any immediate hope of a sex life with his wife was when he said sarcastically that he presumed she thought God was a woman.

Soon after that his dalliance with Susan Medlidge came to light. Since Lorraine's forgiveness included a heavy session in front of the altar, after prayers in which Gary was obliged to beg God's forgiveness, he believed all might yet be well. But a little later Yvonne phoned with her news and Lorraine dashed to her side and then brought her back to their home.

It was about now that an idea formed in Lorraine's mind. Yvonne wanted to kill her husband. She probably didn't mean it, just a natural reaction to the fearsome and heartbreaking news, the sort of thing any wronged spouse might say, but Lorraine's mind was wandering into 'an eye for an eye' country.

Gary was always fiddling with the car and anything else mechanical he could get his hands on. He'd learned much in the army. Lorraine, whose state of mind was possibly already teetering on the side of mental illness, asked him if he wished to prove himself, show himself to be worthy of her forgiveness, and earn a particularly exhilarating and satisfying experience in front of the altar, with or without candles and prayers.

Mr Pratt needed an accident. Could Gary do something to the car that wouldn't look suspicious? At this stage death was not the goal required, but a few decent injuries definitely made the spec.

Yvonne was in such a degraded and shattered state that she agreed to the measure without proper thought. So Gary drove to Suffolk and surreptitiously carried out work on Mr Pratt's car not likely to appear in the service manual. Mrs Pratt, knowing her husband was going out later, not only persuaded him against his better judgement to have a pint, she laced that and other innocent drinks with spirit, liberal helpings into the bargain.

He was too busy to take any notice. Even his morning cornflakes had been given the mildest smattering of *Gordon's*. Any out-of-place aroma was ignored.

Unfortunately, the accident proved fatal although, thankfully, nobody else was involved, just the car and the tree, and the investigators could not be certain anything had been tampered with. The tree survived but Mr Pratt did not. The post-mortem revealed him to be over the limit.

The widow was beyond caring what happened to him, and returned home to make the funeral arrangements, not even realising that she was culpable in his murder. That realisation came later.

Mr Wimbush's life took an upturn, for he found his wife more passionate and adventurous than ever, and was at a loss to explain it. That is, until he noticed she became more aroused if they talked about death. She asked him about the various ways of killing and detailed accounts almost always resulted in a visit to the altar in the spare bedroom. But what came to worry and disturb him was the way she became frenzied with excitement if he spoke of death during their love-making.

Of course, being a mere male, Gary was overcome with the change that had occurred in Lorraine, the frequency and improvement in sex being of greatest note, but with the passage of time he began to tire of having to talk of stabbings, shootings, and strangling while otherwise enjoying intimacy. It was now he started to think Lorraine might be, in his basic terms, a little ga-ga, and it frightened him.

After they moved from Matlock to Barrow things calmed a little and Gary was delighted to find some pleasure with a female companion, a customer of his. This relationship, harmless to start with, became warm, romantic and tender, delicious kisses being the prime sustenance of their togetherness. Eventually they went to bed. It was a gentle and sensitive experience, all the more appreciated by Mr Wimbush who was heartily sick of the rampant love-making, if you could call it that, he shared with Mrs Wimbush, complete with the now obligatory tales of murder.

Unfortunately, from their point of view, the bed they chose for this excursion belonged to him and Lorraine, he thinking that Lorraine was away for the day. She wasn't and, hearing noises upstairs on her return, crept to the bedroom and surprised the lovers. There was no row. The woman was permitted to dress and leave the premises while Lorraine looked on having ordered Gary to stay where he was.

Then she stripped and set about her husband. It was the most wonderful time of his life, the sensations were unbelievable, the passion was explosive, and Gary was left exhausted and out of breath but happy beyond words. Lorraine forgave him and he couldn't believe his luck. The next day she suggested a picnic in the Lake District and packed a delightful spread.

They drove out to Wastwater where the rocky Screes launch themselves almost vertically straight up from the water on the opposite bank. A fearsome and daunting yet extraordinary vision. It was a lovely spring morning and they walked hand in hand, sure of their love, and returned to the car to picnic on the rug beside it. After their meal another walk. Lorraine came back alone and drove home alone. There was every chance his body would never be found.

Later a Victoria Wollardson from Kents Bank turned up on the doorstep looking for him and was obviously surprised to find Gary had a wife. She tried to pretend she was a client of Gary's but it was all too clear Victoria had been more than a customer. No matter for she wouldn't find him now and, in any case, he'd be no use as a lover. Well, no use at all. Lorraine said she hadn't seen him for weeks, not heard from him, and left it at that.

May you rot in hell, my bastard husband, she thought to herself. At least I have all my money back, and it was the idea of the money that sowed the seeds of a money-making masterplan. In bed that evening she indulged in one of her most absorbing fantasies as she took care of her own needs, and enjoyed a side-splitting orgasm. It was like yesterday in her memory, and she dwelt on each aspect of Gary's murder in turn.

Throwing the rope around his neck. At first he thought it was a game, her sort of game, and he pulled a face and made some horrible squealing sounds. Lorraine smiled and her feelings intensified as she recalled what happened next. His expression, having gone from pale to red to bluish, looked so serious. Gone was the fun element. Then came the realisation, then the abject terror, and finally the pain and surrender; it was all etched in his face. She laughed out loud at the height of her pleasure as she visualised his limp body falling to the ground.

It was such moments that fuelled a new fantasy that was to become an actuality.

Why not set up a service for people who wanted straying partners punished? She discussed the concept quite openly with Yvonne and in due time coerced her friend into setting up the operation. By now Yvonne had accepted her loss and her guilt and knew she could either go along with the scheme or risk conviction as an accessory to murder if she went to the police.

Yvonne was now in every sense a man-hater. There was nothing she liked better than tailing wandering spouses, but the ensuing divorce left her feeling empty. It wasn't justice in her world.

A successful private eye she'd gone into business as a dominatrix and enjoyed magnificent satisfaction inflicting pain. But it was too 'controlled'. So she came round to Lorraine's way of thinking and decided to set the wheels in motion; she could do it, had the computer skills, and it was just a case of hiding access in such a way that only those seeking the information would find it.

All very clever. It had the added benefit of true money-making potential, a bonus indeed!

It came to pass that Ms Pratt, or rather Eve Parr and Evida Prada, carefully spread the word amongst clients who were not the most legitimate or principled of characters, and by such roundabout means Nathan Kethnet and Neville Gradling came to hear of it. Daryl Pequeman was actually a one-off client of Evida's during a business visit to east Suffolk. Then, right out of the blue, Jayne-Marie Panahan contacted her with regard to William Bailey and his lover.

Bullseye!

Needless to say Yvonne wanted William stabbed but it had to be Phyllis Downport; that was the way of things. JMP knew nothing of the business Lorraine and Yvonne had concocted but the service was just what she wanted.

It was Lorraine who came up with the idea that customers should hire a private eye to obtain proof of infidelity as that was sure to spread the range of suspicion with the police. The fees were low in order to attract trade, with a small deposit up front and the balance a safe time after the completion of the client's order. But post-crime blackmail had always been in Lorraine's mind, which is why they selected the wealthy as their customers. Two potential clients had been turned away before they could get in too deep and determine exactly what was afoot.

However, enquiries about Nathan Kethnet and Neville Gradling had resulted in them being given five-star status once their wealth was established, with Yvonne offering services to Jayne-Marie directly. The scheme had been aimed, loosely and broadly speaking, at reducing the male population, so the despatch of Phyllis was a departure from the norm. Not to worry, because JMP had all the dough, masses of it, so she was a strong target for blackmail.

Lorraine regretted fitting Daryl Pequeman's requirements into her schedule, but Yvonne had pleaded with her believing that he too had pots of money especially as he had tipped Evida handsomely after being all but scarred for life. How anyone could enjoy being on the receiving end of such treatment was beyond her. How on earth do you keep all the bruises from your wife?

Of course, being on the giving end was very enjoyable for Evida aka Yvonne!

Although Lorraine regarded the faithful Mr Pickles as a complete plonker she also had some respect for him if only due to his sadness over his mama. Since his mother had killed her unfaithful husband Lorraine and Yvonne felt a certain bond between them, and had taken the overweight dumpling (as Yvonne called him) under their wings, nurtured him, brainwashed him (not a tricky task) and released him to do their bidding.

And so it was that Lorraine returned to her hotel bedroom and had an early night.

***

John Wapernod could not get over the idea of a suitcase stuffed full of used notes. It amused him continuously. We knew exactly what he was thinking every time there was a muffled chuckle.

Occasionally it was a guffaw.

"David, David, nobody does that anymore. Not been seen in crime fiction or TV or movies for donkey's years, for heaven's sake.

"David, David, David," he would exclaim amidst much mirth, "if you were writing a crime novel and included a suitcase stuffed full of readies no publisher would touch it. This isn't happening, please tell me it isn't happening." And he'd dissolve into fits of laughter his head shaking from side to side.

But it was happening, and it was happening to us.

"It's not real," he exclaimed, "and I'm half inclined to think that it's a feint of some sort. At the last moment Neville will be given an account to transfer the money to. Drawing all that cash out is a dead giveaway; bank's certain to notify the police. And while they and we chase shadows the money will be moved electronically leaving Neville with his suitcase and its precious cargo!"

"That being the situation we ditch Nev to the police ourselves," I volunteered. But we looked at each other knowing he might be right. "I know John, what's a killer going to do with half a million in cash? Well, my guess is live very comfortably for the rest of her life. I'm not convinced she wants a lot of money showing up anywhere, for example in a bank account. Too easy to trace. Keep a stock of notes under the proverbial mattress and simply spend a few bob every now and then. If Nev was given the details of an account the police could trace that pronto."

"Point made and point taken, David." We seemed agreed. Then DS Okafor phoned.

"Talk of the devil, nice to hear from you Holton."

"Bollocks. I'm not hearing from you and that's the trouble, David."

"Nothing to report."

"More bollocks. You're up to something because we won't do anything. But you know from experience, David, we don't publicise what we're going to do anywhere, let alone on social media, so don't imagine we're all fast asleep cos you can't hear us ticking."

Never thought that for a mo, Holton. So that sounds like you think *I'm* up to something and I think *you're* up to something. A score draw, wouldn't you say?"

"Keep me posted David. Pur-lease."

"I'm off your mailing list, Holton, so I'll be sending you no mail."

"Sounds like the end of the perfect relationship. And I was really getting to like you."

"Tell me about Yvonne Pratt, Holton."

"Nothing doing David." I actually sensed he was trying to tell me that Suffolk weren't acting on my advice, so small wonder he was seeking other tips, or better supporting information to those already supplied.

"Rest assured, you'll be the first to know if anything shows up. Promise." For my part his ensuing silence confirmed that he understood my 'coded' message as I'd understood his. I also knew that meant he was now one hundred percent aware I was up to something!

I relayed my news to my colleagues in detection. John, always smart and well-groomed, had an air of an old fashioned headmaster, and spoke in pleasant, crisp tones, his voice never raised and never betraying anxiety or panic.

"Mmm ... a good job you didn't tell him about the suitcase David, for he would've had you certified without further ado." We all smiled. Kenny was the antithesis of John, managing to look scruffy even when smartly dressed, as he was now. His voice was one of excessive eagerness, full of emotion relevant to the subject or moment, and generally lacking the grammatical correctness displayed by John. But I'm a one to talk!

"Well, that means we're on our own, guys, unless your pet copper is having us all watched. In fact he only needs to watch you Dave. Nope, can't buy into that. But he might, just *might* be watching uncle Neville."

"Yes," I agreed with a weary sigh, "that's the problem Kenny." We sat in silence for a while, contemplating the unknown and hardly relishing a task that could prove beyond us and that might result in a dismal outcome and dire failure. But we had to try.

Then came the phone call.

The number wasn't identified, the voice was male, muffled as if to disguise it, and with notable presence of mind I swiftly switched to loudspeaker so John and Kenny could hear.

*"We know what you're doing. Stop it now. Go away and leave well alone. You're in danger. Leave us alone and we'll leave you alone. We know who is in this with you and you'll suffer. Let sleeping dogs lie. I mean it."*

"Could be a wrong number," Kenny smirked, demonstrating what he probably believes is a ready wit.

"Or......" John's use of a single conjunction said more than a thousand words.

"Or it could be someone on behalf of the killer, or it could be a rogue copper, or it could be a crank," was my contribution, uttered after a short spell of mental consideration.

"Or," Kenny observed, "it might be uncle Nev. Let's say he's been frightened off and wants us disbanded." John and I looked at him then at each other. John spoke next.

"The fact is gentlemen, we don't know and we can't be sure it is actually anything to do with us, but I vote we ignore it. What do they know, what *can* they know? That I'm here with you two? That we have a mission before us to find the killer and return Neville's cash? The only thing we're sure of is that it's not one of us!"

That eased rapidly rising tensions. Of course, only the three of us knew exactly what we were up to. Even Laura didn't know, and the police couldn't know either, in spite of Holton Okafor having his suspicions. Lorraine couldn't know, and Neville couldn't have any idea what we were planning.

"Odd point though," I intervened, "that he started by saying 'we' and ended up saying 'I' – what do you think John, anything significant?"

"Just a matter of speech, but it could mean that he's a lone wolf and spoke of 'we' to add gravity to the message. The thought of two or more people might pose a greater threat to us in the context of the message, I suppose."

We went back to thinking in silence. Later on John and Kenny set off for their hotel, little knowing that they would be staying to the east of Sittingbourne while Lorraine was staying to the west. I collected Laura and brought her home for a fish and chip supper. So while she was enjoying that her sister, who should've been home in Carlisle, was devouring a pub meal less than ten miles away while my fellow 'team' members tucked into an excellent dinner at the Hempstead House hotel.

The stage was thus set for the events of the following few days.

It was the also the evening Daryl Pequeman set off for what he assumed would be his last walk on planet Earth.

# Chapter Thirty One
# Silloth

I had asked Laura why, when her long lost sister was coming down for just two nights she should want to visit an old friend. I knew the real reason, of course, but Laura did not and the question perplexed her.

"Well, she's not that well off, you're paying for her train ticket, and you can't blame her using the opportunity to see someone. She'll be here all afternoon and evening when she arrives, and all afternoon and evening the next day. And by the way I hope you're buying us dinner that night."

"Am I invited?"

"Nope, you know the deal."

"And I pay for someone who can afford to buy and run an expensive car."

"I don't know what that's about Moncks, but maybe I'll find out, maybe she'll tell me when she's ready. You said I don't have to chase her over it, haven't you?"

The conversation had swung away after that and returned to more personal matters, all far removed from the murders and Lorraine's trip to Kent. Laura was working in the morning, which suited everyone, before we were due to meet her sister at Sittingbourne around 2 p.m. Kenny and John were coming over and we were going to do some research into the missing lady but more importantly discuss tactics.

It was clear the suitcase exchange would be the day after, the morning Lorraine was supposedly going to her friend. I'd already made my excuses with Laura. She knew John and Kenny were down, didn't want to be excluded, and was making life very awkward. But I said they had come for a conflab over the murders, assured her she wasn't being marginalised but that I was taking the opportunity to use them to help me dig for Gwendoline Ford, sister of Daphne Carter.

"Being sidelined, Moncks. You always get me to help. I'm going to sulk." Not that I'd ever known her to sulk but it set the tone for the rest of the evening, and that night, although we shared a bed and a conciliatory cuddle, nothing else happened between us. Of course it felt to her as if I was pushing her aside and it was hurting me, for I didn't want it to be that way, but I knew that if Lorraine was the killer it would be like a bomb going off in her mind, and definitely in our friendship. So I didn't want to be too close.

I was aching because I really did not know the best way to play it, and I simply could not be open with her. Lorraine pleading poverty was concerning her but she was doing her best to hide the worry. They were bound to drink plenty and alcohol loosens the tongue, often after it has loosened the brain. Laura might well ask questions and, worse still, might get answers.

That evening Daryl told his sister and mother that he wanted some air and set off on his suicide mission towards Monsal Dale. It was dark and he could barely make out the road but he was so focused and single minded that it didn't even bother him when he stumbled now and then. He had taken to humming a tune that he was composing en route, a fairly innocuous piece comprised of a few random notes strung together in a curious melody, and it was doubtful he realised he was doing it.

The van came from behind him at speed and lit up Daryl's road for him. He took no notice. He was dressed for death, in a dark coat and trousers, with no acknowledgement of the principle 'wear something light at night'. The driver was over the drink-driving limit, as was proved later, and going much too fast for what was little more than a country lane. Daryl woke up to the fact the van was there when the vehicle was no more than twenty yards from him. All might have been well, as the driver had seen him and moved out the way, had not Daryl, for some inexplicable reason turned to his right and stepped into the van's path.

The collision made a terrible noise, but the driver did at least stop and call for an ambulance, rushing back to the prostrate figure of Mr Pequeman to provide whatever assistance he could, in truth very little of value.

Thus, while Lorraine, Laura, David, Kenny and John were tucking into their meals at various venues Daryl Pequeman was being rushed to hospital, still alive but badly injured. It was an ignominious end to an attempted suicide, and a truly unsuccessful one, for he was destined to survive. He had no documents such as ID on him so it wasn't until his sister reported him missing that the authorities were able to put two and two together later that night.

And while all this was going on Royal Mail had ownership of a letter that was going to condemn him when it was delivered the next day.

The next day was bright and sunny but cold, chilled by a nasty easterly that swept across the Garden of England. I took Laura to work and Kenny and John arrived. There was such a sense of apprehension, a feeling of trepidation laced with fear and excitement, that it was almost tangible.

Soon after twelve Lorraine phoned to say she was walking from Euston to St Pancras. I'd already noted the delay due to an 'incident' at Lancaster. Her masterplan was coming adrift, my worst suspicions were stacking up. I drove to Sittingbourne with Laura and Lorraine was waiting. Surprise, surprise, and about the time the train she should've been on, if innocent, was arriving into London. The girls greeted each other while my stomach revolted. I felt quite ill.

A trouble free journey, apparently. We drove back to Laura's flat where I left them and returned to Kenny and John at mine with the news. I was giving Lorraine a lift back to Sittingbourne in the morning so that she could see her friend who would pick her up from there. How very convenient!

My visitors returned to their hotel early evening. Alcohol was off the menu; we'd need our wits about us the next day. And the next day dawned quickly.

***

I watched Lorraine cross over to the Forum, the town's small shopping centre, and immediately noticed Kenny following her. He phoned to say she was back at her car and was making phone calls. John was nearby in his car, ready. My phone rang; Neville.

"Got to stand by for instructions, Dave, and I don't mind telling you I'm scared. Not for me, but for whoever gets selected for rough treatment if you screw up." He did indeed sound like a bag of nerves.

"It's okay, whatever happens you're in the clear. We ain't the police Neville. You wanted me in, I'm here, I've got help, and we'll make it count." He rang off; those instructions would follow soon.

John wasn't near Lorraine's car for tailing purposes, just to pick up Kenny and take him to his.

Laura phoned. Oh gawd, please get off the line, please leave me alone!

"Hiya Moncks. Whaddya doing? Look, sorry about me little sulks, so pleased to see Lorraine and I haven't asked about the car or anything, cos you say it's not the right thing to do, like, and she'll tell me when it's the right time, I know. Anyway, sorry lover boy." It was difficult to believe that we'd gone through most of this in five separate phone calls last night!

"That's fine, as I said last night. Our business partnership is not dissolved and I have taken a shine to cuddling you especially in bed. Is that alright?"

"Sure am, sweetheart. Don't forget you're chauffeur tonight." How could I forget?

"Of course I won't Law. Be there at seven. Got to go, bye for now."

"Yeah okay, love and kisses lover boy."

This was starting to turn my stomach, and the anguish I was feeling for Laura, especially as I was now deceiving her, was almost intolerable.

Then it was Neville and most of his dialogue was made up of obscene words. This was a man in a state. When he calmed I was able to note the details.

"Flint Lane, near Lenham. Know it?"

"No, but I'll find it."

"Got to go now, just hurl the suitcase into the woods at a junction, God knows where, it's the middle of nowhere, and get out of there, go home and ring from my landline."

"Brilliant Neville. That means she'll be on site ready to collect when she knows you're safely home. All we have to do is make sure she doesn't think the police are there. And we're not going to intervene, and that's because we know where she's going. Safe as houses, mate. Leave it with me and call after the drop and again when you phone from home. Understand?"

"Yeah, yeah, okay Dave, anything you say. But keep my family safe."

So that's what a combination of fear and blind panic sounds like, I thought! I rang John as arranged and he had Kenny with him. Both had Satnav. I'm rather proud of the fact I don't use it and can find my way around.

We met up near Bapchild to the east of Sittingbourne and studied the maps.

From there we set off for Teynham, Lynsted and Doddington, where we let John proceed on his own towards Flint Lane, a backwater on the North Downs above Lenham, while we headed south to the village itself. John was least likely to arouse suspicion and might've easily have passed as a country gentleman, definitely not an undercover cop.

He phoned Kenny, keeping my phone open for Neville.

"She's parked in West Street," We looked at the street map. It junctioned with Flint Lane. Then Neville called.

"Just dropped. There's a junction here, that's where I had to dump the case. Going down towards the A20, okay?"

"Great Nev. We're here and on to it. Trust me."

"Okay, okay, I'll ring her."

Kenny relayed this to John who had parked a good distance away and was observing the junction from a hidden vantage point. We waited. John couldn't be sure if Lorraine was now on foot watching the area so he stayed out of the way.

He knew of quiet country lanes back home in Devon, but there was something almost eerie yet stimulating about this location. Narrow lanes, few places to pass, plenty of potholes lying in wait. Rolling Kentish countryside either side of the road for the most part, and here woodland, ideal for Lorraine's purpose. A handful of buildings dotted along the way, occasional footpaths crossing the landscape, and all atop the Downs from where exquisite views across southern Kent and the Weald could be enjoyed. The sound of birds but otherwise the sounds of silence. Rarely a vehicle, rarer still anyone on foot. Unspoilt countryside, today desecrated by the presence of a serial killer.

John's mind wandered to many things. This woodland, in its serenity and beauty, was still menacing and he could imagine all kinds of weird goblins hiding behind the trees and bushes ready to rush forth gushing with hideous laughter as they surrounded and mocked him.

Still, it was a good place to hide himself.

He'd have loved to check the suitcase. But he would have his chance, he was just longing to see this wonderful marvel of a bygone age, a case packed with used notes!

Neville called to confirm he'd rung from home. By arrangement we were now covering the three exit routes from Flint Lane with me well out of the way near the Marley industrial site close to Lenham. John confirmed the pick-up, case now in the boot, and that she was driving down the hill towards me and the A20. She knew me, knew my car, so it was no good me trying to tail her, but thankfully she had obviously been happy the police were not about.

John regained his car and by prior agreement returned to her parking area on the outskirts of Sittingbourne where she duly arrived later on. Here he could observe her and follow her to the station. As far as he knew she hadn't removed the case from the boot, and we had to hope it was still there although there was a faint chance it had been passed to an accomplice.

Somehow I didn't think so. It was her money, she wasn't going to risk losing all or some of half a million to someone else when she had the cash, real cash, in her grasp.

Sure enough she took the branch train back to Sheerness. Kenny and I arrived at her car and he confirmed what I hoped would be the situation; he could unlock the vehicle, overcoming the alarm, and retrieve the suitcase which would then be taken to my home, ready for stage two. And that is what happened. I realised then that to be good at this job you occasionally had to bend the rules, break the law, and Kenny was adept at that. I was not ever going to be able to do it.

Small wonder he had a grey past! But he was an absolute ace, and he got results.

Back home John had his moment of glory, and took photos presumably to decorate his autobiography. He was happy with a capital H. Here it was; a suitcase full of notes. He was on cloud nine.

Surely they were traceable? Surely the bank had a record? Was Lorraine counting on that not being the case?

I phoned Nev, said we had the money back, and that he had nothing to worry about, for nothing now would come back on him. He'd done as he'd been told. Lorraine thought the case was in her car boot from where it would appear stolen.

"Money back later, Nev," I said, "once the heat has died down. The main thing is to trap the killer, get the person arrested and out of your life. Speak soon." And I hung up.

We had a celebratory drink as we looked at the open case. Kenny had an idea.

"Listen, kiddoes, half a mill. Let's divide it and go our separate ways. Buy a house of your own with that, Dave!" We all laughed. There were several further suggestions as to the fate of the money and how it's distribution might benefit each of us, but then normality returned.

"She's bound to check the boot before driving off," John ventured.

"Yep," I agreed, "but I'm counting on her not checking the contents. No reason to. Kenny's going to put the case back exactly where he found it, the car's supposedly locked and alarm-protected.

"Yeah," ventured Kenny, " but suppose she *does* check, suspects you and arrives here or even takes her own sister hostage?"

"Chance we have to take. At least she won't report the theft to the police," I stated.

"True," John realised, "*Very* true. In fact I fancy she may need a change of underwear! Nasty shock that, but worse still to realise your cover is in some way blown".

"Certainly would be with her knickers off," Kenny remarked, maintaining his usual light-hearted approach to any situation, and encouraging dirty laughs all round.

My friends went back to their hotel, via the BMW, and a superb dinner accompanied by fine wine, of that I was sure, and I took Laura and Lorraine to the *Tudor Rose* in Chestnut Street near Sittingbourne. My fare for the evening was beans on toast and no alcohol; I had to drive the girls home.

I felt a sad and lonely person that night. I lay in bed for a long time, longing for the touch, the feel, the sweet smell of Laura McCaffield, and worried myself sick, not about what I had planned for her sister and for me, but for Laura and how all this might affect her. Eventually sleep overcame me. I wanted to be there for her knowing she might reject me, and I hated myself for it, and hated what I had to do. There was no doubt now, Lorraine was the ruthless killer, pursued by the police and hunted down by me, and I was going to hurt Laura however this all turned out.

There was surely no way our relationship could survive this.

They had been so happy when I picked them up at the *Tudor Rose*. It had been a wonderful evening, full of fun and laughter they told me, and their light inebriation added to their warm spirits and good humour. I was in turmoil. Oh Laura, dear Laura, your sister is a merciless killer who is probably insane. You cannot imagine how I felt, knowing Lorraine was in my little Fiesta behaving as if nothing had happened when I knew she was a cold-blooded killer.

No surprise that I threw up when I got home.

I had also reflected on Kenny Parrett during my time alone. We had raided the blue recycling wheelie for heavy material like newspapers to fill up the suitcase. I was hoping Lorraine would not open it.

Kenny was proving to be an asset but not one to respect the law. He had easily accessed a top of the range car, disabling its alarm, without making it obvious to anyone who might be looking, and taken the case and now replaced it the same way. The vehicle was once again locked and alarmed. If he could do it then car thieves everywhere could help themselves.

I was right to have my doubts and I knew positively that the stories surrounding his shady past were based in truth, plus there was probably more that hadn't come to light or at least not to the attention of the police. Adam was correct to warn me. I felt mildly disgusted, like someone who has taken hold of something nasty and rushed to wash their hands. Kenny was above board in that I actually trusted him in our investigation, but I couldn't wait to be done with the relationship.

He never hesitated to act against the law, but possibly because he believed that the right outcome justified the processes involved, and I was as guilty as he was in this latest venture. It suited his cavalier attitude, his sense of adventure, and it forced an adrenalin rush that not only drove him on, it also concentrated his mind so that he didn't make mistakes. So there was much to admire but much to condemn; no wonder the police didn't like him.

His skills (such as with Lorraine's car) had to have been acquired somewhere, indicating a very dark past indeed, and the likelihood he had mixed with some unsavoury characters in his time. Having said all that I could not have done without him, for there would've been no way of achieving what we had.

Together with John, who seemed to know more about the legal angles, we logged, photographed and recorded every aspect of our day's work, essential when presenting the evidence to the police. John had surreptitiously snapped

Lorraine retrieving the suitcase. This guy is first-rate I concluded, and had to accept that I probably wasn't the right man for a career as a private eye, those feelings engulfing me more than before. I didn't want to think right now what else I might do; that worry would come later, if it turned out there was a 'later' for me.

The worst was yet to come, the danger, the dread, and there were moments when all I wanted to do was hand everything we had to the police right away and let them sort it out.

*** 

In the morning I drove both girls to Sittingbourne station and witnessed their sad farewells, Laura in torrents of tears as the train's doors closed and it moved off. John would be waiting for Lorraine's return; presumably she was going to Rainham and back. I took Laura home.

And the postman delivered Daryl's letter. There was nobody there, Daryl's sister and mother being at the hospital, so it settled on the mat to await discovery, a discovery that was a long way off.

Back at my place I was sickened by my thoughts over Laura as I watched the sad figure sitting on my settee, head in her hands. I wanted to explain everything, tell her what I was going to do next and why, and be there to hold and comfort her as the pain took hold, and I could do none of these things, not least because she might turn against me, perhaps even violently. I couldn't blame her if she did. Her reaction was what I feared most.

But was I afeared for me or for her? I didn't know but I was aware I was on two sides of the fence and that's a difficult situation for anyone to be in.

"Moncks," she sighed, raising her head from her hands, and searching me out with sorrowful red eyes, "she wouldn't talk about Matlock or Gary, said it was all in the past, wanted to forget, and asked me not to ask again. I've got to tell you this, Moncks, cos I don't know what to make of it. I nearly mentioned it yesterday but it made more sense then.

"You know, like, the National Rail website? Well I found I could track her train and according to that her train was well late, some incident at Lancaster, yet she phoned on time. Well, I reckoned she'd got an earlier train, missed the Lancaster business, and I took that for granted. I didn't challenge her, well, she's me sister ain't she? But I did kind of casually ask about her journey and she said it went very smoothly, all to plan."

Her words were spoken in a soft, mournful, whimpering voice, as she hung her head.

317

"Well, David, I couldn't challenge her could I? But I don't understand. And I never found out why it was important to go and see her friend yesterday morning. I wanted us to be together, why didn't *she*?" Her miserable face was pleading with me for the answers, almost as if she knew I had them. I've never felt so horrible in my life. Her eyes, cheerless and dull, were begging me for the answers, maybe even the truth, and I was sitting there hoping she couldn't see through my facade. And she'd called me David, maybe suggesting that was her way of seeking a closer intimacy and the prospect of a better solution.

"Don't want to go to work," she announced, head down. "I'll phone in sick."

"Up to you, but I have to go out. I've cases to attend to...."

"Why don't you want me doing them with you? And what's the real reason them guys are down here? It's all to do with the murders, ain't it? And I don't count anymore. You three blokes, all men together, all up for the job, don't want some woman along, do you? Spoil the masculine fun. Ex-druggie, ex-con, the sooner you're shot of me the better. Now ain't that right?" Her indignation only fuelled the horrid feelings churning inside me. Then she leapt to her feet.

"Okay, I'm history, pal. I'm off. You won't see me again. You nasty little sod, better off a million miles from you," she bellowed as she raced for the door, catching up her coat as she went. For a second I stood stunned, then plaintively cried after her.

"Laura, come back here. Stop all this nonsense, for heaven's sake." She opened the door and glanced back and I called to her. "Laura, I love you, come back, please."

"No you don't." And she slammed the door and was away. Well, perhaps it was for the best in the circumstances. Get this vile mess cleared up and then see how she was. As I sat in the dining room at my computer I remembered I'd said that I loved her. Did I mean it or was it just a spur of the moment comment?

Somehow I had to put all of this on the proverbial back-burner and concentrate on the matter in hand. I was not the only one in a state of shock.

DS Holton Okafor was so shocked he slumped into a chair, his eyes agog.

*"Half a million quid!"* He exclaimed in a loud, high-pitched voice. "He withdrew *half* a million quid, wheeled it out of the bank in a suitcase, and they let him do it, sir?"

"That's it Holton, and never thought to tell us until now. I expect they had to have a top level conference to get this far! Client confidentiality taken into account especially as Gradling's a very good customer. No, it's not funny, but it's time to pay Mr Gradling a visit. Coming?"

"You betcha sir! Wonder if that private eye's mixed up in this?"

"What makes you say that?" Okafor realised that in his shock he'd said the wrong thing, but now was not the time to make a clean breast of his association with David Canbown.

"Just this story's set to run and run, and I suspect everyone. Something's going on out there, sir, and we're excluded. A gut feeling, nothing more."

"Well, Mr clever-clogs Gradling has some explaining to do. Let's get going."

***

John reported Lorraine had come back to Sittingbourne and was walking to her car. I held my breath.

"She's opening the boot, putting her own case in, closing boot, and she's getting in the driving seat. Kenny's at the end of the road, motor running." Well, at least we'd got over that hurdle. Kenny was going to follow her if he could, hopefully around the M25 and to the north, then he was returning home. John still had work to do in Kent. He had all the gen and, of course, the money. What I hoped he didn't have was the desire to abscond with the lolly!

In Suffolk, and in defiance of orders, DS Stephanie Broome had turned up on Evida Prada's doorstep knowing full well she was there and expecting Stephanie's colleague.

"Well hello Ms Pratt, or is it Ms Prada? Are you a private investigator tonight or a dominatrix?"

"Police harassment now, Sergeant, to add to a growing list of misdemeanours on your part. I'll notify Ms Bhatia. You appreciate I am doing nothing wrong. You know how it works as well as I do, and how we are just on the right side of the law of the land."

"I'm obliged to you for telling me so much when you don't know why I'm here."

"Fancy wasting so much valuable police time tracking me down just to find out about my hobby. What about the resources and savage cuts your lot are always bleating about? You could be better employed solving burglaries or directing the traffic."

"I simply wanted to confirm that you were Evida, which I have done. I take it you are also Eve Parr. Either way, there are some things that don't go down too well on the cv of a private eye, especially when all has been revealed to the public."

"Empty threats. So if there's nothing else I'll be closing the door with you on the outside. Mind you, I could close it with you on the inside if you'd like a free sample."

"I shall look forward, Ms Pratt, to closing a door with *you* on the inside quite soon."

"Thank you. I shall advise Ms Panahan of your actions so she can speak to your superiors."

"Why bother? They know I'm here."

"Bet they don't." And the door was slammed shut.

Broome had a restless, sleepless night. Yvonne Pratt just had to be involved in the murders somewhere. Pure instinct was forcing Stephanie on, the very same intuition that had been the bedrock of her rise in the police, the very same desire to apprehend those who broke the law and to bring them to justice. Her career was going to take her to the very top, she knew that, and she knew she was damn good at her job.

Right now that career could be on the line, but she had to find a way to drive this one forward with her bosses. She had to get to Yvonne Pratt if she was to get to Jayne-Marie Panahan. She would call Okafor in the morning, hoping against hope he'd got more out of Canbown.

And in the morning, as Lorraine drove north towards Derbyshire in possession of a suitcase full of recycling, DS Broome collected a mammoth surprise from her colleague in Kent.

*"What?"* she squealed, as shocked and stunned as Okafor had been. "Half a *million* in *cash* .... *wheeled* out of the bank .... in a *suitcase* .... you're having me on Holton. Not April the first is it?"

"No Steph and I'm telling you the truth. Can't talk for now, with the DI going to Gradling's. We'll be in touch and you can let me know how you're getting on."

That would have to do for now. She sat back, wide-eyed in surprise, and contemplated the meaning of all this. Gradling was being blackmailed. She spent the morning like a cat on a hot tin roof waiting to hear how things were progressing.

John Wapernod had a mobile and a simcard he rarely used. Untraceable in every sense. He advised me to get a card myself for the same purpose, and I popped into Tesco for that reason as well as for some fuel. I'd packed a few things and I was heading north, guessing that Lorraine might feel more confident on home ground when it came to a confrontation. Kenny phoned from services on the M1 to say he'd lost her; no chance of keeping up with a super-charged killer in a super-charged BMW! But that was fine.

At an appointed hour John was going to make an anonymous call to Lorraine to advise her of the situation and how her fortunes were about to be revised. I was sure she'd swallow the bait. John had demonstrated how he could disguise his voice when he practised the message.

*"I have your money. Five hundred thousand. When you get back to Carlisle we can discuss its return. Fifty-fifty sounds good from where I'm standing. You get half, I get half, and we walk away and forget all about it. Surely you'd be happy with a quarter of a million rather than nothing.*

*And it also buys my silence because I know all about you Lorraine. So I give you your share and we say no more about it. I'll call you later."*

Lorraine had already learned one thing guaranteed not to improve her temper or weaken her resolve. Mr Pickles did not have good news from Devon and there was an angry recognition that she was going to have to get killing again. Not once did she ask herself if it had all been worth it, was still all worth it, or question her wisdom in using blackmail. JMP had paid up, so why did the men have to be so tiresome and difficult? Typical men, she decided.

And talking of which there was that ghastly man Pequeman who'd gone to pieces because his wife took her own life. It wasn't Lorraine's fault, for pities sake, but it would have to be Lorraine who sorted it out.

Apart from Nathan Kethnet's act of alpha male rebellion Lorraine had two other problems and she didn't know about either just yet. Daryl Pequeman was in hospital, in intensive care, and beyond her reach, and Yvonne was about to report her visit from William Bailey to tell her the tap had run dry. And lying on Daryl's doormat was his confession in which Evida Prada's role was described.

\*\*\*

I am growing to hate the Dartford Crossing and the M25. They only exist as a means of torture for drivers. So it was with welcome relief that I turned onto the M11 and up to my beloved A1.

Near Peterborough I pulled into services and had a leg stretch and a coffee. Normally I would've indulged in a spot of lunch but my stomach was having none of it, being too knotted over my feelings about Laura. I checked my phone and there was a text from her. Might as well get it over, I thought, as I clicked the buttons.

*"Did u mean it"* was all it said. I replied, without stopping for consideration and without employing any wisdom *"I love U"*. Within seconds there was a

response. *"Come make love then."* How I wished I'd hesitated before sending my first message. I decided to ring instead.

"Laura, look I'm sorry, but I'm near Peterborough on the trail of that missing sister, y'know, the woman from Minnis Bay. I'll only be a day or two at most. I just didn't get the chance to explain, did I? I want us to get back together, and make a success of what we do together, I really do."

I waited and waited. Then she spoke.

"This the truth Moncks? Cos don't mess me about. Been so lovely with sis. Wish I could see more of her, but wish she wasn't so cagey about her past. But I want to be with you and work with you. I thought we made a great team, y'know, *Cagney and Lacey* like. But don't sod me around."

"It's the truth Laura." Oh how I wanted to confess all knowing it would not only end our affair but that she would alert Lorraine. I didn't know how to handle it, I just didn't, and it would be magnified a thousand times when she discovered what I'd known all along. For now I had to play it like this because it was more vital to nail the killer.

I promised to ring that evening and we blew kisses down the phone and said our goodbyes, and my stomach turned. This was agony to the enth degree. I hated myself and my heart was tearing itself apart.

Back in Kent John had left a message on Lorraine's voicemail. My scheme was under way. No going back.

Around the same time the two detectives arrived at Neville Gradling's palatial country pad. Jacqueline admitted them and showed them into a lounge, offered them drinks which they politely declined, and left them to await Neville.

"Wonder why she bothered putting any clothes on," the DI commented, "Not that I'm supposed to say things like that these days! Just barely seemed worth her while, barely being the operative word." Okafor smiled. He made no remark but he didn't need to.

Meanwhile John had phoned me to say the message had been sent. I'd left him with the keys to my bungalow so that he had some sort of base for the next stage, and that is where he went together with a take-away lunch. It gave him the opportunity to catch up on some of his own work while he waited. Later his 'anonymous' phone rang and a woman's voice screeched at him.

Liberally laced with obscenities it went something like this.

"Who the hell are you? Where's my money you filthy toe-rag? I don't know what you're on about. I'm not sharing anything with you. Who are you? How dare you take my money? I'll have it all back and I'll kill you, you moron. Now where's my money, you filthy little bastard?"

So that's what a woman scorned sounds like, John mused.

"Lorraine, when you get back home to Carlisle tonight please ring again and further discussions can begin. Goodbye and safe journey." He rang off and ignored the next call. She left no message. Good, he thought, now she can have a jolly old stew in her own juice. I'll call up David with the news, which is what he did.

Still worrying us was the anonymous call *I'd* received, not that there was a lot we could do about it. But it rankled. It had to be someone with some sort of connection; it might then merely be a 'fishing' call where the person was making assumptions and hoping to press all the right buttons, and that scenario might be allied to a police officer warning us off, for whatever reason.

Would the police have enough to go on if we handed in our file now? Would they be prepared to take any action? It had to be a fait accompli. Of course, we didn't know they were after Neville following his extraordinary cash withdrawal, or that Daryl's confession was gathering dust on a doormat in a remote part of Derbyshire. Thus it could be said that we should've given them all the material we had and taken a step back.

But we were stupid enough to believe the only way of trapping Lorraine was to use amateur labour, so immersed were we in our skills as private eyes, and in our faith in our approach. Only we could achieve what the police could not. Sensibly, if I'd gone straight to Okafor surely they would've investigated Lorraine fully; our evidence was convincing.

If common sense had come into it we would've realised that we were taking part in an illegal activity that could get us into serious trouble with the law. Laura was right; three boys playing cops and robbers. Three men behaving like arrogant, self-assured, know-it-all bastards.

Oh yes, we were the three to be reckoned with, the A-team, the all-stars, and we were going to clean up the country, or at least rid it of a serial killer. What idiots we were, playing at being James Bonds, carrying out covert operations as if we were attempting one of those computer games that are so popular these days, and doing it all without any thought for the law or for reality. I would have plenty of time to reflect later and to know the wisdom of Laura's condemnation.

It was true. We'd been completely carried away by some sort of desire to be heroes, solving a major crime by ourselves, just as one might see in a TV crime drama, and bringing the evil to justice while the police looked on appreciatively. Real life isn't like that, and we should've known better. The thrill of the detective work and the hunt was more like fun than serious endeavour and we could end up paying a high price.

*** 

If John felt Lorraine reacted like a woman scorned then he could only begin to imagine the frightening rage she flew into after the call. Her temples throbbed, her face was screwed up in anger and blazing bright red; she spluttered lewd oaths as she thumped her steering wheel and the spittle covered the dashboard as she struggled to form the words through snarling teeth and lips.

Fortunately for her she was in a near-deserted part of the car park, and gradually the tempest subsided and her head collapsed onto the wheel as her violent breathing started to regulate itself into a more measured series of deep inhalations. Nobody saw her, nobody came to see if she was alright, if she needed help.

With a mighty sigh she sat upright and stared at the roof. Then she looked straight ahead. Resolve came upon her in that instant. Still enraged but in a much more controlled way she tried to make sense of what might've happened. Who had her number, that was a good starting point, and she immediately rang Laura. Steaming with anger she roared into the phone.

"Law, listen, who's got my number apart from you and David?"

"Lorraine, is that you?"

"Of course it's me, you soddin' stupid slut. Who have you given my number to?"

"Lorraine, what you on about? Don't start calling me names. What's this about then?"

"Law, just give me an answer," she screeched. Laura recoiled in horror, unable to understand why her sister could behave like this.

"Pet, I don't know, only me and David I guess."

"And who would that berk David tell?" Laura felt an abominable sensation flood her mind, and her stomach churned. Lorraine had called her out of the blue to shout at her about her phone.

"Why would he tell anyone, Lor, he'd have no need to. What's happened?"

"A bloody nasty anonymous phone call, that's all, and I'm upset and angry because it's a guy who knows an awful lot about me. Your depraved little detective would know these things. How you can like a weak little wanker like that I don't know."

"Lor, please calm down. David's alright, I know he is. He wouldn't phone you and he'd have no reason to pass your details on."

"God give me strength. Okay, I'll sort it out myself. Cheers." And she hung up and a stunned and unbelieving Laura threw her hand to her mouth as the tears fell from her eyes. What on earth was wrong? What was the call about? Why had Lorraine attacked her verbally in such a crude manner?

She slipped slowly down onto a stool, sobbing profusely and asking why, why, why? through the tears. Even in Laura's biased mind the sister she had found and now loved was not behaving well at all.

There was the business about the car, then the train she wasn't actually on, and her visit to a friend when they had so little precious time to share together. Now she had used the most vile language to berate her, shouting abuse down the phone, accusing David of investigating her and arranging an anonymous call. Why? Why? *Why?*

Poor Laura was seeing Lorraine in a different light and it bothered her beyond reason. Was there so much more to her sister than she knew, were there matters she'd rather not know? She wanted to think well of her but there were nagging doubts, doubts that had been in the background and easily dismissed before now, doubts that kept surfacing and causing anxiety.

So David had looked into her, then he must have had some suspicions, reasons for delving.

This wasn't how it was supposed to be. This was all horribly shocking.

***

It was a day for shocks.

Neville Gradling was struggling with his. The officers confronted him about the cash and, of course, he had no answers.

In the end he gave up the unequal battle and came up with a pack of lies about how he'd been threatened by a woman who wanted the money or she'd murder one of his family.

"Nothing to do with the killing of Alistair Bourne-Lacey then?" asked the Inspector.

"No of course not. Came right out of the blue. People know I'm wealthy."

"Why didn't you tell us?"

"She told me not to. Go to the police and someone I love gets it, you know the form."

"And it never occurred to you that withdrawing half a million in cash and waltzing out of the bank with the money in a suitcase might arouse suspicions? Oh Mr Gradling, you're beyond belief."

"Well, that's what I did...."

"And where's this suitcase now?"

"I don't know. I had to go to Flint Lane, near Lenham, and chuck it in some woods. When I got back I had to call her to say it was there."

"Right, let's start there. Come with us Mr Gradling and show us exactly where."

"I can't, I've got business to attend to..."

"Right away, if you please sir. We'll go now." Gradling knew better than to argue. His only problem was whether or not to reveal that he'd hired David Canbown to get his money back and find the blackmailer. Better keep quiet, he decided, especially as it was very much to do with Alistair Bourne-Lacey's demise.

Lorraine had worked herself into such a state that she called up Yvonne on her ordinary phone and not the 'business' one she normally kept hidden. She issued forth with such a tirade as soon as Ms Pratt answered that the recipient switched to loudspeaker and laid her phone on her desk while the caller rattled on, and continued with some other work on the computer. Eventually Lorraine ran out of steam. Not a good time to go into details about William's visit, Yvonne knew.

"I don't even know your personal number, do I? But fair to say I do now...."

"Don't be facetious. Listen, and get this right first go. Daryl Pequeman, speak to him, find out where he is and get back to me. You're a private investigator, so find out about this Canbown guy, and I mean more than you already know. If you haven't given out my number then either it's my stupid sister or this Canbown idiot. Or, of course, either of them could be behind my anonymous message." She ended the call leaving Yvonne looking at the phone.

Well, clever girl Lorraine, she thought. Go all the way to Kent, risk the entire operation and our safety from the law, and come away with recyclable material. How very environmentally friendly! An unusual blackmail payment, I'll grant you, and I'm pleased I'm not due a share of that lot.

It took Yvonne some time to establish where Daryl was and what he was doing there. In the meantime she took a call from Mr Pickles. Oh dear me, she sighed, it's all unravelling and all because of this ridiculous blackmail nonsense. This was about the time Daryl's sister arrived at his house and found the letter.

She recognised the writing and more out of curiosity than anything else opened the item with the intention of a quick scan with a read to follow later.

Within seconds she'd collapsed in shock and fallen to the floor in horror. As she pulled herself together she read the letter again and again. So had her brother been on the way to Monsal Dale, or did he decide to be run over instead? Either way he had not succeeded in committing suicide. But he had paid to have Rosie's lover slain. And arranged it through this woman Evida Prada.

She was alone, knew where the brandy was kept, and wailing bitterly poured herself a glass only to discover she didn't like brandy. Still, it was supposed to be good for shock, wasn't it, and good medicine never tastes nice. Flustered, unnerved and shaking she dashed outside to take some deep breaths of fresh air while she weighed up this astonishing new situation.

Her brother had hired a hit man. It could not be so. Going back inside, a little calmer but still mortified by the contents of the letter, she took another measure of medicine and came to a hideous decision. She couldn't betray the brother she loved. She would destroy the letter and forget all about it then Daryl, once he recovered, could rebuild his life. Yes, that was what she'd do.

Lorraine had booked into a motel for the night so had steam coming out of every orifice when she learned of Daryl's predicament. She checked straight out and drove directly home to Carlisle inclusive of a relatively minor altercation with a police patrol car. On the M6 north of Preston, and anxious to get home, she hit ninety-five unaware an unmarked car was on her tail.

When she was stopped she thought she'd turn on the feminine charm only to discover the officers were both female. Oh well, she thought, in this day and age worth a try, and turned on the feminine charm anyway, having undone the top two buttons on her blouse and hoisted her skirt hem up to an indecent level. Whether it was that, or the officers were in a good mood, she escaped with a warning and took the rest of the M6 more sedately.

She called Yvonne who only had bad news, she divulged it all now, and listened in silence to the private eye with her brain starting work on the solutions, there being no time to lose.

"Ring Gradling direct. Don't let on what I've told you. Give him thanks for the money and say we'll be in touch regarding the next payment. Check his reaction, you're good at that Yvonne. Leave the rest of this to me. My God, someone is going to suffer! And I *mean* suffer. If you so much as get a sniff that Gradling's double-crossed me he'll be my next victim.

"Mr Pickles will be made redundant after this; I've no further need for him, they obviously don't take him seriously, so he can be next on the list. It'll save on redundancy payments to say nothing of National Insurance contributions! Daryl

I must think about, but in the meantime I have some pressing business with some nerd."

"You sure you don't want me to come up there?"

"No, definitely not. We've taken too many risks as it is. Just making these phone calls goes against my professional grain, Yvonne."

Lorraine went upstairs, tossed off her clothes and showered very thoroughly indeed, as if she wanted to wash the dirt of all that had happened from her body. She slipped a silk dressing gown around her and walked downstairs to the kitchen and made a cup of tea. No alcoholic medicine for her; she needed all her wits about her now.

***

The Officers, having been shown the disposal point by Neville Gradling, radioed in for a forensic team and escorted their passenger, much against his will, to the police station where they intended to hold him for questioning. They had to wait while his solicitor, Tanya Barkett, a fiery individual with an encyclopaedic knowledge of criminal law, and enthusiasm beyond measurement, drove over from Sandwich.

Okafor took the opportunity of a break to call Broome with the news.

"So he's trying to say it's just straightforward blackmail. Doesn't get us very far, does it Holton?"

"No Steph, we need a break, and I don't fancy our chances with this joker given the solicitor he's got. Only met her once and that was enough."

"Any joy at all with Canbown?"

"Nope, and I've left three messages to call me today. Any news from Geoff?"

"He says nothing doing but he'll have a quiet word with John Wapernod, the private eye in the Edward Nobbs case, you remember. Maybe Nathan Kethnet's being blackmailed, not that Wapernod will know, I suppose."

"Keep me posted. Something's in the air, I just know it is, and if I find Canbown's mixed up in this I'll nail him alright. These bloody private investigators, need shooting sometimes, they do. Think they're better than the experts. If I catch Canbown do you want to watch as I tear him limb from limb?"

"I can guess how you feel Holton! The answer's yes if I can join in."

After allowing herself to breath comfortably and with her temper firmly under control Lorraine picked up her phone and rang the number. John answered. He knew what to do.

"Listen. I don't know who you are but you think you've got the whip hand and I'm telling you that you haven't. I'm lethal when roused and I'm going to kill you in the most prolonged and painful way possible, you filthy, detestable weed."

"Thank you madam. I'm not prepared to debate the status of either player in this game, but the rules are so simple a child of five could understand. You name the place, the date and time, and I'll be there to give you a cool two hundred and fifty thousand pounds. Nobody else will be there; you return home with your share and I walk away with mine. What's so hard to understand in that?"

"Listen creep. I'm not doing business with anyone I don't know. You might be the police and I could be walking into a trap. Daft I am not, and only a miserable weak excuse for a man like you would think so."

"Okay Lorraine, it's all mine and you forego any cash at all. Still, it does follow that neither of us will be going to the police. And if I was a police officer, since I know what car you drive and where you live a personal call, an arrest and an investigation would be every bit as good as a trap. Ends up the same way, with you in custody. Why would I hang it out like this? I've told you, you get half and that's the last you'll hear of me. Surely a quarter of a million's better than nowt?"

Lorraine was thinking quickly. Perhaps her tame police officer could discover if this was genuine or a stitch up. She'd call her.

"I'll ring you later. Have some business to attend to."

"Take all the time you need. I'll be around the Carlisle area later and at your disposal."

"Listen. If I take you up on this I want a couple of friends undercover checking out the location. Any objection?"

"Yes. That way I lose my half to your friends. Nothing doing."

"Ring you later."

John knew she would have assistance anyway. But it was a chance to be taken. After all, she'd have no way of knowing if David had help on site. He rang Canbown and then had a call himself, and it was that call that raised the excitement levels in Suffolk and Kent.

\*\*\*

Yvonne Pratt was drawing a blank and not liking it very much. Gradling, she was told, wasn't at home and his wife (it was assumed) had no idea when he'd be back. So she rang David Canbown and got his voicemail. Drats! Then she turned to the computer and started researching the Kent private eye, again with very limited success.

After a pause for thought she tried remembering the name of the girl he was with. It was Lorraine's sister but what was her first name? Then it came to her, Laura McCaffield, and so began a search for David's bit-on-the-side as she'd termed her.

John Wapernod was mentally preparing himself for the next task. It was arguably the most important one and he had to get it exactly right, and do so the next time he spoke to Lorraine. It was such a vital element to the project that he had to handle it delicately and with great presence of mind, but he was quietly confident because he was that sort of person. The last call didn't ring any alarm bells for he was completely engrossed in Lorraine.

***

"Stephanie? It's Geoff."

"Hi Geoff, and everyone calls me Steph."

"Thanks Steph. Just called Wapernod, mainly to ask if he'd heard from Kethnet, and he mentioned he's in Kent. On business. Didn't pursue it any further, but that's a mighty coincidence."

"Isn't it just. I'll call Holton right now. Any chance I can pass on Wapernod's number?"

"Sure Steph." And he passed on the details. Within seconds DS Broome had left a message for DS Okafor who was engaged grilling Neville Gradling.

Yvonne rang Lorraine.

"Your sister's got some record, hasn't she? Take you it knew."

"Knew she'd been inside. Why are you asking? What's she got to do with it?"

"It's what she might have to do with David Canbown that interests me. I didn't even know you'd got a sister till they turned up in Matlock. I take it you didn't want to be found."

"I'd love to know how they found me, but there's more important matters now. Was that the only reason you called?"

"Occurred to me that if she's not as clean as the driven snow she might be useful, y'know, letting us know what Canbown's about, especially if he's being naughty, and particularly as she's got her family ties to think of. Not going to shop her sister, is she? Not going to want you arrested."

"I'll sleep on it. Anything else?"

"No." She didn't mention that DS Broome had visited Evida Prada. Not the time to do so.

And in Kent life was becoming very tricky for Neville Gradling. The Inspector persisted.

"Mr Gradling, you're a self-made man, a millionaire, fingers in all sorts of pies, and I know that means working with ready cash sometimes. But you watch your money like a hawk and you wouldn't waste a penny. Do you deny that?" There was no visual response from either Gradling or his solicitor, so he continued. "You're careful with money, that's one of the reasons you're worth a fortune. Occasionally you get a security firm to collect cash from the bank, for wages I understand, that sort of thing, but the banks are very cautious about large withdrawals for all the reasons I've stated.

"And then you arrange a personal withdrawal and wander out of the premises with the loot stashed in a bloody suitcase. No security. It's not you, it doesn't fit. Try and appreciate my problem, Mr Gradling. You say you flung it into the bushes, but that might tie in with money laundering, or even a payment for a really shady business deal that you wanted kept quiet. Then, when we challenge you, out comes this story about blackmail."

"I told you Inspector. I was frightened for my family, for my kids, if you got kids, Inspector, you'd know that kind of fear, and without thinking I made the arrangements with my bank, collected the dosh, and did as I was told. How simple was that?"

"Inspector," Tanya Barkett intervened, "are we going to spend time going round in circles? You have asked the same question various ways and received the same answers. It was blackmail and my client has explained his genuine fear and panic. My client has businesses to run and you are wasting his valuable time. If you have no further questions I do not believe you can hold my client here any longer."

"Thank you, Ms Barkett. Two points Mr Gradling. Blackmailers come back, again and again. They'll bleed you dry, especially as it was that easy to run off half a bloody million! Secondly, this was no ordinary blackmail was it? This was connected to the murder of Alistair Bourne-Lacey with whom your wife was having an affair." Ms Barkett looked ready to explode but before she could interrupt proceedings the Inspector spoke again.

"I know, I know. No more words from me on the subject. I am just going to say this. Mr Bourne-Lacey was taken out by a merciless killer who, as far as we know, has murdered at least three other people, so you will appreciate our desire to track down he, she or they before they kill again. Please understand the gravity of the situation." He was looking Tanya right in the eyes, a manoeuvre not lost on the solicitor. Both had their jobs to do and had the Inspector known it she was hating every minute of it, protecting scum like Gradling.

There was a knock at the door. Message for Sergeant Okafor.

"Okay, we'll have a short break," the Inspector decided, "then I have other relevant questions, so we all stay here for now."

"My client and I would like comfort breaks, Inspector."

"Sergeant, ask the officer to come in and make the arrangements."

A few minutes later Holton was on the phone to Stephanie and learning the news. A few minutes after that he was in an office with his Inspector revealing his relationship with Canbown, and where it had led him.

"Jeez, Holton. Thanks for telling me now. I didn't realise you'd got that close. Not wise, old son, not wise. We're a team. Maverick coppers are for the telly and cheap crime novels. Okay, try and get through to Canbown and if he's home get Sally round for a chat pronto. If he's not I want to know where he is. Leave Wapernod for the mo. I'm an old-fashioned pillock, and it won't be long before me and my sort, already an endangered species, will be gone from the force to be replaced by wiz-kids. And I don't mean you. You're bloody good, Holton, but play by the rules now and don't blot your copybook and you'll get to the top. Off the record you did bloody well, way I'd have done it once, but I wish you'd felt you could share it with me. It's just that someone upstairs will tut-tut if we foul up and we haven't done the job properly, and the muck might fall on your head. They're worried about the way inquiries are launched into everything these days, and the top brass like to keep their noses clean. Pensions to worry about and all that.

"Then there's the com-pen-say-shun aspect. And a load of newspaper guys ready to tell the world and his brother how we cocked up."

"Sorry sir..."

"No, we'll leave it there. Now let's get cracking. On yer bike Holton!"

***

"Why can't you leave the money hidden somewhere and I'll arrange collection at a later date, when I'm sure nobody is watching me." Lorraine was trying a different tack.

"No. I want to meet you. We're kindred spirits, as they say these days. We know right from wrong. And we know it's wrong to commit adultery. My wife, or I should say my *late* wife, went off with someone, so I've suffered the agonies.

Once she was soiled she was dead to me, so I thought she may as well *be* dead. Anyway, that's all irrelevant. This is only about splitting your ill-gotten gains."

"I could cheerfully kill you, whoever you are, and I've a pretty good idea."

"No you haven't or you'd confront me. Out of interest how would you kill me? Strangled with rope like Edward Nobbs? That was how I got rid of my unfaithful wife. Where on earth did you get the strength to throttle a big, strong lad like that?"

"Don't underestimate women. I practised on my husband and enjoyed every second, so much so that I've yearned to do it again. Him and Nobbs, carrying on like that, deserved to die. I submit to such great and uncontrollable sensations, I think that's what they say, when I recall their faces as they died. Yes, even in the dark I was close enough to see Nobbs's face, because I wanted to be."

"I guess Gary, being ex-army, taught you all you needed to know."

"Poignant and apt. He perished by my hand after he'd shown me how."

"And Alistair Bourne-Lacey?"

"Gary had an old gun but he kept it working. Used to take me out and let me have a couple of shots. Improved my aim no end. Alistair was only feet away. Same instantaneous look of fear."

"Laura used drugs. Did you?"

"Yeah, once upon a time. Set me up nicely for doing John Holgarve, y'know, injecting and all."

"But being large on womens' rights you can't have enjoyed stabbing Phyllis."

"No, but same principle. She'd done wrong in the eyes of God but God wasn't around to provide retribution. Here, anyway, what's all this? Twenty questions? This is your life?"

"No, merely general conversation between two people who care about fidelity, two God-fearing people who are committed to their beliefs. Now Lorraine, place, date and time."

"I know who you are. I'm a killer, what makes you think you want to trust me?"

"We'll trust each other because we get a quarter of a mill each and walk away unscathed with our secrets intact."

"You said I could have time. I'll get back to you."

"All the time....." but she'd rung off. John sat back and replayed the recording, and then typed out the transcript before uploading the conversation and burning it to disc. He had what he wanted.

***

I was having second thoughts and a few more after that. There was really no need to be chasing up to Carlisle. If John worked a minor miracle we had all we needed and the file could be handed over to the police, but I had my doubts. They were not going to take kindly to private investigators carrying out a covert plot behind their backs and then presenting them with all they needed to make an arrest.

They might not see it like that. They might look at it a very different way, and arrest us, charge us, and let Lorraine get clean away. No, if I was going to be nicked then I wanted to be absolutely sure I handed them Lorraine on a plate, with no get-out clauses.

Lorraine meanwhile was calling her sister and ready to pour oil on troubled waters. She had some apologising to do, and needed Laura onside.

"Hi pet. How's things?"

"Fine, but missing you Lor. Wish we could spend more time together now we're reunited. And then you ring me and have a right go over nothing."

"Yeah, and I'm sure we will see more of each other. Look I'm really sorry about the call. Just a bit het up at the mo what with seeing you after all these years and all that. Very emotional. Got over-heated."

"Yeah, I understand How's you now Lor?"

"Fine. Just a nasty phone call and I over-reacted. Unforgiveable. Sorry. Now tell me, do I get to be bridesmaid?"

"*What?*"

"Your wedding to David. Top man, by the way, you're a lucky girl."

"Not like that, Lor."

"Come off it, see the way you look at each other, talk to each other. Is it just that you're not going to marry?"

"Straight up Lor, it's not like that."

"Only thing I didn't like about him, probably comes from being an ex-cop, is that he seemed so suspicious of everything. Is he like that with you?"

"Don't know where you get that idea from...."

"I got the idea he thought I was up to something," she added with a nasty and rather pointed snigger.

"You silly so-and-so, nothing like that at all."

"Being ex-cop how does he get on with you being a jailbird and that?"

"No problems. Like I said, I've even helped him in his private eye business."

"Yeah, that keep him busy? What's he doing at the mo, or is that top secret?" Both girls laughed.

"No, he's busy on a case right now, up in the Midlands somewhere, missing sister by strange coincidence. Still, we're good at finding those, aren't we?" After some more laughter and ordinary chit-chat, as you might expect between siblings, they said goodbye, and Lorraine tapped the phone against her chin as she pondered her new knowledge.

Away in the Midlands, eh? I wonder, I wonder ....

***

The police were getting nowhere with Gradling, that is, nowhere of interest, and in light of current developments decided to let him go. If nothing else it would get that Tanya Barkett out of the way!

DC Sally Banner showed her identification and looked at the smartly dressed man who'd opened the door.

"Mr Canbown, David Canbown?" she asked.

"No, I'm sorry, here's not here. In fact he's away on business."

"Oh right. May I ask who you are sir?"

"Of course. John Wapernod. I'm a private investigator, like Mr Canbown, and as we're good friends I'm looking after the shop, in a manner of speaking, while he's away. He should be back in a day or two but I can give you his mobile number."

"Yes, can I check that please? I think he knows Sergeant Okafor and the Sergeant's left a couple of messages. Maybe he has the number wrong. It is quite urgent."

The number they had was right.

"Just a mo, officer, I'll try him now." There was a pause. "Ah David, I have DC Banner with me and she says Sergeant Okafor has left a couple of messages...." There was another pause. Speaking to DC Banner and relaying what he was being told John continued. "He says he has the messages but as he's been busy and the Sergeant did not mention any urgency he's not rung back yet. Would you like to speak to him?"

"No, that's fine, if he'll call now or as soon as, please."

"Did you get that David? Fine. Talk later."

"Where is Mr Canbown?" Sally asked as casually as she could.

"He's in Cumbria, looking for a missing sister. We private eyes often find it's beneficial to follow leads in person, providing our clients are willing to pay, and his customer in this case, a lady in Minnis Bay, is."

"Thank you for your help, sir."

"It's been a pleasure."

DC Banner radioed in. In a matter of minutes not only was Okafor in the picture but Geoff Alcock in Devon and Stephanie Broome in Suffolk were reading the updates. Okafor was talking to Canbown.

"David, get your arse back here now, and I mean now. I want to know what's going on and I want the truth and I want the whole story."

"Nothing doing Holton. You can't order me back. I'm pursuing a lead and if you interfere I'll regard that as restraint of trade."

"David, I can have you arrested up there. We're a widespread operation, you know, and you'd be surprised what I can do. We've come a long way from Black Marias when the only means of communication was a whistle." Sarcasm coursed through his words and their application. "Now be a good boy and come home."

"I'm doing what you wouldn't, if you must know."

"And you're doing it in Cumbria. How lovely. David, David, you must know, from your own experience, that we're actually better at it than you can ever hope to be."

"You sarky sod Holton. You're not doing it at all."

"Had Gradling in. Know all about the money. If he'd involved us and not you we'd have someone in custody by now."

"Sounds like he didn't notify you so you'd have been too late I guess. But then I've no idea what's happened."

"Liar."

"Now, now, not a nice thing to say to a member of the public, and a taxpayer to boot."

"Think about your position, *son*, and get back here. I'll give you twenty four hours and if you're not back and I haven't heard from you it's curtains. *Son.*"

My next caller was Wapernod who first related his visit from DC Banner. I told him about Okafor.

"Think he's bluffing?"

"Not sure I want to put it to the test, John. But I have a gut feeling about him saying I'd got twenty-four hours to get back home, as if he was trying to tell me I'd got twenty-four hours to finish what I was doing."

"Good point David. This fella might be right on the ball. Now, the good news and bad news re the exchange. It's a place called Silloth and it's overnight tonight, and I mean overnight, the wee hours."

We discussed details and our strategy. John would monitor things from my home. He reminded me to check the charge on my phone and a good job he did, it was running low. I really must step up in the world if I'm going to survive in this work, and get an all-singing-all-dancing phone, and perhaps an all-singing-all-dancing brain as well! Wake up, David.

I'd anticipated a drop nearer Carlisle and I was parked outside the city in readiness, but a glance at the map showed Silloth to be not too far away. With sunset not long away I thought I might as well drive over at once as I was on unfamiliar roads, and arrived just in time to witness a most glorious setting of the sun on the western horizon.

It could be the last sunset I'll ever see.

***

I hadn't left my car where Lorraine might easily spot it and now sat hunched in the driver's seat as day turned to night and the temperature plunged accordingly, this cold but dry November night. Before nightfall I'd sussed out the rendezvous point, an obscure lonely and deserted place, made more objectionable and unpleasant by winter. An unloved, untouched bit of Silloth.

There were two texts and a message from Laura so I gave her a ring.

"Hello Law, how are you?"

"Depressed without you Moncks, depressed about me sister. Like being with you Moncks, like working with you, miss you babycakes."

"What's wrong with your sister?" She told me about her phone calls and the nasty way she'd been spoken to, and explained that Lorraine was enraged about some message thinking that I had given her number to someone.

"Did you Moncks?" Actually yes, I had, but couldn't tell her even though every part of me was aching with the craving to reveal everything.

"No. Nothing to do with me. But should she carry on at you, call you a slut and so on? Did she say what was in the message?"

"No, wouldn't tell me anything and she's making me feel cold."

"Tell me."

"Well, it's all the bits of the puzzle, ain't it?" I sensed how disturbed and hurt she was. "Keeping the car from me, not telling the truth about the train down, going to see a mate when we had so little time to spend together, and now shouting at me like I don't matter and something's more important. Could she be in trouble David? I'm so worried all of a sudden."

'David' again. A sure sign of her genuine concern. Yes, my darling Laura, your sister is a self-confessed serial killer without conscience or mercy, who has murdered at least four people and who heads a ruthless if small organisation dedicated to punishing the wicked on behalf of God.

"I have to say this, Law, but I do think she's not all she seems to be, and I reckon you might have to prepare yourself for the truth which may well be unpalatable. I know it's unimaginable and I hope we're both wrong, that there is a simple and satisfactory explanation, because you have to remember you've been parted a long time, and you've probably come as a bit of a shock.

"I know I've got a suspicious nature, Law, but you yourself know she hasn't been straight with you. Just bear that in mind. And sometimes it takes time for people to adjust to new situations in their lives."

"Yeah, know you're right. Spose I want everything at once and it all to be lovely and beautiful, but you're right, we've gone our very separate ways, we're different people, yes it will take some getting used to." This conversation wasn't quite going the way I wanted it to, but then I have to admit I'd given the impression that it all might turn out fine when I knew it darned well wouldn't. How would Laura react to me then? Oh, I'm no good at this.

She sighed in mournful way. But then she changed the subject, taking me by surprise.

"Tell me about your sister David. She died for love, yeah? What was her name?"

"Katie." I paused as the memories returned. "Katie. That was her real name, not short for anything. She and her husband were into Siberian huskies; went racing at Aviemore and in the Kielder Forest in Northumberland. Beautiful animals. But the marriage hit the rocks and they divorced.

"She had two dogs and met another guy through the club they belonged to. Then it got serious. When she got her share of the money for the marital home she went and bought the house next door to her new boyfriend, and it all looked rosy for a while. She must've been very much in love and probably wanted to marry him but he shied away from commitment, and I always thought he was the epitome of the expression laid-back.

"I expect it all became too heavy for him and he packed her in. Good fun when you live next door to each other eh? Katie determined to win him back and dreamed up an absolutely extraordinary scheme involving a botched burglary. One night after he'd gone to the pub she made her preparations little realising how silly they'd look."

The memories from all those years ago are indelibly printed in my mind, rarely shrouded and all too often thrust to the fore. I miss Katie more now than ever before, with our parents long gone and other family members spread far and wide, and basically no close relatives, I'm left with my few loyal friends. Everything about Katie's demise was fresh in my thoughts, the tale so easy to relate.

"The idea was that burglars broke in and tied her up and made off with the valuables like the telly and the hi-fi. Now, my sister, being neat and tidy and one for having everything in good order and in its place, dismantled the electrical stuff and then stacked it all tidily by the door, cables secured behind them. What burglar does that?

"She put a plaster over her mouth, a plastic bag over her head, and using plastic ties managed to secure her hands behind her back. Then she went to lie down outside her former boyfriend's house hoping he'd come back and rescue her and want her again. Much of what I've said is speculation but the result of a thorough police investigation and I have to say it all makes sense.

"Unfortunately she tripped and fell and hit her head on a rock in the front garden. Partly stunned, she vomited but with the plaster over her mouth she choked...." Into the quietness that followed I was conscious of Laura's voice intruding on my sadness.

"Oh David, I'm so sorry. That's awful. Oh your poor sister, she must've been in hell. David I really am so very sorry, truly I am. If only I'd known, but thanks for talking about it." I don't think I'd ever wanted to tell Laura but tonight, with an uncertain future, it strangely seemed the right thing to do. Little did I know that when we ended our chat she'd call Lorraine overcome by a mixture of horror, revulsion and her sadness at my tale, and relate the story to her. A fatal move.

John called with the time and exact place. He had a further role to play with the police. We went over all the details again. I'd forgotten about the charge on my phone despite topping it up earlier and I should've realised it wouldn't last forever. Then came another anonymous call.

*"Pack it in, it can only end in tears. Go home. Clear off while you can."* I let John know. He was becoming very wary.

"David, someone, *someone* out there knows. Are you going through with this?"

"Yes. Has to be done. Got to nail her tonight. If you take everything to the police she'll scarper, Let's face it, she could temporarily lose herself in Scotland in next to no time, even if she dumps the BMW. We have no idea if she can easily disguise herself but my guess is that yes, she can, as I'm confident it's happened. And she has more than one identity, remember?"

"I do, and I agree, but I have to confess to being a bag of nerves David."

"You and me both. Now, brass tacks; she'll call when she's in Silloth."

"Yes, but if there's anything suspicious she'll turn straight round. Tonight she said she'd forego all the cash to ensure her personal safety. I don't believe her."

"No, neither do I, but we must also take into account, John, that she's not a paid assassin as such, she's doing it for religious reasons as well, and because she thinks adulterers should be punished, blah, blah."

"You believe all that do you?"

"If she's round the bend, yes." I heard John chuckle.

"I think *you're* round the bend David. Good luck."

***

Yvonne's tame police officer had provided very little inside info, but what few snippets were available were potentially valuable and Yvonne was all for grabbing tidbits and then seeing if two and two could be forced to make four. Handy Evida Prada having a Detective Sergeant as a customer, as the poor woman would not want her promising police career wrecked by revelations that she visited a dominatrix.

The DS had some limited access to Operation Corkscrew, as it had been named, and was aware Gradling had been interviewed again, and that David Canbown was a concern. She was also able to furnish the intelligence that John Wapernod was staying at Canbown's Minster home. So the police clearly thought there was a connection between Canbown and Gradling and the five hundred thousand pounds. She relayed the information to Lorraine who told her it was Canbown's last few hours on Earth.

In Kent, DS Okafor was fretting. Trying to disguise his voice he'd now sent two anonymous messages to Canbown, and speaking as himself had tried to coax him home. He knew he had to do something, but what? No good talking to the Inspector. He'd had a warning, but he liked the private eye, had felt a true bond of brotherhood between them and couldn't just desert him.

Was Canbown leading them to the killer? Hang on a moment. Hang on a moment! Was that what this was all about? Was it about Holton Okafor solving the clues and riding over the hill at the vital moment, just like the cavalry in those westerns? Was it Canbown's intention that he should piece things together and take action as appropriate? His train of thought was interrupted by a call from Steph in Suffolk.

"This is between you and me, Holton. Operation Corkscrew, been an unauthorised access up here. We know the DS and my boss is looking into it. Oh Holton, I'm hoping this leads back to Yvonne, I truly am."

"You mean this DS might be slipping gen to Ms Pratt?"

"Could be."

"Shhh .... I mean, damn and blast, that's what my Inspector, who's a bit old-fashioned so he tells me, always says." They both laughed.

"You home or work Steph?"

"Home."

"Great. There's an email coming via my Samsung Galaxy phone-in-a-million about our forthcoming date. And you're not backing out. Dinner for two, on me." Broome understood and waited eagerly by her home computer. What she read blew her mind away. It was, of course, nothing to do with dinner.

Within minutes Holton Okafor was receiving a call from John Wapernod.

"Up to you, Sergeant. I'll meet you at a place to suit you and the time I shall give you. There's no options, either you do or you don't."

"Is this about......"

"Sergeant. Yes or no?"

"Okay. Do I have to be alone?"

"No, of course not, and it can be a police station for all I care. Probably better if it was." Holton was shocked and took a moment to recover.

The appointed time arrived. It was very dark, very quiet and nobody else seemed to be about at this ungodly hour. Silence. It's always amazed me how beautiful and yet daunting silence can be, particularly when allied to total darkness, and here on the Cumbrian coast, just north of Silloth, it was as astonishing as it was frightening, and whilst my apprehension had curiously vanished altogether the silence replaced it with something indefinable.

I knew Lorraine would've surreptitiously checked the area out, perhaps already observed me, making sure I had no obvious back-up. Tricks she might have learned from Gary being ex-army.

I checked my watch and suddenly remembered the charge on my phone, as I was intending to call John and leave the line open. Alas, no charge. Bugger! I had a large holdall with me, crammed full of dry mixed recycling, this season's blackmail must-have, and I set it on the ground as a mighty thud sent me flying, a blow that left me unconscious.

When I started to come round I was suffering from a terrible headache, the result of a whack on the head, and there was something covering my mouth. Tape I guessed. It was too dark to see anything but as I came to I realised my head was in some sort of bag, and I was lying face-down on the ground, my hands tied behind my back. I felt sick.

As I stirred a female voice whispered from close by.

"Hello David. Laura told me all about Katie and as I like my killings to be appropriate I've decided to start the ball rolling this way. Good isn't it? How does it feel to be trussed up like a turkey and about as dead? As you're not likely to vomit I'm going to take the bag off and slit your throat. Gary showed me how. This is how your sister must've felt, bound hands behind her back and utterly helpless. Oh, I've checked the bag. Thanks for the recyclable material. I don't care about the money; I've written it off.

"I understand they may be introducing a deposit return on plastic bottles, so I'll recoup a few bob. I wonder who knows you're here. There's nobody else here, I checked, so it'll be too late when anyone arrives. Now, let's deliver you to your maker."

Gone was the voice she knew Laura would recognise that day in Carlisle. Then she spoke Laura's language and that was all part of an act. Now her words were spoken in a more cultured way, forever an actress in an unreal world. Not that it bothered me now facing a most unpleasant death at the hands of this deranged animal.

It was about the time John Wapernod met Holton Okafor. John handed over the files, the money and explained where David Canbown was.

"Good job we're on the same wavelength, Mr Wapernod."

"What do you mean?"

"Got my colleagues in Cumbria on standby, which is what you intended if I've read this right. I think they'll be needed don't you? Wish you bloody amateurs would keep your noses out of our business. This could all have been sorted out and done properly, you bastards."

"Whatever you do to us we deserve it. We accept that. But I still think we've done more than official activities could've hoped to achieve."

"You've achieved nothing yet, except bloody chaos."

"Tonight we hand you a killer and the evidence you would never have collected."

"So you hope."

"Sounds as if you do too, Sergeant."

*** 

Did I have any chance at all? I'd learned some self-defence in the police but was it any good when you were already tied up and helpless? The plastic bag was removed and Lorraine shone a torch in my eyes.

"Still there David? Good. At least Laura won't be a widow, although I expect she'll be heartbroken. She loves you to pieces David, thinks the sun shines and all that. You'd have made a beautiful couple, you know, and tonight I am going to wreck my sister's future."

She put the torch down and in the darkness I could see the faint glint of the steel blade of the knife.

# Chapter Thirty Two

# **Aftermath**

There was a brief scream and the sounds of a struggle but I couldn't see a thing. I was vaguely aware of the distant sound of emergency sirens.

The plaster was torn from my mouth with a ruthless and unfeeling regard for any hairs that it might take with it, so it extracted an involuntary yelp.

"Shuddup, you ungrateful sod" the voice intoned, a voice nonetheless laden with gentle humour.

"Where is she?" I whimpered.

"Tied up, she's going nowhere. Here, let's get you untied and sitting up, you little hero, you." It was still very dark, or course, moonless, and I could hardly make out a thing. The cold didn't seem to matter at all. "Don't worry, I didn't hurt her, though God knows she deserved it."

The sirens were much nearer. Lorraine's torch was still glowing where it had fallen and was the only source of light. It seemed a weird piece of inanimate normality in an extraordinary and unbelievable scenario that was all too alive and real.

"Got to explain this to the police now."

"Yeah, but how's John getting on?"

"Done his bit, me old son, and I'll tell you this, I reckon that Holton Okafor's on the ball. He's been on your side for a long time, that's my view." I sighed with relief. "Yeah, and he understood your coded messages, not that he's planning on thanking you any time soon."

He sat on the grass next to me close to the writhing figure of a prostrate Lorraine who was cursing us with a stream of vile invective and swearing filthy oaths with equally unpleasant language. After a while I spoke.

"You know what Kenny? I want to see the sunrise, so what are my chances?"

"Zero mate, we'll both be in custody, so make the most of this fresh air now."

***

In Kent the police had Lorraine's confession but it proved no more than the impetus for a full outpouring of her admissions of guilt once she was being interviewed. She knew the game was up and, saying she had no need of a solicitor, gave a full account of her murders and the background.

In Suffolk the police set about the traitor in their midst and consequently were at last able to set about Yvonne Pratt, Ms Pratt having kept all the dodgy dealings hidden in the businesses belonging to her alter egos, Eve and Evida. The sums of money running through Evida Prada's account relating to Jayne-Marie Panahan were sufficiently substantial for a warrant to be issued to set about the business-woman.

In its turn Kent police were able to arrest Neville Gradling. The police *setting about people* was the order of the day.

In Cumbria I faced a savaging at the hands of the local force, well deserved I might say, but I was to be returned to Kent who would decide what, if any, charges I would face. Frankly, I was more concerned about Laura's reaction, not least because the story had decorated the front pages as well as the TV news. I was in for a total surprise, but a very welcome one.

I hadn't been allowed to contact her, didn't have my phone, and wouldn't know more until I was back in Kent much later.

***

Kenny Parrett had been part of the plan. His personal skills would be put to the test; keeping hidden until Lorraine struck was key, but he'd watched, quite captivated, as she'd walloped me over the head with the same balustrade spindle used on John Holgarve and, as he waited just feet away ready to spring into action, saw Lorraine put the plaster over my mouth, the bag over my head and tie my hands behind my back. He accurately assessed Lorraine wanted words with me before she executed me, so he waited to see and hear what happened.

His eyes were more accustomed to the pitch black dark, and he was also able to see more anyway once Lorraine switched on her torch.

I was brought back to Kent, interviewed, charged with 'obstructing the police' and released.

But my car was in Silloth, not that the police were sympathetic although Holton Okafor offered to run me to Maidstone West station. It gave us the chance of a chat.

"I don't think you'll get more than a fine, maybe just a caution, perhaps they'll even drop the charge David. I'll do my best."

"You've done all you could Holton."

"Well, I picked up the clues I suppose, but I've got one angry boss and my career to rescue."

"Sorry mate. But at least you've got Lorraine, a confession and..."

"Yes! A bag of recyclable items!" We both had to laugh.

I'd looked at the texts and listened to the voicemails. Laura's most recent messages pleaded with me to come home, and as quickly as possible. When I finally spoke to her I realised how desperate she was to see me and how much she needed me right now. As we said our goodbyes I could sense the relief, sadness and urgency, and wanted to magic myself to Sheerness in a flash to be by her side. But I couldn't get there any quicker.

Back at Minster John was waiting and Kenny was heading south from Cumbria, home to Derbyshire after his own session with the boys in blue. A reunion and a few pints was the way things were looking. John had been held, arrested, released without charge and drove to Sheppey to await my return. I had to do the journey by train, and not an easy journey by any means.

That evening I sat alone with Laura in her flat snuggled up together. I couldn't have anticipated her reaction but it was definitely one of amazement and disbelief, yet she was utterly calm, resigned to the situation, almost as if she herself had known what Lorraine was. I think she suspected something unpleasant without realising how dreadful it might be.

The most important aspect, from my point of view, was that she wanted me and didn't blame me for her sister's arrest. In a way that was a real surprise, albeit a relief.

Few words were spoken; none was necessary. Laura was struggling to come to terms with the fact she had unintentionally provided her sister with the inspiration for my method of despatch, and was mortified that Lorraine came so very close to seeing me off, and in such a sickening manner.

She seemed more concerned that her sister, her *own* sister, had almost killed the man she now knew she loved beyond mere words, and tried to murder him *knowing* what he meant to Laura.

"Thank Kenny for me," she said, "I owe him everything, saving the bloke I love like that." At first she'd wanted to disown her sister, as Lorraine had done to Laura all those years ago, but she quickly relented. "I'll be here for her, write to her, that sort of thing, go and see her if she wants me. Important that, not treating her like she treated me. But I'm pleased you're safe, David, and I know you couldn't tell me what was going on, but you did it right, did it right, top dog."

We'd snuggled closer. I thought back to the events of the last hours.

John had dropped me at Laura's before setting off for Devon, declining to share some time together, sensing we needed to be alone. Another day, he'd said. Bring Laura and have a holiday my way, he'd suggested. We were all feeling empty and cold, devoid of enthusiasm, just wrapped up in a bizarre nothingness that came from incredulity about Lorraine and the way things had turned out.

Me, John and Kenny had discussed tactics in a private manner, whispering in the garden and communicating when apart with unused and untraceable mobiles, the advantage of the simcard system, and it was Kenny who devised the ambush in which I was the live bait. Okafor had indeed read the signals and, through his bosses, alerted the police up north; it just needed John's last piece of the jigsaw to set the wheels in motion, even though they were angry at our intervention.

DS Broome got the news that made her day, her week, her whole year, and was directly involved in the raid on Yvonne Pratt and the premises used by her alter egos, Eve and Evida. The computer systems, especially those of Evida Prada, once thoroughly explored, produced the evidence needed to go to town on Neville, Nathan Kethnet, Jayne-Marie Panahan and Daryl Pequeman.

Thankfully the news media were not informed about Nev's half a million and Nev himself was led to believe that the police recovered the money from me when I was arrested. That left me free of any retribution his family and 'colleagues' might have otherwise heaped on me. Phew!

I was equally pleased to find myself and my cronies largely left out of the media stories. Our roles were minimised and we were all grateful in a way, not one of us being portrayed as a hero. The concept seemed to be that a member of the public had his life saved by a quick thinking man, and that the police moved in to catch the serial killer involved in the nick of time, the result of a great deal of police investigation during Operation Corkscrew. Further arrests would follow.

Kenny deserved a medal, I thought, but I must admit to being dismayed that he stood back and watched developments rather than pounce, so interested was he in what Lorraine was up to. For heaven's sake, Kenny, she might've stabbed me while you were trying to see what was going on!

His answer was that he had assured himself she wanted me to be conscious and to talk to me before finishing me off. That turned out to be an accurate assessment but then he was not the unconscious body lined up for the chop!

"My poor parents," Laura said in that quiet, soft and seductive tone she has, "raised a right pair of criminals, didn't they? Sorry mum and dad, not your fault." The weak humour was her way of dealing with the pain and horror the episode had induced.

"Main thing is, Law, at least you've reformed and you're leading a blameless and successful life now. I'm sure your mum and dad would be proud of what you've achieved once you put your mind to it. And Moncks is proud of you too." We snuggled even closer. "And I'll tell you what, Law, I'm nothing special, a right arsehole, and I haven't treated you well. I've done things in my past that perhaps aren't squeaky clean and yet I thought I was better than you, mainly cos I was a bloke. Blind prejudice. No excuses."

"Yeah, well, you're on the right road now, Moncks, the road to redemption if I've got the correct word." And we both chuckled. "Funny how you look at drug taking though. We both love a good drink and it can be a killer. There's drink-driving where someone else can get killed, and people can behave strange and violent when they've had a few like. Yet you don't see it as the same as cannabis, crack and heroin, do you? They're not legal but alcohol is. Both can do yer head in, ruin yer organs, wreck lives."

She'd produced an argument I had no answer to, not that I felt like explaining my views.

"You see Moncks, I've had to drag meself out of the gutter. When I've talked about being top bitch it's because I really did want to prove I was a better person than you and that you couldn't manage without me. I wanted to prove that a woman, even one that's been regarded as lowly pond-life in her time, could eventually be better than a man. I appreciate your support but there are some aspects I've needed to do for myself.

"Like refusing to share a joint with Shel. Not told you that, but I did decline. Took all me strength cos it was good stuff. The aroma was so so tempting. But it was like that time in the pub when I noticed things you hadn't, and watched them girls in the Ladies. It gave me an advantage over you. I was an empowered woman, that's what they call us, ain't it?

"But somehow I've come up short in my quest to break through the glass ceiling. That's another expression I've learned. And just when I think I'm there this bombshell with me sister comes along."

"Well, Law, I think of you as being very much my equal. The thing is we both bring different strengths to our relationship, both work and play, and our relationship is improved for it. Combine those strengths as we're doing and we're not only bloody invincible but we're moulded more tightly together, and that's beautiful.

"You've proved yourself top bitch, top tec, top woman. Look how good and invaluable you've been researching things, and your record keeping is the best. As far as I'm concerned you've crashed through *my* glass ceiling about the time I was nose-diving the other way! And you don't arf kiss nice!"

"You don't arf say nice things, Moncks! Notice you didn't mention those lousy photos I took of Jackie and Alistair!" We snuggled up even closer, if that was possible, absolutely united. "Tell you what I've always liked about you,

Moncks, you ask me to do something and leave me to it and never check up I've done it right. Appreciate that.

"Anyway," she added, "I got such plans for us. We's gonna be a success whatever we do. We're going to be entry-pruners."

"What?"

"Entry-pruners."

"*What?*"

"Entry-pruners. That right innit?"

"Think you mean on-tray-prer-ners, it's pronounced."

"Oh gawd. Why can't everything be in the Queen's English, fer flips sake! It's like that Motor Oper ... Oper ... Oper ... Operanders thing you mentioned."

But I knew deep down the Lorraine business had hit her hard, pulled the carpet right out from under her, and that she might even need professional help in the times ahead. I couldn't imagine her feelings and it was remarkable, in my eyes, that she'd pulled through this far without going completely to pieces.

I also knew that I had learned many things from my partner not least how to be a better human being and not be so judgemental and intolerant. I learned from her that the sun can shine from the saddest eyes, that all kinds of people make up the world we share with each other, and the world is a better place for it if we open our eyes and minds to see and understand.

Additionally Laura showed me that I'm not the good cook I thought I was, and proved that I really wasn't much good at washing and ironing either, but she says I'm improving. Praise indeed!

I've never liked lasagne or risotto but Laura's homemade specials converted me. I'm now prepared to try other dishes I don't like and have found, thanks to her exquisite culinary skills, other meals I would once upon a time never have gone near.

We have learned from each other. Laura taught me to listen, an important life-skill. Even with our different backgrounds I now accept I can learn from anyone, especially my partner, if I have an open mind and a will to do so. None of us knows it all. She's brought so much into my life and I would've denied myself the opportunity right on day one if I'd walked away from that shelter in Sheerness and left her behind forever because of my prejudices.

How different Kenny was to John yet both were great guys, salt of the earth, and damn good detectives. Kenny married with kids, John gay, maybe bi. What did it all matter as long as they were happy? Me and Laura, what did anything matter other than us being the people we are and enjoying a loving relationship?

When we made love it was sensational and exquisite because we were *in* love. Another lesson I learned from Lovely Lady Laura was that I didn't know the half of it when it came to sexual pleasure (having been a typical male I thought I did, of course). She launched me into space where my feelings hurtled around a kind of brightly lit fairyland, she interrogated all my senses and drove me to a distant heaven I had never dreamed of, and unleashed a level of passion in me that must've laid dormant since my birth!

She taught me how to thoroughly explore her ....... no, wait a mo, too much information! You don't want to hear all this......

More to the point, you're not going to!

In the days that followed the news media seemed far more interested in praising the police for a successful operation, carried out in the face of extreme difficulty and with few clues, and in Yvonne Pratt's other professional pursuits. In fact the red tops made that aspect their main front page stories. Headlines such as 'Evil dominatrix beaten at last' and 'Dom Evida caned by police' were in frequent evidence.

It was probably to Laura's benefit that Yvonne was making the front pages, as it deflected attention from any family Lorraine Wimbush might have had.

We went back to sleuthing less lethal matters and found the missing sister which bagged us another cosy little cheque, but otherwise business was slow. A couple of minor cases arrived and we found we liked the lack of adventure they presented. Laura continued in her part-time job in the Dockyard and I started to consider what else I could do.

One evening Laura was looking doleful and drawn and I guessed Lorraine was weighing heavily on her mind and mercilessly gripping her emotions.

"Can't get over me sister being round the bend like that," she said in a grey, dull, quiet voice and with a barely discernible shake of the head. "Wonder why we say round-the-bend?"

"Well, I think it originated up north somewhere. The Victorians were sensitive about things like being able to see a lunatic asylum from the road, so they planted trees at the front and curved the approach road so you couldn't see the building. So anyone taken there was going round-the-bend."

My explanation broke the spell and she cheered up a little. Just a little. The next day we had some good news.

The police dropped the charge against me and I was pleased Holton and I became friends, so good came of it all.

In fact he and Gilly went out for dinner with me and Laura and, much to my surprise, both girls got on famously. As me and Holton were driving the girls did have the extra bonus of being able to consume alcohol and that no doubt added to their good humour, but generally the four of us hit it off splendidly anyway.

Adam rang to say, light-heartedly, he'd strangle me at the first opportunity, that I should know better but hey, brilliant, well done, he was proud of me. "One in the eye for the sods that forced a good copper out of the police," he'd commented.

Laura and I considered the possibility of moving away, pooling our resources and renting a place together somewhere you can get a whole lot more for your money, but we knew we needed a plan regarding employment and that might be a dicey aspect, especially for Laura. I had to take the train to Cumbria to collect my car and decided that, on reflection, attractive though Silloth as a charming resort remained, it had bad memories for me.

I promised to take her to Shrewsbury for a break so she could see 'Laura's Tower' and be photographed next to it. Having looked up Shrewsbury and Shropshire online she decided she fancied a holiday there being somewhere not associated with recent unpleasant escapades.

"There's a village in Shropshire called Knockin," I informed her, "and yes, there is, or was, a Knockin Shop. Seriously." She didn't believe me but I had actually seen it myself. "There's the whole of Scotland to be explored. If Derbyshire and the Lake District opened your eyes imagine your reaction to the islands and highlands. None of it featured on the trail of terror; it'll be all new and fresh.

"And that's without considering Northumberland, Yorkshire, Wales. The list is pretty much endless. We'll be pushed to fit it all in during our lifetimes!"

"Not goin' abroad, Dave, bad memories an' all. Like it here with you. You can take me places in Britain and I can learn things." Not going abroad suited me right down to the ground. "You mean we might be doin' more things together, like going on holiday? D'you mean that David?"

"Absolutely. One hundred per cent if it meets with Top Bitch's approval."

"It do, it do, it sure do little Monkey."

There were days when we hugged, quietly and without words, conscious of the depth of our sorrow and heartbreak, and our incomprehension of what had happened to Lorraine.

It was our way of coping.

There were times when we talked at length, sometimes about Lorraine and her crimes, sometimes about the events leading to that awful climax and her arrest, sometimes about the other characters involved in the sorry saga, not least the victims.

It was our way of coping.

There were days when we appeared carefree and full of fun. Probably just a facade. We would laugh at silly things and reminisce about John and Kenny and the humour they brought to the situation.

There were times Laura wanted to be alone and I respected that and gave her space which she appreciated. She told me she sometimes felt a kind of loneliness she couldn't explain but I said that was perfectly natural and all part of the horror and heartbreak. Often we would just hold each other tight.

It was our way of coping.

And the really good days were coming more frequently.

We spent Christmas at my rented bungalow, alone apart from a small supply of *Bollinger*, and we cooked our Christmas dinner together amidst great alcohol-induced mirth, but on the strict understanding Laura was head chef. I had to make do with being the proverbial bottle-washer!

By agreement we bought each other a selection of small, inexpensive presents to fill our stockings. One or two daft things, you know the form, plus bars of chocs etc., each item individually wrapped.

But my stocking (actually a pillow case) also contained a 'thank you' card with seventy five pounds in cash, the money she'd offered me right at the outset. I said I'd add some more and we'd open a joint savings account at the Post Office, which is what we did and which pleased Laura no end.

"A joint account, Moncks. Wow! But not for buying *joints* eh? P'raps joints of meat. Blimey, me first joint account. Can't get over it. I've arrived. This is livin'. 'Ere, give us a kiss."

The New Year was also greeted at my abode, and at midnight, glasses of cheap *Pinot Grigio* in hand (no spare dosh for champagne this time!), we stood on the patio and watched the fireworks going off all around us. And a day or two later it was back to work.

We had been working on one of our cases at my place and it was one of those times, ever increasing in number, when I felt that I couldn't take my eyes off her, she was seriously affecting me like that. We did work well together, knew instinctively what the other was thinking more often than not, and shared a sense of humour that was rising to the surface at every opportunity now the recollections of that terrible business started to fade.

After a fabulous dinner, which Laura prepared and cooked at her insistence, and which was complimented by a notably crisp *Frascati*, we sat and enjoyed another episode of *Pride and Prejudice* from our DVD collection. Afterwards we cuddled closer still and partook of a particularly pleasing and sensual kiss that succeeded in enflaming our passions further.

Drawing back I looked at her lovely little face, her eyes smouldering in that beautifully feminine way that ignites all my fires, and tenderly flicked away the hair that hung across those eyes. She let me do it without a flinch and without glancing away.

"I told you never to do that again," she scolded, with raw mischief illuminating her words. She might have had the text *'I'm feeling frisky'* tattooed on her forehead!

"No, that's not quite what you said," I corrected her. She looked puzzled. "What you actually said, in so many words, was don't do that again unless there's a marriage proposal attached."

She stared at me, then laughed, then cried, laughed again, cried once more, then kissed me, then spoke.

"You serious, cos don't mess top bitch about." I nodded once.

"Gawd Moncks. You just made top bitch happiest girl in the world," and as more tears of joy fell we kissed again. "Just wish you'd waited till I proposed to *you*," she spluttered through our kiss.

It was my turn to cry. Relief? Joy? It didn't matter. I was in a place I wanted to be.

# Epilogue

Daryl Pequeman didn't rebuild his life. He was a long time recovering from his accident and despite the fact his sister told him the letter was destroyed he simply couldn't face the guilt, and confessed in the face of damning evidence from the files of Yvonne Pratt or rather Evida Prada.

Strange how enraged he became when he discovered Rosie's infidelity. He visited prostitutes and, of course, a dominatrix, yet never saw that in the same light. Weird how people can do that, condemn others without looking at themselves.

And it's a bit late discovering that you really love someone, with all their faults, once they are dead. But perhaps there would've been no way back for Daryl and Rosie as a couple, who knows?

Lorraine was thoroughly examined at length to see if she was fit to stand trial and finally it was decided she wasn't, although it appeared to be a close call. She's in a secure unit so at least she's off the streets as it were. David remained convinced, as did most of the police officers on the case, that someone who could meticulously plan such a scheme and carry it off so decisively, so completely, and make sure they left precious few clues, could not possibly be mentally unfit for trial.

If Lorraine's mental state was open to professional medical debate there was no such excuse for Ms Pratt who bore the brunt of the prosecution and faced a long sentence. Gradling, Kethnet and Panahan were in the same boat and were also staring at life behind bars. Unsurprisingly the search of Yvonne's computer and business records earlier in the investigation drew a complete blank because that wasn't where the bad stuff was kept.

William Bailey's life was ostensibly shattered and beyond repair whereas Cathy Kethnet and Jackie Gradling soon rose above their broken hearts and the shock of learning their husbands had hired a killer to embark on the enjoyment of a great deal of freedom. And money.

However, William Bailey made a come-back.

He had a massive business empire to run and he discovered he could absorb himself in his work to the exclusion of emotional agony. His earlier knowledge of Jayne-Marie's crime was never disclosed so it was assumed he was an innocent party. But if any good can ever come from evil William also immersed himself in his anonymous work with the homeless and those less fortunate than others, and again he learned it could relieve his own pain, so perhaps there was redemption of a sort.

For poor Rosie Pequeman there was no redemption, well, not in this life, but for Joan Holgarve there seemed nothing but eternal suffering to be endured. At least she wasn't charged in relation to her attack on Barry's car and house. Barry Welahome moved right away from Bakewell, to be on the safe side.

Neither Lorraine nor Yvonne mentioned the business with Mr Pratt's car so the guilt for that particular murder seems to have been buried with Mr Wimbush who, after all, was responsible for the ensuing death. Since it was dismissed as an accident at the time the truth is unlikely to be revealed.

There seemed to be a puzzle (Lorraine never revealed how she came by the knowledge) as to how the killer knew Cathy Kethnet and Edward Nobbs enjoyed bondage as no evidence was presented by John Wapernod in his report to

Nathan. But perhaps it was coincidence as strangulation was how Lorraine despatched Gary, her first victim, and Nobbs was next up. We'll probably never know.

DS Stephanie Groome became a Detective Inspector, the next step on her rise to stardom, and was eventually treated to dinner courtesy of DS Holton Okafor, who made the journey to Suffolk specially. Over dessert she related one moment of mild humour in an otherwise deadly serious investigation. While they were raiding Grayden Optics after Lorraine's arrest, and when she was not in the mood for any messing about or the application of respect for those being searched, she decided she wanted to talk to William Bailey immediately, as in, yesterday.

She barked fiercely to the receptionist "Where's Bill Bailey?"

Back came the reply "He's gone home, Miss."

And in Lancashire Lionel Boldfield made a full recovery from his heart attack and still remained blissfully unaware that his ill-health helped trap a killer.

Some people learned that true love is a beautiful state and can be found where you least think to look. It can just happen, and it can happen to people you might not ever think of as a couple. Occasionally convention has to be set aside, prejudices ignored, and two people, any two people can become as one, locked in the loveliness of everlasting love.

Step forward David and Laura, Georgina and Leonora.

Georgina and Leonora embarked on their new life together and the former discovered that she actually quite liked working for a living, and that it wasn't all that bad not having a great deal of money. It was a bit of a mental and physical struggle at first but, as they say, love conquers all and after a while she put her past of lazy luxury behind her and started to live.

Funny how love can do that for you.

The former Mrs Hayle discovered, as David Canbown did, that you don't need a 'perfect match' to find love, or for that matter friendship. Someone you might discount through narrow-mindedness could turn out to be someone precious.

Mr Pickles vanished without trace and is still wanted. It's always possible Lorraine polished him off but since her confession included the death of husband Gary it appears unlikely that she wasn't prepared to have him counted among her victims had he been one. Gary's body, or its remains, was found during a detailed search, so Mr Pickles is the only outstanding strand to the whole business. He never visited his mother again or got in touch by any medium.

John Wapernod saw an appreciable increase in business when his reputation was enhanced by an article in his local paper praising his role in the serial killer affair. Ever modest, the self-effacing private eye declined an interview on local radio, but he did get to date the producer, an effervescent, outgoing man, who shared John's love of walking Exmoor.

And their shared walks became more frequent, as did other meetings, so maybe, just maybe John has found the man of his dreams.

Hero of the hour, Kenny Parrett, returned to near anonymity and the joys of family life vowing to write a murder mystery loosely based on his adventures. He said that if it was ever made into a film he hoped David Tennant would play him.

John improved his relationship with his constabulary whereas Kenny was regarded with even more wariness by his.

The three private eyes are planning a reunion at the same hotel in Derby where John and David met Yvonne, although obviously the latter will be missing. Partners will be invited this time and that will be of great interest and excitement for Laura McCaffield, or Laura Canbown as she may be by then. Happily John will be able to translate the menu!

And that leads us neatly to David and Laura.

Ah now, that's another story ......

# Author's Afterthoughts

I am familiar with most of the places that take part in this story especially Flint Lane on the Downs above Lenham. The wooded drop point for Neville's suitcase is indeed both wondrously beautiful and frighteningly eerie! It is an inspiration in itself. A place for elves and pixies, harmful spirits, and yet a place of enticing and enchanting loveliness, of peace and calm.

A special corner of unexplored Kent, of which there is still much.

I feel almost sad for involving such a spot! But then I must also apologise to the other venues of crime mentioned in this book should they feel in any way maligned and degraded.

Hemel Hempstead figured in my youth but at a distance that made it a kind of mysterious entity. My father was a gloriously titled Non-Ferrous Metal Merchant and once a year he hired a lorry to go and collect some materials from this weirdly named town which I didn't get to visit personally until much, much later. I'm sorry if HH doesn't seem to come out of it well in this tale, it was not my intention to denigrate it or its residents, it might merely read like that in the context of the book.

There is much action set in Derbyshire and that is an area that I loved from childhood. Part of the Dales is in Staffordshire of course, but it is a region of Britain that I shall never tire of, and I can honestly say I have no particular favourite place although the view above the Monsal Dale viaduct would be a frontrunner.

You can stand at Monsal Head and imagine a steam hauled express flying out of the tunnel and across the viaduct.

I have enjoyed many a fine visit to Castleton (Ye Olde Cheshire Cheese is a pub to die for!) and the Hope Valley, Matlock and Matlock Bath, Bakewell and Dovedale, the Snake Pass, among towns, villages and countryside too numerous to mention.

The Lake District is synonymous with beauty, both dramatic and picturesque. The daunting Screes rising sharply and hauntingly almost straight up from Wastwater make the location seemingly ideal for inclusion in a book on dark deeds! Of the high passes Newlands and the Hardknott are my favourites but inevitably the Kirkstone is highlighted in this saga. Buttermere and Rydal Water are my all time greats amongst the lakes themselves but largely miss out on a mention, as does so very much of this most attractive of areas.

Still, plenty of other spots are included. I've also taken the step of putting Kent's Bank and Silloth into the narrative as although they are technically outside the National Park they serve as a reminder that there is much to see beyond the normal boundaries, proving Cumbria is a very wonderful district.

There is a special place in my heart for East Anglia, particularly the wonderfully picturesque Essex/Suffolk border region, not that there is too much detail in my book. Once again, my apologies, this time to Woodbridge which I am sure has done nothing to deserve being the venue for Evida Prada's dungeon! Sorry folks.

As I said at the outset the police officers, their ranks and police procedures detailed herein are strictly imaginary and simply suited to the chronicle of events, so I must also apologise to those forces mentioned for taking them in vain. It is not a reflection of my strong admiration and respect for our upholders of the law.

Similarly I mentioned in Chapter One the Association of British Investigators; there is a great deal more to gaining membership than I suggested, but my comment was more in passing rather than an important part of the story. No disrespect to the excellent ABI is intended.

Some historical points and descriptions given go back to the time when I ran my own British coach holiday company and so adored taking my clients to the places I knew and loved. Much of it comes from my tour commentaries and, as these are not delivered under oath, may contain some minor inaccuracies!

Derbyshire was frequently on my itineraries, and a very popular autumn weekender was my unique 'Nooks and Crannies of Essex and Suffolk' where we often got off the beaten track going where many coach firms feared to tread! Thank you to my excellent drivers at the time.

The shelter on Sheerness seafront is real. I often walk there and its mere presence was the inspiration for the meeting of David and Laura, and can therefore claim to be at the very heart of the genesis of this story.

Amongst the research I did carry out for this book I tried to ensure no such firm named Grayden Optics actually existed, but I may have missed something. Once again apologies are in order if I've slipped up. Similarly I do try to use invented names for some of the principal characters, but I cannot do this for everyone involved so inevitably names in more common usage crop up.

I'm dedicating this book to my publisher Tim, and to the NOG. Thanks for everything.

# Other books by Peter Chegwidden available from Amazon

Peter writes across various genres bringing his own style of humour to bear although there is one serious work, Kindale, which is set in 18th century east Kent. There's bound to be something for almost everyone; crime stories, tales of espionage, charming 'cat's tails', a selection of short stories of all kinds. Quite a choice!

## THE CHORTLEFORD MYSTERY

Death comes to the Kent countryside and a quiet unassuming village soon becomes the centre of attention. All kinds of characters abound in a cosy tale of murder told with humour, pathos and satire.

Indeed this is very much a work about the characters themselves with the villagers truly at the forefront, as are their 'visitors', the police and media representatives including an ambitious local reporter.

*Available as Kindle e-book and in paperback*

## DEADENED PAIN

A satirical work lampooning the crime novel genre. Almost everything you've come across in such works is parodied, including bigotry, horror, red-herrings, love interests, red-tape, the law, double-crossings and more.

A most unlikely police force tries to solve crimes including murder and the large scale organised supply of drugs. On the face of it the team is a collective recipe for disaster, yet somehow they blunder along and it is the female officers who rise to the fore at the eleventh hour.

The story begins with a robbery at a local garage in which, rather oddly, very little was stolen, and gathers pace when a terribly mangled body is discovered. Detective Chief Superintendent Luke Fuselage, the epitome of uselessness, swings into action as the body count starts to mount with his squad facing the inevitable race against time.

There is a serious message about illegal drugs. There's a real mix of characters to get your teeth into and a host of varied incidents taking place before the dramatic life-or-death climax is reached.

*Available as Kindle e-book*

## KINDALE

It is the late 18<sup>th</sup> century, the threat of war with France as Napoleon rises to power, and a mysterious man, Oliver Kindale is on his way to Kent.

He is not in any way an officer of the law but he is very definitely a man on a mission. Could the very fate of England be in his hands?

A tale of mystery, intrigue and espionage played out in east Kent.

This is a time of rampant smuggling and although Kindale is not pursuing the free-traders their paths inevitably cross. An outlaw is establishing a reign of terror and fear, and his presence in Kent at this stage is of keen interest to Kindale, as is a Frenchman recently arrived in Dover.

e-book and paperback

## TOM INVESTIGATES and TOM VANISHES

Two delightful "cat's tails" to warm the heart.

These are not stories about cartoon or any sort of animated cats, they are about the cats we see round our neighbourhoods every day. Maybe even your own cat! They behave just as we see them but in these stories we learn what they are thinking and hear what they are saying.

In *Tom Investigates* a tabby called Tom leads a group of cats in solving a crime, overcoming a fearsome foe, and indulging in a little human match-making.

In *Tom Vanishes* the cat himself is accidently shut in a car boot and taken miles from home. The story details his efforts, and those of his friends back home, to return him to where he belongs.

Various incidents are encountered including one development Tom could never have bargained for.

Tom Investigates available as e-book and paperback

Tom Vanishes available as e-book.

There is no bad language, nothing to offend. So just get in touch with your feline side and enjoy the fun.

*Available as Kindle e-book*

## SHEPPEY SHORT STORIES

A collection of 18 short stories based on Kent's Isle of Sheppey, with the central theme being "relationships".

There is variously humour, poignancy, sadness, love and satire at the heart of these Tall Tales from north Kent.

Here's one of them, entitled **A Battle of the Sexes** – *a tale with only one winner.*

\*\*\*

Davy looked out from under a furrowed brow and exhaled noisily.

It was taking longer than he hoped to saw through the tree trunk. His arm was aching. At moments like this he regretted having an open fire and found himself dreaming of the gas fire he had secretly promised himself. One day.

They had central heating, but they enjoyed the warmth and glow of a log fire, especially the roaring log fire variety, and it was cheaper than heating the whole bungalow unnecessarily. It made winter evenings in the lounge more than tolerable; they actually became desirable. Warm and cosy. Draw the curtains, put the day away, settle down for a lovely, warm night until bed time.

So he and Janice made wood gathering into a hobby and combined it with the exercise of a good walk whenever they could. The beaches, especially between Warden Bay and Leysdown, provided a happy hunting ground particularly during the winter months, and the timber was, after all, quite free of charge.

Sometimes there would be a windfall.

On one occasion they had stopped their car just outside Eastchurch having spotted some 'roadkill' as Davy would insist on calling it; a few pieces of wood that had probably, quite literally, fallen off a lorry. As they loaded the boot a voice called out to enquire if they wanted some more wood.

The voice came from a contractor working on renovating a roadside property and he and his mates had quite a quantity of wood removed from the cottage, including a wooden fire-surround. They were faced with its disposal so why not give it to a couple of foragers?

Everybody won, and Davy and Janice went home with a car full.

It was rare for them to miss an opportunity. This particular tree trunk, the one putting up such stiff resistance to Davy's best sawing efforts, had been discovered on the Shingle Beach and he and Janice had carted it back to their Minster home by hand, he one end, she the other. The project had required some rest en route and had taken them the best part of an hour from seafront to their domicile. Well, it was worth it.

Janice was baking some scones for tea and preparing her homemade jams as well as a little cream on the tray. They would enjoy them in the lounge. Davy was ready for a break and swiftly and happily responded to her call that tea was ready.

"Just don't like winter," he commented, "with its short days and long, dark evenings. Yuk. I reckon I've got that s-a-d, or whatever they call it. Hate bloody winter, and there's nothing on the telly worth seeing. Gawd, all those Freeview stations and we still can't find anything much!"

"I know love," Janice added soothingly, "but we've got some videos and DVDs and that, and the fire for cold evenings, and summer won't be long coming."

"I know, I know pet, but you know what I mean, dark at half four and if we haven't much to do of an evening, well, I don't know. Hate winter."

"Well, love, we can always have a Scrabble, and y'know, it would help if you could get into a good book..."

"Yes, I understand that, but you're well catered for, all those romantic novels, blimey, must be the same story retold hundreds of bloody times..."

"No, no it isn't, not a bit of it..." Janice retorted with a grin and chuckle. "Why don't you come up the library, have a good look round, get a handful of books, all different types, y'know, all different types of books, fiction, non-fiction, you know. Doesn't cost a penny, just take them all back later. And you might just find one you enjoy. You ought to give it a try, love."

Davy knew the form. He would eventually give in, so he thought if he did so right away, without argument, he might earn a brownie-point. A mate of his had once expounded a piece of simple philosophy. 'If you know you're going to lose, don't waste time, lose.'

So Davy said he would go with Janice next time round, and promptly changed the subject. This was also in accord with his mate's philosophy. 'And when you lose, change the subject completely. Takes the other guy's mind off victory, see.'

It worked just as well in marriage, Davy knew. What Davy probably didn't know was that Janice was wise to all his tricks. Her own philosophy, duly applied, was that you start by suggesting an idea and leaving it to ferment in a man's mind. Over a period of time a husband will weigh the issue up, in a man's way, and consider the problems of not agreeing to the suggestion. A man will know, she felt, that you will return to the subject periodically and occasionally use it in your battery of criticism when things are a little heated.

It worked on Davy. Today it took him seconds rather than weeks to come to the right conclusion. Janice smile inwardly. It was, after all, for his own good! There was the added advantage that her husband had applied his own philosophies to proceedings and had therefore decided he had won, whereas he had in fact lost.

"I think we're the ones out of touch," he ventured, "I think we're the odd ones out. Most people must like what's on the telly, cos they wouldn't put it on if nobody watched it. Bloody rubbish. Games shows, so-called reality tv, detective series, violent films...."

"Football, crickct, golf..." she interrupted, determined to light-heartedly kick a man when he's down, and keep him underfoot.

"Yes, yes, I know, but that's not often, is it?" he responded, grittily trying to make a hopeless point.

"Mmmm .... like Sunday morning, Tuesday evening, two matches Thursday night, they don't count?"

Davy thought for a moment.

"Well, Sunday's only highlights and Tuesday's game was rubbish..."

"Oh yes, I had forgotten that. Rubbish because the Spanish team beat the English team, maybe?"

This discussion was going nowhere and for Davy, floundering in a stew of his own making, another change of tack was needed.

"Could always have a week away somewhere. You know, get away from the four walls, have a break. Get a nice, warm, self catering cottage..."

"Ah, yes, Davy, a nice break. Self-catering. Me doing all the cooking and everything. Yes, a nice break from routine, that."

Whichever way he twisted Davy found himself frustrated. Every attempt at conversation led down a cul-de-sac into impending misery and doom. Janice was clearly in the mood, in the mood to keep him firmly in his place. She was up for it and he was in for it. No escape.

"These scones are de-bloody-licious," he quoth, hoping this change of subject was not going to be laced with the potential for scorn and retribution. "You make a mean scone, girl, they really are first class. Delicious with a capital D."

At the eleventh hour he had managed to steer his sinking ship away from the rocks and into calmer waters. He and Janice munched their way through their refreshments and washed the scones down with hot tea.

"Ooooo ... I don't understand you," Janice started. "How can you drink tea with so little milk in it? God, that looks disgusting. Horrible colour," and she pulled a face that further expressed her revulsion. Davy's ship had just been torpedoed.

Back to the tree trunk.

Big mistake.

As he strode out of the lounge Janice enquired if he was going to take the tea tray out and do the washing up. He knew he was snookered. She had made the scones, he must clear up. Whoops! Any brownie-point gained earlier had now been eradicated from the scoreboard.

And so he did the clearing up and did so with his proverbial tail between his legs. Game, set and match to Janice.

***

That evening they sat and read, Janice buried in her Emma Blair novel, Davy in the newspaper's sports pages.

"Did you know," he enquired, "that Emma Blair was actually a bloke?"

"Yes" came the simple answer.

"Mmm ... odd that, a bloke writing romantic novels."

"Why not, dear? Some fellows are romantic souls and anyway his novels are stories, well written, beautifully crafted stories, tales with depth. Romantic novels aren't necessarily about romance the narrow way you see it. These stories can be about tragedy, sadness and loss as well as life's uplifting experiences."

Davy considered this. Janice's explanation, he reasoned, could've come straight from one of her books. Long-winded. Ten words where one would've done! She continued.

"You see, dear, some of my books are even set in real places and often during real events. Some of the historical novels are the best. The characters react to real events in the same way we do, on a day to day basis, like some are set in the war years, that kind of thing."

I asked her, Davy thought, if she knew Emma Blair was a bloke, and I get a whole lecture on romantic novels. Gawd. Now where was I? Oh yes, this story on Manchester City.

"What brought that on?" Janice added.

"What on?" he responded, with all the foolishness a man can muster and all the folly he can demonstrate.

"About Emma Blair," she persisted.

"Oh, don't know, just something I learned. Wondered if you knew."

"Yes I did. Came to light when he won a literary award, so I believe. What are you reading about, darling? Not Emma Blair I take it?"

"Nope, Manchester City actually."

"Very intellectual. That'll improve your wide diversity of knowledge."

Her eyes didn't leave her book. But there was a wicked grin decorating her visage.

He decided it was pure sarcasm and went back to reading but found he wasn't concentrating. His wife had got under his skin. It wasn't deliberate. It was nothing that threatened their relationship, their devoted love for each other, but she just had that annoying ability to, well, annoy him!

"I'm gonna make a cuppa," he announced, "if you fancy one too, love."

"Not for me at the mo, thanks darling. We're due our pills in half an hour and I'd like a drink then. But you carry on, pet. I expect you'll have another one when you take your pill."

Davy sat back in the chair and breathed in heavily, exhaling noisily and at length. If Janice noticed there was no sign.

She's done it again, he thought. Uncanny. Only said I was making a cuppa but I'm in the wrong again, making it half a bloody hour too soon and making me feel bad about it. And I don't even know why I'm feeling bad about it! Strewth.

"Are you going, dear?" she said in a very pointed manner as if to suggest she knew she had come out on top yet again.

"Nope, leave it half an hour," he replied grumpily.

"Well, you can have a drink now, doesn't matter to me, no need to get the grumps."

"I am not grumpy. I'll leave it for now."

Pause.

"You *are* grumpy."

"I'm not."

"You *are*, y'know."

"If I am it's you that's made me grumpy."

And with that one sentence Davy instantly recognised that he had fallen into the age old trap and was now stuck in defence mode with abject apology the only possible route out. Game, set and match to Janice. All because he'd asked about Emma bloody Blair.

***

Later they climbed into bed, their evening run.

Janice put out the light and snuggled down and Davy snuggled up behind her, instinctively putting his arm around her and his hand on her stomach. There was a scream.

"That's *freezing*," yelled Janice, "put it somewhere and get it warm. Bloody hell!"

"I had put it somewhere warm," he retorted, "you're like toast."

"Well, you're *freezing*. How did your hands get so cold? We've had the fire blazing tonight. You need gloves. Keep away. Just let me go to sleep."

"But I want a cuddle."

"Cuddle, cuddle, cuddle, all I hear at bedtime. I just come to bed and just want to be quiet and go to sleep."

"You're the one making all the noise."

"It's your fault, coming to bed with cold hands."

"Cold hands don't make me noisy."

"Aw, you stupid man. Now let me get to sleep."

"What about my cuddle?"

"In a minute I'll be wide awake and won't be able to get off for hours, and I'll just have your snores to listen to while you sleep soundly. And don't you dare pass wind; this bed's clean on today, fresh sheets and pillows."

"Just want a cuddle before we settle down. Wazzat got to do passing wind?"

Davy lay back and in doing so inadvertently dragged the quilt across his wife.

A death wish could never have been more clearly made flesh. He was skating on the very verge of starting something akin to a world war in domestic relationship terms.

"Stop fidgeting," she ordered, tugging the quilt back. His nose was itching. He tried ignoring it. The more he tried the more it itched. He was lying perfectly still. He tried screwing up his nose and then his entire face but all to no effect. Finally, overcome, he reached up and scratched his nose.

"Stop *fidgeting*," came the squeal. He tried not to move. Now his ear itched. He was afraid to breath, let alone contemplate any slightest movement. He wrestled with the problem mentally for some time until, once again, the itching became too much. Unable to dream up a more appropriate solution he found himself with no choice but to scratch.

He waited. There was no sound. Dare he consider a sigh of relief?

"You, you, you *wretched* man," she bellowed, "now I'm wide awake."

Pause.

"Can I have a cuddle then?"

If his scratching had lit the blue touch paper his request had depressed the detonating plunger. He shook with fear as Janice slowly turned over onto her back. There was silence. Horror was his companion. He dreaded the next tirade.

Eventually she spoke. Quietly, almost in a whisper.

"I'm wide awake, Davy. So why don't we do something more intimate than cuddle?"

And that is what they did.

A score draw the amicable outcome.

**Sheppey Short Stories** is available as an e-book. There are seventeen other tales including those entitled The Bungling Burglars; Having Cake and Eating it; Going Straighter; Infrastructure; The Extremely Merry Widow; Getting the Bird, and many more.

**As yet unpublished:**

*Dead Corrupt* and *Dead Departed*, the sequels to *Deadened Pain*, completing the trilogy of crime novel parodies based in the fictional district of Paslow, somewhere in the south-east.

*After Hugh* follows recently widowed Hannah as she struggles to cope with her extended family and their troubles whilst coming to terms with the loss of her beloved husband Hugh.

Gradually she comes to realise how much Hugh influenced her life and opinions, and as she begins to think more widely for herself becomes a different person and finds contentment and happiness.

# THE UNLOVED ROSE - A childrens' short story

A tale of love conquering prejudice, and understanding overcoming fear.

There was a girl in Molly's class that Molly didn't like. The other pupils didn't like her much either. You see, Rosie wasn't perfect. Sadly she'd been born with a face that was different to other girls faces. Her upper lip had a curl in it, her nose was slightly to one side, and her right eye looked smaller than the left.

She had trouble speaking, or rather she had trouble getting people to understand what she was saying as she couldn't form the words properly. Behind her back, and occasionally in front of her, Molly and her friends would cruelly imitate her voice and then giggle a lot.

One day, on her way home from school, and holding her mother's hand, Molly told her mum about how they'd teased Rosie because of the way she looked and spoke. Mum was horrified.

"Molly, the poor girl can't help the way she looks and speaks. You should be kind to her and you certainly shouldn't tease her. I'm very upset that you've behaved like that. You should resolve to be nice to her from now on, and do it for me." Molly stayed silent and the matter was not raised again. If anything Molly resolved to carry on being rude to Rosie and never to mention it to mum. If she hadn't said anything in the first place mum wouldn't have been annoyed.

*** 

Molly lived with her mum and dad and young brother Jude in a small semi-detached house with a small garden front and back. Mum was a keen gardener and loved the time she could spare to work in her little bit of heaven as she called it.

And the back garden in particular was always a mass of colour during the summer months. Molly enjoyed helping mum and tried to learn the names of the flowers but with very limited success, hardly surprising for one so young. She liked daffodils and tulips (they had easy names) but her favourites were the roses, all different colours and so pretty. Yet she never touched one, not since she reached out to take one in her hand and cut herself on the prickles.

She'd asked mum why something so beautiful could be so dangerous, why something so lovely could hurt her and cause her to cry.

"That's just nature's way of protecting the roses from any creatures that might threaten them," she'd replied. "You're not a threat, darling, because you want them to live and be wonderful and bring colour into your life. You love roses, don't you, but you've learned to simply be careful. Mummy handles the roses with these thick gloves. Roses are proof that even something that looks unpleasant with those sharp prickles can actually be something quite gorgeous. We shouldn't always take things at face value, you know, take things as we see them. Often there is much more than what we can see."

***

Angelina was a rose bush of the Warm Wishes variety. She'd grown up over the years in a far corner of a garden in a residential area.

But Angelina was a sad rose. Often in the morning the dew dripping from her petals and leaves mingled with the tears she cried. For there was nobody to see and admire her beautiful orange flowers, her children.

The reason for this was that the current property owners were not gardeners and they'd taken no notice of anything pretty growing in their garden. Down the bottom of their garden brambles had grown up everywhere and almost completely obscured poor Angelina. She loved her children as she called them, the young buds that opened into a glorious mass of astonishingly lovely colour throughout the summer, a delightful shade of soft, tender orange. Silky petals that formed into fabulous flowers, just as roses should be.

And nobody ever saw them.

But she was wrong, because next door Molly's mum saw them and one day she pointed them out to Molly.

"Can't we cut them, mummy, and have them indoors?"

"No darling, that's stealing, but I'll have a word with our neighbours and see if they mind us having one or two. If it's okay then I might try and take a cutting and see about growing one in our garden."

Molly was thrilled.

A few days later they were down the garden, Molly's mum having obtained permission to take cuttings. The rose was difficult to reach and the brambles were all around it, but with her gardening gloves on her hands and a thick woolly worn especially for the purpose, she managed to snip four flowers and take one cutting while Molly looked on.

"Ouch," she said as she stepped back, for one of the rose thorns had just caught her face. It was the slightest nick but Molly was so upset she burst into tears.

"It's alright darling. Mummy's okay, mummy's okay," she said reassuringly as she dropped the roses and hugged her daughter. "The rose didn't mean to hurt me, I just didn't take enough care. You see it's still a beautiful rose, Molly, we just have to be careful and see beyond the thorns."

The flowers themselves were added to some dahlias from their own garden, a bit of greenery for extra decoration, and then they were put in vase and made a splendid display in the lounge. Mum potted one cutting with a view to planting it in the garden the following year.

For once Angelina's tears were tears of joy. Her beautiful blooms were not only being admired, some were being cared for, and she was happy at last.

***

A couple of days later Mum was putting a little water in the vase when a thought occurred to her.

"Molly, y'know that girl at school you told me about, she's probably a bit like our roses. All you see are the thorns, not the lovely flower."

"And her name's Rosie, mum. But she's ugly like those nasty thorns...."

"No she's not ugly, darling. She can't help the way she looks and you have to learn to look beyond just what you can see. Then you might see beauty. Everything has a beauty of its own, my love, just like the orange rose we rescued from next door's brambles. Why don't we invite Rosie round after school one day?"

"Oh mum, do we *have* to? I don't like her."

"How do you know? You've never tried to get to know her, have you?"

"Oh mum, I don't want to." And her bottom lip curled outwards to give her face a sulky appearance.

"Well, let's just do it the once, darling. Do it for mummy?"

"Oh, alright then, but I still don't want to." If Molly had stamped her foot it would've been quite in place given her look of annoyance.

So Molly sulked. Invite Rosie round? What would her friends Suzi, Jayde and Fleur say? Still it would only be for an afternoon, and hour or two, as her mum had said. Let's get it over with, then Molly could tell her close friends how horrible Rosie truly was.

***

At the school gates the following morning Molly showed her mum Rosie and her own mum who were just walking over. As the girls walked into school, separately it has to be said, Molly's mum started talking to Rosie's mum and arranged to have the girl round for tea later that day, with mum invited too.

When Molly walked out and fell into step beside Rosie and their mothers she could hear Suzi and Jayde making unpleasant comments about her as well as Rosie. She wanted to run away, she wanted to curl up in a ball, she wanted to be anywhere apart from being alongside Rosie.

The two girls didn't speak all the way home. Molly just wanted to get it over with.

Once indoors the visitors noticed a lovely spread on the table in the lounge. Molly's mum had prepared a few special goodies during the day and while the adults chatted the girls tucked into their treat, but without a word passing between them.

They went to Molly's room to play and slowly but surely they started talking. Once they discovered they liked being together, playing together and nattering together the time went all too swiftly and they were sorry when they had to part.

But the following afternoon the four went to Rosie's and this time they played in the garden. It was rather larger than Molly's and she loved being shown around, especially as she knew the names of some of the plants that Rosie didn't.

"That's a dahlia," she revealed, pointing to a particularly large crop of flowers, "but I don't know how it's spelled, only that it's got an H in it, but I don't know where." Rosie was impressed anyway, regardless of where the H went. "Do you know what that one is Rosie?" she exclaimed, looking at a plant she didn't know the identity of. Neither girl did. Both rushed to the flowerbed and Molly reached out to touch the lovely blue flower but cried out, withdrew her hand and recoiled from the bed clutching a finger and squealing.

"Let me look, let me look," Rosie pleaded taking the finger in her own hand. "Molly, you've got a rose thorn stuck in your finger. Here let me." And she slowly, tenderly and very gently eased the thorn from Molly's finger. The pain stopped at once and Rosie placed the finger in her mouth saying, "This'll make it better. Then we'll go in and get you a plaster."

And that is what they did.

While Rosie's mum put a plaster on her finger Molly told Rosie all about the orange rose in her own garden, and about how her own mother had said that if you look beyond the prickly thorns you can see a thing of beauty. Then came the words that warmed both parents and moved them close to tears.

"Rosie, I thought you were ugly, but I've looked beyond your thorns, the thorns that, like the roses, you cannot help having, and I can see a beautiful flower. Isn't Rosie beautiful mummy? Please be my friend Rosie, my special friend. I want you as my beautiful flower." And the two girls hugged as their mums looked on and shared knowing glances.

"Mum, wasn't Rosie terrific with the rose thorn? I love her. She made me feel better and I know the rose didn't mean to hurt me."

In the days ahead Molly stood up to Rosie's tormentors and in time Suzi, Jayde and Fleur changed their tune and also became friends with Rosie.

And so Rosie became as loved as Angelina's blooms.

The five girls were rarely seen apart, and Angelina was able to smile as her 'children' – her precious blooms were cherished at last for their simple loveliness.

An unloved rose loved at last. In more ways than one.

19803038R00222

Printed in Great Britain
by Amazon